NEW YORK REVIEW |
CLASSICS

OTHER WORLDS

TEFFI (1872–1952) was the pen name of Nadezhda Lokhvit-
skaya, born in St. Petersburg into a distinguished family that
treasured literature. She and her three sisters all became writers.
Teffi wrote in a variety of styles and genres: political feuilletons
published in a Bolshevik newspaper during her brief period of
radical fervor after the 1905 Revolution; Symbolist poems that
she declaimed or sang in Petersburg literary salons; popular
one-act plays, mostly humorous or satirical (one was entitled
The Woman Question); and a novel titled simply *Adventure
Novel*. Her finest works are her short stories—collected in
Other Worlds and *Tolstoy, Rasputin, Others, and Me*—and
Memories, a witty, tragic, and deeply perceptive account of
her last journey across Russia and what is now Ukraine, before
going by boat to Istanbul in the summer of 1919. Teffi was
widely read; her admirers included not only such writers as
Bunin, Bulgakov, and Zoshchenko but also both Lenin and
the last tsar. In pre-Revolutionary Russia, candies and perfumes
were named after her; after the Revolution, her stories were
published and her plays performed throughout the Russian
diaspora. She died in Paris.

ROBERT CHANDLER's translations from Russian include
Alexander Pushkin's *The Captain's Daughter*; Nikolai Leskov's
Lady Macbeth of Mtsensk; Vasily Grossman's *An Armenian
Sketchbook*, *Everything Flows*, *Stalingrad*, *Life and Fate*, and *The
Road* (all NYRB classics); and Hamid Ismailov's Central Asian

novel, *The Railway*. His co-translations of Andrey Platonov have won prizes both in the UK and in the US. He is the editor and main translator of *Russian Short Stories from Pushkin to Buida* and *Russian Magic Tales from Pushkin to Platonov*. Together with Boris Dralyuk and Irina Mashinski, he has co-edited *The Penguin Book of Russian Poetry*. He has also translated selections of Sappho and Apollinaire. As well as running regular translation workshops in London and teaching in an annual literary translation summer school, he works as a mentor for the British Centre for Literary Translation.

ELIZABETH CHANDLER is a co-translator, with her husband, of Pushkin's *The Captain's Daughter*; of Vasily Grossman's *Stalingrad*, *Everything Flows*, *An Armenian Sketchbook*, and *The Road*; and of several works by Andrey Platonov.

OTHER WORLDS
Pilgrims, Peasants, Spirits, Saints

TEFFI

Translated from the Russian by
ROBERT CHANDLER,
ELIZABETH CHANDLER,
and others

Edited by
ROBERT CHANDLER

NEW YORK REVIEW BOOKS

New York

THIS IS A NEW YORK REVIEW BOOK
PUBLISHED BY THE NEW YORK REVIEW OF BOOKS
435 Hudson Street, New York, NY 10014
www.nyrb.com

Illustration on page xx: Nicholas Millioti, portrait of Teffi, c. early 1930s; courtesy
private collection, Moscow.

Library of Congress Cataloging-in-Publication Data
Names: Tëffi, N. A. (Nadezhda Aleksandrovna), 1872–1952, author. |
  Chandler, Robert, 1953– translator.
Title: Other worlds: peasants, pilgrims, spirits, saints / Teffi; translated by
  [Robert Chandler and 9 others].
Description: New York: New York Review Books, [2020] | Series: New York
  Review Books classics | Translated into English from Russian.
Identifiers: LCCN 2020015022 (print) | LCCN 2020015023 (ebook) |
  ISBN 9781681375397 (paperback) | ISBN 9781681375403 (ebook)
Subjects: LCSH: Tëffi, N. A. (Nadezhda Aleksandrovna), 1872–1952
  —Translations into English.
Classification: LCC PG3453.B8 A2 2020 (print) | LCC PG3453.B8 (ebook) |
  DDC 891.73/3—dc23
LC record available at https://lccn.loc.gov/2020015022
LC ebook record available at https://lccn.loc.gov/2020015023

ISBN 978-1-68137-539-7
Available as an electronic book; ISBN 978-1-68137-540-3

Printed in the United States of America on acid-free paper.
10 9 8 7 6 5 4 3 2 1

CONTENTS

FOREWORD

There are writers who muddy their own water, to make it seem deeper. Teffi could not be more different: the water is entirely transparent, yet the bottom is barely visible.

—GEORGY ADAMOVICH[1]

IT IS NOT unusual for a writer to be pigeonholed, but few great writers have suffered from this more than Teffi. Several of her finest works are extremely bleak, but many Russians still know only the comic and satirical sketches she wrote during her first years as a professional writer, from 1901 until 1918. Few critics have recognized the full breadth of her human sympathy, her Chekhovian ability to write convincingly about people from every level of society: illiterate peasants, respectable bourgeois, monks and priests, eccentric poets, bewildered émigrés, and public figures ranging from Lev Tolstoy to Rasputin and Lenin. Teffi also has a remarkable gift for writing about children, for showing us the world from the perspective of a small child.

Throughout her life, Teffi was a practicing member of the Russian Orthodox Church. Both Orthodox Christianity and Russian folk religion, with its often poetic understanding of spiritual matters, were important to her. And she recognized that many of her finest stories were those inspired by these themes. In December 1943, she wrote to the historian Piotr Kovalevsky: "Which of my things do I most value? I think that the stories 'Solovki' and 'A Quiet Backwater' and the collection *Witch* are well written. In *Witch* you find our ancient Slav gods, how they still live on in the soul of the people, in legends, superstitions, and customs. Everything as I encountered it in the Russian provinces, as a child."[2]

Teffi made few such direct statements about her work. I know just one other passage in a similar vein:

> During those years of my distant childhood, we used to spend the summer in a wonderful, blessed country—at my mother's estate in Volhynia Province. I was very little. I had only just begun to learn to read and write—so I must have been about five. [. . .] What slipped quickly through the lives of adults was for us a matter of complex and turbulent experience, entering our games and our dreams, inserting itself like a brightly colored thread into the pattern of our life, into that first firm foundation that psychoanalysts now investigate with such art and diligence, seeing it as the prime cause of many of the madnesses of the human soul.[3]

These two statements have guided our choice of stories. We have translated all but one of the stories from *Witch*.[4] We have included the two other stories Teffi mentions: "Solovki," an account of a pilgrimage to the Solovetsky Islands in the White Sea, and "A Quiet Backwater," which incorporates a memorable monologue about the patron saints of various birds, insects, and animals. And we have chosen ten other stories on similar themes, many of them from the first of Teffi's more serious collections, *The Lifeless Beast*. For the main part, we present the stories according to their order of publication. The one exception is that we begin with "Kishmish," which was written much later. This short, semiautobiographical story serves as a perfect introduction to many of the main themes of *Other Worlds*.

This is the first time that Teffi's more "otherworldly" stories have been brought together in this manner. Our hope is that this will allow readers a clearer sense of the depth of understanding beneath her often dazzling wit and brilliance.

*

Teffi was well aware of how often her work was misunderstood. Her preface to *The Lifeless Beast* begins:

> I do not like prefaces. […]
>
> I would not be writing a preface now were it not for a sad incident.
>
> In October 1914 I published the story "Yavdokha." This melancholy and painful story is about a lonely old peasant woman. She is illiterate and muddle-headed and so hopelessly benighted that, when she receives news of the death of her son, she is unable to grasp what has happened. Instead, she wonders whether or not he will be sending her money.
>
> One angry newspaper then […] indignantly scolded me for laughing at human grief.
>
> "What does Madame Teffi find funny about this?" the newspaper asked indignantly. After quoting the very saddest passages of all, it repeated, "And does she consider this funny? And is this funny, too?"
>
> The newspaper would probably be most surprised if I were to tell it that I did not laugh for a single minute. […]
>
> And so the aim of this preface is to warn the reader that there is a great deal in this book that is not funny.[5]

Several of the stories in *The Lifeless Beast* seem startlingly modern. The journalist's misunderstanding shows us how far beyond the conventions of her time Teffi had moved. Yavdokha has no companion but a hog and is hunchbacked from living in a hut that has sunk deep into the ground. She lives five miles from the nearest village and is alienated both from the other peasants and from everything to do with the Russian state. After someone has read out a letter informing her of her son's death she repeats the word "war"—but it is unclear if she even grasps what the word means and she certainly does not take in that her son has died. Yavdokha could have stepped out of one of Samuel Beckett's last plays.

Curiously, misunderstandings not unlike the journalist's are a central theme of *The Lifeless Beast*. In some stories, the misunderstandings arise from differences of social class; in others, it is the young and healthy who fail to understand the old and needy; in still others it is adults who fail—or do not even try—to understand children. Teffi's portrayal of human failings is unflinching; in "Happiness," she describes happiness as an "empty and hungry" creature that can survive only if fed with the "warm, human meat" of someone else's envy. In a smaller number of stories, however, she evokes moments of genuine love and compassion. In "Daisy," a seemingly inane aristocratic lady enrolls as a military nurse because that is the fashionable thing to do, quickly becomes involved in her work, and, to her surprise, is deeply moved by the gratitude of an uneducated soldier she helps to treat.[6] "The Heart" follows a similar pattern; Rakhatova, a frivolous actress, thinks it would be entertaining to confess to a simple, poorly educated monk before receiving Communion in a remote monastery. She is taken aback by the monk's spontaneous joy when she says she has not "committed any grave sins."

> The eyes now looking at her were so clear and joyful that they seemed to be flickering, just as stars flicker when their clear light overflows. [...]
>
> "Praise the Lord! Praise the Lord!"
>
> He was trembling all over. It was as if he were a large severed heart and a drop of living water had fallen onto it. The heart quivers—and then all the other dead, severed pieces quiver too.

As always, Teffi's imagery is carefully developed. The last sentence refers back to the scene that greeted Rakhatova and her friends when they arrived at the monastery the previous day:

> The peasant was hacking at the fish with a broad knife. [...]
>
> Then the peasant took a bucket and poured water over the pieces of fish and the severed head. There was a sudden move-

ment in one of the middle pieces. A twitch, a quiver—and the whole fish responded. Even the chopped-off tail jerked.

"That's its heart contracting," said the Medico.

Born in 1872, Teffi was a contemporary of Alexander Blok and other leading Russian Symbolists. Her own poetry is derivative, but in her prose she shows a remarkable gift for grounding Symbolist themes and imagery in the everyday world. "The Heart" is entirely realistic and at times even gossipy—yet the story is permeated throughout with Christian symbolism relating to fish. In "A Quiet Backwater," she achieves a still more successful synthesis of the heavenly and the earthly. Toward the end of this seven-page story a laundress gives a long disquisition on the name days of various birds, insects, and animals. The mare, the bee, the glowworm—she tells a young visitor—all have their name days. And so does the earth herself: "And the Feast of the Holy Ghost is the name day of the earth herself. On this day, no one dairnst disturb the earth. No diggin, or sowin—not even flower pickin, or owt. No buryin t' dead. Great sin it is, to upset the earth on 'er name day. Aye, even beasts understand. On that day, they dairnst lay a claw, nor a hoof, nor a paw on the earth. Great sin, yer see." In a key poem—almost a manifesto—of French Symbolism, Charles Baudelaire interprets the whole world as a web of mystical "correspondences." In a less grandiose way, Teffi conveys a similar vision. She was, I imagine, delighted by the paradox of the earth's name day being the Feast of the Holy Spirit—not, as one might expect, the feast of a saint associated with some activity like plowing.

The Lifeless Beast is notable for its striking imagery and bold rendition of peasant speech, and for being one of a very few treatments in Russian literature of the First World War as experienced by civilians. Teffi's insight into human selfishness and viciousness never wavers. Nevertheless, she remains true to her faith in Christian love—as practiced by Daisy in a field hospital, as experienced by Rakhatova through Orthodox ritual, and as embodied in the generous, restorative understandings of folk religion.

*

In early 1920 Teffi settled in Paris. Russian émigrés throughout the world were quick to set up publishing houses and Teffi was one of their most valued authors. In 1921 alone she published five books: two miniature selections of articles and stories, in Berlin; a collection of comic sketches, in Shanghai; the short-story collection *Black Iris*, in Stockholm; and *A Quiet Backwater*—which includes most of the stories from *The Lifeless Beast*—in Paris.

Teffi's high standing is still more clearly shown by her publications in periodicals. "Ke fer?" (Que Faire?)—a brilliant evocation of the Russians' sense of alienation in Paris—was published in April 1920, in the first issue of the important *The Latest News*. And "Solovki"— an almost Bruegelesque account of the widespread practice of mass pilgrimage to holy sites—was the first item in the first issue (August 1921) of the glamorous, lavishly illustrated journal *The Firebird*, which featured work by almost all the best-known émigré writers and artists. These two publications serve as markers to the twin paths Teffi would follow for the next fifty years. Many of her stories are about the mishaps and absurdities of émigré life; others are about a long-lost past.

"Solovki" was republished in *Evening Day*. Teffi's following collection, *A Small Town* (Paris, 1927), is not represented in *Other Worlds*, since most of the stories deal with her émigré present—the "small town" of Russian Paris—rather than her Russian past. We have, however, included three stories from *The Book of June*. Like "Solovki," the title story is a sympathetic account of overwhelming religious experience. Here, however, Teffi enters more deeply into the heroine's inner world, into her most inarticulate thoughts and feelings; it is one of Teffi's most sensitive treatments of adolescence.

Most of the stories in *Witch* bear the titles of folkloric beings—for example, "Wonder Worker," "The House Spirit," or "Rusalka" (a female water spirit resembling the Lorelei). Some of the stories are grim, some fanciful, some sober and philosophical. Some are realistic, with only the merest hint at the supernatural; in others, the supernatural motifs are more pronounced. Sometimes a character tries all too transparently to cover up his or her misconduct through some implausible supernatural explanation; sometimes it is the rationalist skeptics who appear foolish and blinkered. One piece, "About the House," is hardly a story at all—more like a chatty retelling of a scholarly article, with a brief anecdote tacked on at the end.

All the stories are presented from the perspective of a Russian exile. Often the tone is nostalgic. Sometimes there is a note of bewilderment: Could such things truly have happened? Could such a world as old Russia really have existed?

Witch is a coherent and self-contained collection. Its main themes, however, are anticipated in "Wild Evening" and "Shapeshifter," the last two stories in *The Book of June*. The central character of these two stories—and also of the first and last stories of *Witch*—is clearly modeled on Teffi herself. In 1892, aged twenty, Teffi married a lawyer by the name of Vladislav Buchinsky. We know little about her years as a young wife and mother, living in small provincial towns, but we know from statements Teffi made later that she was deeply unhappy.

"Wild Evening" is about fear of the unknown; except for an opportunistic peddler, everyone in the story—the young Teffi, the monks, even the horse—is in a state of terror. All around lurk threatening forces—darkness, cattle plague, the unclean dead. "Shapeshifter" may represent Teffi's fantasy of a different course her life might have followed; a stranger's chance intervention prompts the Teffi figure to decide *against* marriage to a lawyer who has much in common with the real-life Buchinsky. The opening, title story of *Witch* shows us a young husband and wife feeling more and more exasperated with each other as they grow ever more afraid—though neither will admit it—of a maid suspected of witchcraft. And in "Wolf Night," the concluding story of *Witch*, we glimpse this same husband and wife perhaps a year or two later. The husband has grown even more resentful and evil-tempered, and the wife—now pregnant—is overwhelmed by nightmares of the house being surrounded by wolves. Ten lines before the end of the story, the husband says to the wife, "Please! Do me a favor! Go and stay with your oh so clever mother. A fine way she must have brought you up, to make you into such a hysteric."

Teffi did not ever go back to her "oh so clever mother," though it is possible that her husband may have uttered some sarcasm similar to the above. All we know for sure is that in 1898, probably on the edge of a breakdown, Teffi abandoned her husband and three children and moved back to Petersburg to begin her career as a professional writer. There is little doubt that this rupture—which she very seldom spoke about—was a source of almost unbearable guilt and pain. Nevertheless, the words she wrote nearly fifty years later to her eldest daughter have the ring of truth. After saying she had been a bad mother, Teffi backtracks: "In essence I was good, but circumstances drove me from home, where, had I remained, I would have perished."[7]

At the heart of *Witch*, framed by these stories drawing on her unhappy life as a young woman, stands a group of six stories in which Teffi moves further back in time, to her own childhood. At one level, these can be read as a fictional treatment of folk beliefs in Volhynia (now part of western Ukraine). At the same time, they constitute a memorial to Teffi's younger sister Lena, the closest to her of her six siblings. Lena had died in 1919, and Teffi writes movingly about her death in *Memories*, which she completed only shortly before the stories in *Witch*. In both books, Teffi portrays herself and Lena as inseparable.

One of these stories, "The Kind That Walk," is a study of anti-semitism—and of xenophobia more generally. Teffi deftly shows us people's blind fear of Moshka, an honest and competent Jewish carpenter; she is equally deft in evoking the fascination with which she and Lena listen to the adults' wild talk about how Moshka, many years earlier, had been dragged off by the devil. Many of the other main characters in these six stories are domestic servants. Teffi's mother and some of her elder siblings appear now and then, but it is the children's Nyanya, or nanny, who is the most important authority figure.

There are also two stories set mainly in Moscow and Petersburg.

The longer of these, "The Dog," begins with the narrator, Lyalya, recalling idyllically happy summers as a teenager on a country estate in the company of friends and admirers. In *those* days, she says with pained emphasis, she was carefree and high-spirited. She had felt briefly troubled, however, by the intense feeling with which a shy young boy called Tolya once swore eternal devotion to her, promising always to remain her "faithful dog." A few years later, Lyalya falls in with the bohemian crowd who frequent the Stray Dog, the famous Petersburg cabaret where all the major poets of the time used to give readings. Somehow, almost inadvertently, Lyalya takes up with Harry Edvers, a particularly odious pseudo-poet who later ends up working for the Cheka, the Bolshevik security police. In the story's final scene she calls on her "faithful dog" for help—with dramatic results. Lyalya concludes,

> That's the whole story; that's what I wanted to tell you. I've made nothing up; I've added nothing; and there's nothing I can explain—or even want to explain. But when I turn back and consider the past, I can see everything clearly. I can see each separate event and the axis or thread upon which a certain force had strung them.
>
> It had strung the events on the thread like beads and tied up the loose ends.

"The Dog" is convincing on every level. As an evocation of a lost childhood paradise, the first pages bear comparison with the work of Teffi's friend and colleague Ivan Bunin. As a reckoning with the febrile cultural world of prerevolutionary Petersburg, it anticipates Anna Akhmatova's *Poem Without a Hero* (written 1940–1965). Like Akhmatova, Teffi sees the bohemian abandonment of traditional moral values as having paved the way for the brutalities and duplicities of Communism. And the denouement provides a fine example of a writer drawing on the occult not for exotic ornament but as a source of psychological truth. The huge dog's sudden appearance may be mere chance; it may be a real embodiment of Tolya's loyal and resolute spirit; or it may be Tolya's spirit prompting Lyalya toward an act that requires superhuman powers. Teffi has taken care not to exclude any of these possibilities. Unlike the "certain force" spoken of by her narrator, she does not tie up the story's loose ends.

In the letter quoted earlier, Teffi says of *Witch*, "This book has been highly praised by Bunin, Kuprin, and Merezhkovsky. They praised it for its artistry and the excellence of its language. I am, by the way, proud of my language, which critics have seldom commented on."[8]

Teffi's pride is justified. Along with Andrey Bely, Ivan Bunin, Vladimir Nabokov, and Andrey Platonov, she is one of a number of great twentieth-century Russian prose writers who were also poets but whose poetic gifts found their truest expression in prose. It is difficult, though, to define what makes Teffi's language so remarkable. She makes skillful use of repetition, often using a single word as a leitmotif for an entire story. In "Wild Evening," for example, she uses the adjective "*dikii*" (wild) of a horse's eye, of the night, of a person, and of the dangerously high seat of a two-wheel carriage. In "Rusalka" she repeats "*mutnyi*" (murky, cloudy, troubled) more and more often in the course of the story; she uses the word especially often in relation to the two sisters' troubled visions in the last pages, when one of the housemaids either drowns or turns into a *rusalka* and the girls fall ill with scarlet fever. It is also true that Teffi has a fine ear for the linguistic peculiarities of people from different social groups—ranging from Volhynia peasants to Russian émigrés in Paris; it is not for nothing that the satirist Mikhail Zoshchenko, as a novice writer, noted down some of Teffi's most striking coinages and malapropisms.[9] Nevertheless, the 1920s was a rich period for Russian prose and none of the above is enough to make Teffi unique.

What truly sets her apart is her lightness of touch. More than Vladislav Khodasevich, more than Akhmatova or any of the Acmeist poets, it is Teffi who has inherited the grace and fluency of Pushkin. She can write as simply and tautly as Hemingway—but without the least sense of willed tightness. She can write long, complex sentences dense with embedded participial clauses, yet these sentences, unlike apparently similar sentences in the work of Bunin, retain a conversational quality. Some of her more unreliable narrators come out with phrases as memorably absurd as characters out of Zoshchenko—yet even here there is a difference. Zoshchenko's sentences seem brilliantly constructed; Teffi's appear simply to have happened. It may be for this very reason—her success in creating an illusion of naturalness—that Teffi's language has received so little scholarly attention.

Many of her greatest contemporaries, however, were well aware of her gifts. Zoshchenko studied her intently; Bunin admired her; Mikhail Bulgakov borrowed from her Civil War articles for his *The White Guard*. And Georgy Ivanov referred to Teffi as "a unique phenomenon in Russian literature, a true miracle that people will still be wondering at in a hundred years' time, crying and laughing at once."[10]

The last two pieces in this collection are "Baba Yaga" and "Volya," two essays from *Earthly Rainbow* (published six months before Teffi's death), in which Teffi asserts her profound Russianness. Baba Yaga is the name of the archetypal Russian folktale witch and the word "*volya*" is used for what Teffi understands as a peculiarly Russian kind of unbounded emotional freedom. Both essays end with a heartfelt cry. Baba Yaga, confined in her wintry hut, longing for wildness, freedom, and open spaces, cries, "*B—o—r—i—n—g*." And in the last lines of "Volya" the aging Teffi remembers herself as a young woman, waving at the spring dawn and crying out, "*Vo-o-o-ly-a-a-a!*" Shortly before this, she has heard a boy on the other side of the river singing his heart out. The last line of his song—"Sing *Volya, Volya, Volya!*"—is described as "heartrending, piercingly joyful, like a sudden yelp, coming from somewhere too deep in the soul."

Teffi is indeed one of the most graceful of Russian writers. It seems likely, however, that this grace is a way of managing an almost unbearable burden of pain. There are a great many heartfelt cries in these stories. Some of these cries and desperate screams seem almost infectious, so agonizing that those who hear them can't help but let out similar screams. The epileptic sleigh driver in "Shapeshifter," for example, lets out a cry with "something so terrible about it" that the narrator screams too, jumping up from her seat and almost tumbling out of the sleigh. And the narrator of "Witch" describes, at some length, the scream of a guinea hen "wailing for her slaughtered mate." She continues,

> This isn't easy to explain to you, but such a cry of inconsolable despair, above the dead little town, in the silence of that trackless steppe, was more than any human soul could bear.
>
> I remember coming home and saying to my husband, "Now I know why people hang themselves."
>
> He screamed, clutching his head in his hands.

In the last pages of "The Book of June," Katya lets out repeated screams of terror: "Katya had no idea what made her keep on screaming like this. Some kind of lump seemed to be filling her throat, making her gasp and wheeze and scream out Grisha's name." And two of Teffi's very finest works end with still wilder cries. The heroine of "Solovki" gives herself up to a prolonged scream during a service in the main monastery church: "What mattered was not to stop, to expend more and more of herself in the cry, to give herself to it more intensely, yes, more and more of herself: *Oh, if only they didn't get in her way. Oh, if only they let her keep going...* But it was so hard. Would she have the strength?"

One of the most painful passages in all Teffi's work is the last page of her autobiographical *Memories*, her account of her final, irrevocable departure from Russia. It is the summer of 1919 and she is on her way to Istanbul, on a boat leaving Novorossiysk harbor:

> From the lower deck comes the sound of long, obstinate wails, interspersed with words of lament.
>
> Where have I heard such wails before? Yes. I remember. During the first year of the war. A gray-haired old woman was being taken down the street in a horse-drawn cab. Her hat had

slipped back onto the nape of her neck. Her yellow cheeks were thin and drawn. Her toothless black mouth was hanging open, crying out in a long tearless wail: "A-a-a-a-a!" Probably embarrassed by the disgraceful behavior of his passenger, the driver was urging his poor horse forward, whipping her on.

Yes, my good man, you didn't think enough about whom you were picking up in your cab. And now you're stuck with this old woman. A terrible, black, tearless wail. A last wail. Over all of Russia, the whole of Russia . . . No stopping now . . .

These cries and wails differ in tone. The boy's "sudden yelp" in "Volya" is "piercingly joyful," whereas the gray-haired woman in *Memories* is mired in despair. In at least one respect, however, the cries are all too similar. All are painfully raw; all come from "somewhere too deep in the soul." It is as if these characters have been flayed. Layers of protective skin have been torn away and what should be hidden lies dangerously exposed.

Teffi's grace seems all the more precious when we understand that it was both a protective cloak and her way of trying to keep her footing. It may perhaps have been what enabled her, unlike many of her contemporaries, to preserve her balance and sanity throughout a seemingly never-ending series of catastrophes—the First World War, the Russian Civil War, the viciousness of émigré political infighting, and life under German occupation during the Second World War. If Teffi liked to refer to herself as a witch, if she identified at the end of her life with Baba Yaga, this may be because she was hoping to charm the inner and outer darkness, to cast a spell on it that might keep it at bay.

—ROBERT CHANDLER

PART ONE

from *Earthly Rainbow* (1952)

KISHMISH

Lent. Moscow.

In the distance, the muffled sound—between a hum and a boom—of a church bell. The clapper's even strokes merge into a single, oppressive moan.

An open door, into murky predawn gloom, allows a glimpse of a dim shape, rustling stealthily about the room. Now it stands out, a dense patch of gray; now it dissolves, merging into the surrounding dark. The rustling quietens. The creak of a floorboard—and of a second floorboard, farther away. Silence. Nyanya has left—on her way to the early-morning service.[1]

She is observing Lent.[2]

Now things get frightening.

Barely breathing, the little girl lying in bed curls into a small ball. She listens and watches, listens and watches.

The distant hum is becoming sinister. The little girl is all alone and defenseless. If she calls, no one will come. But what can happen? Night must be ending now. Probably the cocks have greeted the dawn and the ghosts are all back where they belong.

And they belong in cemeteries, in bogs, in lonely graves under simple crosses, or by forsaken crossroads on the outskirts of forests. Not one of them will dare touch a human being now; the Liturgy is being celebrated and prayers are being said for all Orthodox Christians. What is there to be frightened of?

But an eight-year-old soul does not believe the arguments of reason.

It shrinks into itself, quietly trembling and whimpering. An eight-year-old soul does not believe that this is the sound of a bell. Later, in daytime, it will believe this, but now, alone, defenseless, and in anguish, it does not know that this is a bell calling people to church. Who knows what this sound might be? It is sinister. If anguish and fear could be translated into sound, this is the sound they would make. If anguish and fear could be translated into color, it would be this uncertain, murky gray.

And the impression made by this predawn anguish will remain with this little creature for many years, for her whole life. This creature will continue to be woken at dawn by a fear and anguish beyond understanding. Doctors will prescribe sedatives; they will advise her to take evening walks, or to give up smoking, or to sleep in an unheated room, or with the window open, or with a hot water bottle on her liver. They will counsel many, many things—but nothing will erase from her soul the imprint of that predawn despair.

The little girl's nickname was "Kishmish"—a word for a kind of very small raisin from the Caucasus. This was, no doubt, because she was so very small, with a small nose and small hands. Small fry, of little importance. Toward the age of thirteen she would suddenly shoot up. Her legs would grow long and everyone would forget that she had ever been a kishmish.[3]

But while she still was a little kishmish, this hurtful nickname caused her a great deal of pain. She was proud and she longed to distinguish herself in some way; she wanted, above all, to do something grand and unusual. To become, say, a famous strongman, someone who could bend horseshoes with their bare hands or stop a runaway troika in its tracks. She liked the idea of becoming a brigand or—still better—an executioner. An executioner is more powerful than a brigand since it is he who has the last word. And could any of the grown-ups have imagined, as they looked at this skinny little girl with shorn flaxen hair, quietly threading beads to make a ring—could any of them have imagined what terrible dreams of power were seething inside her head? There was, by the way, yet another dream—of becoming a dreadful monster. Not just any old monster, but the kind of monster that really frightens people. Kishmish would stand by the mirror, cross her eyes, pull the corners of her mouth apart, and thrust her tongue out to one side. But first she would say in a deep voice, acting the part of an unknown gentleman standing behind her, unable to see her face and addressing the back of her head, "Do me the honor, madame, of this quadrille."

She would then put on her special face, spin around on her heels, and reply, "Very well—but first you must kiss my twisted cheek."

The gentleman would run away in horror. "Hah!" she would call after him. "Scared, are you?"

Kishmish had begun her studies. To start with—Scripture and Handwriting.

Every task one undertook, she learned, should be prefaced with a prayer.

This was an idea she liked. But since she was still, among other things, considering the career of brigand, it also caused her alarm.

"What about brigands?" she asked. "Must they say a prayer before they go out briganding?"

No one gave her a clear answer. All people said was "Don't be silly." And Kishmish did not understand. Did this mean that brigands don't need to pray—or that it is essential for them to pray, and that this is so obvious that it was silly even to ask about it?

When Kishmish grew a little bigger and was preparing to make her first confession, she underwent a spiritual crisis. Gone now were the terrible dreams of power.

"Lord, Hear Our Prayer" was, that year, being sung very beautifully.

Three young boys would step forward, stand beside the altar, and sing in angelic voices. Listening to them, a soul grew humble and tender. These blessed sounds made a soul wish to be light, white, ethereal, and transparent, to fly away in sounds and incense, right up to the cupola, to where the white dove of the Holy Spirit had spread its wings.

This was no place for a brigand. Nor was it the right place for an executioner, or even a strongman. As for the monster, it would stand outside the door and cover its terrible face. A church was certainly no place to be frightening people. Oh, if only she could get to be a saint. How marvelous that would be! So beautiful, so fine and sweet. To be a saint was above everything and everyone. More important than any teacher, headmistress, or even provincial governor.

But how could she become a saint? She would have to work miracles—and Kishmish had not the slightest idea how to go about this. Still, miracles were not where you started. First, you had to lead a saintly life. You had to make yourself meek and kind, to give everything to the poor, to devote yourself to fasting and abstinence.

So how would she give everything to the poor? She had a new spring coat. That was what she should give away first.

But how furious Mama would be. There would be a most unholy row, the kind of row that didn't bear thinking about. And Mama would be upset, and saints were not supposed to hurt other people and make them upset. What if she gave her coat to a poor person but told Mama it had simply been stolen? But saints were not supposed to tell lies. What a predicament. Life was a lot easier for a brigand. A brigand could lie all he wanted—and just laugh his sly laugh. How, then, did these saints ever get to be saints? Simply, it seemed, because they were old—none of them under sixteen, and many of them real oldies. No question of any of them having to obey Mama. They could give away all their worldly goods just like that. No, this clearly wasn't the place to start—it was something to keep till the end. She should start with meekness and obedience. And abstinence. She should eat only black bread and salt, and drink only water straight from the tap. But here too lay trouble. Cook would tell on her. She would tell Mama that Kishmish had been drinking water that hadn't been boiled. There was typhus in the city and Mama did not allow her to drink water from the tap. But then, once Mama understood that Kishmish was a saint, perhaps she would stop putting obstacles in her path.

And then, how marvelous to be a saint. There were so few of them these days. Everyone she knew would be astonished.

"Why's there a halo over Kishmish?"

"What, didn't you know? She's been a saint for some time now."

"Heavens! I don't believe it!"

"There she is. See for yourself!"

And she would smile meekly as she went on eating her black bread and salt.

Her mother's visitors would feel envious. Not one of them had saintly children.

"Are you sure she's not just pretending?"

Fools! Couldn't they see her halo?

She wondered how soon the halo would begin. Probably in a few months. It would be fully present by autumn. God, how marvelous all this was. Next year she'd go along to confession. The priest would say in a severe voice, "What sins have you committed? You must repent."

And she would reply, "None at all. I'm a saint."

"No, no!" he would exclaim. "Surely not!"

"Ask Mama. Ask her friends. Everyone knows."

The priest would question her. Maybe there had, after all, been some tiny little sin?

"No, none at all!" she would repeat. "Search all you like!"

She also wondered if she would still have to do her homework. If so, this too might prove awkward. Because saints can't be lazy. And they can't be disobedient. If she were told to study, then she'd have to do as they said. If only she could learn miracles straightaway! One miracle—and her teacher would take fright, fall to her knees, and never mention homework again.

Next she imagined her face. She went up to the mirror, sucked in her cheeks, flared her nostrils, and rolled her eyes heavenward. Kishmish really liked the look of this face. A true saint's face. A little nauseating, but entirely saintly. No one else had a face anything like it. And so—off to the kitchen for some black bread!

As always before breakfast, Cook was cross and preoccupied. Kishmish's visit was an unwelcome surprise. "And what's a young lady like you doing here in the kitchen? There'll be words from your mama!"

There was an enticing smell of Lenten fare: fish, onions, and mushrooms. Kishmish's nostrils twitched involuntarily. She wanted to retort, "That's none of your business!," but she remembered that she was a saint and said in a quiet voice, "Varvara, please cut me a morsel of black bread." She thought for a moment, then added, "A large morsel."

Cook cut her some bread.

"And will you sprinkle a little salt on it," she continued, looking up as if to the heavens.

She would have to eat the bread then and there. If she went anywhere else with it, there would be misunderstandings. With unpleasant consequences.

The bread was particularly tasty and Kishmish regretted having only asked for one slice. Then she filled a jug from the tap and drank some water. Just then the maid came in.

"I'll be telling your mama," she exclaimed in horror, "that you've been drinking tap water!"

"She's just eaten a great chunk of bread," said Cook. "Bread and salt. So what do you expect? She's a growing girl."

The family was called in to breakfast. Kishmish couldn't not go. So she decided to go but not eat anything. She would be very meek.

For breakfast there was fish soup and pies. She sat there, looking blankly at the little pie on her plate.

"Why aren't you eating?"

In answer she smiled meekly and once more put on her saintly face—the face she had been practicing before the mirror.

"Heavens, what's gotten into her?" exclaimed her astonished aunt. "Why's she pulling such a dreadful face?"

"And she's just eaten a great big chunk of black bread," said the telltale maid. "Just before breakfast—and she washed it down with water straight from the tap."

"Whoever said you could go and eat bread in the kitchen?" shouted Mama. "And why were you drinking tap water?"

Kishmish rolled her eyes and flared her nostrils, once and for all perfecting her saintly face.

"What's gotten into her?"

"She's making fun of me!" squealed the aunt—and let out a sob.

"Out you go, you vile little girl!" Mama exclaimed furiously. "Off to the nursery with you—and you can stay there on your own for the rest of the day!"

"And the sooner she's packed off to boarding school, the better," said the aunt, still sobbing. "My nerves, my poor nerves. Literally, my every last nerve . . ."

Poor Kishmish.

And so she remained a sinner.

Translated by Robert and Elizabeth Chandler

PART TWO
from *The Lifeless Beast* (1916)

SOUL IN BOND

AT THE Dvuchasovs' country house, their old Nyanya was readying herself for death; she had been doing this for ten years.

In summertime, a small kitchen was put at her disposal. It was a little timber-board room next to the dairy where they made curd cheese. In winter, with the master's family gone to the city, she would move herself to the corridor in the main building. There, in a corner behind a dresser, she would sit or lie on her trunk and carry on with her dying until spring.

Come spring, she'd pick a dry, sunny day, stretch a rope between a pair of trees out in the birch grove, and air her burial clothes: a long yellowed linen shirt, a pair of embroidered slippers, a pale blue belt—embroidered with a prayer for the repose of the dead—and a small cypress-wood cross.

For her this was the most interesting day of the year. She'd wave a stick around, trying to keep the gnats off her burial clothes, and talk to herself about different cemeteries—which were dry and which damp—and about what kind of shoes it's best to put on the dead, so they won't make the floorboards creak at night.

"Nah then, Nyanya," a servant might chuckle. "Mekk sure ye mind that shirt, eh? Not gooin to last thi much longer than twenty year, is it? Tha'd 'ave to mekk thisself a new 'un, wouldn't ye?"

Come winter, though, she'd be left all on her own in the empty echoing house. All day she'd sit in her corner behind the dresser. In the evenings she'd drag herself to the kitchen to drink tea with the caretaker woman.

*

Nyanya comes and sits herself down. And starts talking. A long rambling story, and she seems to have left out the beginning. At first, the caretaker tries to make sense of it all, but after a while she gives up.

"…An' she come to the old biddy's daughter-in-law…" Nyanya mumbles on, pursing her lips to stop a nub of sugar falling from her mouth.[1] "She come an' says, 'I want to mekk misself some spiced bread—'ere, Matriona, gi' us some cardamom, would ye?' Nah, why would I 'ave any cardamom, eh? So I tells 'er, you leave ol' Matriona alone nah, there's a good lass. Stop mitherin, and go and pester summn else. Aye, that shut 'er up, good n' proper."

"Oh Nyanya, who're you goin' on about nah?" says the caretaker. But Nyanya doesn't hear.

"And what's to fret about, anyway? I've lit me lamps, stood up to pray, and bent to each corner. 'Nah then, old soul stealer,' I says to 'im, 'Can ye hear me dahn there? You leave me in peace while I'm prayin. After that, do as you will, for thine is the power an' the glory, as they say.' An' I know he can't touch me."

"Oh, my days!" says the startled caretaker. "Him dahn there an' the power and the glory—the words ye come out with…"

"'Ere. See that cockroach o'er thiere—bin followin me, it has—pitter-patter-patter. What's he up to, eh? Night before last, I 'eard summat else. Floorboards in t' drawinroom. Creak creak creakin, they were. So I'm lyin there, neither wake nor sleepin—summat in between. But then I sees it all, allus keep one eye open, don't I. An' in comes our late master. Aye, he's proper raging, all reight. Slippers slip-slappin on t' floor. Goes into t' dininroom. Winds up clock. Trrk-trrk-trrk. Even rightens clock hands wi' his fingers. Well, whiere'll he go nah, I wonder. He's still slip-slappin them slippers of 'is, mind. In a reight rage. 'Not good,' he says, 'not good at all.' An' way he goes —back through the drawinroom, back to 'is study, I reckon. Meanwhile that blessed cockroach's still witterin on in me ear! Witter-witter-witter. 'That's enough,' I tell 'im. 'I 'eard it all misself, din't I?'"

"Oh, Nyanya. What ye on about, luv? And just as it's nightfall, an' all. Only…did ye really see the late master?"

"No one believes. Nowadays, no one believes in owt. Tekk that lackey they brung from Petersburg. He only goes and leaves his knife lyin wi' t' edge facing up! I tells 'im, 'Wha' d'ye do that for, ye berk? Ye tryin to please the Wicked One, or what?' Well, he falls about, laughin. Nope, no one believes in owt these days, I tell thi. And then wha' did the old master die of? That's reight! And don't think I din't tell 'em, and all. I told 'em all straightaway.

"Yes, they'd brung that new German lass. 'Sposed to teach the little 'uns, she were. Well, I goes into her room, and wha' do I see? She's only gone and spilt needles all o'er the floor. And nah she's try-ing to pick 'em all up again. 'What's tha up to?' I ask 'er. I look at 'er face. Summat not reight. Then she goes an' says some strange word at me. It's not Russian. Well, I goes straight to her ladyship and tells her everything—that strange word n' all. Her ladyship only laughs, though. 'What of it?' she says.

"Two days later, n' the master tekks ill. Pins n' needles all over. Like summat's prickin 'im. Well, I know wha' that is, don't I? So I tells her ladyship: 'Tekk them needles off that German lass. Drop them in vitriol and wait till they dissolve. Then gi' it to t' master to drink. That'll tekk the needles out of him, all reight.' Did she listen? Did she 'eck. Fore thi knew it, he were dead n' buried. That's grand folk for ye—ne'er believe us simple folk. They're all the same—each n' evry one of 'em. 'Ere. If I were to count 'em nah, I'd say I've known a good five 'undred, or so. An' they're all the same. Oh, aye."

"Pour us another cuppa, would ye?"

"Eh, there goes that cockroach again. Nah, back in t' day, there were this chef. Used to work 'ere. Very good chef he were, too. Mas-ter paid a pretty penny for 'im. He were reight nasty tho'. Baked cockroaches into our pies. On purpose like! We was so upset, but no use gooin n' cryin bout it to t' master. He really liked that chef.

"So thiere we were, fastin for Holy Week, worried there'd be roaches in us Easter bread. Cryin we were. Anyways, off we go to church, confess us sins like, and what d'you know—one of the girls ups an' tells holy father bout this cook. Then t' cook hisself comes to confess. Oh, ye shoulda seen his face as he come out. All ashen like. Shekkin, he were. Din't say a word to us, mind. Just baked Easter kulich[2] as normal. Hahsomedivver, come the Liturgy—and he's nowhiere to be found. We searched n' searched, o'course, but couldn't find hide nor hair of 'im. So anyways, we sit down to break the fast. Summn cuts into t' kulich—an' thiere inside lies a dead finger. It were his—the cook's! Aye, that's roaches for ye. Pour us a splash, would ye?

"…Two years we spent workin on that shawl. Four girls doing the lace, each her own corner. That shawl were meant as a special gift— our master's wife had to grovel before the Tsaritsa, to get their daughter into one of 'em institutes. And, sure enough, girl got in. She were no fool, her ladyship, oh no. And she'd nivver hit one of us girls across the reight hand—she wanted us to go on mekking lace for her, din't she? Your left arm, mind, she'd pinch it raw. We all had left arms mottled as chintz. And all us girls wound up lopsided to boot. She'd start us early, ye see—five years old and she'd already 'ave us at our embroidery frames: reight shoulder up, left shoulder down, so you can push the needle up from underneath.

"The old master were a serious 'un. He'd sit thiere all quiet, embroiderin slippers wi' worsted. He did a pair for her ladyship, and the aunt, and other family, an' all. And when the girl were all done at her institute, he went and embroidered her a whole screen! Serious, he were. His son though were a proper joker. Once he come home from t' regiment and, in mid night, he drags our little Steshka out of bed by her plait. 'Sing, my beauty!' he goes. 'Sing me songs from the Volga country!' Poor Steshka, not even twelve yet. Well, the silly girl took fright—fainted thiere and then. Out cold, she were. It were two days before she were herself again. But he jus' laughed. Aye, a reight joker! Nah, when my eyes started to fail, they passed me on to his wife. Needed me for t' little uns, ye see. A good woman, she were too. Ever so gentle. Slender. And she used to walk on tippy-toe, like an angel. Ludmila Petrovna, her name were.

"Her 'usband tho, he were a brute. Treated us proper cruel. He'd start beatin ye—and then he'd get carried away. There were no stoppin him.

"Our Ludmila Petrovna, she used to 'ave this gentleman cousin of hers call round. Quiet one, he was. The pair of them, they'd spend hours togither. Always cryin, they were—Lord knows what about, mind. And he wrote 'er letters, too. She'd give 'em me and ask me to hide 'em away. I've nivver learnt to read misself, so o' course I couldn't make head nor tail of 'em. And I'd nivver show 'em to another soul. She trusted me, ye see.

"Oh, and did we love her. She allus defended us simple folk. An' when that brute of hers were in one of his rages, she'd throw 'erself at his feet. Aye, we really did love her.

"Anyhow, this one time, our master sets out for t' evening. Back then, we had this coachman, a lad called Naum. 'Well, Nyanya,' he says to me, 'I'm telling you that afore tonight's ovver, I'll be ten rubles better off.' And off they drove. Then the quiet one calls round. He an' her ladyship sit in the dining room, cryin they were. Naum, meanwhile, he says to the master, 'What do you think goes on when you're not at home, master? Shall we go back n' find out?' So back comes the master. An' sure enough he flies into a rage—smashes up evry plate in t' house. The quiet one, though, he slips out, dun't he. And thiere I am in t' nursery. I can hear our master going at it like thiere's no tomorrow—and I'm thinkin, 'Lord have mercy on my poor soul! Happen it's time to confess me sins.' So, I wait till he's calmed down a bit, then I tekk all 'em letters, run to our master, an' throw misself at his feet. And I tell him, 'I'm not a plotter,' I says. 'I'm not the sort to go against her master.' And after that—Lord help us! Her ladyship, our poor angel, didn't last another year. The master, he gave her hell for them letters. As for Naum, our master had him shaved an' packed off to t' army. That were a good laugh all reight— so much for Naum an' his ten rubles!

"You died, my Ludmila Petrovna, my bright one, our defender. You prob'ly even walked into Paradise on tippy-toe. Now I shall die too. My body will be dressed in us burial clothes. It'll be laid in t' ground. And I shall go up to Paradise. And my gentle one will be thiere to meet me. She'll plead for me before God. 'Here,' she'll say, 'is Matriona, my children's old Nyanya, now come before thee. In life she were me faithful servant. She were bound to me in serfdom and she served me devoted, as a soul in bond should. So grant her, good Lord, a place 'neath thy bosom and let her warm her little soul reight through to the bones—may she run free nah an' never know want! Amen!'"

Translated by Robert and Elizabeth Chandler,
Pavel Gudoshnikov, and Sian Valvis

CONFESSION

THE FIRST week of Lent.

Singing is forbidden, and so is skipping.

From the glass-fronted cupboard where they have been banished, my dolls watch my sufferings with round, frightened eyes: this afternoon, at four o'clock, I will be taken to make my first confession.

Nyanya is breakfasting on pea kissel[1] with sunflower oil—a dish that looks tasty but tastes nasty. I have often asked to try it, always hoping that maybe this time I'll like it.

I'm in low spirits. I'm frightened. Yesterday Nyanya told me I mustn't tear my stockings at the knees. I must stop riding horseback on the chairs and generally give up my unbridled ways. She ended: "Just you wait till you go to confession! The priest'll take you outside, harness you to a cart, and have you pull it round and round the church."[2]

Naturally, I didn't want to lose face. I pretended to take this calmly and said that I couldn't care less if I had to pull a cart. Inside, though, I was scared stiff.

Of course I knew perfectly well that torn stockings and riding on chairs were only trifling sins, but I had something more serious on my conscience—a proper grown-up sin. I had broken the eighth commandment: Thou shalt not steal.[3]

The theft had come about almost of itself. I happened to go up to Nyanya's windowsill and catch sight of a round bun, a *vatrushka*. One side of it was oozing jam. I wanted to check whether or not the jam went all the way through. So I inspected it. By the time the inspection was over and I'd come to a definite conclusion, there was only a tiny morsel of bun left—so tiny that leaving it on the windowsill would have looked positively unseemly. I had no choice but to finish it.

Nyanya puzzled for a long time over the bun's disappearance while I sat quietly at the table, stringing beads to make a little ring. It was only when Nyanya's ruminations abruptly switched to me—after drawing a blank elsewhere—that I resolved to put her off the scent.

"Nyanya dear, I think *the master* must have eaten it."

Nyanya and the house spirit—the master—were old foes. He often scattered her sewing needles or spat in the stove to stop the firewood catching. Even more annoyingly, he would place her thimble right under her nose and then make her look elsewhere. Poor Nyanya would get down on her hands and knees and fumble about under the bed and the chest of drawers. Until the master tired of his game, there was no chance of her finding the thimble.

And so the mystery of the vatrushka remained unsolved and I myself had long ago buried it under layers of more recent smaller-scale sins; but now that I was facing my first confession, I remembered everything and was overcome with terror.

Not only had I stolen something but, more terrible still, I had blamed the theft on the totally innocent house spirit. I spent the whole morning in painful reflection. After lunch, the six-fingered scullery maid came in and made three deep bows to Nyanya, saying, "Forgive me once, forgive me twice, forgive me thrice." Then she came over to me and did the same. Nyanya had answered, "God will forgive." I understood that I should make the same reply, but somehow I felt too ashamed. And when Nyanya reproached me for my silence I came up with a lame excuse.

"I couldn't speak."

"And why ever not?"

"I'm too hungry."

This sounded so stupid that I shed a few tears, hoping this might make my nonsense go down a bit better.

Before going to church I was taken off to the schoolroom and told to ask forgiveness from my older sisters and their governess, with due Christian humility.

The governess, a stout, whiskery Frenchwoman, had ample reason to be apprehensive about my visits to her domain. She asked sternly, "Well, what can I do for you?"

I curtsied and said, jamming three fingers into my mouth to hide my embarrassment, "*Madame, pardonnez-moi, je vous en prie.*" The governess's eyes darted around the room as she tried to guess what misdeeds she would now have to scold me for. But when one of my sisters put her in the picture, her French sentimentality got the better of her. She threw up her hands and exclaimed, "*Oh! Oh! Je te pardonne, ma fille.*"

This was too much to bear. She was not *my* governess; her strictly limited authority extended only as far as my sisters—and now here she was, suddenly daring to address me familiarly, in the *tu* form, and even to call me her daughter!

My humility instantly gave way to enraged indignation.

"How dare you call me *tu*, you stupid creature?"

The church is deserted but for the shadowy figures of some old women huddled by the wall.

Tiny and stooped, sighing noisily, they shuffle after the caretaker, questioning him in toothless, spluttering whispers and jingling their copper coins.

Someone hurries by, heels clacking, walking not on the thin strip of carpet but over the flagstones. The sound echoes, a long moan floating up into the cupola.

"I have sinned!" I say to myself, "I have sinned!" My left temple throbs and the candle trembles, drooping from the heat of my hand. "I have sinned! I have sinned! How will I ever admit it? How will I tell him? And is it even possible to tell him? Probably he won't want to listen to me at all."

I'm standing right next to the screen. From behind it comes a soft, calm voice. I'm not sure whether it's the priest or the tall bearded man who'd been waiting in front of me.

It'll be my turn any moment. I hope that the tall man will keep on confessing for a long time. Please let him be a great sinner. After all, there are people, robbers for example, who have committed so many sins that a whole lifetime isn't enough to tell them. Perhaps he'll keep on confessing and confessing and I'll be dead and at peace before he's finished.

But then it dawns on me that it would also be wrong to die without having confessed. I don't know what to do. I hear a rustling behind the screen, then footsteps. The tall man comes out. I scarcely have time to marvel at his calm expression before someone nudges me toward the screen—and there I am, standing before the priest.

My mind goes blank with terror. My one thought is that I mustn't start crying.

I hear the priest's questions but I can hardly make sense of them and I answer goodness knows what. I feel my mouth wobbling… Mustn't cry, mustn't cry!

"Have you been unkind to your sisters?"

"Yes, I have sinned, I have been unkind."

"And to your brothers?"

"My brothers?"

How on earth can I admit that I have been unkind to my brothers as well? What an appalling thought! I'd better just say nothing. Especially as I have only the one brother, a brother who hit me on the head with a ruler because I couldn't rattle off "I-wish-you-good-health-sir" like they do at the military cadet school when they salute the officers.

Better just to say nothing for a while.

There's a smell of incense. Solemn and soothing. The priest speaks softly, he doesn't scold or reproach me. But—what about Nyanya's vatrushka? Am I really not going to tell him? But then how can I tell him? Where will I find the words?

No, I won't tell him.

Up on a table that is almost taller than I am, something is gleaming. It must be a cross. How can I stand before the cross and tell the priest about the vatrushka? It's all so shameful, so silly, and so unseemly.

Now the priest is asking another question but I can't make out what he says. Now he's gently tilting my head forward, placing something on top of it.[4]

"Father, Father! I ate Nyanya's vatrushka. It was me. I ate it and put the blame on someone else."

I'm trembling from head to foot and I'm no longer afraid of crying. I'm no longer afraid of anything.

It's all over for me. I no longer deserve to be called a human being.

Something tickles my cheek, then brushes the corner of my mouth. Something salty. But why doesn't the priest say anything?

"It's not right to do that sort of thing," he says.

He goes on talking but I don't take anything in.

I come out from behind the screen.

Now I want to kneel in front of the icon, cry my eyes out, and die. It would be good to die now, after making a clean breast of it.

But here's Nyanya, the same humdrum look on her face as always. Why's she looking at me like that? She's going to tell everyone at home that I cried and my sisters will start teasing me.

I turn away and give my eyes and nose a firm rub with my kerchief.

"Of course I haven't been crying. Cry? Why would I cry?"

Translated by Sara Jolly

YAVDOKHA

for A. D. Nurenberg[1]

ON SUNDAY, riding back from the village, Trifon the miller's worker turned into the gully, stopped by Yavdokha's little hut, and handed her a letter.

"From thi son," he said. "From t' army."

Goggle-eyed and scrawny, tall but a little stooped, the old woman stood there and blinked. She didn't take the letter.

"But . . . mebbe it's not for us, tho?"

"Postman says it's for Yavdokha. In t' woods. Tekk it. From thi son, it is. From t' army."

The old woman ran her fingers across the letter, turning it over and over. There were calluses on her fingers and the nails were broken.

"Gi it a read, would tha. Mebbe it's not for us."

Trifon held the letter between his fingers too, then returned it to her.

"I can't read, can I? Get along to t' village. Summn there'll read it thi."

With that he rode off.

Yavdokha went on standing there. She was blinking.

Her hut had sunk down into the earth, as far as the little window with its shattered pane that broke the light into rainbows. But she was tall and spindly, not meant for such a hut. That, evidently, is why fate had bent her spine—after all, she could hardly spend every hour outdoors.

Yavdokha blinked. Back in the hut, she tucked the letter behind the blackened icon.

Then she went outside, to see her boar.

The boar lived in a dilapidated shed stuck onto the side of her hut. At night Yavdokha could hear him scratching his flank against the wall.

She would think lovingly, "Aye. 'Ave a good scratch nah. No scratchin laters, when tha's scran for t' Yule feast."

It was for the boar's sake that she got up each morning, pulled a thick canvas mitt onto her left hand, took an old sickle, now worn to a thread, and went out to cut the tough, fibrous nettles growing along the track.

During the day she would take the boar to root about in the hollow; in the evening she would drive him back to the shed, scolding him loudly, as if hers were a proper, well-run household where—praise the Lord!—all was in order.

It was a long time since she had seen her son. He was working in the city, far away. And now this letter from the army. Which meant her son had been taken to the war. Which meant he wouldn't have sent her money for the holiday. Which meant no bread.

Yavdokha went over to the boar, blinked, and said, "Remember me son, Panas? He sent us a letter. From t' army."

After this she felt calmer. Still, she lay awake for a long time that night—and then, in the morning, she heard the heavy tramp of boots.

She got up. She peered through a crack. Soldiers—a great many soldiers, all gray and silent. "Whiere they gooin? An' why? Why they not sayin owt? Wha' they so quiet for?"

She felt a sense of horror. She lay down and pulled the blankets over her head. And, once the sun had risen, she got up to go to the village.

Out she went. She looked around and blinked. This was where the soldiers had passed. All mud, all churned up. As if someone had pounded the path with a pestle. Everything along the verges now trampled to the ground.

"They've gon n' trod on t' boar's nettles. Trod 'em reight into t' ground, they 'ave!"

And off she went, tall and scrawny, kneading the mud with her feet and her makeshift staff, all the eight versts[2] to the village.

The village was celebrating. The girls were making a bridal wreath for Ganka One-Eye. She was about to be married to Nikanor, son of Khromenko. This Nikanor was going to the war, but the Khromenkos were getting old and they needed a daughter-in-law to help out in their hut. If Nikanor were killed, they'd never get one. And so the girls were weaving a wreath for Ganka One-Eye.

Ganka's hut felt stuffy. There was a smell of sour bread and sour sheepskin.

Red-faced and sweaty, eyebrows bleached by the sun, the girls sat squashed on a bench around the table. They were picking through ribbons and cloth flowers, turning them over and looking at them from each side. And with all the might of their robust young bodies, they were bawling out a song of the fields.

They had fierce faces and flaring nostrils; they sang as if hard at work. But this was an outdoor song, a song of open spaces, a song meant to carry from field to field. Here, in this cramped hut, it was squashed and deformed, throbbing against the tiny, clay-sealed windows, beating against them, unable to find a way out. But the young lads and older women crowding behind the girls seemed not to notice; they just squinted, as if something were blowing in their eyes.

"Hoy! Hey! Ho-o-o! Hoy! Hey! Ho-o-o!"

Whatever the words they yelled, they all sounded like "Hoy-hey-ho-o-o!" The girls were belting it out.

Yavdokha tried to squeeze in through the door. A woman turned to face her.

"Got a letter. From me son, Panas," said Yavdokha. "Sent it from t' army."

The woman didn't reply, or maybe just didn't hear; the girls were really making a racket.

Yavdokha decided to wait. She found herself a spot in the corner.

The girls fell silent—abruptly, as if stifled—and over by the door a fiddle began to scrape. Like a rooster with a sore throat. Rattling along behind it, as if trying to overtake it, was a tambourine. Everyone pressed back toward the door, and out into the middle of the hut stepped two flat-chested girls. They wore loose-fitting sleeveless waistcoats over their blouses and their bellies stuck out in front of them. They embraced, then danced and stamped, sometimes hopping and skipping as if they'd just stumbled. They circled the hut twice.

Everyone made way for a young man. He tossed back his greasy blond locks, squatted down, and began to move in a circle, now extending his pigeon-toed feet in their bast shoes, now scooping them back underneath him. He seemed not so much to be dancing as crawling clumsily and pitifully about, like a grotesque cripple who'd gladly stand upright if only he could.

He completed his circle, then straightened up and edged back into the crowd.

And then everyone was calling out, "Come on, Sakhfeya, ol' girl! Gi us a twirl! Goo on!"

A little old woman in a thick shawl tied like a turban shook her head and gestured dismissively. *She* wasn't going to dance—not for the life of her.

"Why they pesterin 'er?" muttered a few outsiders, who weren't in the know. "She's jus' an ol' biddy!"

But those who knew better went on calling out, "Come on, Sakhfeya! Gi' us a twirl! Goo on!"

All of a sudden, the old woman made a wry face and began to laugh. Turning toward the icon, she said, "Well, all reight then. But first le' me ask forgiveness." She crossed herself, bowed low before the icon and repeated, "O Lord, forgive us. O Lord, forgive us. O Lord, forgive us!"

Then she turned around again and said with a little smile, "I've prayed me sin away."

And her sin certainly called for prayer—no two ways about it! The way she winked, the way she cocked her head, the way she held her arms akimbo! You should have seen her!

Then a gangly young man leaped forward and began showing off his fancy footwork. But no one so much as looked at him. Everyone was watching Sakhfeya. And Sakhfeya wasn't even dancing. She was just standing and waiting her turn, waiting for this young man to reach her. He was the one dancing—and yet all the dance was in her, not in him. He was light on his bast-shod feet. His movements were deft—but the old woman was something else. Each of her veins was alive, each little bone was at play, every drop of her blood was charged. All eyes were on her, not on the young man. And then it was *her* turn. She spun around—and took off! Phew!

Not for nothing had this old woman prayed before the icon. Sin like hers can cost you dear in the next world.

But Yavdokha was squashed into her little corner. She couldn't see—which was perhaps just as well.

Once she'd caught her breath, she pushed her way out to the space by the entrance.

There she found Nikanor, the bridegroom. He was teasing a dog with a little stick.

"Ere Nikifor! Mebbe tha can read this. It's from our Panas. Sent us a letter from t' army."

Nikanor hesitated—he was enjoying himself and didn't want to be interrupted. Then he dropped the stick and took the letter. He tore a corner off the top, peeked inside, then carefully inserted a finger and opened the envelope.

"Aye, it's a letter, all reight. I'll read it ye: 'Auntie Yavdokha, I bow to you, respectfully. Wishing you good health. We're still going, still marching on. Very tired. But not too tired, mind. Your son, Apanasy, has gone to his rest. Maybe he were wounded, but don't get your hopes up. Cos he's gone to his rest. From Phillip Melnikov, who you know.' That's all."

"Pilipp?" asked the old woman, wanting to be sure.

"Aye, Pilipp."

She thought a little and asked, "Who's bin wounded then? Pilipp?"

"I dunno, do I? Mebbe Pilipp. Who knows. There's lots that's bin killed. War, in't it."

"Aye . . . war," she said. "Ere. Could tha read it again for us?"

"I can't now. Come back on Sunday an' I'll read it ye then."

"Reight then. Sithee Sunday."

She tucked the letter into her bosom, then stuck her head into the main room again.

"Wha' is it?" asked a young man as he elbowed her out of the way. It was the man who'd been lurching and lumbering about earlier. "What's up wi ye?"

"It's from us son. Panas. Sent us a letter. From t' army. Pilipp Melnikov's bin wounded—or mebbe he hasn't. There's lots that's bin killed. War, in't it."

In the evening, as she made her way back to her little hut, slipping now and then on the churned-up, slimy track, she was thinking two thoughts: a sad thought, and a calm thought.

The sad thought was: "They've gon n' trod on 'is nettles."

And the calm thought: "Panas sent us a letter tho. He'll send us money, too. Aye, an' when it comes, I'll get us some bread, eh?"

And that was all.

Translated by Anne Marie Jackson,
Robert and Elizabeth Chandler, and Sian Valvis

A QUIET BACKWATER

EVERY sea, every great river and stormy lake has its quiet backwater.

The water is clear and calm. The reeds don't rustle, and there are no ripples on the smooth surface. Anything there is an event—the mere touch of a dragonfly's wing, or that long-legged dancer, an evening mosquito.

If you climb the steep bank and look down, you'll see at once where this quiet backwater begins. A line has been drawn with a ruler.

Farther out, in the open water, waves toss and turn. They rock from side to side, as if in madness and pain, and suddenly, in a last despairing leap, they throw themselves toward the heavens, only to crash back down into the dark water, leaving the wind to snatch at clumps of maddened, impotent foam.

But in the backwater, this side of the sacred line, all is quiet. Instead of waves rising in mutiny, flinging themselves heavenward, the heavens themselves descend to the water, in clear azure and little puffs of cloud in the daytime, and with all the mystery of the stars at night.

The estate is called Kamyshovka—Reed Bank.

Evidently, it once stood on the bank of a river. But the river retreated and left behind it, as a keepsake or forget-me-not, a small, blue-eyed lake that is a delight to ducks—and a mass of stiff reeds growing in the front garden.

The main house is abandoned; the doors and windows are boarded up.

Life lingers on only in the lodge—a cross-eyed, lopsided little building.

Here live a retired couple—a laundress and a coachman. They are not idle; they take care of the estate.

In her old age the laundress has sprouted a beard, while the coachman, subdued by her dominant personality, has turned into such an old woman that he calls himself Fedorushka.

They live simply. They speak little, and since both are hard of hearing, each always has his or her say. And even if one of them does hear the other, they understand only hazily, so they keep to what is near and dear, what they lived through long ago, what they know well and have already recalled many a time.

Besides the coachman and the laundress there are other souls living on the estate: a cunning mare who thinks only about oats and how she might work less, and a glutton of a cow. There are chickens too, of course, though it's hard to say how many—you can't say there are four, but neither can you say there are five. If you throw them some grain and are careful to say, "Come an' have your fill! God bless!", then four chickens come running. But just you forget that blessing and along comes a fifth. Where it's come from no one knows—and it gobbles up all the seed and bullies the other hens. It's big and gray, and it doesn't want to be blessed.

What a worry it all is! The grain belongs to the master and mistress. Sooner or later the mistress will come and ask, "Who's been pecking up my grain? Four beaks or five?"

What will they say?

They are both afraid of being called to account. It had been a hard winter and they had gone through a lot of firewood. Fear had set them thinking: across the river lay piles of state-owned timber ready for the spring floating. They harnessed the mare, drove across the river, and brought back a load. And when they got through it all, they went back for more. What could be more wonderful than having such fine wood there on your doorstep! Even the mare, for all her cunning, didn't pretend to be tired. She hauled the wood with pleasure.

And then—would you believe it?—came a summons from the magistrate.

"Why did you steal the wood?"

"Why d'you think? To heat t' stove, of course. We've got through all our own wood already. And when 'er ladyship comes, she'll be reight cross."

The magistrate could have treated them worse. He didn't curse or swear—but he did tell them to return the wood. Why did he have to be so mean and stingy? Yes, he'd brought them nothing but trouble.

And how had he found out, this magistrate? They hadn't seen anyone when they were fetching the wood. Apparently it was the tracks from their sled—going straight across the river to the timber and then back to their door again.

Tracks? Weren't people cunning nowadays? The things they could figure out!

It's a warm day. Four red hens, properly blessed, are pecking at crusts of bread.

The table has been brought out onto the porch. They're going to drink tea. They have a guest from the village—a girl called Marfa, the coachman's first cousin once removed. Today is Marfa's name day.

She's a large girl, white, big-boned and slack-jawed. Her pink name-day dress is so unbearably bright that it verges on blue. The day is clear and fine. The sky is the bluest of blues, the young grass is a garish green, and the yellow flowers in the grass are like little suns—but the girl's dress outshines everything.

The old laundress looks at the dress. She squints and screws up her eyes. The girl's bearing, she feels, lacks dignity.

"Here. Wha's tha fussin about for? Stop being silly now, and mind yer manners. It's yer name day today. That means yer angels'll be lookin down on you from t' sky. And there's you, wigglin yer tail side to side, like an heiffer."

"Wha's up wi' ye, Nana Pelageya? I've not budged an inch since I sat down."

The old woman screws up her eyes at the dazzling dress. She can't understand why it so troubles her eyes.

"Go an' fetch t' samovar."

The old coachman appears. His face is anxious, his brows knitted—the imprint of spending time with the cunning mare.

"She's only gone an' finished the oats again. Doesn't matter how much I gives 'er, she eats the whole lot, she does. Cheeky mare! There's men that's less cunning, I tell ye. She'll outwit the lot of us. Our mistress won't be best pleased, I'll bet."

"Aye, an' she'll take it out on you, all right. The stores are near enough empty! 'Er own fault though. I mean, how else can I feed a peasant the whole winter long? It's not cheap, I tell you. Give 'im some spuds, an' he'll ask for butter. Give 'im porridge an' he'll want grool an' all. Does a peasant mind how much he eats? All *he* thinks about is how to fill up his belly."

The coachman nods sympathetically and even heaves a sigh, although he does half sense that the peasant in question might be himself. But that's the way things are. Deep in his soul he feels a certain awe before this peasant nature of his.

"Aye, peasants is peasants, all reight. Is a peasant goin to try and eat less?"

Then Marfa came back with the green-stained samovar.

"Tea's ready. Come an' sit at the table!" she said.

The old woman began blinking and screwing up her eyes again.

"Who's you talkin to? Who is it yer callin to t' table?"

The girl's jaw dropped. "Why—you, Nana. An' you, Grandad."

"Well then, that's wha' you should say. There was another woman, called folk to t' table. 'Come in for yer tea,' she says. 'It's on the table.' But what she didn't say, mind, was: 'Come in for yer tea, *Good Christians*!' An' wha' d'ye know, she got all sorts comin through: out from under t' stove, and out from behind t' stove, from t' sleepin shelf, from t' bench, an' from under t' bench. All t' unheard an' unknown, all t' unknown an' unseen. Great eyes peerin, great teeth chatterin. 'Tha's called us in, so now tha's got to feed us.' Well, what were she to do? Can't feed all of 'em, can she?"

"So what happened then?" The girl's eyes widened.

"Well, you know."

"Well, what?"

"Well, they did what they do."

"What did they do?"

"They did what they 'ad to, and that's the end of it."

"But what was it they 'ad to do, Nana?"

"Ask too many questions—there's no knowin who'll answer."

The girl hunched up in fright and looked away furtively.

"Wha's tha fidgetin for?" said the old woman, squinting at the bright pink of the girl's skirt. "And on yer own name day, an' all. Yer name day is yer saint's feast day—it's a holy day. A bee's name day is the day of Saints Zosima and Savvaty. A bee's a simple creature—but they don't buzz or sting on their name day. Just sit tight on their flowers an' think on their angel, they do."

"Horse's name day is the day of Saints Frol and Lavr," interrupted the coachman, blowing on the tea he'd poured out into his chipped saucer.

"An' the bird has 'er name day on the Feast of the Annunciation. She won't mekk a nest, won't even peck for grain. She'll just 'ave a little sing. Quiet, mind. Respectful."[1]

"On Saint Vlas's day we pay our respects to the cattle," the coachman interrupted again.

"And the Feast of the Holy Ghost is the name day of the earth herself.[2] On this day, no one dairnst disturb the earth. No diggin, or sowin—not even flower pickin, or owt. No buryin t' dead. Great sin it is, to upset the earth on 'er name day. Aye, even beasts understand. On that day, they dairnst lay a claw, nor a hoof, nor a paw on the earth. Great sin, yer see. Any beast knows its name day. Even the glowworm—his day bein Saint John the Baptist's day. Blows on his little flames an' prays to his angel. An' soon after comes Saint Aquilina's day—that's when red berries have their name day. Yer strawberries, yer raspberries, yer currants and brambles. Yer cranberries and cowberries. Every woodland creature, even the tiniest, has a name day. On Saint Aquilina's day, you won't catch a fox nor a wolf, nor even a hare, layin a paw on a red berry. Even the bear's careful. Doesn't want to bring down trouble. Sniffs around before every step."

The girl seemed frightened again. She was looking away to one side, tucking her flat feet under her pink skirt. Snuffling and sighing.

The coachman wanted to have his say too.

He did not know much. He'd been in the army. Long ago. They'd had to push back the enemy. And then push on somewhere else. And somewhere else again. Where? Who knows? You can't remember everything.

"Three year, I were away. An' then I come home. 'Hello, Fedorushka,' says me wife. So do the bairns. Then I looks in t' corner, an' what do I see, but a cradle. A cradle with a nursling. Well a nursling's a nursling. Next day, I ask me eldest, I says, 'Now then. What's that bairn in t' cradle?' 'Oh, that's the littl'un,' she says. All reight, if it's a littl'un, it's a littl'un. Day after, I ask the eldest, 'An' where did this littl'un come from, then?' 'Granny brought 'im us,' says she. All right, if it were Granny, then Granny it were. He gets bigger, this littl'un. Petka, they call 'im. An' he grows up, quick enough. Last year, his son got married. Petka's, I mean. I still never learned where he came from. Mind you, they'll all have forgotten by now, I dare say."

"There's lots I can't remember," murmured the old woman. "Don't remember when it's the cow's name day. Right bothersome, that is. I'm old now, forgettin it all. Still, it's a sin to upset a being on its name day, in't it?"

They shut the gate behind the pink girl. The day was over. It was time to go to bed.

It had been a difficult day. You can't fall asleep straightaway after a day like that. After guests have been around, you always sleep poorly. The tea, and the talk, and the finery, and all kinds of fuss.

"Now, when oh when is it the cow's name day? You'll see now, I'll not remember, an' then I'll go an' upset the cow on her name day, won't I? An' that'll be a sin. An' the cow, bless 'er, she can't say owt, can she? Up on high an angel'll weep."

It's hard being old! Hard!

Outside the window, the night is a deep blue. It calls something to mind—but just what, it is impossible to remember.

The reeds left behind by the river rustle softly.

The river has gone elsewhere. It has forgotten the reeds.

Translated by Robert Chandler,
Anne Marie Jackson, and Sian Valvis

THE HEART

THEY HAD to walk a whole eight versts through the bog.

There was a way around the bog, but it was a great deal farther, and there were no horses to be had in the village—they were all at work out in the fields.

And so they set off through the bog.

It was a narrow path, winding from tussock to tussock. Soon, though, things got harder still. They had to keep to a slippery walkway—two small logs lashed together, or just a bundle of sticks, squelching up and down in the bog.

The grass on either side was a bright, poisonous green and it was oddly short, like the manicured lawn of some English park. Here and there gleamed a shy, stunted birch, quaking and virginal. It was clear that these spindly branches were never going to be bent and that no one would ever tread on this poisonous grass. The monastery bog neither dried out in summer nor froze over in winter; there was no time of year you could go straight across it, whether on foot or on horseback.

They walked single file. Were they to meet someone coming the other way, they'd be in trouble; the narrow walkway was very slippery indeed.

Fedosya Fishergirl went first. She had a sharp nose and sharp eyes, a narrow, black-toothed smile and angry nostrils; when she was agitated, they looked pale.

The nickname "Fishergirl," as if from the operetta,[1] did not fit her at all, but she had once inherited a tattered fishing net and she managed now and again to catch some bream and a few orfe before a holiday. She would sell them and spend the money on drink.

The villagers envied Fedosya. They saw her as dangerously crafty and wily, almost a witch, and when they got drunk, they would threaten to burn her place down. All because of the fishing net.[2]

Fedosya walked barefoot, with a light tread. She had slender, sinewy calves, like a racehorse, and she kept looking from side to side, moving her head like a bird.

Tripping and stumbling along behind her was the Medico, a thick-lipped medical student wearing a calico peasant shirt that hung down outside his trousers. Dangling from one pocket was the yellow lace tail of his cigarette case.

After the Medico came Polosov the schoolteacher. He looked languid and greenish; there was something of the bog about him.

Last were the two women—Lykova, a local landowner, and the actress Lyolya Rakhatova. They were walking almost side by side, holding on to each other.

At first they let out little squeals as they slid and swayed along, but then, either realizing that this made no impression on the gentlemen or else simply getting used to it all, they stopped worrying about losing their footing. Instead, they just chattered away to each other, whispering and laughing.

Both of them liked the Medico. At first, they hadn't. It was, in fact, because they thought him a bit simple that they'd invited him along on this pilgrimage. He wasn't the kind of man to make them feel awkward or embarrassed.

Here, though, in the bog, things were different. Suddenly they both found that they liked him. And each tried to hide this unforeseen turn of events from the other by laughing nervously and making fun of the Medico. What seemed to amuse them most of all was the dangling yellow tail of his cigarette case.

The Medico glanced back at them now and then, sensing that their little snatches of laughter had something to do with him, and not knowing whether to take offense or be flattered.

At the sight of his plump, pink face with its beatific smile, the two women would nudge each other and giggle. This, of course, made them giggle still more.

The walkway grew still more difficult. Each step required careful thought—legs were aching and knees trembling.

The greenish teacher suddenly went into a squat, then began to jump up and down. The walkway bent beneath him. The whole bog turned springy, quietly trembling and diddering.

"Polosov! What are you doing? Stop it!"

It was frightening. Hidden under the velvety green carpet lay sticky, treacly, quagmiry death.

But it was bright and cheery all around. There were laughing green leaves, crosshatched by white sticklike birches, and quick midges dotted the air with gold.

A quiet hum shimmered over the bog. It seemed to be the bog itself that was humming, ever more clearly, ever more loudly.

"What on earth's that?" asked Lykova.

The teacher stopped for a moment. "Long ago, the bog must have swallowed up some city, and now its bells are tolling," he replied. In an embarrassed mumble, he added, "There always has to be some legend or other, doesn't there?"

Fedosya turned her beak-like nose toward them. "They're aringin at the monastery."

"The monks are ringing the bells," said the Medico, "so that if someone starts to drown in the bog, they can be saved."

"So they'll hear the bells and stop drowning?" the teacher asked sarcastically.

"They're aringin at the monastery," Fedosya repeated. "Vespers. Only it's so weird round here there's no tellin where the sound comes from. A woman from the village once dropped her shawl here—an' while she was bendin to pick it up, the Shishkun span her reight round."

"The *what*?"

"Y'know…the Bogle, He Who Lives in the Bog. So, when she looked up again, she was lookin the wrong way, not where she'd been lookin before. And then our good woman—she just wandered around in circles. First this way, then that way. The same wherever she looked—nowt to guide her. Even the bells weren't comin from any one place. The Shishkun was catchin the blessed sound an' smotherin it in the bog. Tryin to keep a Christian soul from reachin the monastery, he was. So the poor woman was in torment. Her hair turned gray—and not just her hair but her woolen shawl too. Just like that! Can you imagine? Beyond words!"

The Medico laughed. "Our Fedosya is something else! Tell us, are you all fibbers in your village? Or is it just the old bats?"

Fedosya turned around. Her eyes darted from face to face, looking for understanding. Not finding any, she forced a cheerful grin and said, "I'm only tellin what others tell me."

Rakhatova suddenly slowed her step, letting the others go on ahead. She put her hands over her eyes and turned around several times. She listened. All around she could hear a slow, even hum. The bog seemed to be swaying beneath her feet. She felt very scared.

"Must be this way," she said to herself. She turned around again and uncovered her eyes.

No one to be seen. She had got it wrong. Now she felt scared to turn the other way—what if she found herself all on her own now?

"Hello-o-o-o!" she shouted.

Behind her she heard the guffaw of the Medico.

"You and your games! You knew perfectly well where we were!"

"This bog. I can't bear it. When will we ever get there?"

All of a sudden, the monastery buildings sprang up out of nowhere. It was hard to believe that a few stunted birches could have hidden them for so long.

The place seemed deserted. The monks must have all been in the church. There was just a blind old man with a wooden begging bowl, sitting against a bright white wall. Hearing footsteps, he bowed his head and began intoning his despairing chant.

"He's putting it on," said Lykova.

The Medico crouched down, peered into his blind eyes, and rapped out some Latin term.

"Beautiful! This beggar lends such character to the scene!" said

Rakhatova the actress, looking from side to side. As if by way of explanation, she added, "Grinbaum stopped by a few times during the winter. Grinbaum the artist. He's very talented."

The teacher threw a small copper coin into the beggar's bowl. Feeling a twinge of envy, Fedosya shook her head and whispered, "These blind fellows can be really dangerous. Aye. Sometimes they gather in droves an' commit dreadful crimes."

In a corner of the monastery yard, close to the kitchen, two broad-shouldered monks and a peasant in a peaked cap were cleaning and gutting a huge catfish on a wide wooden board. The peasant was hacking at the fish with a broad knife. One of the monks was holding it by the hook piercing its snout; the other was watching, grunting at each blow of the knife.

Then the peasant took a bucket and poured water over the pieces of fish and the severed head. There was a sudden movement in one of the middle pieces. A twitch, a quiver—and the whole fish responded. Even the chopped-off tail jerked.

"That's its heart contracting," said the Medico.

Lykova let out a shriek. The monks looked up, watching disapprovingly as she fled.

The evening went by very pleasantly.

They sat on the stone steps of the monastery guesthouse and chatted away.

Out of respect for the gentlefolk, Fedosya Fishergirl perched a little lower down, on a log.

First, they told all kinds of stories about monasteries and monks. Then the greenish teacher suddenly mumbled a risqué joke and the conversation began to roll freely and boldly along, as if reaching a broad, well-traveled road. Full speed ahead!

A stout monk passed by on his way to the storehouse. He was jingling a set of gigantic plain keys.

"Here to prepare for Communion?" he asked.

This made them laugh still more. The Medico was convulsed, shaking his bowed head as if he were a bull.

"Actually, that's not such a bad idea," said Polosov. "Preparing for

Communion in a monastery is quite something. You'll hear passages from their book of devotions. They've come up with sins beyond our wildest dreams. Honest to God, it's truly intriguing."[3]

Rakhatova the actress decided to prepare herself for Communion.

"Aye," said Fedosya. "You can confess at first light, take Communion during the Liturgy—an' then we'll all be on our way."

And it was back to telling risqué jokes.

Lykova and Rakhatova were huddled close together, a little apart from the others. They were all pretending that their enjoyment of these funny stories was entirely straightforward, that the jokes were not any funnier for being told on the grounds of a monastery.

The Medico was sprawled out on the steps. Wanting to touch him, Rakhatova kept stretching out her legs.

The others kept trying to get Lykova to join in the joke-telling.

"You must, you really must! Remember we're in a monastery. They've got strict rules here—everyone must pull their weight."

"Too bad we can't sing here," said Rakhatova. In a barely audible voice, she began to sing, "With te-e-enderness, with fi-i-iery passion . . ."

Then she remembered she was an actress. Why wasn't the Medico taking an interest in her? Feeling put out, she said, "Time we all went to bed."

"Aye!" Fedosya said quickly. "Or tomorrow we won't be able to get up at all."

There was a small window in the thick stone wall and it was left open all night. Lykova and Rakhatova could hear Fedosya. Interrupted now and then by a gruff voice, she was whispering away: "That's just it, Father, that's just it. There are relics of many kinds. Some lie hidden in crypts. Others are seen in the light of day. An' sometimes they be hidden again. Your miracles, Lord, are beyond all words!"

Extreme fatigue, and Fedosya's whispering, made it hard to get to sleep. And then, the moment you closed your eyes, there were myriads of golden sparks—that swirling column of midges over the poisonous green of the bog.

Getting up in the morning felt harder still. Every limb, every joint was stiff and aching.

The men were still asleep.

Lykova, Rakhatova, and Fedosya set off toward the church across the damp morning grass.

They walked past the wooden board where the two monks had been gutting the catfish. Scales and fins still lay scattered about on the ground. The monastery rooster was pecking at them crossly.

Inside the church, four village girls, a look of frightened piety on their faces, were huddled against the wall, and a very old monk was fussing about by the lectern. His white hair was tinged with green, and his cassock was a faded brown.

"She's come to confess," said Lykova, nodding toward Rakhatova.

The monk fussed about still more busily, as if unsure how to reply.

"Probably you want the abbot to confess you?" he said in a whisper.

"No, no," said Lykova. "We don't mind who it is."

The monk hesitated. He looked troubled. "No, the abbot . . . surely, you'd rather it was the abbot . . ."

"He doesn't dare," Fedosya whispered. "He doesn't dare."

"No, I want it to be you," Rakhatova said decisively. The whole business had already begun to bore her.

The monk darted away, stumbled, then made toward the screen.

"Now the entertainment begins," Rakhatova said to herself, watching him open his book of devotions.

But the monk still seemed troubled. He kept hesitating. Seeing Rakhatova trying to look at his book, he covered the pages with his trembling, gnarled hand.

"Have you been obedient to your elders?" he asked.

"He takes me for a little girl!" thought Rakhatova—and began to imagine what a funny and entertaining story she could make out of all this.

The monk asked a few timid questions, to which Rakhatova replied perfunctorily. She was still amused by his attempts to stop her looking at the words of his book. "What's got into him? He wants to protect me—me of all people! Seems he's gone dotty in his old age!"

"Have you committed any grave sins?"

"No!"

The monk said nothing. She looked at him—and she too fell silent.

The eyes now looking at her were so clear and joyful that they seemed to be flickering, just as stars flicker when their clear light overflows.

Nothing was clear but those eyes. There was a mist over everything else. She could barely make out the gray of his beard, tinged green with age, and the ancient, faded fabric of the tall klobuk on his head.

All of a sudden, his whole face quivered. It broke out into delicate ray-like wrinkles. Like the face of a child, it broke into a joyful smile—all of it, first the eyes, then the hollow cheeks with their taut, dry skin, and then his crinkled mouth. And his hand began to quiver more and more rapidly, with ever smaller, finer movements.

"Praise the Lord! Praise the Lord!"

He was trembling all over. It was as if he were a large severed heart and a drop of living water had fallen onto it. The heart quivers—and then all the other dead, severed pieces quiver too.

"Praise the Lord!"

Rakhatova closed her eyes.

"What is all this?" she wondered, addressing the sweet, ineffable tenderness she now felt. "Not going to start crying, am I? No...it's just that I'm tired...overwrought. That's it, I'm overwrought!"

They left the monastery on a peasant's cart.

The Medico took the reins from the peasant and did his best to gee-up the horse. In return, the horse tried to slap him with her tail. Polosov slept. And Fedosya gave her opinion of the monastery.

"A very bad monastery indeed. The monks can't leave off their tobacco. Sniffin and chewin away, no matter what. Klobuks on their heads—and they stuff their noses with snuff. It's beyond words! They set thirty village women to work on their vegetable plots—an' don't lift a finger themselves. Beyond words! A depraved monastery—they've really let themselves go, they have. Last week they had to drag two drunk monks out of the gulley—barely managed to bring them round! Beyond all words!"

Rakhatova and Lykova said nothing.

Translated by Maria Bloshteyn and Robert Chandler

PART THREE

from *Evening Day* (1924) and
The Book of June (1931)

SOLOVKI

for Ivan Bunin

THE SEAGULLS from the shore accompanied the steamer for a long time. After a while they grew tired and began coming down more often onto the water, barely grazing it with their breast, spinning around as if on the point of a screw—and then wearily gliding off again, leading first with one wing and then with the other, as if taking long strides.

From the stern, pilgrims threw them bread. Many of them came from far inland. It was their first encounter with the sea and they were astonished by the gulls.

"What strong birds!"

"What great big birds!"

"But people say you can't eat them."

When the boat reached open sea and the shore it had left behind was no more than a low, narrow strip of pale blue, the gulls dispersed. Three last greedy birds took a few more strides, begged again for bread, veered off somewhere to the left, called to one another, and disappeared.

The sea was now empty and free. In the sky shone two diffuse bands of crimson: one not yet extinguished, still red from the departed sun, and one now catching fire from the rising sun. The steamer, lit by their silvery-pink light that cast no shadow, was cutting aslant through the waves; from the deck it appeared to be sailing sideways, skimming weightlessly over the water. And high in the air, fastened to the mast, swaying gently against the pink clouds, a golden cross marked out the boat's path.

The *Archangel Michael*, a holy ship, was carrying pilgrims from Arkhangelsk to the Solovetsky Monastery.[1]

There were a lot of passengers. They sat on benches, on steps, and on the deck itself, conversing quietly and respectfully, and looking with awe at the golden cross in the sky, at the boat's steward—a monk in a faded, now greenish cassock—and at the gulls. They sighed, yawned, and made the sign of the cross over their open mouths.

Up on the bridge a monk in a sheepskin coat and a black skullcap kept coughing hoarsely, calling to the helmsman—his commands as abrupt as the gulls' cries—and then bursting out coughing again.

Waves were beating rhythmically against the hull; the crimson glow had faded; the birds had flown away. The drama of setting sail was now over and the passengers began to settle down for the night.

Peasant women hitched up the calico skirts they had starched for the holiday and this unusual journey, and then lay down on the floor, tucking in their legs and their heavy, awkward feet. The menfolk were talking quietly in separate groups.

Red-haired, thickset Semyon Rubaev came down the ladder and joined the men. His wife remained alone, sitting on one of the steps. She didn't move or even turn her head. She merely gave him a sideways look, full of mistrust and resentment.

Semyon listened for a while to the other men. A tall, curly-haired old man from White Lake was talking about the smelt they now caught there. "We've a damage now. A damage. Engineers built it. They needed earth for this damage. They took earth of mine."

"What damage? You're not making sense."

"For the damage . . . the da . . . For the dam." The old man fell silent for a moment, then added, "I'm in my nineties, you know. Yes, that's how it is now."

Semyon didn't care in the least about the old man's age, nor about the smelt in the lake. He wanted to talk about his own concerns, but he didn't know how to bring them into the conversation; it was hard to find the right moment. He looked around at his wife. She was sitting sideways to him, looking away. He could barely see her broad face and the pale, taut line of her mouth.

And then nothing could hold him back. "Well, we come from near Novgorod. From the Borovichy district. Penance, a church penance—that's why I've brought 'er along with me."

He stopped. But since no one asked him anything, he eventually began again: "Penance, confession an' penance.² Varvara, ma wife. No light matter, I 'ad to take it to the district officer."

Varvara got up from the step. Baring her white teeth like a vicious cat, she moved a little farther away, then stood beside the rail, resting both elbows on it.

There was nowhere farther to go. The pilgrims sitting on the deck were densely packed. She could hardly use their heads as stepping stones.

Now at least she could no longer hear all that Semyon was saying. The odd word, however, still reached her.

"The whole village were complainin . . . There weren't one lass that Vanya Tsyganov . . . The officer . . . Ma wife, Varvara . . ."

Varvara hunched her shoulders. She was still baring her teeth. Semyon was still talking, talking, talking: "Varvara, aye, Varvara . . . 'We just kissed,' she said . . . A court sentence weren't possible. But a penance, a church penance . . ."

For ten months Semyon had been telling this story, over and over. And now, like clockwork, all through this journey. On the iron road, at every station where they'd stopped, in the pilgrims' hostel at Arkhangelsk, wherever there were ears to be filled, he had told it once more. Since the day all this began, since their neighbor Yerokhina had run back from the fields, pulled off her kerchief, and wailed out that Tsyganov had wronged her—and then old Mitrofanikha had rushed out and yelled that her granddaughter Feklushka was being pestered by Tsyganov too, that Tsyganov wasn't giving the girl a moment's peace. Other women of all ages appeared, all white with fury, kerchiefs slipping off their heads, all cursing Tsyganov and threatening to lodge official complaints and have him driven out of the village. And then Lukina had caught sight of Varvara at her window and shouted out that Varvara had been with Tsyganov too. She'd seen them out in the rye: "Them two, walking side by side! Arms around each other!"

And from then on, work had been forgotten. Semyon had done nothing but tell this story.

He went along as a witness for Yerokhina. He told the officer about Varvara and demanded that she be brought to trial and punished. He dragged Varvara around with him and wherever they went—on the road, in country inns and town lodgings—he had gone on telling this story. At first he had spoken gently, calling her "Varenka," the same as ever. "So, Varenka, tell me how all this came to happen. All o' the circumstances."

"How *wot* happened? Nowt happened."

Then he would go purple all over, his red beard seeming to fill with blood. Choking with fury, he would say, "Bitch! Snake! How dare you? How dare you speak so to yer wedded husband!"

And all day long Varvara had busied herself around the house, not exactly working, more just fussing about in one corner after another—anything to get out of earshot, anything not to hear.

As for Tsyganov, he was nowhere to be seen. He had gone off to the city to work as a cabdriver. The women began to calm down. Only on the river bank in the evening, as they beat the damp linen with their bats, the young girls sometimes sang a jokey song from Saint Petersburg:

> Vanka, Vanka, wot you done wi yer conscience?
>> Where be yer heart of hearts?
> Wasted 'em both in the taverns
>> for love o' billiards an' cards.

Their voices sounded thin, almost mosquito-like.

As for Semyon, he went on and on questioning Varvara and repeating his story. And Varvara fell more and more silent. When the officer asked her about Yerokhina, her only reply, delivered in a tone of true Novgorod obstinacy, was "Nowt to do wiv me."

And so life went on. In the daytime Varvara hardly spoke. At night she kept thinking things over, reliving that day again and again. She had heard screaming women; she had seen their white-hot, vicious fury. The devil had gotten into them. And what a lot of them there had been. Even pockmarked Mavrushka had shouted out, as if bragging, "D'ye think he didn't touch *me*? No, he touched *me* all right. Only *I* hold my tongue. But if you all speak, then *I'm* speakin too!"

Her pockmarks, evidently, had not counted against her. The lads had jeered, "Oh Mavrushka, Mavrushka! And her wi t' body of a bear!"

Yerokhina, for her part, had lamented, "Eight year, believe me, I've kept a hold o' me honor—and then . . . along come this fiend an' he snatches it from me!"

All shaking in jealous rage. All shouting, as if bragging, "Me too. Aye, me too!"

A sly fellow with the nickname "Tomcat" had smirked mischievously and said, "You lassies be in a right state. What's eatin you, then? Eh?"

He seemed to have hit on something.

They reached Solovki as the bells were ringing for Matins.

On the shore to meet them were monks and seagulls.

The monks were thin, with severe faces. The gulls were large and plump, almost as big as geese. They waddled about proprietorially, exchanging preoccupied remarks.

Unloading and disembarking took a long time. Some of the pilgrims were still packing their knapsacks when the wife of the elderly fisherman returned from the Holy Lake, after bathing in its icy waters. She had put on a clean linen shirt and was smiling beatifically, her lips purple with cold.

The hosteler, a tall monk with a neatly combed beard, was dealing with the new arrivals, arranging who should sleep where. Since there were crowds of pilgrims and little space, the Rubaevs were put in part of what had once been a room for gentlefolk. This had whitewashed walls and two windows, but it was now divided into three by partitions. One part had been given to a teacher and his wife, and the biggest part—with three beds and a sofa—to a party of four.

The head of this party was an Oriental-looking abbot. Handsome and well turned out, he had chosen, for convenience while traveling, to abandon his monastic dress for that of an ordinary priest: "People, I understand, have little love for monks, and they criticize them for everything: *Why's he smoking? Why's he eating fish? Why's there sugar in his tea?* But how can a man observe the rule when he's on the road? Dress as a priest—and you don't tempt people to judge."

Together with the abbot were a merchant, a lanky young gymnasium[3] student, and a hypocritical old bigot of a public official. All three were family.

The remaining little cubicle, with no window, was allocated to the Rubaevs.

The pilgrims spent the rest of the day either attending church services, looking around the monastery, wandering about the forest or along the seashore, walking down the long, musty hostel corridor—with its damp and grimy, finger-marked doors, weighted to slam heavily shut—or visiting the little monastery shop and haggling over the price of icons, small cypress-wood crosses, and prayer belts for the deceased.[4]

There was one very tall young man whom it was hard not to notice. He was smartly dressed, with a new peaked cap and patent leather boots, and he had come for healing; he suffered from spasms that repeatedly wrenched at his mouth, forcing it open. It was as if his jaw were in the grip of a vast, insuperable yawn; he would involuntarily stick his tongue out and slobber all down his chin and neck. Then the fit would come to an end and his mouth would close, his teeth snapping together like those of a dog that has caught a fly.

Accompanying him was a short little fellow who could have passed for the impresario of an exotic theater troupe. He wore a silver chain that hung down over his round belly and he bustled about excitedly, taking evident pride in the young man's illness and proffering explanations: "Keeps on yawning, he does. Several years now, yes indeed. He's the son of rich people. Make way, make way now, if you please!"

The monastery courtyard was full of gulls. They were round and placid, like household geese. They sat between gravestones and on the track leading to the church. They weren't afraid of people and didn't get out of your way—it was for you to walk around them. And on the back of almost every one of them was a chick—like a fluffy spotted egg propped on two thin little twigs.

The gulls called out to one another in quick, curt barks. They always began loudly, then gradually quietened, as if losing hope. They sat crowded together around the monastery and did not fly anywhere. It was very cold. The small rectangular Holy Lake was swollen with gray-blue water. One gull went down to the lake and gazed for a long time, with a suspicious eye, at the violet ripples. Some way off, a chick was cheeping importantly, as if imparting advice. The gull stretched out one foot, touched the water, quickly withdrew the foot, and twitched its head a little.

"Too cold, old girl?" asked a young monk.

Against the gray sky swayed lopsided trees; their branches, reaching toward the sun like arms stretched toward a distant dream, grew only from their southern side. The northern side, gnawed by cold breaths from the throat of the Arctic Ocean, remained naked and sickly all summer, as in winter.

Down by the harbor some young men, with faded skullcaps over thick strands of curly fair hair, were throwing pebbles in the water and scuffling with one another. They were like puny young bear cubs, fighting clumsily and without anger. Pomors,[5] from villages along the mainland coast, they had been brought to the monastery to labor for a year or two in fulfillment of vows made by their mothers. "Aye, 'e'll serve t' Lord—and 'e'll earn 'is keep too."[6]

And there were solitary monks wandering along the shore. Now and again they would stop and look at the water, as if waiting for something.

One after another the gray-blue waves uncoiled, splashing against the brown rocks, filling hearts with a leaden sadness.

Along with the other pilgrims, the Rubaevs went to the church and then on into the forest. Monks in faded cassocks emerged from the little chapels. They seemed to struggle to understand even the simplest questions. If someone asked, "Which church is this?," they would reply, "How?," then smile affably and withdraw to gaze at the water.[7]

Outside the chapel of Saint Philaret, the pilgrims took it in turn to lift the long stone that had once served Philaret as a pillow. They balanced it on their heads and walked three times clockwise around the chapel—a cure for headaches.[8]

In the farthest of the little chapels, ten versts or so from the monastery, the pilgrims were met by the very oldest elders of all. They were barely able to put one foot in front of the other, barely still breathing.

"But how, good fathers, do you walk to the church?"

"We go, good people, but once a year. On Easter Sunday, yes, to Holy Matins. That day we all meet together—from cliffs, from woods, from bogs, from t' open fields. Every one of us goes—and they count us up. As for food, we get by. They bring us our bread."

The hostel was no place to sit in for long. The Rubaevs' cubicle was dark and damp. Semyon would come in, sit down on the bed, and start to drone on once again: "Mind you tell it all. As God is your witness. Each and every circumstance. Tell everything, or woe betide you!"

Varvara did not reply.

Behind the partition the merchant and the gymnasium student kept demanding more hot water for their tea. The official was sighing piously.

Behind the other partition the teacher's wife was criticizing the ways of the monastery: "They just stand there and stare at the water. Will that save their souls? And at table they defile themselves with mustard.[9] Will that save their souls?"

And then they would all wander up and down the shore again, or along the monastery corridors.

They looked at the paintings of the Last Judgment and the Parables of Our Lord. A huge beam planted in the eye of the sinner who so clearly beheld the mote in his brother's eye. The temptation of beauty, illustrated by a devil—with a rather appealing canine muzzle, shaggy webbed paws, a curly tail, and a modest brown apron tied around his belly[10]—and his charming legend: as the brothers were praying in church, this devil had slipped unseen between them, distributing the pink flowers known as house lime. Whoever received a flower found himself unable to go on praying; tempted by the spring sun and grasses, he would steal out to freedom[11]—until in the end the devil was caught by the Holy Elder. And portrayals of every kind of ordeal and hardship, of sins and torments, sins and torments...

Toward evening they were called to the refectory. The women sat in a separate room.

To one side of Varvara was a woman covered in scabs. Sitting opposite her was an old woman with a nose like a duck's beak. Before dipping her spoon into the communal bowl, she would lick it all over with her long, flaccid, rag-like tongue. They ate salt-cod soup and drank bland monastery kvass[12] with a faint taste of mint. A monk read aloud to them in a dismal monotone—"Lechery, lechery, the devil."

There was no night. The partitions did not reach the ceiling and the Rubaevs' windowless stall was lit by a wan light that cast no shadow.

The hypocrite official got up at cockcrow and, in reproach to his companions, began bowing and crossing himself before the icon. With loud sighs—part whistle and part whisper—he repeated, "Woe is me, O Lord, O Lord—for my loins are filled with mockings."[13]

The abbot awoke, shamefacedly put on his clothes, and left the room. The merchant held out for a long time but couldn't get back to sleep. In a loud, clear voice, as if to the student, he said, "You get some more sleep! Yes. It's too early for church. Not even the monks have gotten up yet." He then repeated all this—really, of course, for the benefit of the hypocrite official, who was by then creating more of a disturbance than ever.

The official finished praying, looked around censoriously, sighed, and turned away. There are sights best not seen, he appeared to be saying.

Varvara had had a bad night. There was no peace anywhere and the seagulls kept calling to one another with their dismal barks. Toward morning she dozed off. She saw a field of rye and a cart. There on the cart was Vanya Tsyganov, laughing: "'Ere again, are ye? Well, there'll be no getting away this time." He got down from the cart, took her by the shoulders and looked into her eyes. "Ashamed? As if yer a maiden!"

Not a good dream, and it left her with a sense of dread.

Once again everyone went off to the church or out into the forest. After the service, Semyon sat down beside the teacher, on a bench outside the hostel, and was soon telling his same old story. Varvara went back to the room. The student was alone there, sitting at the table and eating curd cheese from a large clay bowl. On his face was a look of sly embarrassment.

"Want some?" he said to Varvara. "I got it from the dairy. I'm famished. All we get in the refectory is cabbage soup seasoned with holy relics." He giggled.

"No, thank you."

The student stopped eating and looked at Varvara intently. With an awkward smile, blushing and giggling, he said, "You're quite a woman, you know. As for that husband of yours . . . And your eyes— your eyes are gorgeous. But sit yourself down, for the love of God."

Varvara looked straight into his bashful but laughing eyes and felt a sense of horror. It seemed as if she was looking not at a young student but at Vanya Tsyganov—and was unable to get away from him.

"O Lord, O Lord! What is all this?"

She wanted to tear her hair, to weep and wail.

Slowly, still looking the student straight in the eye, Varvara backed toward her door.

"Is th-that where you s-sleep?" the student stammered, still blushing.

Varvara heard footsteps out in the corridor. She locked her door, sat down on the bed, and listened to her heart trembling. The merchant and the hypocrite official came back, caught sight of the curd cheese, and were incensed with rage.

"Huh! Like that, is it? Can't even last three days?[14] Well then, what's stopping you? Eat! You bought that cheese—so you eat it!"

"I've had all I want."

"Eat that cheese!"

Both men felt the same craving. And the stronger their craving, the fiercer their rage.

"Eat, I say!" hissed the official. "You bought it—so you eat it!"

"What's wrong with you?" the merchant chimed in. "If you know no shame, then eat all you want!"

The two men swallowed down their saliva, unable to take their eyes off the cheese.

During the afternoon a large-winged boat flew in, bringing Pomor women from the mainland coast. So high were the waves that no one even saw the boat draw in to the pier.

The women spilled out onto the shore. They were a bright, loquacious flock, in pink, green, lilac, and pale blue dresses, with pearl rings on their headbands. They had fair eyebrows and the eyes of seagulls or mermaids—round, yellow eyes with black rims and black dots for pupils.

The women chattered away and laughed. The pilgrims watched from a distance, the men twisting their beards between their fingers.

"Them Pomors are a rich lot. They catch fish, they shoot animals for their pelts, they gather down from eider ducks. No wonder they go around in pearls."[15]

A woman in a rose-lilac dress, with a yellow-eyed child on her back, was teasing a gull, holding out a piece of bread, then withdrawing it, repeating, "Bread for t' gull-bird? Bread for t' gully-bird?"

The gull, who also had a child on her back, stretched out her neck crossly.

The seagull and the woman—two of a kind, and with the same yellow-eyed children—both understood that this was a game.

"Mock away, mock away!" people called out. "But wait till she's up above yer head! See what she does to you then! Them gulls can get mighty cross."

Toward evening a gale blew up. As if through a funnel, it blew straight down the icy throat of the Arctic Ocean, shaking the trees, twisting skirts and cassocks around legs, stopping people in their tracks or knocking them to the ground, flinging sea foam against the hostel's windows. Flocking swiftly together, the Pomor women got back on board and hoisted sail. Pink, lilac, and pale blue dresses swirled in the wind. The boat had no thwarts and no gunnels—the women simply stood on the planking. Someone cast off. Two young lads got out their squeeze-boxes and began to play; pink, lilac, and pale blue skirts swirled and danced near the edge of the boat. The following wind filled out the sails, driving the boat on so fiercely that, for a moment, the entire stern rose high above the waves. The wind snatched the song away, brought it back, carried it off again—and then blew everything into the sea, burying both boat and song under a huge, turbid wave that smelled of fish scales. A few minutes later the pilgrims were pointing to a tiny craft now rounding a distant headland.

"Look—already there! They're a desperate lot, them Pomors."[16]

That evening in the refectory the old woman with the flaccid tongue was once again licking her spoon. The monk with the nasal voice read the same words about lechery, sin, and the devil. The yawning youth was once again led through the yard. A new group of pilgrims appeared—old women in black, smelling of cod and incense.

The gulls in the yard seemed cross, and something was frightening them. The gale was making their feathers stand up on end, and they were squealing shrill complaints.

Semyon took Varvara to confession. And, just as when she'd been questioned by that officer in Novgorod, her soul closed up in blank, obstinate misery. Back then, she had said, "Nowt to do wiv me." Now, in the church, she fastened her eyes on the bronze clasp of the Gospels, repeated to the priest, "I have sinned, I have sinned"—and said no more.

No one in the room slept long that night—thanks to the hypocrite official, who chose to prolong his devotions until the second cockcrow. He groaned, prostrated himself, and intoned his prayers in a noisy whisper: "Lord, Lord, who art present even in the uttermost depths of the sea. Even there thou art present." Seven beds, from seven corners, creaked angrily back.

But the official inadvertently overslept. Eventually, he got up along with everyone else and sat down by the window, trying not to catch anyone's eye. And then, still not looking at anyone, he sidled off to church.

The church was thronged with people. There was a smell of cod, sheepskin, something sour, and melted wax. Candle flames swayed before the flat, dark faces on the ancient icons; where the saints' hands emerged from their gilt covering, the paint had long ago wrinkled and blistered from the touch of thousands upon thousands of lips. As they went past the holy relics, the pilgrims gazed with awe and horror at a deceased *skhimnik*, a monk who had followed the most extreme of the monastic rules: all that could be seen of him, poking out from a black shroud embroidered with bones, was the tip of a waxen nose, along with some wisps of gray beard and two bony hands.

High above everyone rose the head of the yawning youth, mouth suddenly gaping open with a groan and then snapping shut. The wind knocked at doors and windows, bursting into the church, then howling as it withdrew. Now and again white wings swept past the windows—and a mermaid's round yellow eye would peep in.

In the alcoves the monks' silent, shadowy figures were barely stirring, as if their prayer beads had gone stiff in their fingers. A ripple passed through the congregation as people stepped back to let the communicants through. The choir was already singing the Cherubic Hymn,[17] the boys' high voices soaring up to the cupola, when a woman began shrieking frenziedly, "Kuda-a-a! Ku-u-da-a-a! Ku-da-a-a!"[18]

Her shrieks grew ever more piercing, ever more violent.

"Possessed," whispered the peasant women. "Possessed good n' proper!"[19]

Then someone else let out a scream and a wail—and began to bark like a dog, not letting up.

Varvara clenched her hands tight. The chandelier swayed, slid to one side—and she felt her legs and shoulders begin to shudder, swiftly, violently, while her whole face stretched as if clinging tight to her cheekbones, and her stomach swelled, climbing right up to her throat, and a wild scream flew out from somewhere deep and dark, twisting her whole body, tearing her body apart, smashing red lights against the crown of her head: "A-a-i-i! Da-a-a! Da-a-a!"[20]

A fleeting thought: *Should I stop?*

But something made her tense herself more and more powerfully, forcing her to cry out more and more loudly, to clench her whole body, to will on the convulsions. The words didn't matter. The first sounds to burst out had been "A-a-i-i!" and "Da-a-a!"—and so she had gone on. What mattered was not to stop, to expend more and more of herself in the cry, to give herself to it more intensely, yes, more and more of herself: *Oh, if only they didn't get in her way. Oh, if only they let her keep going...* But it was so hard. Would she have the strength?

"A-a-i-i! A-a-i-i!" *If only ... if only ... How sweet ... how sweet that would be ...*

Someone's feet, next to her cheek. A strip of rug, a flax rug.

Am I lying down now? Oh, who cares? I can't keep going now. But another time. Another time, somehow ...

And suddenly she was being lifted up. She was being hoisted by hands under her shoulders—and there before her eyes was a vast golden chalice, vast as the world.

"Varvara," someone was saying beside her.

"Varvara," she heard someone else repeat.

And a sharp golden spoon, also vast, was parting her lips and knocking against her clenched teeth.[21] Her teeth unclenched of their own accord, a gentle quiver passed through her arms and legs, and her head fell forward; she could no longer hold it up. Small beads of sweat were cooling her forehead.

How sweet! Oh, how sweet!

And her whole body became empty. As if everything heavy, swollen, and black had left with the scream.

They seated Varvara on a bench outside the hostel. She had turned suddenly thinner. She had thrown back her head, her hair uncovered, and she was smiling with a look of exhausted bliss.

Not daring to go at all close, the other pilgrim women were looking at her in fear and awe, just as they had looked at the deceased *skhimnik*. Semyon was also looking at her in speechless fear and awe. And Varvara was saying in a delirious voice, her words coming out in fits and starts, "Oh, my darlings! All of you! What sweetness! Lord God! My dearest Semyon! And now—a long, long way, on foot, to Saint Tikhon of Zadonsk.[22] How dear the sky is. Sweet sky, bright sky. And the gulls . . . the dear gulls . . ."

Translated by Robert and Elizabeth Chandler

THE BOOK OF JUNE

A VAST country house, a large extended family, the spaciousness of the clear, bracing air—it could hardly have been more different from her quiet Petersburg apartment stuffed with carpets and furniture. Katya at once felt exhausted. She had been ill for a long time and had come to the country to convalesce.

Katya was staying with one of her aunts. This aunt was hard of hearing and so the whole house was constantly shouting. The high-ceilinged rooms reverberated, dogs barked, cats meowed, maids from the village clattered plates, and the children shouted and squabbled.

There were four children in all: fifteen-year-old Vasya, a bully and tattletale studying in a Novgorod gymnasium, and two small girls, home from boarding school for the summer. And then there was the eldest, Grisha, who was the same age as Katya but was staying with a school friend in Novgorod. He would be back home soon.

They all talked about Grisha a great deal. He seemed to be a general favorite, even something of a hero.

The head of the family, Uncle Tyoma, who was plump and had gray whiskers, looked rather like a large cat. He was constantly teasing Katya. "What's the matter, my little goose? Are you bored?" he would ask with a smirk. "Just you wait, young Grisha will be here soon. He'll really turn your head!"

"Nonsense!" the aunt would shout (like all deaf people, she spoke louder than anyone else). "Katya is from Petersburg—she'll hardly be impressed by a mere Novgorod student. Katya my dear, I'm sure you have throngs of admirers. Come on now, admit it!"

And she would then wink at everyone. Knowing that all this was meant to be funny, Katya would attempt a smile, with trembling lips.

The two girls, Manya and Lubochka, gave her a warm welcome and reverentially inspected her wardrobe: a blue sailor jacket, a smart dress (starched piqué), and some white blouses.

"Ooh! Ooh!" repeated eleven-year-old Lubochka, sounding like a windup doll.

"I love Petersburg fashions," said Manya.

"All so shiny, like silk," Lubochka chimed in.

They took Katya for walks. Beyond the garden lay a marshy river dense with forget-me-nots. A calf had drowned there.

"He was sucked under. The bog sucked him under and that was it. We never saw him again—not even a bone. We're forbidden to swim here."

They swung Katya on the swing. But when Katya was no longer a novelty, things changed. The two girls even began to snigger at her behind her back. Vasya made fun of her, too, coming out with all kinds of stupidities. He would walk up to her, perform an exaggerated bow, and say, "Mademoiselle Catrine, please be so good as to explain to me how you would say 'gulch' in French?"

All very tedious, unpleasant, and wearying.

"Why is everything so ugly here?" Katya kept asking herself.

They ate suckling pig, carp with sour cream, and pies with burbot. A far cry from the crisp, delicate grouse wings she enjoyed at home.

It was the housemaids who milked the cows. If you called them, they yelled back, "Wot?"

The girl who served them at table was huge. She had a mustache and looked like a soldier squeezed into a woman's blouse. Katya was astonished to discover that this gigantic creature was only eighteen.

It was a relief to escape to the small garden. Clutching a slim volume of Alexey Tolstoy with an embossed cover, she would read aloud:

It isn't he who holds you spellbound;
It's not his own perfection that attracts you.
He's nothing more than an occasion
For secret dreams of torment, bliss, and rapture.[1]

Every time she came to the last words, her heart skipped a beat. Tears would have been sweet.

"Coo-ee, Katya! Tea-ea time!"

Once again, the shouting, the clamor, the general din. Excited dogs flailing hard tails against your leg. A cat suddenly up on the table, its tail flicking across your face. Animal heads. Animal snouts and tails.

Grisha returned shortly before Midsummer Day.

Katya was out when he arrived. Later, as she was going through the dining room, she glimpsed Vasya through the window. He was talking to a tall young man in a white naval jacket and with a very long nose.

"Auntie Zhenya's invited a cousin to stay," she heard Vasya say.

"What's she like?"

"A blue-ish idiot."

Katya moved quickly back from the window. "Blue-ish? Or did he say 'foolish'? How very strange." She went outside.

Long-nosed Grisha greeted her cheerily, stepped up into the porch, and peered out at her through the small porch window. Screwing up his eyes, he made a show of twirling an imaginary mustache.

"What a dolt," Katya said to herself. She sighed and walked on into the garden.

At dinner Grisha was rather boisterous. He kept picking on Varvara, the huge girl with the mustache, telling her she had no idea how to wait on the table.

"Enough of that!" said Uncle Tyoma. "Just look at you—that great beak of yours just keeps growing and growing."

And Vasya, always the bully and troublemaker, declaimed in a singsong voice:

Monstrous nose, awful nose
With room inside its flaring holes
For fields and farms and villages,
For cupolas and palace halls.

"Such great big boys," yelled the deaf aunt, "and they still keep on squabbling!" Turning to Auntie Zhenya, she went on, "Two years ago I took them with me to Pskov. It's a historic city and I wanted them to see something of it. I had things to do in the morning, so I went out early. Before I left, I said, 'Ring down for some coffee and then go and have a look around. I'll be back for lunch.' I get back at two—and guess what! The blinds are still down—and they're both still lying there in bed. 'What's the matter with you?' I ask. 'Why are you still in bed? Have you had your coffee?' 'No.' 'Why on earth not?' 'Because this blockhead wouldn't ring for it.' 'So why didn't you ring yourself?' 'Me? Why? Why should he lie in bed while I run around at his beck and call?' 'But why should *I* have to do all the work!' says the other blockhead. And so the two of them just lay there until two o'clock in the afternoon."

The days went by, noisy as ever. With Grisha back home there was, if anything, even more shouting and arguing.

Vasya had an air of constant grievance. He seemed full of spite and was rude to everyone.

One evening at dinner, Uncle Tyoma, who in his youth had greatly admired Alexander II, showed Katya his huge gold watch with a miniature of the tsar and tsaritsa inside its lid. He told her how he'd made a special trip to Petersburg in the hope of somehow getting a glimpse of His Majesty. "He wouldn't have traveled that far just to see me," Vasya muttered crossly. "That's for sure."

Grisha grew ever more indignant about Varvara and her mustache. "She comes bantering on my door in the morning with those great fists of hers—and that's my whole day ruined."

Vasya shrieked with laughter. "*Bantering*! I ask you! I think he's trying to say *battering*!"

"She's no maid, she's a guy. A male peasant. I'm telling you, I don't want to wake up to the sight of her. End of story."

"He's upset because they've gotten rid of Pasha," Vasya shouted. "Pasha was very pretty."

Grisha leaped to his feet, red as a beetroot. "I'm sorry," he said, looking at his parents but pointing at Vasya. "I cannot sit at the same table as this relative of yours."

Grisha took no notice of Katya at all—except once, when he saw her in the garden with a book in her hands. "May I inquire what you're reading?" he asked with exaggerated politeness. He then went on his way before she could answer.

Varvara happened to be passing by, too. Bristling like an angry cat and glaring at Katya with eyes that seemed almost white, she said, "So young ladies from Petersburg like good-looking boys, do they?"

Katya did not understand this, but she felt scared by the look in Varvara's eyes.

That evening Katya spent a long time with Auntie Zhenya making pastries. It was the eve of Saint Artyom's day—the name day of Uncle Tyoma. When they'd finished, she went out into the yard to look at the moon. Not far away, in the wing, she could see a light in one of the windows. Standing on a log she must have just put there herself, Varvara was gazing into the room.

Hearing Katya's footsteps, she beckoned and hissed, "Here!" Seizing her by the arm, Varvara pulled her up onto the log.

"Look!"

Vasya was lying fast asleep on a small sofa. Grisha was lying on the floor, on a straw mattress. He was reading, his face very close to the book, and the book very close to the candle.

"What is it?" Katya asked in surprise. "What are you looking at?" Varvara hushed her.

Varvara's face was both tense and vacant. Her mouth was half open and her eyes were staring. She seemed bewildered, transfixed.

Katya managed to free her arm and get away. Varvara really was very strange.

The following day the house was full of guests. There were merchants, other landowners, and the abbot of the nearby monastery—a huge, broad-browed man who looked like one of Vasnetsov's warriors.[2] He arrived in a two-wheeled carriage and talked all through the meal about crops and haymaking. Uncle Tyoma kept complimenting him on his management of the land.

"What weather!" said the abbot. "What meadows! What fields! June! Wherever I go, it's as if a book of untold wonders is being opened before me. June!"

These words made an impression on Katya. She listened to the abbot for some time, hoping he'd say more in this vein. But he spoke only of the price of fodder and the purchase of a small area of woodland.

That evening, Katya sat in front of the mirror in her chintz dressing gown. She lit a candle and studied her thin, freckled face.

"I'm boring," she said to herself. "Everything's boring, so boring."

She remembered the word that had upset her: Blue-ish. It was true. She was blue-ish.

She sighed.

"Tomorrow's Saint John's day. We'll be going to the monastery."

Everyone was still up and about. Behind the wall she could hear Grisha, playing billiards in the games room.

Suddenly the door burst open. Varvara tore in, red-faced, her teeth bared in a wild grin.

"Not asleep yet—an' why not? What ye waiting for, eh? I'll put you to bed meself. Aye, I'll put you to bed right now."

She grabbed hold of Katya, held her tightly, and began to tickle her, laughing loudly as she ran her fingers over the girl's thin ribs. "Not asleep yet?" she kept repeating. "An' why not?"

Katya could hardly breathe. Letting out little shrieks, she tried to escape, but Varvara's strong hands held her fast, fingering her, twisting and turning her.

"Let go! I'm going to die! Let go of me!"

Her heart was pounding. She was choking. Her whole body was screaming, struggling, writhing.

And then she glimpsed Varvara's bared teeth and white, glaring eyes. This was no joke and no game. Varvara was out to harm her, perhaps to kill her. Varvara was unable to stop herself.

"Grisha! Grisha!" Katya yelled desperately.

Varvara at once let her go. Grisha was there, standing in the doorway.

"Get out, you fool. Have you gone mad?"

"Can't I 'ave a little fun?" Varvara said feebly. Everything about her—her face, her arms—had gone limp and droopy. She staggered out of the room.

"Grisha! Grisha!"

Katya had no idea what made her keep on screaming like this. Some kind of lump seemed to be filling her throat, making her gasp and wheeze and scream out Grisha's name.

Still screaming, her legs still jerking convulsively, she reached out to Grisha, flung her arms around his neck, and pressed her face to his cheek. Wanting protection, she was still calling out, "Grisha! Grisha!"

Grisha sat her down on the sofa and knelt beside her, gently stroking her shoulders through her chintz gown.

Katya looked into his face, saw the embarrassment and confusion in his eyes, and wept still more bitterly.

"You're a kind man, Grisha. You're very kind."

Grisha looked away a little. A thin little arm was fiercely embracing his neck and his lips were somehow brushing against it. Timidly, he kissed Katya in the crook of her elbow.

Katya was now still. Grisha's lips were strangely warm. This warmth was spreading beneath her skin, ringing sweetly in her ears, and suffusing her eyelids with a heaviness that made them slowly close.

Then she herself moved her arm to his lips, and Grisha kissed the very same spot once again. Again Katya heard the sweet ringing, and felt the same warmth, and the heavy, blissful languor that closed her eyes.

"Don't be frightened, Katenka," said Grisha, his voice faltering. "She won't dare come back now. If you like, I can stay in the billiard room. And you can bolt your door."

His face looked both kind and guilty. A vein stood out in the middle of his forehead. Somehow, the guilt in his eyes was frightening.

"You must go now, Grisha! Go!"

He gave her a scared look and got to his feet.

"Go!"

She pushed him toward the door and bolted it after him.

"Oh God! Oh God! This is awful."

She raised her arm and cautiously put her lips to the spot Grisha had kissed. It felt warm and silky. She could taste vanilla.

Her strength failed her. She began to tremble and moan. "Oh . . . oh . . . oh . . . How can I go on living? Lord help me."

The candle on the table trembled and guttered, swaying its black flame.

"Lord help me. I am a sinner."

Katya put her face to the dark rectangle of the icon and joined her hands in prayer.

"Our Father who art . . ."

But these weren't the right words. She did not know what words would allow her to ask God for she did not know what, and to speak to him about what she did not understand.

She closed her eyes tight and crossed herself.

"God forgive me," she began.

And again she felt that these weren't the right words.

The candle went out, but the room only seemed brighter.

Dawn was drawing near. This white night would soon be over.

"Lord, Lord," Katya repeated, and pushed open the door to the garden.

She dared not move. She was afraid of clacking a heel or rustling her dress, so ineffable was the silvery blue silence around her. The magnificent groves of trees were still and silent, as only living, sentient beings can be still and silent.

"What's going on? What on earth's going on?" thought Katya, almost paralyzed with fear. "No, I've never known anything like this." Everything was breaking down. The trees, the still air, the invisible light—everything was overflowing with some sort of extreme power, something insuperable and beyond our ken, for which we have no sensory organ and for which there are no words in our language.

Katya was startled by a burst of sound. It was quiet, yet so sudden that it seemed loud. At once strong and delicate, there was no knowing where it sprang from. It flowed from goodness knows where and spilled over, bouncing back up like the most delicate of silver peas. Then it broke off.

A nightingale?

After this, the voices—"their" voices—grew still quieter, yet still more intense.

And "they" were all as one, all in concert. Only this little human creature, rapt and terrified, was alien. "They" all knew something. While this little human creature could only think.

June. She remembered the book of untold wonders. June.

And her small soul tossed about in anguish.

"Lord! Lord! To be in Your world is terrifying. What am I to do? And what is this? What is all this?"

And she kept searching for words, kept thinking that words would soothe and resolve.

She crossed her arms over her thin little shoulders, as if she were not herself, as if wanting to protect the fragile little body entrusted to her and to bear it away from the chaos of bestial and divine mysteries that had engulfed it.

She bowed her head in obedient despair and spoke the only words that are one and the same for all souls, great and small, blind and wise: "Our Father . . . Hallowed be Thy name . . . Thy will be done."

Translated by Robert and Elizabeth Chandler
and Kathryn Thompson

WILD EVENING

AFANASY Yevmenievich had a textile stall in our town market. He had inherited it from his peddler father and the sign still read, YEVMENY KHARIN, KNOWN AS MINA.

People would say, "I bought some green linen from Mina's—for a skirt." No one ever referred to the stall as Kharin's.

Afanasy was a sly fellow. If customers were present, he would speak in peddlers' slang.

"Afanasy Yevmenievich," his assistant would ask, "how much is velveteen for the lady?"

"Say, one and a half khroosts,"[1] Afanasy would reply. Khroosts—not rubles. And the lady, of course, would be none the wiser.

Or he would say to his assistant, "Tell 'er to stir 'er stumps. Say I need to lid the *dudorka*."

Who'd have guessed he was talking about shutting up shop for the night?

I myself was once taken in by his patter. I let him palm me off with a totally useless *tarataika*.

"You're in luck today, my good lady!" he began. "I've got a *tarataika* that's just right for you, a miniature English charabanc. I'd stake a claim to it misself, as people say, only the boss won't let me. Brand new an' high up—the height of fashion. On the small side for my line of business—but you'll find nowt better for an afternoon drive. No, not even if you get a carriage made to order. Let us know when you next decide to go up to Gorushka. I'll take ye there in it—you can try it out for yesself!"

71

After that, he kept sending his boy around to ask when I was going to visit Gorushka.

In the end, we agreed on a time. Afanasy came around for me.

It was a two-wheel *tarataika*. Black. Tall as a scaffold. The seats were crazily high up, so your knees were almost level with the front rail.

"Real chic!" said Afanasy. "Grand as they come!"

Our ride went quite well.

"Smooth and swift, in't it?" Afanasy enthused. "And ye can see everythin from up 'ere! And people can see you! Couldn't be grander, I say!"

His sly green eyes narrowed. His reddish beard moved in the breeze. I yielded.

But he couldn't drive me back; he had urgent business to attend to. "Yer friends can tekk you back," he said. "As for the *tarataika*, I'll send it around in the evening. Please arrange for the down payment."

Two days later I ordered Raven to be put in harness and I set off to Gorushka on my own.

Getting into the *tarataika*—I soon realized—was going to be a nightmare. The step was almost waist height. And Raven was a nervy, skittish horse. He was always jerking about, which made it difficult to get into even the most comfortable of carriages. Still, I could always ask someone to hold his head for me.

It was uphill all the way, which was why the estate was called Gorushka—or Little Hill.

The family who lived there were very sweet: a shortsighted young man who needed binoculars when he went out picking mushrooms, and two young ladies. One was considered a beauty and the other a freak, but, though I knew these ladies many years, I never managed to work out which was which.

Raven was skittish as ever. He seemed spooked by rooks, by puddles, and by heaps of crushed stone on the side of the road. The wind picked up; the telephone cable began to hum.

When I got to the hilltop estate, I found the gates locked. There was no one there. And the house was some distance away, down a long avenue.

I couldn't go and open the gate, since Raven would never allow me to climb back up onto my scaffold.

I shouted, waited a bit, then shouted again.

The trees swayed and bent. The wind shook their crowns, as if combing their forelocks.

Raven's mane fluttered this way and that way. He raised his head, seeming to listen. And then his head suddenly turned—and he fixed me with a huge, wild, yellowish eye.

A black bird flew into the air. As if casting a spell, it traced a large circle, passed swiftly overhead, and disappeared beyond the forest.

All as bleak as bleak can be. I was close to tears.

The moribund estate, the flailing trees, the ominous bird, and Raven's huge eye, wild, vicious, and frightened. I could sense his fear. And suddenly he careered off downhill.

I understood at once how smart Afanasy had been. It was not for nothing he'd wanted to make a quick sale and been so eager to take me on the long climb up to Gorushka. This was not a vehicle in which to descend a hill. Everything was out of kilter—everything sloped forward. The seat was so high that your feet barely touched the floor. The leather cushion was hard and slippery—and forward-sloping. Staying seated was barely possible. I tried bracing my knees against the boards in front—but soon my knees were trembling and my legs aching all over. Going right down onto the floor was more difficult still—the space was too narrow.

The wind howled. My horse was frightened. And there was nothing to hold on to.

Somehow or other I had to make my way to the monastery. Then someone could hold on to Raven while I turned the cushion over. It might be less slippery if I wasn't sitting on the leather.

It began to get dark.

At last I saw the white shape of the bell tower. The monastery itself was some distance away, but the monks had built a small well house by the side of the road, with an icon inside and a cross on the roof. There was always a little old monk there, speaking to passersby, collecting money from them and noting down the names of those they wished to be prayed for.[2] A little old monk in a worn habit, always with his small notebook. Nannies sometimes used him as a threat, to frighten their charges: "If you're not asleep soon, I'll take you to the ragged priest. He'll set you to turning the well wheel. That'll teach you!"

He might be little and old, but he could certainly keep hold of Raven for me.

I drove up to the well and stopped. Not a sign of the ragged priest with the notebook.

I waited. I called out.

No one.

I could hardly believe it. As if the whole wide world had come to an end.

Once again, Raven took to turning his head, looking from side to side. Once again, I sensed his fear. Wanting to reassure him, I called out in a deep voice, "Easy boy! Easy boy!"

At that, I felt still more frightened. Everything was frightening. Night—a wild night—was setting in. There wasn't a living soul anywhere. The wind howled. And I was alone in the world, calling out in a deep voice from the top of a black scaffold.

I made up my mind.

I got down from my seat. I tied the reins to the well column and began to walk toward the monastery.

The wicket gate in the wall turned out not to be locked. I couldn't believe my luck. I walked calmly and confidently up to the low white building that was the monastery guesthouse. I could hear voices inside.

The door was ajar.

At first I thought there were just two people at the table, and a boy standing beside me in the doorway. A solitary icon lamp and a dim light from the window. Then I glimpsed several more people, sitting around the room on benches.

And the two people at the table were women, probably pilgrims. One—an old woman in a white kerchief—was sipping tea from a saucer. The other, her head uncovered, had long, straight hair that hung below her shoulders. Looking more closely, I realized that this was in fact a young man, wearing a cassock and tall boots. But his face was strange and rather feminine—large and oval, like an egg, with everything pointing upward. Even his eyebrows were raised, as if he were listening to something in intent surprise. Broad bones, and a flat chest and belly. He sat there, looking up at the ceiling, not saying a word. His skullcap was lying on the table beside him.

"Here!" said the old woman, pushing a teapot toward him. "Drink deep if to good you will keep!"[3]

"Bless you," the lad replied in a whisper. "But I've no thirst on me."

"Hides his voice too," said somebody on one of the benches, evidently continuing some long conversation. "But why? What's up with the fellow?"

On a bench by the door—I could see more clearly now—a man in some kind of homespun coat, or maybe a cassock, swayed forward a little. His face was crisscrossed with wrinkles, as if he were constantly squinting. Locks of hair hung down over his eyes and his beard seemed to grow from as far up as his eyebrows. I couldn't make out his eyes at all; it was as if his eyebrows were his organs of sight. In his hand was a long whip.

"So, where did this fellow first join you?" he asked, turning to the old woman.

"This morning," she answered reluctantly. "As I were leaving the monastery. The Antony Dymsky Monastery."

"Yes, yes. From the other side. Just what I thought." And he called out in a loud voice to the boy standing beside me, "Locked the cowshed?"

"Aye."

"And barred it?"

"Aye—an' closed t' gate."

"Keep on guard, then!"

One of the other monks got to his feet. The ragged priest—I recognized him at once.

"And who might you be?" he asked.

I told him my name, then asked, "Did you really not recognize me?"

He said nothing.

The boy in the doorway let out a startled whistle. "Our Father treasurer, he told me she were dead."

The old woman looked scared. She crossed herself and began sweeping crusts and scraps off the table and into her bag.

"No," I said. "I'm alive all right."

"Oy, you!" someone shouted at the boy. "Stop scaring people."

"And what's brought you here so late at night?" asked the same voice, now addressing me.

"I've left my horse outside," I replied. "By the gate."

There was some whispering and the boy darted out, no doubt to check my words.

"A stake through the heart," muttered the shaggy man with the whip. "An aspen stake for evry one of 'em. Or there'll be no end to it all."

"Which was your monastery?" someone asked the young man with the long hair.

The young man got to his feet without a word. Leaving his skull-cap on the table, he went out to the porch.

"Anything else?" someone asked the old woman. "Notice anything else about him?"

This angered the old woman. "Why ye pickin on us? I've already said. I'd just left the monastery. And there he were. The road's open to all, in't it."

"Why ask *her*?" sneered the shaggy man. "Them two's in cahoots."

The boy returned. "Aye," he said, "there's a horse outside, by the well."

I wanted to rest longer. My legs were still trembling from the ride. But there was something horribly sinister about this little room with its shadows and voices, with its words I couldn't understand. And that long-haired being that had just left the room so strangely? And people saying I was dead, then seeming to doubt me when I said I was alive. All like some burdensome dream.

"Gone, has he?" asked the shaggy man.

"Yes, she has," the boy replied. "Bolted off, she did. Almost flying. Mebbe she really is flying?"

"We should wake Father Safrony," someone said.

"I'll check the cowshed," said the shaggy man. He got to his feet.

His legs were so short he could have been walking on his knees. I felt queasy. My head was spinning.

"Please come with me," I said to the boy. "I want you to hold my horse while I climb in."

"Yes, go along with her," said the ragged priest. And he too got to his feet.

We set off toward the main gate.

"How come you didn't recognize me?" I asked the priest. "I passed this way only the other day."

The priest strode on ahead, not saying a word.

I turned to the boy. "But who was that fellow with the long hair?"

The boy looked all around him. "Wait—wait till we're past t' gate."

"What do you mean?"

The ragged priest was already standing by the well, book in hand. He bowed. I placed an offering on top of the book.

"Pl . . . pl . . . plague," the boy said in a whisper.

"What?"

"Her wi the hair. Plague, cattle death. She's come from t'other side. From t' lakes and t' monastery—that's where the plague be."

"The plague?"

I turned the cushion over and climbed in. Raven jerked the *tara-taika* forward and to one side.

It was all as awful as before. My legs began to ache.

The telephone cables hummed. The crushed stone murmured.

The road was still clearly visible, but to either side lay only blue darkness.

Once again I was alone, sensing Raven's fear.

No one had responded when I called out at Gorushka. They hadn't heard me at the monastery gate. They'd said I was dead . . .

The cables hummed and howled. I thought I could hear shouts.

Raven snorted and shied to one side. I almost fell to the ground.

In the middle of the road stood "Cattle Plague"—huge, wild, and terrible.[4] Long hair whipped by the wind. Flailing her arms about. Half shouting, half singing in a hysterical, heartrending voice:

> White sheets of snow
> Lie on every field.
> The only field still lying bare—
> Is the grief I feel.

Raven leaped forward and tore off toward the town.
Soon I heard the clatter of carriage wheels on cobbles.
The old coachman was waiting for me by the gate.

"Easy, easy now...What's up wi ye?" he said, wiping Raven's neck with the flap of his caftan. "Smelled a wolf, did ye? All atremble, all atremble. Or were it a shapeshifter? Eh? A shapeshifter?"

"Fyodor," I said, "quick. Get me down. I'm not feeling well."

Translated by Robert and Elizabeth Chandler

SHAPESHIFTER

IT WASN'T by chance that I found myself in that snow-swept small town. Nor was it because I wanted to see my country aunt. I was there for romantic reasons; I'd taken rather a liking to Alexey Nikolaevich.

He had spent the whole autumn in Petersburg—visiting us on occasion, dancing with me at every party, and "bumping into" me at exhibitions. And as he was about to leave (having just been appointed a magistrate in that unprepossessing small town), he had told me he loved me and asked me to be his wife.

I asked him to give me time to consider his proposal—which is how we left things.

Most of my relatives seemed to think well of him.

My granny said, "Well, *ma chère*, he has impeccable manners. And he's a lawyer to boot."

One of my aunts said, "No flies on you! Barely out of college—and you've already landed yourself a husband!"

Another aunt said, "He seems rather dim, and he's got money too. What more could you ask for?"

He wrote me letters—long ones—and the passages about me were quite interesting. But for the main part, he wrote about himself and the complexities of his soul. He even described his dreams, which were full of esoteric visions. Awfully tedious.

And then came the invitation to visit this country aunt, and so I decided to go and test out my feelings.

This little town was sixty versts from the nearest railway station, and as godforsaken as they come. The buildings were all of wood, the river was blanketed with snow, and on the far bank stood a monastery.

I happened to come at a time when the place was unusually lively—because of a meeting of the local *zemstvo*.[1]

My suitor, however, was out of town, investigating a case someplace far away, in the village of The Lakes, near his own estate.

For something to do, my aunt took me along to the meeting, introduced me to the other women, sat me down, and told me to listen.

The hall was fairly large and full of people. In the middle was a group of local doctors and other dignitaries sitting around a table covered in green felt. They all had thick whiskers and bushy eyebrows and were wearing frock coats that looked like something out of the previous century.

They were talking loudly, arguing with one another. A little old man with a lisp was getting very worked up, constantly repeating, "I'm an old man and I can no longer make eloquent speeches." It sounded, though, as if he were saying, "make elegant peaches."

Then someone embarked on a lengthy speech about the importance of restructuring the hospital, since it was wrong for the lavatory to be located next to the operating theater. A lady sitting beside me giggled, nudged me with her elbow, and said, "What piquant details—whatever's next!"

A little apart from the others, just beyond the shaggy doctors, was a strange man. His face was oddly thin, with a small, shapeless beard. He looked, if such a thing is possible, dazzlingly pale. Sitting there with his eyes closed, he could have been dead. I stared at him for a long time. Suddenly, as though sensing my gaze, he opened his eyes, looked straight at me, and then closed them again. He looked at me like that several times, always somewhat questioningly, as if in surprise.

"What are you doing, making eyes at that young doctor?" asked my neighbor, the genteel lady who had just been giggling and nudging me. "I wouldn't bother with him. No one here gives him the time of day. They say he's some sort of were-creature."

In the evening, my aunt had visitors. Among them was the most prominent of the town ladies—a widow. Her carriage was drawn by two white horses, and because of these horses she was known as "the priestess." She was the town's chief gossip, and so she already knew that the pale doctor had caught my eye.

"You could do better than that, my dear!" she said. "No one around here can stand him. The peasants say he's a shapeshifter. Where his eyes fall, they say, crops fail."

She went on to say that this doctor—Oglanov by name—had not lived in these parts long, only a little over a year. His grandfathers and great-grandfathers had all lived here and been rich and well known, but the family house was now almost falling down. Nevertheless, that was where the doctor lived—although his own father had never been seen in these parts.

It was a big stone house, a frightening place with all sorts of legends attached to it; some of them had even been written down. A troublesome serf girl, apparently, was once immured alive—in one of the walls of the main hall. And there had once been a large cellar; the great-grandfather of the current Oglanov had secretly kept ten Jews there, forging banknotes; he'd smuggled these Jews in from somewhere in Austria. The authorities somehow caught wind of all this and the great-grandfather heard that there was likely to be an official investigation. Without saying a word to his Jews, he ordered piles of bricks to be placed in the courtyard beside each of the air vents to the cellar. Meanwhile the Jews just carried on working, with no idea what lay in store for them.

Soon Oglanov's men reported that the district court was on its way. In those days the legal authorities simply went straight to the place in question, just like that. Oglanov summoned his masonry serfs and ordered them to seal up every last air vent. When the court arrived, Oglanov gave them a splendid welcome. For five days on end they all feasted, while the unfortunate Jews down below suffocated to death. And since the house appeared to have no cellar at all, no one suspected a thing. And then off the court went.

After that, Oglanov never so much as unsealed the cellar. He went on living in that dreadful house as if none of this had ever happened. And his son lived there too; they were both fantastically wealthy. But the grandson—our doctor's father—was brought up in Petersburg, where he squandered the family fortune. And then, years later, this degenerate—the current Oglanov—had shown up out of the blue, to work as a doctor.

A letter arrived from my suitor, inviting me to The Lakes. He wanted to introduce me to his family.

My aunt made no objections. "Only you can't go all that way on your own," she said. "We must find you a traveling companion."

In small towns, such things are arranged quickly. Somebody was sent somewhere, somebody else then knocked on our door, and so on. We were told that, since the *zemstvo* meeting was over, the delegates were now going their separate ways—so there was sure to be someone who could take me to The Lakes. After a few more exchanges, I learned that Dr. Oglanov would be coming around for me after breakfast. He too was going to The Lakes and—as it happened—would be joining my Alexey Nikolaevich there to attend a postmortem.

I would be traveling with the Shapeshifter.

"Who knows?" I said to myself. "It might even be rather entertaining."

I waited a long time. By the time the doctor called, it was getting dark. He didn't come up for me, though; he stayed outside.

Felt boots were pulled onto my feet. I put on my fur coat and—on top of that—I was bundled into one of my aunt's old traveling cloaks. I must have looked quite a sight!

Out on the street, instead of the elegant troika I was expecting, I found two rather unkempt horses, harnessed in tandem to a shabby old sleigh.

The doctor greeted me morosely, not even looking up. I could barely see his face behind the collar of his fur coat. He covered my legs in a blanket that smelled of rancid sheepskin.

"This'll keep you warm," he muttered. "It's a wonderful blanket."

That was all he said.

He truly did have a dark presence: where his eyes fell, crops might well fail.

For a long time, we traveled in silence. I began to doze off. It was all very boring: the long, white road; a cold, lilac sky; and the squeal of the runners.

"...is that so?"

The Shapeshifter was speaking.

"What?"

"I've heard you're going to marry this magistrate—is that so?"

His pale, thin-lipped face was turned toward me, but he was looking down at the ground.

"I don't know," I said. I felt confused.

He fell silent again. And then: "Oh well. He's rich and stupid. A good catch, I suppose."

"What's it to do with you?" I asked.

"Just bear in mind," he said, after another long silence, "that his wealth won't mask his stupidity forever. One way or another, his evil stupidity will make itself felt. Not that it's any concern of mine, of course."

"Why say such things then?"

He turned sharply toward me—as if to meet my eye—but then buried his face in his collar again.

"Yes, yes...it is a little strange of me," he muttered. "You're right."

After that, we both fell silent again. There still remained a long, long way to go. The white anguish of the boundless snows, the monotonous jingle of our bell, the motionless, evil figure beside me—all this made my heart ache. The driver swayed silently in his seat, as if dead. Ahead loomed the dead of night. I wanted to ask if we'd be arriving soon, yet somehow I lacked the strength to speak.

It was particularly disgusting to have that "wonderful" blanket of his over my legs. Yes, everything about this journey felt wrong! Why had I agreed to travel with the first person who came along? My stupid aunt should never have let me.

I fell asleep.

I woke to the sound of barking. We were approaching a large house.

"I have to pick up my medical instruments," said the Shapeshifter.

"This is my home. Come inside. Warm up a bit while we wait for fresh horses."

I didn't want to go in. Why hadn't he told me we'd be stopping at his home? But I had no choice.

A huge stone house. Boarded-up windows—all except three or four. A grand main entrance, flanked by columns—but we stopped outside one of the wings. A man in a sheepskin coat, holding a small tin lamp, let us in and led us rather nervously down a long corridor and through an echoing hall. Patches of damp made strange shapes on the walls. And huge shadows raced along beside us, one overtaking another.

Heavens! This was the house where people had been walled up alive.

"Here we are!" said the Shapeshifter, who had been walking behind me.

The room was almost empty. A sagging sofa, a leather chair, and a small table. It could have been a prison cell.

The Shapeshifter put his hand to the stove and said something to the man in the sheepskin. They both went out.

I sat on the chair. The room felt cold and damp. I sat there in my fur coat.

The man in the sheepskin brought in an armful of firewood and thrust it into the stove. He blew and wheezed over it for a long time, filling the room with smoke. Then he brought me a glass of tea and a few sugar lumps on a saucer. After that, he disappeared, eventually coming back with some fried eggs in a pan, a slice of bread, and an old iron fork. The giant frying pan could have fed five people. Then, to my surprise, he brought in a jug of water, a chipped wooden basin, a bucket, and a rough towel. He placed the basin on the sofa, as if that were quite normal, then put the jug on the floor. "There," he said—and off he went.

It all seemed more ghastly than ever.

My enormous shadow flickered on the walls. The table, the lamp's orange glow, and my own face were all reflected in the black window. But could I be sure it was *me*? Why was my face so pale and narrow?

I screamed. It was *him*—the Shapeshifter, looking at me from behind his fur collar! I jumped to my feet—and it was me again, my own reflection. But I was still terrified. I ran and hid in a corner where I could no longer see the window, and quietly began to cry.

The man in the sheepskin came in again and said that the horses were now ready.

Once more: dancing shadows, ghosts swooping and swerving along the walls, chasing one another as they tried to hide from the feeble lamplight.

In the courtyard stood an open country sleigh and two horses in tandem. A skinny young man was sitting up on the box.

"I ordered a covered sleigh," said the Shapeshifter. Morose as ever, he wrapped me up again in his blanket.

"Aye, but summ'n else has took it," the young man replied. "P'lice officer."

We set off. The horses plodded along pitifully. We went through a little forest, down a small hill, and out onto a dismal, empty steppe.

"Doesn't your master ever feed the horses at all?" asked the Shapeshifter.

The driver gave a start, turned to look at us, and said, "Oh aye, he gives 'em a bit nah 'n then."

His face looked strange, his mouth twisted yet gaping open, as if he were guffawing madly.

"Idiot! What do you keep twitching about for?"

"Nothin . . . I weren't doin owt," the driver mumbled—and turned forward again.

Never-ending bare steppe, with only a thin strip of forest far away to the left. The wind blew and blew, reaching under the doctor's vile blanket, creeping up the sleeves of my coat.

"Why've you taken us so far out?" shouted the Shapeshifter. "You should have stayed close to the shore."

Once again, the driver started and turned to face us. "Fancy a swim, does tha?"

"What!"

"Can't ye see?" said the driver, pointing his whip toward some long patches of black in the snow near the edge of the forest.

"Patches of thaw," muttered Oglanov. "But why did your master send *you* out today? Wasn't there anyone else?"

"Well, Igor's with t' p'liceman, in't he?" the driver replied, with a twitch of the shoulders.

"Stop twitching, you scoundrel!" the Shapeshifter cried wildly.

I couldn't bear it any longer.

"Doctor," I began, "why do you keep shouting at him? It's horrible!"

"Keep out of it," Oglanov answered under his breath. "It's the only way to restrain him."

I had no idea what he meant and I was afraid to say any more. I just asked about the patches of thaw.

"We're driving over a lake. Our route takes us across four lakes, one after another."

Up another hill, through another forest—and then back down again. Snow and wind—and more snow and wind. There was no end to it all. The sleigh plunged and swerved. I shivered and began to feel sick, as if I were out at sea, in a nasty swell.

"There! Yonder!" said the driver. He turned toward us and pointed his whip somewhere off to the right. I could see three dark spots moving along the snow, one after the other.

"What are they?" I asked.

"Word 'as it, they're at yer beck n' call!" the driver yelled at Oglanov. Then he turned forward again, toward the horses. He was mumbling, but I heard one word clearly: *Shapeshifter.*

Or did I imagine it?

"Wolves?" I whispered.

"Don't worry," said the doctor. "It's all right. They won't dare come close."

Then the driver let out a cry. It wasn't even so very loud, but there was something so terrible about it—some note I'd never heard before—that I too screamed and jumped up from my seat, almost tumbling out of the sleigh. As for the driver, his head drooped forward and he began to fall to one side, with strange jerks and spasms.

The Shapeshifter grabbed him by the shoulders, leaned right forward, seized the reins, and halted the horses.

"Just as I feared," he said crossly.

Very gently, he laid the young man down in the snow. He twitched about for a while, then went still. The Shapeshifter lifted him up, placed him on his own seat in the back of the sleigh, and wrapped him in a fur blanket.

"Is he dead?" I asked timidly.

"Epilepsy," Oglanov answered abruptly. He got up onto the box and took hold of the reins.

And it was back to more wind and snow, all the while with that lifeless body beside me. By then, I was in a bad way. My legs were frozen, and I felt dizzy and nauseous. I began to sob.

"Not much farther!" said the Shapeshifter. "Soon we'll be at the warden's."

More snow. More wind. The sleigh dipped and dived, its runners creaking under the strain.

I'm dragged up some steps. Then I'm lying on the floor, on a straw-filled mattress. "Quick," says an old woman in a peasant headdress. "Get 'er some vodka!" Then someone's rubbing my feet, my teeth knock against the thick rim of a glass, and something's burning my throat.

"It's all right, it's all right," someone is whispering.

The face of the Shapeshifter—now sorrowful, tender, and attentive.

"You poor girl," I hear. "You'll have a hard time with that fool of yours. You took offense . . . I know . . . But he'll make life hell for you, you silly, silly thing. I feel for you."

I cry and cry. I don't want to stop.

Gentle hands stroke my face, then wrap me in something warm. If the hands go away for a moment, I cry more loudly, to bring them back again.

Protect me! I want to say, but I can't get the words out. My head spins. I'm falling asleep.

And then—morning. Bright day peeks in through a tiny, ice-covered window. Last night's old woman is grating something into a basin.

"You've woke up, then?" she asks. "Well, let's get thi up an' make thi a brew. Only, we drink willow-herb tea round 'ere. Or Saint-John's-wort. Me ol' man's gone into t' village, to fetch thi some 'orses."

"Is it far to The Lakes?" I ask.

"No, luv. Not far at all. Fifteen versts or so."

In a corner behind the stove I catch sight of the Shapeshifter's blanket.

"What's that?" I ask. "Under the blanket?"

Why had I got into such a state? What was it had frightened me?

"It's Fedka, the driver. He's took a turn, but he'll soon be reight. It's t' fallin sickness, in't it."

The doctor had even given the driver his sheepskin blanket—his pride and joy.

I remember the outlandish pan and the iron fork. I feel racked by shame. If only out of politeness, I should have at least tried those eggs. I had behaved badly.

The old man comes back with fresh horses.

As I leave, I quietly stroke the blanket, as if apologizing for the disgust I'd felt earlier.

Later that day, in a grand drawing room full of furniture upholstered in red corduroy, I had to listen to Alexey Nikolaevich. Tall, stupid, utterly alien to me, and idiotically jealous at my having traveled with Dr. Oglanov—he made quite a scene. And when I told this stupid and evil man that I didn't love him and had no intention of marrying him, his eyes bulged.

"I don't believe it!" he said—and he did indeed sound incredulous.

I never saw Dr. Oglanov again. But now and then, if I happen to recall our encounter, I find myself wondering... Did that sly Shapeshifter take on the guise of a perfect gentleman, someone uniquely kind and affectionate, just so that he could ruin my chance of happiness with a splendid husband by the name of Alexey Nikolaevich?

Translated by Robert and Elizabeth Chandler and Sian Valvis

PART FOUR

from *Witch* (1936)

WITCH

SOMETIMES, when you think back, you can't help wondering: Were people really like that? Was life really like that?

Needless to say, you couldn't ever talk about all this to a foreigner. He wouldn't understand, and he wouldn't believe a word you said. But a real Russian—if he hasn't forgotten his past altogether—he's sure to accept it as truth, and he'll be right.

I'm going to tell you a story I heard from a very respectable lady. It's a story I didn't find in the least surprising. We've certainly all seen things a great deal stranger!

"This happened," my friend began, "some thirty years ago..."

Or perhaps not quite so long ago. At the time, we were living in a little steppe town where my husband was a magistrate.

And what a dull place that little town was! Full of dust in summertime, and in winter the snowdrifts would bury the streetlamps; in spring and autumn it was so muddy that a whole troika almost sank out of sight in the cathedral square, and the horses had to be pulled out with ropes. I remember our cook going out to the baker's in boots that came right up to her thighs. And one evening, my husband and I were out visiting and stayed too late, and by the time we left the house, the street was so deep in mud there was no hope of crossing it. Luckily there was an inn on our side of the street, so we spent the night there, and the next day someone found a cart to take us back home.

All as boring as can be.

The government clerks used to go to one another's houses to play cards. There was a club, too—a wretched place. Sometimes there'd be a cardsharp who'd clean out everybody's pockets, and even that was a welcome event. Unfortunate, perhaps, but at least it gave us something to talk about.

The women mostly stayed at home. What else could they do?

I remember, one day I was wandering around late in the evening—I'd gone out because I was so bored—and the moon was shining, and everything was quiet, so very quiet... Not a light in the windows, and a warm breath of wormwood blowing in from the dim, moonlit steppe. And trembling over the quiet streets—the frantic scream of a bird. I'd already been told that this was the doctor's guinea hen, wailing for her slaughtered mate. A three-note call, again and again, the last two notes a tone higher than the first. This isn't easy to explain to you, but such a cry of inconsolable despair, above the dead little town, in the silence of that trackless steppe, was more than any human soul could bear.

I remember coming home and saying to my husband, "Now I know why people hang themselves."

He screamed, clutching his head in his hands. The look on my face must have been frightful.

However, we led a peaceful life, and we were a close family. I was about nineteen at the time, and my little Valechka was one and a half. She had a Nyanya, a little old woman who'd lost count of her age—she'd been born a serf on my aunt's estate. Our apartment was cozy, the walls hung with framed pictures of my college friends and my husband's fellow lawyers.

The servants in this little town were dreadful. All the women were tobacco-smoking drunkards, and at night they would wait at their windows for the local Don Juan—a water carrier with no nose.

But with my maid, I'd been rather lucky. She was a quiet girl, pockmarked and fair-haired, with an uncommon gift for finding lost objects.

"Ustiusha," I might ask, "you haven't seen my keys, have you?"

She'd think a moment, then go straight to the kitchen, get the broom, slide it under the sofa, and bring out the keys.

Another time, I said to her, "Remember, Ustiusha? Last year there was a scrap of velvet ribbon lying around on my dressing table. Where can it have got to?"

Ustiusha thought a bit, went to an armchair, slipped her hand between the seat and the back, felt around, and brought out the ribbon.

All this, of course, was both helpful and entertaining. What's more, she neither smoked nor got drunk.

She got on all right with the other servants, though I have to say that, even if there weren't any quarrels, they did look somehow askance at her—as if they suspected her of something or were a bit afraid of her. Our cat, however, was openly hostile. As soon as Ustiusha came into a room, the cat would leap up, arching her back. Her fur would stand on end, and she'd streak out of the room and hide away in some corner.

"What's going on?" we wondered. "Does Ustiusha hit her?" But that seemed unlikely. She was such a quiet girl, walking around with downcast eyes and always very respectful.

All very good, but I must admit she had some strange ways. It's hard to say just what it was. A kind of absentmindedness, perhaps. For instance, you could send her out to buy bread rolls, and she'd come back with a cockerel. What were we supposed to do with a cockerel at teatime?

One evening we'd invited some guests around—Dr. Mukhin, the police inspector, and their wives—for a game of vint. Everything was ready and we were expecting them.

Then someone seemed to ring, and we heard Ustiusha go to the front door, but no one came in. Then another ring, and again—nobody. "Very odd," said my husband.

We called Ustiusha. "Who was that?"

"The inspector with his wife, and Dr. and Mrs. Mukhin."

"Why didn't they come in?"

"I told them you'd gone to bed."

"Why on earth? You knew very well we were expecting guests. We sent you out to get candies. We'd put out the lace tablecloth!"

Ustiusha didn't say a word. She stood there looking down at the floor, all plump and yellow—an absolute turnip.

"What on earth made you do that?"

"I'm sorry."

And that was all we could get out of her.

Again and again we made up our minds to sack her, but we were always afraid that her replacement might be even worse.

But one day she did something utterly unforgivable. It was carnival time, the week before Lent, and we'd invited people, perhaps about fifteen of them, to come and eat pancakes. Everything was ready, we were just sitting down at the table, when I began to worry that there might not be enough salmon.

The grocer was next door, and I quietly said a few words to Ustiusha.

She hurried out. After a while, we started on the pancakes. For some reason it was the cook who was serving us, not Ustiusha.

I slipped out into the kitchen.

"Where's Ustiusha? Why isn't she serving us?"

"She won't be doing any serving, madam. She's gone to her village for a wedding."

"A wedding! I just asked her to go to the shop."

"Well, on the way she met a friend who told her there was a wedding in her village today, so she bundled up a few things and off she went."

I'm sure you can imagine our astonishment.

Ustiusha stayed away for four whole days. Full of resentment at her barefaced insolence, we didn't, for one moment of that time, stop talking about her.

"I'll speak to her," said my husband, puckering his brows. "I'll tell her, 'Ustiusha, answer me, clearly and categorically—'"

"Just listen to you," I interrupted. "*Clearly and categorically*... You don't have a clue how to talk to ordinary people! I'll speak to her myself—"

"You? Are you capable of giving anyone a serious talking-to? You'll get nowhere at all—you'll just start hemming and hawing. We have to be forceful. I'll say, 'If your position as a maid—'"

"No, I still say, keep out of it. We need to give it to her straight: 'Ustiusha, be off with you!' Simple as that."

We argued a long time, each defending our right to sack Ustiusha.

I asked the cook to find us another maid as soon as possible.

"Whatever for?"

"What do you mean? Because I'm sacking Ustiusha."

The cook smiled enigmatically. "You'll never sack her!"

"Why do you say that?"

"Because every night, she whispers on you, and she burns scraps of paper, and blows smoke up the chimney. You'll never get rid of her."

I laughed and told my husband.

"What a primitive lot they are! All their witchery and superstitions—it's a disgrace. And it's not as if she can't read and write."

We told our cook that she absolutely must find us a new maid, and we went on arguing about which of us would do the better job of sacking Ustiusha.

"Anyway, what is all this about burning scraps of paper and blowing smoke up the chimney?" I asked.

"Primitive folk have any number of superstitions—relics of medieval times," my husband explained. "Still, I wouldn't have expected nonsense like that from Ustiusha."

"Perhaps it was just the cook telling stories? Perhaps she wanted to get rid of her, so she could put forward some friend of her own?"

"Maybe. But there's no gain from guessing. What we need to do, without wasting another minute, is to get rid of her. And I'll see to that myself."

"No, I'll see to it."

"And I sincerely beg you not to contradict me."

On the evening of the fourth day, my husband and I were sitting by the samovar. I was knitting Valechka a pair of mittens, I can remember quite clearly. My husband was playing patience. And the cat was sitting on the table looking at the cream jug with half-closed eyes.

Suddenly the cat shot up, arching her back. Her fur stood on end, and she sprang off the table and fled into the drawing room. The door curtain parted and in came Ustiusha. Quiet, plump, sallow, the same as ever. She went over to my husband, kissed him on the shoulder, then went over to me and kissed my shoulder too.[1] She turned to the dresser, took out some cups, and slowly left the room.

"So why didn't you . . ." I hissed.

"But I thought," my husband muttered in embarrassment, "I thought *you* were going to."

"Good God! You kept shouting at me, saying it had to be you who got rid of her! Now what? Now I don't even know how to bring up the subject with her."

Then Ustiusha appeared a second time. She stood calmly by the door and asked, "May I give yesterday's pie to the washerwoman?"

"Yes, of course," I replied.

"Yes, yes, please do," said my husband.

What made him butt in just then, when he never took any interest in household matters and certainly knew nothing whatsoever about any pies?

"Well, now what?" I asked in bewilderment.

"Perhaps it'll all go better tomorrow," my husband mumbled in some confusion. "You just tell her in the morning that her services are no longer required."

"Why me? Tell her yourself. You're the head of the household . . . Maybe it's because she blows smoke up the chimney. You daren't sack her!"

"Don't talk nonsense," he snapped angrily, and left the room.

After that, everything went quiet. But not for long. Soon our house witnessed an event so dramatic that people in that little town probably still talk about it. (But ne'er a word of this after dark!)

I really don't know if there are words to tell you about all this—the most important event in our lives in that province. It'll seem so very odd, in this day and age.

Well, not long after Ustiusha's strange absence, our cook unexpectedly left us. It was very mysterious—all of a sudden she handed in her notice. She made up some story about wanting to retire to her village but then just stayed in town. Everyone saw her there.

"Why did she leave?" I asked Nyanya. "Perhaps we weren't paying her enough. She should have said something, and we'd have given her a raise."

"She was getting more than enough," Nyanya replied. "She could search for years and never find a job like this one. 'You could live with a mistress like ours forever and a day,' I heard her say. 'Never weighs up the butter nor counts the eggs—an absolute ninny is our mistress! Life's good here.'"

"So why did she leave, if she was happy with her pay?" I asked, pretending not to hear the last part.

"She was swept out."

"Swept out?"

Nyanya came closer and whispered, "Cook always kept her things in the kitchen, locked in a cupboard. Last Saturday she goes to get a clean blouse, and would you believe it, there on top of her things lies a broom. So she throws her belongings together and runs—fast as her legs'll carry her."

"But how can a broom get into a locked cupboard?" I asked in surprise.

"Well, that's just it! If you're being swept out, best not stand about!"

As I've said, Nyanya was very old, and it was probably this that gave her a look of great wisdom: a downturned mouth and eyes peering out from under deep brows. But she was phenomenally stupid. For instance, she once said to little Valechka, "Look, if you don't do as I say, I'll go back and work for the Korsakov children! They still love their old Nyanya and miss her."

Now the Korsakov children were so old by then, they'd lost their wits. One—a general—had retired from service; the other had taken to such wild living that he'd been placed under legal guardianship.

And Nyanya loved all kinds of scary stories.

Once she told us she'd seen a water spirit with her own eyes.

"I was living with your auntie, and I took Lizanka for a walk by the river. Suddenly I hear a whooshing noise—like someone's fired a cannon—and all the water's whirling around. Lucky I had the littl'un with me—her angel soul kept me safe. Else I'd have been dragged down underwater, no doubt about it."

Some time later I asked my aunt what she thought had really happened.

"It was just the coachman bathing."

Nyanya used to talk all kinds of nonsense, but this time there was no getting away from it: the cook had left because of the broom.

I told all this to my husband. He was annoyed that we'd lost a good cook.

"It's probably Ustiusha again. We should have gotten rid of her long ago. I'll have a word with her some day soon. I'm sick and tired of her."

"So am I," I said.

And so we all but made up our minds to sack Ustiusha.

But then one evening my husband was out at the club. I was sitting in my room getting ready to go to bed, but something made me uneasy. It might have been the wind howling in the chimney. The spring had been nothing but blizzards and snowdrifts, truly vile.

The wind howling. The stove door rattling. Sheer misery.

Suddenly Nyanya came in, her lips pursed and with her look of great wisdom.

"Heavens, Nyanya! What's up?"

She came closer, looked back over her shoulder, and said, "Mistress, dear mistress, have you been in the dining room this evening?"

"No," I said, "I haven't. Why?"

"Well—go in, and you'll see. As for me, say what you like—but I won't be staying here no longer."

Not knowing what to think, I followed Nyanya to the dining room and stopped by the door. Everything seemed quite normal. Just a room like any other room, with a lamp on the table.

"The chairs! Can't you see?"

I looked around. The chairs were positioned around the table, but back to front, with their seats facing outward and their backs against the table. All twelve of them.

"And this thirteenth chair! How did that get here?"

Sure enough, there was an upholstered chair that I'd never seen before, standing on its own at the head of the table, in the place of honor.

"How come? Why?"

Nyanya remained grimly silent.

"Could it have been some little game of Valechka's?" I asked.

"An eighteen-month-old child—moving such heavy chairs! Not likely!"

I felt lost. This may seem funny today, but at the time, I assure you, it was chilling. The room seemed completely unfamiliar. Even the lamp—there was something strange about the way it was burning. And that thirteenth chair, God knows where it had come from.

I said timidly, "Nyanya dear! Shouldn't we turn the chairs the right way round?"

That really did frighten her. "What are you saying? How can anyone move them now? *He's* been here. Why, he's sat on them all himself, each and every one of them!"

"But what's going on, Nyanya? Why's all this happening?"

"Why? Because we're being turned out."

"Turned out?"

"Yes, turn about and get out! Here's the floor, and there's the door! Turn around and get you gone!"

"Nyanya, dearest," I asked in horror, "where's little Valechka? Is she asleep?"

"Yes, Valechka's sleeping. This very evening she was asking for milk," Nyanya replied grimly. After a silence she added, "When the Korsakovs' little Yushenka was dying, he kept asking for tea."

By then I couldn't bear it any longer. I dashed out into the hall, grabbed my fur coat off the hook, and rushed to the club to find my husband.

My nerves were so taut that when a dog yapped at me from behind a fence, I screamed and broke into a run. In my terror, all the houses looked unfamiliar to me, and I almost got lost in our three or four little streets.

I got to the club. Someone went to fetch my husband.

"Things aren't right at home," I stammered. "Chairs turned round . . . Thirteen chairs . . . Nyanya says we must leave at once. Valechka's been asking for milk."

And I burst into tears.

My husband listened aghast, not understanding a word.

"Wait a minute," he said finally. "I'll go back in and have a word with the police superintendent."

"Be quick!" I shouted after him. "Little Valechka's at home all on her own."

The superintendent came out at once. I stammered out to him everything I knew. My husband looked on in embarrassment, mumbling some rubbish about women's nerves, but the superintendent was very professional and businesslike. After clearing his throat a few times, he said he'd come back with us straightaway. Then he'd get a clearer idea what was going on.

Our superintendent was an old, experienced bribe-taker, an easygoing fellow who liked to live and let live.

We set off for our house. Feeling doubly protected—by my husband's love and by the arm of the law—I felt calmer. On the way, the superintendent questioned us about our servants. We said that our new cook seldom left the kitchen, that our maid had been with us for over a year, and Nyanya forever and a day.

We entered the house and opened the dining-room door.

Despite my double protection, I was immediately gripped by the same sense of terror.

The superintendent stood still in the doorway.

"Has everything been left untouched?"

"Yes, yes."

"Hmm . . . It's a good thing you didn't touch anything. Get the servants to come along now. One by one."

Nyanya shuffled in, looking wise as ever.

"Well, old woman, tell us all you know."

To my surprise, Nyanya denied all knowledge of anything.

"I don't know nowt, and I don't want to know. But wild horses won't drag me into that dining room."

The superintendent looked at her with respect and told her to call in the next person.

Next came the cook. Sounding very sleepy, she answered everything with "Nothing to do with *me*," hiccuped, and went out.

Then it was Ustiusha's turn.

The superintendent drew himself up to his full height, then swooped down—eagle-like.

"You turned the chairs round. Why? It's an abomination!"

Ustiusha stood there—tight-lipped, eyes cast down.

"I never touched nothing. Cleared the table, then went back to the kitchen."

"And where's that thirteenth chair from? Answer me, you wretch!"

"I never took nothing, and I don't know nothing."

"We'll soon see about that!" Turning to my husband, the superintendent asked, "Have you got any earth anywhere?"

"My personal estate is in Mogilyov Province," came the bewildered reply.

"No, no, that's not what I meant at all . . . Now, come here, you wretch." The superintendent seized Ustiusha by the elbow and dragged her over to a potted aspidistra.

"Now then. Pick up some earth and eat it, if you're so innocent."

Ustiusha obediently picked up a pinch of earth and began to chew.

"Good for you!" said the superintendent. "You may leave."

And Ustiusha calmly left the room.

"Well, seeing she ate earth to back up her story, that means she's in the clear. That'll do for now. I'll send you one of my men, and he can spend the night in your front hall. Anything untoward—inform the station at once. And now permit me to kiss your hand—and please don't worry. We've known worse tangles than this."

And off he went.

My husband and I were left on our own, with no idea what to do. We looked into the nursery. Valechka was asleep. Nyanya was lying on her back, as if blowing flies off her lips—she too was clearly asleep.

"We could have a look in the dining room, if you like?" I said.

"Why? What good will that do?"

My husband evidently didn't like the idea.

We went to bed. But we didn't put the light out.

I'd just dozed off, when—

"Can you hear?" whispered my husband. "Isn't there someone walking about in the dining room?"

"N-no, I can't hear a thing!" I whispered back.

He was sitting up now, listening for all he was worth.

Then, beneath the window, a knock.

"Who's there?" my husband yelled in terror. "Who's there? I'll shoot!"

This was met by another knock.

"Don't say a word, for God's sake!" said my husband. "A man could go crazy like this."

He got up, put out the light, crept up to the window, drew back the curtain, and looked out.

"Someone's standing out there!" he said in a broken whisper.

Suddenly the door opened and a tousled head poked in.

I leaped up with a scream.

"It's me! It's me!" stammered Nyanya. "*He's* walking around the house. Himself. Now we're done for."

"Who? Why?"

"Someone must have invited him here to dine. He'd have sat on that upholstered chair. Only I shut the door and said a prayer on it. So he couldn't get in!"

"Quiet! Quiet!" my husband whispered. "The doorbell!"

Someone was indeed quietly ringing the bell. And a second time.

We tiptoed along the corridor.

And again!

"Who's there?" shouted my husband. "Speak—or I'll shoot!"

There was a voice outside, but we couldn't make out a word. Then we heard "Your Honor" and "Superintendent." That was reassuring.

We opened the door a crack. A policeman!

"Mr. Superintendent sent me to keep watch here."

"What are you doing walking around the house, you idiot?"

"I didn't want to disturb you by ringing the bell. I knocked at one window, but some old lady started making the sign of the cross over me. Then I knocked at another window, and some other woman wailed at me and threatened to shoot. So I decided to ring the bell after all."

"Come in, come in, my dear fellow," said my husband. Turning to me, he added, "Give him some vodka to warm him up."

He was, I think, far from happy about being mistaken for a wailing woman.

Next morning my husband woke me and said, "Of course it's all a load of nonsense—Nyanya and her magic spells. But since you're getting yourself into such a state, the best thing is for you to hurry up, get your things together, and go and stay at your mother's along with Nyanya and Valya. You've been wanting to go for a long time. I'll dismiss the servants, and I'll go and stay with the Marshal of the Nobility.[2] He was begging me to go and stay with him only last night. Very soon the doctor's apartment will fall vacant—it's a far better apartment than this one—and we can move in there. Incidentally, that upholstered chair comes from the hall, it used to stand in the corner, and we'd quite forgotten about it. Not that that changes anything, and since you're so set on visiting your mama, I think this is the right time."

He himself, of course, was not in a state at all—though he kept shifting from one foot to the other and chewing his mustache.

"I'm not getting myself into a state," I replied. "I'm not some superstitious peasant woman; I'm an educated lady. But since Nyanya won't stay in this house at any price and I really can't do without her, I've no choice but to go away. And for the time being, I think, we'd better keep the door to the dining room locked. I'm not frightened, of course, but—"

"I locked it last night," my husband replied. He was on the verge of saying more, but he blushed and stopped.

Now, thinking back over all this, I reckon that Ustiusha must have been tidying the dining room that evening and forgotten to put the chairs back as usual; and then, seeing the trouble this caused, with the police and all, she understandably enough took fright and didn't dare confess.

On the other hand, if I were superstitious, I should probably think that however stupid this may seem, we still ended up being "turned out"—turned out of our home and driven away. You may laugh all you please, but the truth is that things didn't work out sensibly and reasonably, as educated people like ourselves always want them to. They ended up very different indeed, more in line with Nyanya's dark notions.

Our apartment stood empty all year: no one wanted to live there. Then it was rented out as a post office.

Translated by Nicolas Pasternak Slater

VURDALAK

On the far side of the village, about one and a half versts from our estate, lived our priest Father Savely Giatsintov, in a little house by the churchyard.

It was an old tumble-down house, no more than a shack, wattle and daub like all the other village houses. Except that, unlike the peasants' homes, it wasn't thatched with straw but roofed with wooden shingles.

There was a small parlor with three windows. These little windows looked straight onto a thicket of lilac trees, so that the light inside the room was green, and the people in the room seemed green too, like the dead.

The parlor led into a little bedroom, from which a serving hatch opened into the kitchen. And there was another little room that had no definite name. It was where they kept various sacks and tubs, and Aunt Ganya, the priest's sister, slept there.

Father Savely's family consisted of his wife; their daughter, Lisa, who was our own age; and this Aunt Ganya, whose name was pronounced with a breathy sound almost like "gh"—Ghanya.

He himself was lanky, kind, and very poor. Sometimes he could be seen striding out behind the plow in his high boots and canvas cassock, with his thin pigtails tucked away under a broad-brimmed hat.

His wife was enormous and high-breasted, with a nose like a trumpet. This, no doubt, was why her voice sounded nasal and haughty.

Aunt Ganya rarely appeared at our house, and only for the grandest celebrations. I remember her in a brilliant green velvet jacket with a green neckband.

The parishioners loved Father Savely, though he was sometimes severe.

I remember a scene in church when the communicants were jostling one another as they crowded toward the chalice. He got very cross and shouted at them, "Enough pushing and shoving, you goats! How can Our Lord feed you all at the same time? Get in line!"

Clutching the huge, log-like candles they'd made from dark yellow wax, the "goats" in their peasant overcoats thronged together, frightened but obstinate, their mouths wide open in readiness.

The church was a small one.

The worshipers would bring alms for the clergy. On the floor by the pulpit they would place a brick of fatback with a cross carved on top, or an earthen bowl with a roast chicken in the middle and three long loaves sticking up into the air.

We often saw a girl or young woman kneeling in front of these loaves and chickens and staying there for the whole of the service. This was a penance imposed on them by Father Savely, for some mysterious transgression beyond the understanding of us children.

The church porch was adorned with two large paintings on religious themes, donated by my father. One of them, the scourging of Christ, has stayed with me throughout my life. In the foreground was one of Christ's tormenters, a redhead with his hair standing on end, barefoot, and wearing a bright green tunic. His foot with its improbably well-developed big toe, bearing an enormous lump on its end joint (clearly due to gout), occupied the very lowest point on the canvas, so that when the womenfolk lifted us children up to kiss the image, our lips landed right on this ungodly, unforgettable foot.

Father Savely was assisted in church by his acolyte, who was also the bell ringer. This acolyte was renowned for blowing his nose exceptionally loud, and what's more without the aid of a handkerchief, which aroused the indignation of my fastidious elder sister. In the hope of bringing this outrageous nose-blower to his senses, she had the idea of making him a present of a handkerchief, which he promptly used to get his way with the Eucharist wafer-maker's servant girl. The girl then spent two masses on her knees by the roast chickens, while the acolyte went on trumpeting into his hand as before.

Our friend Lisa, Father Savely's daughter, was an amazing girl. She'd seen the devil several times, and she told such inspired and impassioned tales that she lost weight and became emaciated, as if drained by all this lying. She told us that the chickens and bread and fatback were put away in a cupboard, and that nobody ever cooked meals in their house: if you wanted to eat, you just went and helped yourself from the cupboard. To me this seemed most ingenious, both convenient and luxurious.

"When I'm grown up and married" (my dreams usually started like this) "I'll have a cupboard like that in every room. If I'm hungry in my bedroom, I'll eat in my bedroom, and if I'm hungry in the hallway, I'll eat in the hallway. No fussing about—just poke your head into the cupboard and eat!"

Well, perhaps Lisa wasn't fibbing. Perhaps it was true, and Father Savely's household really was this advanced and sophisticated. It didn't really matter. We believed everything Lisa said; otherwise life would have been far too flat and boring.

Lisa told us how a tailor had once visited them. Back in those days, traveling tailors used to do the rounds of the different estates. They would show up, do all the tailoring anyone needed, and then go on their way.

One of these tailors had come to visit Father Savely. He'd sewn Savely's wife a cloak. But that wasn't the main thing. The important and interesting thing was that he'd secretly eaten up all the rats in the barn.

"Such a shame!" she added.

"And did you see him doing it?" we asked in horror.

"Not likely. If he'd known we were watching, he'd have sliced off our heads with his scissors."

"So how did anyone ever know?"

"Baba One-Eye saw him."

"But how come he didn't kill *her*?"

"She didn't tell anyone, so he never found out she'd seen."

Baba One-Eye lodged with Father Savely and earned her keep by "doing what was needed." In other words, she cooked, washed, weeded, milked, whitewashed the walls, did a little watering, and pilfered wherever she could.

When we came around to see Lisa, Baba would climb out of some cellar, give us a long look, and shed tears of tenderness from her one eye. At the same time she would intone some very strange words: "Little children sitting there, all so tiny as they are, little hands and little feet, eyes that glint all bright and neat, what they know and what they don't, who shall ever tell?"

Baba was supposed to be quiet and meek, but she was a constant presence in Lisa's mysterious tales; she always had a part to play. Baba was supposed to have heard the dead unbaptized babies weeping in the bog; Baba knew that our maid Kornelia "had a fish's tail under her shift"; Baba had seen some sort of green creature down by the mill, catching thunderclaps in his paw and hiding them under his rump. And those devils Lisa had seen, Baba had seen them too, of course, only she didn't want to confess in case one of them did something nasty to her. Because naturally a devil hates it when people catch a glimpse of him. A devil is supposed to be invisible. If he allows a human being to see him, he must be a real bungler.

We respected Baba One-Eye and were a little afraid of her. We respected her all the more after she predicted that not a month would go by before Lisa had either a little brother or a little sister. And sure enough, soon after this, Lisa came around with some astonishing news. A little brother had indeed been born, a beautiful baby, the very image of his mother, and so clever that people couldn't get over their amazement.

"What does he say?" we asked.

"He only talks when nobody can hear him. But Baba eavesdropped. He's got ever such a thin little voice, like a mosquito. 'Time to light the stove,' he said, 'I'm cold.'"

That was Lisa's baby brother all right. Baba One-Eye got the measure of him straightaway.

Incidentally, we never did learn Baba's name. Everybody just called her Baba.

"Baba!" the priest's wife would trumpet through her mighty nose. "Baba! Put on the samovar! Baba! Bring the big pot of milk!"

We ran across to have a look at the baby brother. He was christened Avenir,[1] and nicknamed Venyushka. He was so ugly you wouldn't believe it. A proper spider! With a swollen belly, and long, thin arms and legs that he was constantly stretching out and drawing back in again till it seemed he had at least three pairs of limbs. And his eyelashes were amazingly long and straight, and so damp that they stuck to his cheeks. But the most frightening thing of all was the tufts of hair on his head: fiery red, even bloodred—like that redhead with the whip in the sacred painting. And his big toes stuck out the same as that man's, and like his they were disproportionately huge.

He was a monstrous baby.

Father Savely, however, was very happy. He was walking around the parlor, hands behind his back, quietly humming a "worldly tune," as his wife liked to put it.

"Muh . . . muh . . . muhm . . ."

We knew this sound all too well and often teased one another: "Shut up! You sound like Father Savely, with his worldly tune!"

But Father Savely did not remain happy for long. The baby was weak and frail, and there seemed little hope of his getting stronger. Father Savely began to worry. "This late fruit," he would say, "this late fruit will not absorb sufficient of the sun's juices. He is thin-blooded. He's sickly, and he shakes."

But then everything changed. Unexpectedly, and for the worse.

I have to mention another member of Father Savely's family, his wife's brother.

He wasn't a permanent member of the household but a kind of visitor, the way that schools have both boarders and day boys.

He would simply "turn up." People used to say, "Hey, better not go to the priest's today—his missus's brother's turned up."

Where he turned up from, or why, or what made him eventually go on his way again, I don't think anybody knew. There used to be types like that in the old days, and you came across them in all circles of society, but most often among the merchant class.

This brother was unforgettable. He was enormously tall, with his sister's trumpet nose and a jutting Adam's apple. The clothes he wore were probably hand-me-downs—everything extraordinarily short and tight.

As far as I can remember, he was twenty-six years old, and he was supposed to have been expelled from a seminary, to have gone to the bad and become the shame and terror of his family.

The language people used to describe him was always rude and forceful. Instead of "eating" he "guzzled," instead of "drinking" he "swilled," instead of "talking" he "barked," instead of "laughing" he "cackled." And this wasn't to insult him but probably because the words of common speech were too weak to do him justice, too petty for his epic personality.

I saw him a couple of times myself.

On one occasion he was standing in the middle of the yard, waving his arms as if conducting a choir, and roaring: "Our sea's a lo-o-onely and unfriendly pla-a-ace!"

The other time, he was sitting barefoot on the porch, wriggling his toes and staring fixedly at them, as if in puzzlement.

After a while he said, "What on earth was nature thinking about? Five of them just stuck on at the end—and not one of them's a blind bit of use!"

His health was cast-iron. Aunt Ganya used to tell how she'd roasted a sackful of nuts for winter and left them in the parlor. But he *turned up* and ate the whole sackful at one sitting.

"And what happened then?" gasped her audience.

"Nothing at all. He thumped his fist on his belly and went to bed."

He always turned up empty-handed, sometimes without even a cap on his head. But once he brought a little carpetbag with a worsted pattern on it—the sort of thing old women take with them to the bathhouse. He put it in a corner of the hallway, stayed a short while, and then left, as always, without saying goodbye. Then a peasant from a village ten versts away brought us a note: "Forgot carpetbag. Please immediately seal with named sealing wax and keep hidden till my next visit."

Father Savely was terribly scared.

"A bomb! Dynamite!"

He was on the point of going straight to the police superintendent and "making a clean breast of it." Then he decided to seal the bag, after all. But he didn't possess a seal, let alone a "named" seal. And he'd been strictly instructed to use a named seal . . . So he gave in to temptation and decided to have a look.

But his wife wouldn't let him do this indoors—and, if he did it outside, he might be seen and reported.

So one night Father Savely waited for the moon to come up, then crept out like a thief, behind the barns. He crossed himself and turned the ring of the catch.

Inside the carpetbag, gleaming in the dreamy light of the moon, lay a bottle of beer and half a bottle of vodka. That was all.

It seemed his wife's brother hadn't wanted anyone to know just what it was he so treasured, or perhaps he was worried that someone might help himself. Hence the seal.

The name of this monstrous individual was Galaktion, but he was generally known as Galasha.

Father Savely's late fruit, baby Avenir, was some ten months old when Galasha put in an unexpected appearance. On this occasion he was very smartly turned out, in a demi-cotton frock coat that wasn't even too short for him, and carrying a sort of bundle wrapped in greasy newspaper.

"I've been working as a tutor," he explained straightaway. "Plugging away at the fatheaded son of the Galkins' estate manager. They're sending him off to take some exam."

It was a hot day. After exchanging kisses with the priest and his wife, Galasha went quickly down to the cellar. There, according to Ganya, he "glugged down all the milk from four cows." Baba One-Eye had milked those cows in Ganya's presence, strained the milk in the usual way, and carried it down.

For years to come this tale would be told and retold, and every time the listeners reacted first with disbelief and then with horror.

But Aunt Ganya was someone you had to believe. Nor did Galasha deny it.

"R-r-r-ight," he said. "I drank it all r-r-r-ight. And I'd happily do it again."

As Galasha came up from the cellar, he was intercepted by his sister, who was eager to show off her little Venyushka.

"He's a late fruit," Father Savely was still repeating, "and he shakes. Gets through a lot of food, but he doesn't grow or fatten up, though he has become heavy. Well, Olga, let's have a look at the little fellow. Show him to his uncle."

The priest's wife took the baby from his cradle.

"He's got four teeth already," she said proudly, handing him to Galasha.

Awkwardly, without looking at him, Galasha lifted the baby up to his shoulder. And suddenly, shaking violently, the baby scratched like a cat at Galasha's fine coat and bit his uncle on the neck. Galasha yelled in shock and almost dropped his nephew on the floor. The horrified mother only just caught him in time. Galasha rubbed his neck and stared at Venyushka, his eyes on stalks.

"God, what is this creature?" he muttered. "What a terror. A vampire—a real Vurdalak!"

Venyushka was indeed terrifying. Arms and legs like little sticks. Flame-red hair. And—like a lot of the village children—red scabs all over his cheeks.

And Venyushka had certainly scared the wits out of his uncle—it was almost funny. The childlike giant went all meek and quiet, and he didn't even touch his supper (though this could, perhaps, be ascribed to "glugging down the milk from four cows"). But that night Galasha started shaking so violently that he woke Aunt Ganya, who promptly applied hot cinders to his belly. In the morning he was feverish and delirious.

"He's been raving, saying the most awful things about Venyushka," said Aunt Ganya. "So awful, I couldn't repeat them." And she added, "But I think it's the milk—it's gone to his head."

Whether because of Venyushka or the milk, Galasha took to his bed for more than a month. Emaciated, with yellow skin and sunken cheeks, he was like a giant bone that's been gnawed clean.

They tried every possible cure: vodka with pepper and salt, and infusions of linden flowers, chamomile, and wormwood. Goats' wool was burned by his bedside, and Baba One-Eye twice rubbed him with kerosene. Nothing made any difference. Though he did once punch Baba in the teeth.

Things got so bad, they almost sent for a doctor.

When we came over to play with Lisa, we weren't allowed inside, but through the window we could see a bed in the parlor. On it, under a gray rug, lay a gigantic body with enormous purplish feet.

Poor Galasha was gradually fading away. Meanwhile Venyushka unexpectedly began to thrive. Everybody was astonished and delighted: he ate less yet got fatter. His cheeks filled out and grew pinker, and his arms and legs grew stronger. He was no longer always desperate to eat, and he bounced about so energetically that his mother was afraid to leave him alone in his cradle, in case he fell out. And he started crawling around on the floor.

One day, when Father Savely's wife was in the kitchen, she suddenly heard Galasha bleating like a goat. Running back into the room, she found him sitting on his bed, eyes popping, shaking all over, and yelling. And standing on his crooked legs in the doorway, holding on to the doorpost and swaying from side to side, was little Venyushka. Mouth wide open, staring. The mother grabbed her son—but only just in time. Galasha was already groping around on the floor, searching for a boot to throw at his nephew. God knows what he was thinking. But then, he did have a high fever.

"Vurdala-ak! Vurda-la-ak!" he yelled, or some such nonsense.

They put a wet towel around his head—but still only just managed to calm him down.

That evening, Baba One-Eye went up to Father Savely and said very quietly, "Father Savely! Father Savely! If you sent that little Vurdalak of ours away for nine days, our dear Galashenka would get better."

Father Savely went white. "Whom are you referring to in that way, you wicked woman?"

Thinking he was scolding her for disrespect toward his wife's brother, Baba replied, "Well, I meant Galaktion Timofeich. Only because the poor man's so sick, I called him Galashenka..."

Father Savely was helpless in the face of such innocence, and his anger passed. He looked at Baba and said, with a certain degree of respect, "You're a fool, Baba. You really are."

Next morning, after she'd done all the cooking, Baba went out and was not to be seen again till evening. This was something unheard of.

She returned quite calmly, as if there were nothing the matter, and went straight to Father Savely's wife. "I've just been down to Lychovka. Everything will be all right now. Go out into the garden and dig up some garlic."

Lychovka, everyone knew, was where Poborikha lived—a wise woman, witch, midwife, and bonesetter. You could go to her for advice on anything.

The priest's wife, who'd been wanting to scold Baba for her sudden absence, was pacified. Now she wanted to know what Poborikha had dreamed up.

The main thing was to make sure that Father Savely didn't get to hear of it. If he did, everything would be spoiled.

They threaded some garlic onto a ribbon and hung it round Galasha's neck. Then Baba went to little Venyushka and pushed a clove up his nose. This made him cry.

"Aha!" she said. "Don't like it? That'll teach you!"

That night, Venyushka went into spasms. Probably from fright—Galasha's yells must have been terrifying.

That day proved a turning point. From then on, the child began to weaken, while Galasha grew stronger.

He grew stronger, but he didn't stay around for long. Once he'd put on some weight again, he pulled on his frock coat, went to find his treasure—that bundle wrapped in a greasy newspaper—and left.

Only this time, he did say goodbye. But not to everybody—only to Venyushka.

He walked up to the cradle and looked inside. "Well," he said, "think you got a lot out of me? Damn-all, I'd say!"

And he turned away, spat on the ground, and walked off.

Late that autumn, soon after we left the village, little Venyushka yielded up his soul to God.

The parents grieved bitterly, while Baba One-Eye left Father Savely's service with the words, "Now he's dead, watch out—there's no knowing what he'll get up to next!"

Some years later, I heard a village legend about a priest's terrifying child, who was as little as a kitten, but at night he would climb out of his cradle, grow "right up to the ceiling," glug down the milk from four cows (see how a story gets jumbled!), and if he met anybody on his way, he would gnaw them to death. Then an old wise man, a man of holy life, arrived from Kiev. He read a prayer over the Vurdalak and set his little soul free.

But the best thing of all in this legend was that the person who found out about the priest's vampire child and his tricks was called "Baba Three-Eyes."

The voice of the people, the voice of God, had not only restored to Baba One-Eye the natural eye she lacked; it had also endowed her with a supernatural third eye.

How much of all this was Baba One-Eye's own invention, I don't know. Though I think the part about the third eye could well have been.

Translated by Nicolas Pasternak Slater

THE HOUSE SPIRIT

OUR DEAR old Nyanya had two enemies—an inner enemy and an outer enemy.

The outer enemy was snub-nosed, with colorless eyelashes and no eyebrows. Nyanya called her Elvira Karlovna to her face but referred to her out of earshot as "that Finnish she-devil." This enemy was our governess—the second rung in the ladder of our education. At the age of five we children left Nyanya and progressed to Elvira Karlovna for our early schooling.

Elvira Karlovna taught us the alphabet and the rudiments of Scripture. Her teaching methods were robust; she would administer smacks when appropriate.

I suspect that her own schooling had been sketchy. Her reply to an awkward question would be either a slap or some wise old saw like "Curiosity killed the cat."

One day, I remember, we were reading about how a child was miraculously brought back to life by one of the prophets. "The prophet stretched himself upon the child," we read. So I asked, "But what does 'stretched himself' mean?"

"'Stretched himself' means that he lay on the child head to head, hand to hand, and foot to foot."

This greatly surprised me. "How could he do that? The prophet must have been ever so much taller than the child."

"Yes, but he had holy powers," came the reply.[1]

Elvira's wise old saws all had a somewhat delinquent flavor: "It'll all be swept under the carpet and no one will be any the wiser." "It's not a crime to steal, it's a crime to get caught."

Anyway, Nyanya hated this Elvira with every fiber of her being. Probably there was more than a touch of jealousy in her hatred. Once a "baby" was transferred from the nursery to the authority of this snub-nosed tyrant, to be tormented with schooling and slapping, Nyanya's power was over.[2]

Nyanya's other enemy, her more intimate enemy, was the house spirit, whom she referred to out of earshot as "the master."

What tricks he played on poor old Nyanya! He would put her cotton spool right under her nose—then make her look elsewhere. Nyanya would crawl around the floor searching for it, but the wretched cotton spool was simply nowhere to be found. And suddenly, hey presto—there it was, lying on the table beside her scissors.

Or he would push her spectacles up onto her forehead and she would fumble about in every corner of the room, repeating, "Who's hidden my glasses?"

At heart the house spirit didn't mean any harm, he simply enjoyed playing tricks. He didn't like the stove being lit when the weather was mild and damp. He was thrifty, he thought it a pity to waste firewood. When it was really cold, you could heat the stove to your heart's content but it was no good trying to light it when there was a thaw—the house spirit would just climb into the chimney and blow all the smoke back into the room.

Another favorite trick of his was to push Nyanya's slippers farther under the bed during the night. In a word, he was a prankster—but there was no malice in him.

Although Nyanya was always grumbling about the house spirit, she was ready to admit that they rubbed along together well enough.

"Our 'master' is good-hearted, not like him at the Korsakovs, where I worked before. He was that spiteful we were all covered in bruises. He'd stick feathers in the servant girls' hair at night, and spit in the dough so that the cook just couldn't get it to rise, no matter what. He even used to pinch our mistress in the night! But our fellow's not so bad, he's a cheery soul."

Yes, he was a cheerful, playful soul, so of course he didn't like it at all when autumn came and we children were sent off to the city.

He belonged in the country, he lived in our country home. A long winter on his own would be dismal and lonely. When we started packing and getting ready for the journey he would take to letting out loud sighs during the night. We all heard these sighs and felt very sorry for him.

But what I want to tell you about is a time when the master revealed another side of himself. We learned that he could get very angry indeed and really take it out on someone.

The story begins with an unusual event late one autumn, when my older brothers and sisters had already gone back to Moscow for their studies and only Mama, my little sister, and I were still in our country home. One day, a dirty old britska with a Jewish driver on the box stopped by the front porch. A short, thin lady stepped out, followed by a tiny little girl. The lady spent a long time pulling at her coat, adjusting it with small, quick movements, like a bird preening its feathers. Then she took the little girl by the hand and led her into the house. The girl stumbled awkwardly on her spindly legs. We noticed that one of her stockings was torn and that she had a grubby white handkerchief wrapped around one cheek.

We ourselves were sitting with Nyanya in the dining room and we saw all this from the window.

The lady came in and gave us a frightened look. Then she smiled ingratiatingly, sat the little girl on the sofa, and said solemnly, "Please allow me to speak to Varvara Alexandrovna."

That was my mother.

"The mistress is resting," replied Nyanya.

The lady clasped her hands imploringly. "I won't disturb her peace. But the driver's waiting outside and I do need to have an urgent word with her. Is she through there?" And she pointed to the drawing-room door and scurried toward it.

We watched her make her way through the drawing room and then pause for a moment, crossing herself several times.

She half opened the bedroom door and said solemnly, "Auntie, dearest! I have come to ask for sanctuary. I have nowhere else to go..."

Then she went in and closed the door behind her.

It was all very strange.

Later we learned that she was the wife of some distant relative of ours. That was why she had chosen to address Mama as "auntie."

We never found out what was said in the bedroom. But they went on talking for a long time. Meanwhile we silently watched the very small girl on the sofa. Her feet didn't reach the floor; she sat with her legs awkwardly crossed at the ankles, not moving a muscle.

"What is your name?" asked my sister. Instead of answering, the girl quickly closed her eyes, as if to make herself invisible—and she went on sitting like that, with her eyes tight shut, almost all the time she was there.

She was a strange little girl.

At last the bedroom door opened and Mama emerged, followed by the new arrival. We could see from the look on Mama's face that she was annoyed about something and even rather upset. The lady kept wiping her reddened little nose with her handkerchief and repeating, "What you're doing is wonderful! Wonderful!"

And suddenly, glancing at the little girl, she said, "Oh, I nearly forgot! I have my little child with me. Lusia, make a curtsy to the lady!"

The girl slid off the sofa, plaintively wrinkled up her little face, as if about to cry, and awkwardly bent her knees.

"This is my child!" the lady proclaimed. "And no one shall take her from me! No, never! Not for anything in the world!"

She held her little girl's head close to her. The girl cautiously adjusted the piece of cloth on her cheek. It must have been very awkward, standing like that with her mother squeezing her head—but she just stayed as she was, patiently pressing her lips together and screwing up her eyes.

"Lusia! My child!" the lady continued. "Never, no one—mark my words! We will die together!"

Many years later I came across a mother and daughter who reminded me vividly of this lady and Lusia. It was somewhere in Italy, in the evening, in a railway carriage. A Russian lady, as thin as this one but taller, was saying goodbye to a stocky Italian officer. Leaning out of the carriage window like a snake dangling from the branch of a tree, she exclaimed rapturously, "*Addio! Addio! Io t'amo, o bel idol mio!*"

Her little girl, whom she was squashing against the seat, quietly whimpered, "Mama! Mama! You're hurting me!"

But her mother went on wriggling and writhing. "*Addio! Addio! O la profondità del mio dolore!*"

"Mama, you're standing on my foot. Mama, what are you doing?"

At that moment I saw them both all too vividly: that little Lusia from long ago and her histrionic mother.

They stayed in our home for some time.

Little Lusia hardly ever played with us. She was frail and sickly and always had something wrong with her. We called her "Lusia of the Bandages." At the time she was about six.

She was a quiet child, highly strung but very diligent. She was always writing something, her slate pencil squealing on the board, or stitching some bit of cloth or other.

Her little frocks were torn and grubby—and yet, with their crumpled, threadbare ribbons, they aspired to be stylish. Her mother said proudly that they were her own handiwork.

"I love beauty!" she declared. "And I want to bring up my daughter in the ways of beauty!"

But it was only later on, when she'd grown used to living with us, that she began to speak about beauty. In those first days she seemed rather lost, and as if wanting to curry favor with everyone.

"Your mother is an absolute angel!" she would say. "Yes, yes—she's a typical angel!"

"Nyanya, dear Nyanya, you are a true fount of folk wisdom."

"Heavens! What a graceful little child!" This was with regard to Lena, my chubby dumpling of a four-year-old sister.

Everybody laughed.

"No, I mean it," she would chirp, not in the least put out. "She promises to blossom into a true ballerina."

The lady herself fully blossomed only after my mother's return to Moscow. My little sister and I stayed on in the country for the winter, and she chose to stay on too, until her highly complicated personal circumstances had been satisfactorily resolved.

She completely neglected her daughter, sometimes seeming to forget the child's very existence. And she was peculiar. She recited poetry in front of the mirror, plastered her face with fresh curd cheese before going to bed, and liked to spend time on her own in the grand unheated hall, where she would sing softly to herself in a thin, off-key voice, waltz around for hours on end, and then spend an equally long time weeping, her forehead pressed against the window.

Sometimes she did her hair up elaborately; sometimes she went all day without putting a comb through it. Twice a week a boy was sent to fetch the post, and on those days she seemed particularly on edge. Often she ran out into the rain to meet the boy on his way back.

The lady's name was Alevtina Pavlovna. But on one occasion she said to us, "Please call me Nina. I adore Turgenev."

What Turgenev had to do with it, I have no idea.

As for the little girl, it seemed she loved her mother very much and suffered agonies on her account.

"Mama! You shouldn't dance about in the hall!"

"Mama! Don't do that. And why are you always rubbing curd cheese into your cheeks? You shouldn't, Mama dear, you really shouldn't!"

The little girl had small, pale blue eyes and rather thin hair that curled into silky golden ringlets.

"The *master* loves her," said Nyanya, stroking the child's head. "Goodness, look how he curls her hair!"

There was no one who did not love the little girl. Everyone's heart went out to her.

"Come and sit in my room, Lusia," the housekeeper would say. "It feels warmer with you there."

"And the lamps burn brighter when she's around," Marya the laundress would add in her deep voice.

And everyone would exchange knowing looks.

"The *master* loves her."

One day a letter came for Alevtina Pavlovna. She glanced at the envelope, gave a muffled gasp, and ran off into the hall to read it. And then she spent several days writing something and going from one mirror to another, scrutinizing her face, curling her hair and fluffing it up into any number of different styles. After that, she undid the collar of her shabby dress and tucked it under—a kind of makeshift décolletage.

All the while the little girl followed her mother around fretfully.

"Mama, why is your neck all bare? Mama, dearest, you really shouldn't…"

Then came a second letter. After that, the correspondence appeared to become regular. If there wasn't a letter for Alevtina, it began to seem odd.

And then things really started to happen.

It was late autumn, frosty and resonant—nearly two months since Lusia and her mother had first installed themselves in our house.

The earth had turned hard and the leaves were falling. Everything in the world now seemed clearer and more vivid—as if our eyes and ears had grown sharper. Instead of being out in the garden all day long, we went for walks at set times. Sickly Lusia, however, rarely came with us; mostly she stayed indoors, bandaged up. And her mother had taken to dropping in on Elvira Karlovna. She must have felt the need to unburden herself and there was nobody else around— only servants and children.

She spoke to Elvira for the most part in hints and riddles. She would undo two buttons on her bodice, extract a tightly folded letter, and say, "This letter may cost me my life."

Or she would sigh and say, "There are women whose lives could be straight out of a novel—a Turgenev novel—yet nobody knows a thing about them!"

Unfortunately, we did come to know about this novel.

One evening, dejected and tear-stained, Alevtina went to talk to Elvira. Huddling by the stove, looking not at Elvira but at the dying embers, she mumbled, "He never once let me go out—not even to go skating. Everyone else used to go. Even the elderly wife of the chairman . . . After all, there was music there. There was a band . . . Why did he treat me like that? I was only seventeen at the time. But now I'm twenty-four and life is passing me by."

Elvira paid little attention and went on sorting out skeins of wool, putting them in a chest of drawers. She even left the room a couple of times, but Alevtina just kept on mumbling away, not noticing Elvira's absence.

"Not a single smart dress . . . Why? Seven whole years—and I only once went out to a party . . . I had to get my wedding dress refashioned. It was his boss, so he couldn't not take me. But it made him ever so angry. Naturally, I looked charming. My bare shoulders were truly dazzling. A poet fell in love with me . . . Am I to blame if my looks inspire poems? He threw me out of the house because of those verses and I had to stand outside by the window till morning. Lusia came running after me, she's a true friend. I feel so sad today, so frightened . . . Why does the chimney keep howling?"

Night fell, a strange, restless night. For some reason I couldn't sleep. Someone was howling in the chimney, wandering around the house, tapping on the shutters.

In the next room, little Lusia was crying in her sleep and calling out for her mother. Her mother's bedroom, however, was at the other end of the house, so it was Nyanya who went in to Lusia.

"Nyanya! Who's that, there in the corner? Nyanya! Someone's looking at me through the window. I'm scared."

Later, in the dead of night I heard footsteps and saw a light in the corridor.

I sat up in bed with a loud scream. Nyanya rushed over to me.

The door slowly opened and in came a small girl with her long hair unplaited. She was carrying a candle in her shaking hand.

"Nyanya! Nyanya! It's me! Alevtina Pavlovna!"

That night she really did look tiny. I'd truly thought she was a little girl.

"Nyanya, I'm scared," said Alevtina. Her voice, too, was that of a little girl. "Someone's been walking about all night. They keep sighing. Can I sit with you for a while?"

Nyanya whispered something and took Alevtina into Lusia's room. Probably she made up a bed for her on the little sofa...

When I woke in the morning I heard voices just outside in the corridor.

"It's the master. Heaven knows what's got into him. The horses are well and truly done in. Tangled manes, twisted tails, and all in a lather. It's a bad omen. The groom says they absolutely must put a billy goat in the stables, otherwise there's no knowing what may happen."[3]

"But what *has* got into the master? Seems we're in for trouble!"

"There's trouble's brewing all right!"

"He was sighing all night, wandering about the house."

"But why?"

"There's trouble brewing."

After breakfast we heard the front door slam shut. Someone came running in. How had they managed to drive up to the house without any of us noticing?

As usual, my sister and I were in the dining room with Nyanya. The door flew open and a huge, bearded figure in a fur coat burst in. He bumped into a chair and knocked it over without even noticing. He glanced around the room, then yelled at Nyanya, in a shrill voice, "Tell me where she is, old woman! You lot are hiding her, damn you. You're all in cahoots. I'll take her back under guard. I'll have you all sent to Siberia! I've got the law on my side!"

At this point, needless to say, Lena and I started to howl—but then Alevtina appeared in the doorway. Except that she was white as a sheet, she did not show the least surprise or fear. She gave an odd little laugh, then said very quickly, "Good morning, Kolya! You're behaving very strangely. Here I am. Here we are."

Kolya spun around, knocked over a second chair, caught sight of Alevtina, and froze, eyes wide with astonishment.

"You... you..."

"Yes, it's me! Of course it is. I'm staying with auntie. What else could I do? You were being unreasonable, and it was cold outside. Lusia could have caught a chill. Come to my room—you must need a wash after your journey. Would you like some ham?"

He threw up his hands in bewilderment. "Ham? Ham?" Then he pulled himself together. "How dare you? After... after everything that's happened! Ham? You ask if I'd like some ham!"

He pulled a wallet from his pocket with trembling hands. Scattering receipts and money on the floor, he took out a folded page, opened it, and began to read aloud. "*Dedicated to A. P.* Huh! A. P.!" Kolya was gasping for breath, his whole body shaking.

"*What if, from time to time, in beauteous visions . . .*

"The swine!

"*I dream thy heart is mine to capture,*

"Ugh!

"*Dream I'm belov'd by thee with passion,*

"Some dream, if you please—the cur!

"*Can'st thou forgive this dream of rapture?*

"Huh? I'll give him rapture! A married woman—a mother—and he dreams of rapture! Pornography—from some criminal! What sort of woman would demean herself to accept such filth? Rapture—I ask you!

"*Let not thine anger spill . . .* D-damn him!"

"Kolya, stop it! Kolya, I beg you!" Alevtina's lips were trembling; her voice was thin and quivering. "I entreat you!"

"No, I want everyone to hear this!

"*I know your love can only be a dream . . .*

"Was there ever such a scoundrel?"

It was all frighteningly absurd. A bearded man in an overcoat and a bizarre, shaggy cap, shaking with rage as he read out a tender love poem.

"Kolya! Those verses are by Byron . . ."[4]

"You're lying! As if Byron would dedicate verses to you. It's the work of the tax man. Tax collector Volorybov.

"*Only in dream worlds can I know such love . . .*"

"Kolya, you're killing me. I'm just a poor little bird!"

"A poor little bird!" He sounded astonished. And then, almost without anger, but with evident conviction, he went on, "You're no bird, you're a scheming bitch!"

Alevtina covered her face with her hands and ran out of the room.

Kolya stormed after her, slamming the door behind him.

When the door closed we saw that Lusia had been standing behind it. She was deathly pale, her eyes shut and her little hands folded against her chest . . .

We were taken to the nursery. From there we heard shrieks and a loud crash, like something falling to the ground. Then the housemaid ran in, eyes popping out of her head.

"Quick!" she shouted to Nyanya. "Quick! Pack Lusia's things. He's taking her away. I need to run and tell the coachman to harness the horses."

Nyanya reluctantly began taking Lusia's tattered garments out of the chest of drawers. We didn't dare ask any questions.

Then the maid ran in again, bursting with excitement. "Oh Nyanya, what a to-do! The shed padlock's broken, no one can get the carriage out. They've sent for the blacksmith to prise the hasp off. Whatever's going on? Solid iron! Unholy powers are at work!"

Nyanya gave her a stern look over her spectacles. "Hold your tongue. Maybe someone's just doing what's right and proper."

We were longing to go out and see all these bizarre happenings, but we weren't allowed to.

An hour or so went by and we were beginning to breathe more easily. It seemed they'd never be able to get the carriage out and take Lusia away.

Then came another crash, an unearthly ringing, and a loud yell.

Nyanya leaped to her feet. "That's it—he's killed her."

And she rushed to the door. We'd have run after her but we were too frightened.

Nyanya returned quite distraught.

"Lord have mercy! A window crashed down on him—frame and

all. Our Mikhaila had been putting it in for the winter. He'd hammered in some nails and was about to seal it, but all of a sudden the whole thing came flying out. Crashed straight down on the man, it did. And he only just jumped out the way. If he hadn't . . . Lord, oh Lord!"

"Quick, Nyanya—they're leaving!" Lena shouted, running to the window.

But there was no one inside the carriage. The coachman was just doing a trial run, checking the horses. But for some reason the horses were acting as if possessed—capering about wildly, kicking the front of the carriage. The coachman got tangled up in the reins and his cap fell off.

Later we found out that something had spooked the horses as they approached the front steps. They'd gone tearing off toward the main gate. The trace horse had bolted and the shaft horse had dislocated his shoulder.

"The master pities the girl," muttered Nyanya. "He won't let her be taken away. He's her one true defender—and what he says goes. Them two may be at each other's throats, but why must *she* suffer?"

The gray-blue dusk was already deepening in color when we saw the carriage pass by the window. There was something hopelessly forlorn about this blurred silhouette, about the lowered hood that seemed to give a little jump as the carriage rounded the bend. And then, nothing more—only a gray haze that would soon thicken, darken, and cover over everything.

During dinner we were surprised to hear Alevtina. We'd thought that she'd been in the carriage. But she was evidently in the drawing room and talking to someone.

"I know why he took her away. He wants to finish me off."

Who Alevtina was talking to, I don't know. I suppose it must have been to herself.

"What makes him think a six-year-old girl will be happier living with a retired hussar than with her own mother?"

"Eat up, eat up," Nyanya said in a whisper. "There's nowt there for your ears."

"I won't go, I won't go! I won't go!" Alevtina suddenly shouted.

Elvira Karlovna rushed off into the drawing room, closing the door behind her.

Early the next morning, while we were still in bed, Alevtina came into the nursery. She was wearing the same hat and coat as when she first arrived. She was holding a packet of letters, tied with the lilac ribbon she wore around her neck on feast days—her one little luxury. Her face was very sad and filled with pain.

"Nyanya, you can't read and write. So you won't, you won't read these. I beg you to keep them . . . until I come back. Then you'll be amply rewarded."

She closed her eyes and pressed the packet to her heart. And at that moment she looked just like Lusia. When Lusia wanted to hide from people, she closed her eyes in exactly the same way.

"Nyanya, I have to go and be with my little girl. I can't stay here. When she was being carried off, she turned and said, 'Mama, please don't worry about me.' If it weren't for those words, I might, perhaps, have been able to stay. But that butcher will torture her. I know it. He'll take it all out on her."

She fell silent for a while.

And then: "I can't stay here. Last night the whole house was crying and sighing, crying and sighing like a living creature . . . I must leave . . . Elvira Karlovna has kindly loaned me thirty-two rubles. She too will be richly rewarded. Farewell, dearest Nyanya!"

She was walking dejectedly toward the door when she realized that she hadn't handed over the letters. Her smile seemed as bitter as tears.

"I nearly forgot. Hide them away. Kiss me goodbye. You know I . . . you know I was terribly happy here!"

Translated by Sara Jolly

LESHACHIKHA

"Leshachikha"[1] is a dreadful word.

I probably haven't heard it even once since my early childhood.

Back then, I first learned the word in connection with a very mysterious story, a kind of story that simply doesn't happen any longer.

It is this story that I want to tell you.

In those days, we used to spend our summers in Volhynia, on my mother's estate.

We had few acquaintances there because the neighboring landowners were all Poles; they kept to themselves and didn't even appear very friendly with one another. They peacocked about, each trying to appear the richest and most distinguished.

There was just one neighbor, the old Count I——, who used to call on us now and again; he had met my mother abroad, at a spa town where they were both taking the waters.

I remember this man well.

He was thin and extremely tall, with an entirely white mustache. Whether or not he was bald, I can't say. I was no more than six at the time and I was unable to see the top of his head even when he was sitting and I was standing.

But one detail of his appearance is etched into my memory. On the pinkie of his large, white, rather bony left hand, he had grown a hard, yellowish nail of truly extraordinary length. This fingernail was a frequent topic of conversation in the nursery.

How long would it take to grow such a fingernail? One of us said two years, another twenty, and someone even resolved that it would take at least seventy years—though the count himself was no more than sixty, and that would make him ten years younger than his own fingernail.

My brother swore that he could grow a fingernail like that in four days, if he wanted to.

"Then *want* to, *want* to!" we little ones cried in unison.

But my brother didn't *want* to want to.

The grown-ups discussed the fingernail, too. Such things, they said, had been fashionable in the sixties.

The count was a widower and didn't receive visitors but, driving past his estate, we often marveled at the lovely, centuries-old house and the wonderful park with its quaint little pond.

In the middle of the pond, linked to the bank by a ghostly suspension bridge, was a little artificial island. It was round and green, and a pensive swan used to glide quietly and bewitchingly around it.

And there was never a soul to be seen, neither close to the house nor elsewhere in the grounds. Yet the count did not live alone. There was also the younger of his two daughters, aged about fifteen. I'd seen her at the Polish church where our Catholic governess sometimes took us.

This young countess was pretty enough, but there was something rather coarse about her and just plain wrong, somehow. Her face was like a mask: her eyebrows too thick, her hair so black that it was almost blue, and her skin either too pale or too pink.

She made me think of the evil fairy-tale queen who asks the mirror, "Who's the fairest of them all?"

She dressed plainly and not very attractively.

And then one day the count brought her over to visit us. She was all decked out in a white muslin dress with bright blue bows; she was wearing white gloves and her hair was done up in ringlets. She sat very primly by her father, looking down at the floor but glancing up at him now and then with a spiteful, mocking expression. As if to say: Well, here I am, all gussied up. What *will* you think of next?

To every question, she answered either "yes" or "no." She ate nothing at all for lunch.

That evening, after a long, mysterious conversation with my mother, the count began to say his goodbyes. His daughter sprang joyfully to her feet, but he motioned her to sit down again. "You're staying here tonight, Jadzia. I want you to get to know your new friends."

He smiled graciously in the direction of my older sisters.

Jadzia froze, dumbfounded. Her face turned dark red and her nostrils flared. Not saying a word, she stared fixedly at her father.

He hesitated for a moment, as though confused or maybe even afraid of something.

"I'll come for you tomorrow morning," he said, trying not to look at her. "Now don't you misbehave and embarrass me," he added, switching into Polish.

We all went out onto the porch to see him on his way.

As soon as he drove off in his coach-and-four, Jadzia turned away from my older sisters. She grabbed both me and little five-year-old Lena by the hand and ran out into the garden.

I was thoroughly terrified and could barely keep up with her. Lena was stumbling, panting, and on the verge of tears.

Jadzia ran a long way, into the depths of the garden. Then she let go of our hands and said in French, "Stand to attention!"

She grabbed hold of a tree branch and began to climb.

We looked on in horror, holding our breath.

When she was quite high up, she gripped the trunk between her legs and slid part of the way down. Bits of muslin clung to the rough bark; little blue bows floated through the air.

"Hup!"

And she jumped to the ground.

Flushed with gleeful malevolence, she held up the remains of her dress and said, "He thinks I'm going to wear this to the Munchinskys. Well, he can think again!"

Then she looked at us, burst out laughing, and wagged her finger. "Stand to attention, you foolish little frogs! I'm hungry."

She went over to a cherry tree and started gnawing at a branch, to taste the sap. Then she tore four leaves off a linden tree, spat on them, and stuck them on our cheeks.

"Now go home and don't you dare take those leaves off—you're to go to bed like that! Do you hear? Foolish frogs!"

We grabbed each other's hands and ran like the wind, pressing the leaves to our cheeks to make sure they didn't fall off. That strange girl had really scared us.

Back at the house we began to cry. Nyanya washed us, and our sisters laughed. With our frightened, tear-stained faces, we must indeed have looked foolish.

"Why did you keep those leaves on your cheeks?"

"'Cos she to-o-old us to! She told us to!"

Soon, Jadzia came back too. She walked in with an air of pride, holding together the shredded remains of her dress. She didn't take off her clothes before going to bed; she just slipped off her shoes and turned toward the wall.

Mama said to my sisters, "Ignore her silly antics. It's probably just national pride—she must have decided not to eat or speak in a Russian home. She's completely wild—no governess can handle her. Her father was hoping she'd make friends with you."

At six in the morning, the count's messenger galloped up with a letter. The count wrote that he begged our forgiveness for any trouble we had been occasioned and told us not to worry, since his daughter was now safely back home.

We rushed to the little corner room. Jadzia's bed was empty, the window wide open. It seemed she'd run home during the night—though it was at least ten versts to their estate.

After breakfast, the old count himself came over. Seeming deeply distraught, he apologized profusely.

We, of course, made as though his daughter's antics were endearing and amusing, and told him to shower kisses on his *charmante petite sauvage*.[2] But it was a long time before our anger and indignation subsided.

For four years after that, we saw nothing at all of the count or his unruly daughter. Our next meeting, however, marks the beginning of the wild, outlandish story that I've been wanting to tell you all along.

We were on our way home after some trip, driving through the count's forest.

It was deep, dense forest. As well as lindens, oaks, and birches, you could hear the sound of tall firs (which in those parts are quite rare).

"Whoo-hoo-hoo!" came a cry from a thicket.

"Oo-oo-oo!" came the echo.

"An owl?" we asked the coachman. He didn't answer; he just shook his head and whipped on the horses.

"Whoo-hoo-hoo!"

"Oo-oo-oo!"

"Brigands, probably," whispered my sister. "Or wolves."

Russian children always feel a certain terror in a forest. In a meadow or an open field we'd have laughed it off, but deep in the forest that "Whoo-hoo-hoo!" was frightening. If a forest seems dark, this is not only because of its color but also because of the dark forces that inhabit it.

A child's forest is home to wolves. Not the kind of wolf that hunters go after, like a sinewy dog with a thick, strong neck, but the master of the forest, an all-powerful creature that speaks with a human voice and eats grandmothers alive. Children hear about this creature from fairy tales, before seeing it in pictures, and so to a child's imagination this wolf is fiercer and more monstrous than anything they may encounter later in our humdrum world.

A tiny girl once asked me, "How can trains run at night? Aren't they afraid?"

"Afraid of what?"

"Of meeting a wolf!"

And so we were frightened by this "Whoo-hoo-hoo!" in the dark depths of the forest. We did, of course, understand that it had nothing to do with wolves and that brigands had still less reason to call attention to themselves. But there was something ominous about this cry; it did not sound like the cry of an animal.

The coachman said nothing until we came out into the open. Then he looked around and said, "That was the Leshachikha."

We exchanged startled glances.

"Must be what people here call some kind of owl."

The coachman looked around again. "No," he said severely. "It's no kind of owl—it's a kind of countess. The Leshachikha."

We didn't understand. We said nothing.

"The young *pannochka*,[3] the count's daughter," he said. "When the old count goes hunting, she drives the game toward him—from every corner of the forest. But her cry sounds different today. She must be out on her own—something's amiss!"

We had no idea what might be amiss or why the *pannochka* might be letting out these strange cries. But it was all very weird.

"Jadzia—that wild Jadzia who once came to our house?"

"Must be. But why those wild cries?"

Back at home, we told everyone about this strange incident. The old housekeeper laughed. "So you heard the Leshachikha, did you? Our Gapka was working in the count's kitchen garden and she went over to the pond. Just as she started to fill her bucket, she heard splashing behind a bush. She looked around—and there was the young *pannochka*. She was bathing. All furry from the waist down, she was, like a dog. Gapka yelled and dropped the bucket. And the Leshachikha just dived straight down. Must have dropped right to the bottom."

We found Gapka. She seemed alarmed that we'd heard her story. Her reply didn't make much sense. It seemed she'd been telling tall tales and didn't know how to walk them back.

All this led to much talk about the wild countess. People said that she was sick with love for her father—and that he himself wasn't so very fond of her. Most likely, he was ashamed of her.

Soon after this, the count paid us a visit.

He drove up in his coach-and-four, accompanied not just by one daughter but by two. As well as Jadzia, there was an elder daughter named Eleonora whom we children had never even heard about. She'd been brought up in Switzerland. As a child, she'd had tuberculosis, and it had been out of the question to keep her at home.

Eleonora could hardly have been more different from her younger sister. Pale, a little stooped, and extremely thin, she had ash-blonde curls, her father's face, and a languid manner; her clothes were entirely

Western. Whereas our Jadzia was wearing some hideous dress made from cheap yellow silk—no doubt the work of the local dressmaker. During the last four years Jadzia had grown into a robust young woman. Her eyebrows had joined in a straight line and her upper lip was shadowed by dark hair.

The count was obviously proud of his Eleonora. He called her "Noonya"—his dear crybaby—and he was tender and even a little flirtatious with her. He told us how he'd come alive since her return, how the two of them read and walked together for days on end, and how he'd never let her leave him again.

Jadzia looked gloomy and ill at ease. Her face had turned red and blotchy and she only spoke when her sister was about to say something.

I didn't much like this Noonya. There was something false about her, and she showed her disdain for her younger sister only too plainly. I felt sorry, somehow, for the poor Leshachikha.

I kept very quiet, hiding behind an armchair and barely taking my eyes off Jadzia. I was thinking of her "Whoo-hoo-hoo!" in the dark forest, of her flushing out game for her father. Just looking at Jadzia made my heart thud, but I also felt sorry for her. She was like some horrible wild animal, writhing about after being shot and wounded.

No one else in the room seemed to pay much attention to her. They might even have thought that ignoring her awkward manners and vulgar dress was the best and most tactful way of dealing with her. Anyway, drawing her into the conversation was no simple matter. How does one make small talk with a girl who enjoys terrifying people—a mustachioed young girl who roams about the forest as if she were its guardian spirit?

And so everyone fawned over Noonya, oohing and aahing about her charm and, above all, her likeness to her father.

Suddenly the Leshachikha leaped to her feet. "That's a lie! She's not like him at all. She's hunchbacked, while Papa and I are upright and healthy."

Almost choking with laughter, she snatched up her sister's curls to reveal her hunched, crooked shoulders.

Noonya's face reddened a little as she freed her hair from her sister's grip. But she didn't say anything, merely pursed her lips.

The old count, meanwhile, appeared terribly upset. So upset that it hurt to look at him. He seemed about to burst into tears.

Everyone, of course, began to speak loudly and animatedly, as people do at an awkward moment.

The count, a man of the world, quickly recovered himself and began telling us just how he was going to entertain his "guest from abroad." He would arrange introductions, *pique-niques*, tennis, and hunting parties. His delicate Noonya needed *sport*—in moderation, of course—and, above all, *amusements*.

After her wild outburst, the Leshachikha had drooped and faded; it was as if she weren't even listening.

But as they were leaving, we witnessed an interesting little scene. Jadzia hopped into the carriage ahead of her father and sat down in the place of honor, in the middle of the back seat. Noonya got in next and, pursing her lips again, pointedly sat down opposite her. Then the count took Noonya gently by the shoulders, placed her beside Jadzia, and then sat on the front seat himself. Jadzia immediately jumped up and sat next to her father. She looked wretched and utterly deranged.

My elder sisters were invited to a reception at the count's home, a lunch party the following Sunday, a week after the visit I've just described.

Lena and I enjoyed imagining this lunch.

"Heaven knows what the Leshachikha will get up to!"

"The terrible Leshachikha! Maybe Noonya will make her shave her mustache."

"I wouldn't put it past her to grow a beard specially for the day."

Annoyed at not being invited ourselves, we little ones tried our very hardest to be witty: "Go on and Godspeed! You'll be picnicking on pinecones!"

"The Leshachikha will spit on your cheeks and stick leaves on them!"

But then, two days before this festive occasion, we heard terrible news: Noonya was no longer among the living.

Countess Eleonora, the count's eldest daughter, had died a strange and sudden death—killed by a tree.

The servants already knew what had happened and were discussing it among themselves. We kept hearing the word "Leshachikha, Leshachikha."

But what could the Leshachikha have to do with it?

Then we heard more details: Noonya, who'd never been known to leave the grounds and hardly went out for walks at all, announced one morning that she couldn't read to her father because she absolutely had to go out into the forest. She seemed agitated and in a great hurry, the count said later.

She went out, then disappeared. She didn't come back for lunch. A groom found her toward evening. She was lying on the ground, crushed by a huge tree. Its trunk covered her whole body and all the groom saw was her feet. It was some time before the tree was lifted off her, with the help of a stout rope.

"Leshachikha, Leshachikha!"

The count's servants kept whispering away. Though what the Leshachikha could have had to do with it was more than anyone could explain.

Apparently, she'd been ill that day and hadn't even left the house. Anyway, the whole idea was ridiculous! Even if the Leshachikha had been in the forest, how could she have felled a tree that it then took ten strong men to drag away?

It must, simply, have been poor Noonya's fate to die like that.

We saw the Leshachikha at the funeral. She kept very quiet and did not let go of her father's hand for even a moment.

This whole business would, no doubt, have been forgotten but for a second strange story, two years later, that made this first story appear still more horrifying—and poor Noonya's death a great deal more puzzling and mysterious—than anyone sober-minded and reasonable had been able to believe.

And but for this second story, there would have been no reason for me to tell you any of this at all.

So let me come to what happened two years later.

After Noonya's death, we all somehow forgot about the Leshachikha. The count didn't visit, nor did we hear any news of him.

And then, all of a sudden, everyone was talking about a young woman who had just appeared in our parts.

One of the neighboring landowners had taken on a new steward, and this steward turned out to have a daughter of otherworldly beauty.

Everyone, of course, had their own way of describing her. Our housekeeper, after seeing her in church, expressed her admiration as follows: "Why, I look at her an' think I'll just about burst. Eyes like gems, all atwinkle. An' her face—so clean and honest! An' her smile— jus' like a little birdie's!"

Our steward's wife, who had been educated in Proskurov and was rather grand, said, "She's not bad-looking, of course, but it's early days. Wait and see how she looks in thirty years—then you can judge."

My brother's tutor, an eternal student, was now slipping off every Sunday to the Polish church (and not for spiritual succor). Under questioning, he flushed crimson before saying, "How shall I put it? She appears to have the personality of a true citizen."

As for the old count, he simply fell in love with this "true citizen."

But we did not yet know this when, for the first time in two years, the count suddenly called around one evening, alone and with a rather strange air about him. His eyes very dark and suffused with joy, he seemed almost rhapsodic; he talked only to the younger among us and he asked one of my sisters to sing.

She sang a setting of a poem by Alexey Tolstoy: "Where can I find the words to say, How dear thou art to me?"

This sent him into some kind of crazed ecstasy. He made her repeat the last phrase several times, then sat down at the piano himself and, with a wistful smile, began to play, gently crooning the old romance, "*Si vous croyez* . . ."[4]

He half sang, half spoke the words. And his smile was so sad, so tender and charming, that it captivated not only the young but also the grown-ups.

"What an interesting man he's turned out to be! Who'd ever have thought it?"

"And all these years we thought he was just a dry old stick with an overgrown fingernail. So much for dry old sticks!"

"He's charming!"

"Enchanting!"

And for a long time afterward, we went on warbling in parts the other romance he had sung: "*Que je l'adore, et qu'elle est blonde comme les blés.*"[5]

The count's singing made a particular impression on my cousin, who had just finished boarding school. Blonde herself, she took "*blonde comme les blés*" very personally. For five days after that memorable evening she remained in a state of sweet, tremulous melancholy, eating only apples and going for moonlit walks with her hair down.

A severe cold, fortunately, put an end to all that.

Lena and I were only nine and eleven, but we too succumbed to the all-pervading romantic atmosphere. To give expression to our feelings, we ran into the garden, picked roses, and stuffed them into the count's umbrella.

"He'll open it when it rains—and roses will cascade onto his head!"

Only Nyanya was unmoved. "Tall as a forest tree. You could hang a cow on him to be butchered." However enigmatic her words, she was clearly not enthusiastic.

The housemaid, who'd been listening from the pantry, and the laundress, who'd been standing by the hall door, shared in the general excitement.

The next day, of course, everyone was talking about the count. And that is when it became known that he was in love.

Lena and I, naturally, were first to find out—in the nursery.

We were always quick to learn anything that was meant to be hidden from us: that the housemaid wanted to marry the coachman, that the steward's wife had run out on him twice, and who the gardener's daughter was now making eyes at. More often than not, as we were going to bed in the evening, the housekeeper would come around and tell Nyanya the day's news in a reedy whisper.

Nyanya, to be fair, would always try to make us keep our distance, saying in her strictest voice, "No. What do you think you're doing? This isn't for the ears of children."

At this, we would creep closer still, keeping as quiet as we could.

And so we soon knew all about the count's love for the beautiful young Yanina: how everyone saw him gazing at her in church and everyone knew that his messenger was now delivering an enormous bouquet to her every morning.

"Where do they learn such things!" the grown-ups exclaimed when Lena and I, talking over each other in our excitement, recounted the astonishing news.

Acting as if they'd heard all this long ago, they forbade us from repeating such silly gossip.

We didn't say another word, but it was now they who were unable to keep off the subject.

"The count's in love!"

"Will he marry her?"

"Or love her and leave her?"

"Certainly not. He's been far too open about it all."

And then, a new development: the count had driven in his coach-and-four to see the steward. Our gardener had witnessed it with his own eyes.

"The same as I'm looking at you now, Nyanya," the housekeeper said in her reedy whisper. "The count drove so close to the man that his pants got spattered. He showed me the mud. It's true. The count's going to marry."

Yet more news: the count had gone to see the priest.

Then someone saw the count's pond being cleaned. This too was taken as a sure sign of an imminent wedding.

Then someone dropped some little hint in the count's presence. Rather than denying his intentions, he was said to have smiled.

Strangely enough, everyone seemed to have quite forgotten about the Leshachikha. Admittedly, no one had seen anything of her during this time, but it is still curious that no one gave any thought to the question of how she might feel about the coming event. All of a sudden, she would acquire a stepmother—a charming and beautiful young woman with a smile "jus' like a little birdie's."

Then came startling news. At first, we couldn't believe it. But it was confirmed. In the morning, the count had gone out into the forest with his valet. He did this quite often, more for the poetry of it than because he enjoyed shooting. He would walk ahead, hands clasped behind his back, full of wonder at everything around him and always humming some tune or other—recently, he'd been humming more than ever. His valet would follow with his gun, at a respectful distance of about ten yards. If the count wanted to shoot, he would call to his valet and take his gun. The birds, of course, didn't wait, and upon hearing the count's song, would promptly remove themselves to somewhere quieter—but this did not particularly bother the count.

And so, that morning, out in the forest, the count looked up to admire a wild dove circling about inside a column of light.

"Like the Holy Ghost. Jesus Mary—"

But he wasn't able to finish because he was suddenly propelled several steps forward by a terrible shove in the back. At that very instant, an enormous tree fell to the ground just behind him. The count's valet had saved him—otherwise, he would have been crushed like his eldest daughter, that poor, lopsided young *pannochka*. The valet said later that, had the count not called out to God, he'd have been killed—the valet would never have managed to push him out of harm's way.

And then, yet more whispering: "The Leshachikha! The Leshachikha!"

What kind of accursed forest was this, full of murderous trees?

The count suffered only a minor injury to his leg, but he was badly frightened. He was white as a sheet, all atremble, and unable to walk. The valet carried him on his shoulders until someone saw them and came to their aid.

The Leshachikha, it was said, stood at the window as her father was brought in, but she didn't leave her room. Only late that night did she go downstairs, quietly open the door, and go in to her father.

What happened then, nobody knows. But they stayed together all night.

In the morning, the count's messenger delivered a large, heavy letter to Yanina, along with a single rose. The count also sent a carriage around to collect the notary from the nearest shtetl. The two men then spent a long time drawing up some document; we heard later that the count had bequeathed a sizable part of his estate to Yanina. Apparently, the Leshachikha was in the room throughout—she didn't once leave her father's side.

The next morning, their traveling carriage pulled up, along with the britska for their luggage. Then the old count came out with the Leshachikha. His head was visibly shaking and he was whiter than ever. The Leshachikha was leading him by the hand. As for her own face, it seemed to have shriveled overnight—it was now all eyebrows and mustache.

They got into the carriage and drove off.

Later on, the coachman made out that the count said nothing the whole journey and that the Leshachikha had cried. But no one, of course, believed him. As if a Leshachikha could cry. How absurd can you get!

Late that autumn, we drove past the count's estate on our way to the station.

The park now looked cold and transparent. Through the bare branches we caught glimpses of the house itself, with its blind, chalked-up windows.[6]

A cord had been strung between the two imposing columns of the front entrance. On it hung some fur coats.

The little island in the middle of the pond was scruffy and sodden—as if half drowned.

I kept looking for the swan.

Translated by Sabrina Jaszi

ABOUT THE HOUSE

EVERYONE, of course, is familiar with the house spirit—the *domovoy*.

The *domovoy* is a serious being. He is fair and just, and he takes care of the house, all family concerns, and the stables. For some reason, he's not interested in the other animals—only the horses. That's probably why it's so easy for witches to steal other people's milk; the *domovoy* doesn't protect cows.

This doesn't mean that witches actually slip into other people's cowsheds. What they usually do in order to steal milk is place a harrow upside down in their yard and draw milk from the tines. All they need do is call to mind the other person's cow. Milk flows from the tines of the harrow, and the cow in question dries up.[1]

But all that is women's business—no concern of the *domovoy*. His concern, as we've said, is the house and the stables.

For the western Slavs, and in a few parts of our own country, things are different. They have a number of smaller beings looking after their houses. These little beings are everywhere; they have their homes in every corner, behind the stove, under the bench, in the entrance room, in the larder, in corn bins, under the floorboards. Sometimes they quarrel. They squeal and have little fights. Clever people say that it's mice scampering about. But how can it be mice when none of your fatback's been stolen? Still, know-it-alls always know best.

A Polish woman once told me how, late in the evening, one of these beings drank some of the strainings from a fruit liqueur she'd just made. He overdid it—and forgot the whereabouts of his little home. Wherever he looked, someone was already there. Each of these beings, after all, had their own particular spot. So he rushed about anxiously, squeaking and squealing, and kicking up small clouds of dust. In the end, he got inside a pot that had had sour cream in it. And closed the lid after him. The following day the Polish woman kept hearing little giggles as she went around the house. Evidently, these little beings were having a good laugh. And there were smears of sour cream everywhere—under the bench, on the floor of the stove, and in every corner. The poor fellow must have ended up with sour cream all over him.

These small beings are good-natured. They never do evil, though they sometimes play tricks on you. They sprinkle your salt on the floor or roll your thimble away. They like hiding things: an old man's glasses, an old woman's needle, a young girl's hair ribbon.

When that happens, you must tie a knot on your belt or in your kerchief, or twist some string tightly around a chair leg, and chant:

> Play, little devil, play—
> But give me back
> What you take away!

And he'll do just that. Straightaway. Because they're quick, fidgety folk and there's nothing they hate more than being tied on a leash. But you must never forget to untie the knot once the lost thing's reappeared. If you leave the knot tied, they'll never help you again. And anyway, why torment them?

As long as you behave decently, these little beings are kind and affectionate. They do all they can to warn you of any approaching trouble. But this isn't easy for them. They can't talk. They can only tap and knock. They let out quiet sighs. They rustle about in corners or whimper in chimneys. They twitch a curtain or tug very gently at your dress. Little signs like that are all they can manage.

If someone falls ill, they come out to help. They make such a to-do at your bedside that you can sometimes glimpse them with your naked eyes. Usually, though, they are adept at staying hidden.

I once heard this from a woman who was convalescing: "The doctors told me my temperature wouldn't go up any higher, but in the evening, when everyone left and I was all on my own, I could hear something almost like whispering. From just behind me: 'No, no, she's still in a bad way. Still a lot of poison under the ribs. Here—and by her liver, and to the left…'

"This whispering went on for a long time. They were concerned; they clearly felt sorry for me.

"'No!' I heard. 'She's not yet over the worst!' I turned over very quickly and saw two strange beings. One was like the green leaves of a pineapple, but longer and more attenuated. The other was like a large, flat glass ruler standing on end, with a pleated headdress like a chambermaid's. They both had gleaming eyes, like little beads. When they saw I'd turned over, they darted behind the screen.

"And they were right. I wasn't over the worst. The next day my temperature rose still higher. And I can remember groaning with pain when the fever was at its peak and I tried to turn over in bed. The doctor just said, 'She made an awkward movement.' And then I heard tiny whispers from all around the room: from under chairs and tables, from behind pictures, from behind each flower on the wallpaper: 'An awkward movement. An awkward movement. Whisper-whisper-whisper…'

"Frightened little eyes were gleaming at me.

"'An awkward movement!'

"They were frightened on my behalf. Very anxious indeed. They really are very sweet."

When you move to a new home, you must leave saucers of milk and honey beside the hearth. You must also offer these beings something on the night before Christmas, because this is a sad and painful time for them. It's the eve of their great fall, the eve of the birth of He who took away their human souls.[2] They also need comfort before the beginning of Lent, as Butter Week draws to an end. Fasts, gloom, and churchgoing—they find all that both dreary and hurtful. And you don't want to hurt them, since they're sweet and good-natured.

Not like the *domovoy*. A Russian house spirit can be very bad-tempered indeed. He likes to pinch plump girls. He chokes stout old gentlemen during the night. He's a real martinet—he likes to scare and intimidate. All in all, he's like some petty tyrant of a small landowner. Fanatically conservative about every tiniest matter, refusing to acknowledge anything new. He even goes out of his way to damage new furniture. He makes it split and crack during the night—you can't not hear it.

These little beings aren't like that at all. They certainly don't try to frighten people—they're much too frightened themselves. Life isn't easy for them. Some little fellow makes a home for himself in the cockroaches' corner behind the iron stove, in a spiral of dust. Then someone comes along with a broom—and that's the end of his bolt-hole. Where can he go now? Everywhere's already taken. And if you've lived all your life in a comfortable spot behind a chest of drawers, you're not going to be able to make your home in even the very best of stove vents.

Nor are they in the least scared of innovations. Even something like a golf-club bag suits them fine. They wait till the dust has built up for a while, and then they settle down inside it. All that matters to them is that you should stay in one place—the one thing they can't do is accompany you if you choose to move house.

In the old days, when families lived for centuries in the same nest, these beings all had their assigned places and knew what was what. And everyone—generation after generation—knew that there's something in one room that squeaks, something in another room that keeps tapping away, and that there's a third room where, during the night, it sounds as if someone keeps rolling a nut across the floor.

And nannies went on threatening children—generation after generation of them—with the same dark corner of the nursery: "That's where the *buka* lives. If you're not asleep in good time, he'll give you what you asked for. *Thwack, thwack, thwack!*"

Nannies never described the *buka* or told their charges anything about him. It was left to each child to imagine someone uniquely horrible and frightening.

The *buka* was the nursery spirit. He was in charge of the education of small children and his hour was in the evening, as we were going to bed; his role was to make sure we didn't get up to mischief and went straight to sleep. He belonged to the night. During the day nobody even mentioned him; not even the stupidest nanny would try to threaten her children with him before it got dark.

In the old days, if a family didn't live all year round in one place, but, say, spent the summer in the country and then moved back to the city for the winter, a few of these smaller beings might follow their masters, but most of them stayed behind in their familiar haunts.

And as for some shaggy little creature used to living under the carpet on a grand staircase—what will become of him in the country? He'll catch cold in no time at all. He'll get chilled to the bone from some draft and then sneeze himself to death.

The *domovoy*, of course, is still less likely to go anywhere. As his name implies, he is domestic; he is responsible for the house and cannot be moved from it. If the house is sold to a new owner, or is left to a relative, the *domovoy* stays put. And if he doesn't like the new owners, you can be sure he'll make his feelings known. A *domovoy* may grieve deeply when a family close to his heart, a family that's been around for hundreds of years, moves to another home. But no matter how deep his anguish, he cannot leave the house and go with them. He belongs to the house.

Can these little beings be seen? They can—but not by everyone.

They can only be seen by children, by people in bed with a high fever, and by drunks. And not by any old run-of-the-mill drunk, only by the well and truly blind drunk, by those who can see double.

I once happened to see such a drunkard myself. He was sitting opposite me on a tram, so I had plenty of time to observe him. The poor pie-eyed fellow was obviously infested with these little imps— he kept blowing them off his sleeve, flicking them off his knee, or shaking them from his lapel. From the way he acted, it was clear that they were tiny, not in the least scary, and very boisterous. Judging by what I've heard tell, that's how they appear to everyone who's truly blind drunk.

Beings like that don't even really belong to the house at all. They're just small fry, insignificant beings with no party allegiance or sense of responsibility. They certainly aren't doing the drunkard any harm. If he flicks them away, it's merely because he's embarrassed—their presence shows only too clearly just how drunk he is.

Or maybe he simply finds it disgusting to have such trash settling on him—crawling all over him like flies.

Anyway, even if not all of these beings are particularly pleasant, they are at least harmless.

Whereas the spirit I'm going to tell you about now is spiteful and evil through and through. I wouldn't wish anyone to encounter him.

His name is ... But let's leave that until the next chapter.

Translated by Robert and Elizabeth Chandler

BATHHOUSE DEVIL

Now I shall tell of a most wicked spirit.
The bathhouse devil.

THE BATHHOUSE has always been at the very heart of Russian life. Particularly in the provinces.

Our capital cities have long been building apartments with their own baths, showers, and all kinds of European flummeries, but in the deep provinces, until recently—I mean until the Revolution—you could still find the old-fashioned little bathhouse, with its changing room, soaping room, steam room, shelves, birch-twig whisks, and bowls of water, just like in the days of Tsar Vladimir Monomakh,[1] nothing more modern or fashionable.

But let me be more specific. In big towns, bathhouses used to be built to suit the taste of rich merchants—public baths with separate cubicles, divans, chandeliers, bathtubs, and a hairdresser. I'm not talking about those. Nor about the so-called "black bathhouses" I've sometimes seen in remote country villages and which are almost too dreadful to recall.

A black bathhouse is a tiny log hut with no windows. In the middle of the hut stands a cauldron. It's not built into a fireplace, and the water is heated by a unique, prehistoric method. Stones are made red-hot and then thrown into the water till it begins to steam. The earth floor of the hut is strewn with straw. You sit there and wash yourself. Wild and primitive.

But the most ordinary kind of bathhouse would have belonged to a merchant or tradesman of modest means, in a small township. It would often be somewhere in a kitchen garden, all overgrown with black-currant bushes or raspberry canes. There'd be only one path to it, and a very narrow one at that.

The little windows were invariably crooked, pieced together from bits of broken glass: evidently, that was how they'd always been. And the fragments were jagged. So there'd be a howling draft.

To get to this bathhouse, you had to go past sweet-smelling dill, curly carrot tops, and hairy branching cucumber leaves that displayed their innocent yellow flowers on the outside and jealously concealed their big, juicy cucumbers.

In winter you went in your felt boots, squeaking and crunching along a narrow trench hollowed out between dense banks of snow.

The bathhouse was reckoned an "unclean" place. You weren't supposed to hang an icon there, which was what made it so scary. Nor would anyone ever have taken it into their head to go to the bathhouse alone. Probably that just never happened. Ever since medieval times, God-fearing people have had a disapproving attitude toward washing. It's a sinful business, bothering about your flesh! Even now, in Catholic convents, girls are forbidden to take off their shifts when they wash. And in old Russia there were monks who took a vow never to wash at all.

That, I suppose, is why you weren't supposed to hang icons there.

So since this was such an un-blessed place, anything in the world could happen there. Nowhere was more likely to be haunted.

At Christmastime, young girls would run to the bathhouse to listen under the windows; the wildest ones would go there at night and look at themselves in the mirror. They'd stand the mirror on a table or a shelf and light two candles in front of it. And they'd press another little mirror to their chest, so that it reflected both the candles. A whole avenue of light would appear, a corridor of flame, stretching to infinity. Down that corridor would come the fate that awaited the girl that year. She had to strip to the skin, of course, and be sure to take off her cross.

This kind of fortune-telling is not for the faint of heart. Sometimes, instead of seeing her fate or the man destined to be her love, the girl divining her fortune sees something coming at her that is so very wicked and evil that no magic words will banish it. She throws her mirror onto the floor and rushes out of the bathhouse. But the evil being won't let her out of the door. It chokes her. So, at least, our wiseheads would tell us.

Were-creatures often hang around near a bathhouse. Some brave, seasoned old hand will catch sight of an unfamiliar cat or dog lurking outside his house at night—sitting there, face turned up to the moon—and if he looks carefully, he'll see that it casts no shadow. No shadow at all. And when this brave fellow sees that the cat or dog has no shadow, then of course he'll pick up a stone, sign it with a cross, and let fly at the unholy creature. And the creature will be bound to leap up and run across the kitchen garden, straight to the bathhouse, and vanish there. That's their surest place of refuge.

A little old watchman liked to tell how he was once guarding an orchard at night. The apples had just ripened, so he had to stop the young boys from helping themselves. And suddenly he heard a rustling in the orchard, by the bathhouse, and a strange sound like someone sighing. He thought someone must have been after the apples and then fallen down from the fence.

So he picked up a switch, crept along to the orchard, and had a look.

The moon was full. It had risen from behind the bathhouse and was shining down on the orchard. And the old man saw something moving, but at first he couldn't make out what it was. Then he looked closer and all but screamed in terror. A piglet was running across the orchard, only it wasn't exactly running—it seemed to be skimming through the air, quite low, just above the vegetable plots. And riding on its back was a naked woman. She looked plump and very white, and she was holding on to the piglet's ears as it jolted along, thrashing its trotters in the air, and grunting "Okh! Okh! Okh!"

It was strange that the piglet was flying so very low: Why didn't it either take off, or else run along the ground? The woman was swaying from side to side, her plump white legs brushing against the sticks of dill—it must have felt dreadfully ticklish! It was rather a small piglet—all you could see was its head sticking out in front and a corkscrew tail behind. And that woman must have been quite a weight!

"Okh! Okh! Okh!"

Then they went around the bathhouse and vanished without a trace.

"Why didn't you follow them?" people asked. "You should have run and looked behind the bathhouse!"

"Oh no, my dears, you won't catch me hanging about at night by the bathhouse—I'm not as crazy as that! Know who might suddenly look out at you from a bathhouse? Aha! There you are then!"

A bathhouse is an unclean place, say what you like.

If someone takes it into his head to hang himself, where does he go? Either up to the garret or down to the bathhouse. A dark deed like suicide—somehow it's not so easy in an ordinary living room. While if you go to an empty bathhouse, you'll always find a helping hand.

Afterward, people spend a long time wondering—how did he manage to sling the rope up over that beam? It's not possible, not on your own. There must have been someone helping.

Of course there was. But who?

The bathhouse devil.

The bathhouse devil is an evil creature, the wickedest of all the household spirits. He's never been known to do anything kind or joyful. Only harm.

Say you climb up onto a shelf to steam yourself. Well then, eventually you need to cool down—and quickly. So you reach for the cold water. But the bathhouse devil has switched the bowls around and he makes you pick up the water that's boiling hot. Of course a person with his head full of steam isn't too clear about what he's doing. His ears are ringing and the blood's pounding in his temples. He's desperate for cold water. He snatches up the jug—he's quite sure it's the jug on his left—and pours boiling hot water straight onto his head.

It happens again and again.

Or else, the bathhouse devil likes to tip someone rather portly off the top shelf. Head over heels. Bang-crash-wallop. Down he goes.

"Steamed himself silly!" people repeat.

Maybe he did steam himself silly, that goes without saying—but, even so, he could have just lain there quietly. There have even been cases when a person steamed himself so hard, he gave up his soul to God then and there. Up on the shelf. Without tumbling anywhere.

And then, the bathhouse devil loves making drafts.

No sooner have people worked up a good sweat than he goes and opens the door. At first, no one realizes what's up. They can feel the chill, but with all the steam everywhere no one can make out anything at all.

But the darkest of all the bathhouse devil's dark deeds is poisoning the air. He shuts off the stove vent, though how he manages to do that in full view of everyone is a mystery. By the time anyone realizes, it's too late. People end up being dragged out onto the snow by their legs.

"Who shut the vent?"

"Who poisoned everyone?"

No sense hunting for the culprit. Nobody goes out of his way to suffocate himself. And you know very well who it was. The bathhouse devil.

Well, I once heard a most fascinating tale about this bathhouse devil, and now I shall tell it to you.

I heard this tale from Alexandra Tikhonovna, who lives in Paris, on the rue de Richelieu. And I don't think there are many people who can say that a story about a bathhouse devil has been told them on that magnificent cardinal's very own street.

It all started when Alexandra Tikhonovna's youngest son dropped his scarf somewhere and couldn't find it.

"You ought to tie a knot in the devil's tail, Tishenka, then your scarf would turn up!"

"Shame on you, Mama," replied Tishenka, "believing all that rubbish!"

"Your grandfather didn't believe in anything either," Alexandra Tikhonovna pronounced sententiously. "But when he came face-to-face with a bathhouse devil, then he started to believe all right."

And here's the story she told us, word for word.

We used to live in Olonets Province. My papa was a forester there. We were a big family. There were five of us children, some little, some still littler.

We lived well, in the old-fashioned way.

Papa was a good, solid age—he was already a widower when he married Mama.

Mama was quiet and meek—she'd never have survived in this day and age. She'd have been hassled to death. But back then, life was calm and quiet, especially in our remote part of the world. No cobbled streets except the main road, and only wooden boards for sidewalks. We had a little garden of our own, of course, and a kitchen garden, everything as it should be, our own hens, and cows, and horses. Like living on a grand estate. We didn't have much, but we had all we needed.

Mama had been orphaned, so we had no grandmothers at all. We were governed by the old Nyanya who had once raised Mama. She lorded it over us and she ran the house too. I remember her well. She was a short, crooked, wrinkled creature, who knew any number of clever things—how to cure somebody of the evil eye, or take a jinx off them, or charm away sties. Nobody knows these things any longer—but they work all right. You have to make your hand into a fist, hold it up to the person's face, use your thumb to make tiny crosses over the bad eye, and say:

> Here's a fist to you from me,
> Buy whatever you can see.
> Buy yourself a little ax,
> Hack this thing from front to back,
> Amen, amen, amen.

Then you spit over your left shoulder.

That was how our Nyanya used to charm away a sty, and by the next day it was as if it had never been.

And Nyanya used to cure all sorts of diseases, and always with the simplest of remedies: kerosene, or curd cheese, or wormwood leaves. Once a doctor turned up in our house—not to treat anyone, of course, just to see Papa about buying a cow—and he was simply amazed by our Nyanya. "That old woman," he said, "I bet she's seen plenty of folk off to the next world." But of course we all know what doctors are like. They don't want to acknowledge old women's remedies because it would put them out of business.

Yes, our little Nyanya knew all sorts of remarkable things, and yet (perhaps because she was so old) she'd get confused over simpler matters.

Once, I remember, she went up to Mama and said, "Do tell me, Anyushka, what are these grantchies?"

Mama had no idea what she meant.

"Well," she says, "down there in the kitchen there's a woman from our village, and she says my grantchies are coming to see me. But somehow I've forgotten just what these grantchies are."

It took Mama a moment to understand. Then she explained to Nyanya that it was her daughter's children who were coming—her grandchildren. And not long afterward, her granddaughter Ganka really did turn up, a fat-faced girl with a mark on her nose. It was said that when she was little, her mother took her to the bathhouse, went off to steam herself, and left the child in the changing room. And when she was ready to leave, she found that the girl's nose had been bitten right through to the bone. At first, people said it must have been gnawed by a rat, but they soon realized that it must have been the bathhouse devil. After that, in the village, she was nicknamed "Ganka the devil's titbit." But she was all right otherwise—a quiet sort of girl.

Nyanya was afraid of being accused of favoritism and, to begin with, she was very strict with Ganka, chasing her about the house with a rolling pin. She didn't want anyone saying, "We get in trouble for nothing at all, but it's another story when it comes to family!"

Mama kept this Ganka on as Nyanya's helper.

And so there we were, living in the old-fashioned way. We kept all the fasts. We went on short pilgrimages in the summer. We went to the bathhouse on Saturdays. And we did everything together, as a family.

Our bathhouse was a small one, but clean. Sometimes our watchman would heat it up for us. His main job was guarding the storerooms, but he knew what was needed in a bathhouse. He'd get up a good steam, pouring mint-flavored kvass on the hot stone. And our birch whisks smelled sweet—we always took care to cut them before Trinity Sunday. That way, they kept their leaves right through till springtime, and when they were warmed in the steam, they smelled as if freshly cut from the tree.

Papa didn't like being thrashed with a birch whisk—he preferred things gentler. So he would come along early, undress, and lie on the top shelf. Then we'd come along with Mama and settle ourselves below. And then Nyanya in her shift—grumbling away as she washed, and cursing the bathhouse devil. And truly—maybe because steam's not so good for old heads, or maybe because the devil really did have it in for her—something always went wrong for her in the bathhouse. Once she put Manechka straight into the warm-water tub, still in her felt boots and all; another time she gave Mishenka a cake of soap to eat instead of some spiced apple. Mama heard Mishenka howl, then saw him foaming at the mouth. She was so scared she almost fainted. She thought it must be the falling sickness.

Nyanya made out that it wasn't her fault—what she'd given Mishenka was a quarter of an apple. "I took it from this bowl here," she said crossly, "but the bathhouse devil switched it for a cake of soap."

But Papa didn't believe in the devil and directed terrible curses at the old woman from his top shelf.

Mama, of course, didn't like this at all. An old woman being sworn at, someone not believing in the devil—it was all very upsetting.

Then Papa said we ought to bring Ganka along with us to the bathhouse—otherwise that old witch of a Nyanya would end up crippling every one of us children.

Well, so be it. Nyanya was really quite pleased. Anything she got wrong, she could just blame it on Ganka. She didn't even need to bring in the devil.

So things went on, and then one day, we'd just come back from the bathhouse and were starting to put the little ones to bed when we noticed that Manechka wasn't wearing her cross. It must have gotten left in the bathhouse.

Nyanya, naturally, blamed Ganka, and Ganka blamed the devil. Everyone blamed everyone else. Still, you can't put a child to bed without their cross. And so Ganka was told to go to the bathhouse. Needless to say, she burst into tears. Going off on her own to a place like that—she'd never come back alive.

"You fool!" said Nyanya. "Say a prayer and go. Who's going to touch a fool like you? I'd go myself, but the mistress won't let me."

Off Ganka went.

Suddenly Mama said, "Where's Papa? He was here just now, wasn't he?"

"Yes."

"Wherever has he got to?"

We all began calling him. Where could he have gone, when it was time for tea? After the bathhouse, we always sat down ceremoniously to drink tea, with honey, jam, raisins, and rolls.

But Papa turned up again soon enough. "I just stepped out for a moment," he said, "to rub some snow on my head."

There was snow on his head all right, but he also had a lump over one eyebrow, and his nose was all scratched.

Mama was frightened. "What's happened? You must have bashed your head in the bathhouse. But how come you didn't notice?"

"It was the bathhouse devil!" shouted Nyanya. "I know his ways!"

We all expected Papa to start tut-tutting at Nyanya. Instead, without any argument, he said, "Yes, you must be right. Must have been the bathhouse devil. Who else could it have been?"

Next thing, we heard Ganka howling. What was the matter with her?

We ran off to the kitchen.

Ganka was sitting on the trunk where the cook kept her belongings. She was howling like a banshee.

"I . . . he . . . he . . . he . . . Pinching me like that . . . The old devil."

At this point, naturally, Nyanya took a mouthful of water and sprayed it over Ganka. The girl squealed, opened her eyes wide as saucers—and went silent.

Ganka hadn't managed to find the cross. The steward brought it back the following morning. And we weren't able to get anything more out of Ganka. While she was still howling, she'd kept talking about the devil, but once she calmed down, that was it. She clammed up completely.

"Don't keep on at the girl," said Papa. "Leave her alone—she'll get over it quicker."

Mama seemed rather pleased. "Now," she said, "I dare say you believe in him!"

"Believe in whom?"

"The bathhouse devil!"

Well of course, Papa didn't much like to admit that Mama had been right all along. He mumbled something in embarrassment, about how, of course, all sorts of things happen that the human intellect can't fathom.

And after that evening, he seemed somehow more subdued—and always very affectionate toward Mama.

As for Ganka, once the devil had got at her, she seemed to go quite off her head. She grew cheekier than ever, put on weight, and was constantly bawling out songs:

> Oh Mamenka, I love my Yashka such a lot!
> I'll buy him some cashmere and make him a smock!

Or:

> My love was ariding his white horse one day,
> Shouting "Dear little sweet raisin of mine,
> How I miss you!"

Shiny-faced, but with dull, listless eyes, she bawled out her songs—and kept chewing away; it seemed she always had food in her pocket. Mama even wondered if she was pinching gingerbread from the storage cupboard. But no, nothing was missing.

Nyanya scolded her. "Ganka, you slut, has Satan got into you or what?"

Arms akimbo and swinging her hips, Ganka said, "Some call me Ganka, some call me slut, but you lot can use my full name: Agafya Petrovna!"

Our jaws dropped.

Mama had a word with Papa: Should they sack her, or what? But Papa dug his heels in. "Poor lass, the bathhouse devil gave her a real fright. We can't send her packing now—she needs looking after."

Well, of course Mama was pleased that Papa had come to such a firm belief in the bathhouse devil. So she didn't argue.

All of a sudden, Ganka started wearing ribbons and bows, and boots with smart buttons. How come? Where did she get them? But Papa thought it was better not to ask too many questions. "Anyushka, sweetheart, you know yourself," he said, "there are many things in nature that cannot be explained."

And then, not long after this conversation, Ganka packed up all her belongings.

"I'm off," she said.

She burst out howling, fell down at Mama's feet—and left. Without a word.

She'd gone back to her village, it seemed, and that was the end of it. Nobody was sorry—she'd been a difficult sort of girl. And with that strange mark on her nose. A devil's titbit, indeed.

But six months later we heard through our forest warden, who had been on a distant trip, that at Vanozero (where Papa had timber floats) a new tavern had opened, run by a certain Agafya Petrovna Yerokhina.

"Goodness!" gasped Mama. "Is that our Ganka? The Yerokhins—they're Nyanya's people. Has she got a mark on her nose?"

"Yes. People say she was clawed by a bear."

"A likely story. It was the bathhouse devil!"

Nyanya was summoned. Had *she* helped Ganka get started? Nyanya swore on the cross that never in her life had she possessed enough capital to start opening taverns.

"Well, well, well, that devil's titbit's no fool! It was the bathhouse devil that helped her. Who else could it have been?"

Papa came home—he'd been doing the rounds of the forest dachas—and Mama told him. His eyes almost popped out of his head.

"How can you say you don't know?" Mama asked in astonishment. "She's living right by your timber float, and they say she's built herself a new house."

But this didn't make any sense to Papa. "That Mikhail," he said. "He must have dreamed it all up when he was drunk. We ought to have sacked the old boozer ages ago."

Seeing that Mama was really alarmed, he went on, "Anyushka, you're an intelligent woman. You know very well that if the devil wants something, he'll pull the wool over everyone's eyes. Perhaps there really is an inn there, but evidently I was not meant to see it. I've been telling you for ages, there is much in the world that the human mind is not meant to fathom. So it's best not to try. Even scientists tell us it's dangerous. Peer too hard into nature, they say, and you'll soon end up out of your depth."

That calmed Mama down.

"So," Alexandra Tikhonovna concluded, "that's the sort of thing that used to go on in our part of the world. Today things are different. It's hard to believe in things like bathhouse devils. But Papa was always such a mocker—yet even he quieted down. We children were forbidden even to speak of the 'devil's titbit.' Gave in completely, he did!"

Translated by Nicolas Pasternak Slater

RUSALKA

WE HAD many servants in our large country house. They lived with us for a long time, especially the most important of them: the coachman, who so astonished us little ones when we once saw him eat an entire black radish; Panas, who was our head gardener and the village wise man; our elderly cook; the housekeeper; Bartek the footman; and Kornelia the maid. These were all part of the household, and they stayed with us for many years.

Bartek was a rather picturesque figure. Short, with a distinctive forelock. His walk and some of his other mannerisms were very like Charlie Chaplin's, and he too was something of a comedian. I think he must have been with us a good ten years, since he appears in every one of my childhood memories. Yes, at least ten years, even though he was fired every year, always on Whit Monday.

"It's his *journée fatale*," my elder sister liked to pronounce.

Bartek could never get through this fateful day without running into trouble.

Much was expected of servants in those stricter times. Some of the transgressions for which poor Bartek was dismissed can hardly be described as serious.

I remember one occasion when he let a dish of rissoles crash to the floor. And there was the evening when he spilled a whole gravy boat down an elegant lady's collar. I also remember him serving chicken to a particularly stout and self-important gentleman. Evidently not someone who liked to rush at things, this gentleman studied the pieces of chicken for a long time, wondering which to choose. All of a sudden Bartek—who was wearing white cotton gloves—pointed daintily with his middle finger at a morsel he thought particularly tasty.

The gentleman looked up in some indignation. "Blockhead! How dare you?"

It was Whit Monday, and Bartek was duly dismissed.

But I don't think he was ever dismissed for long. He may, perhaps, have gone on living in some little shed behind the wing. Then he would come and ask for forgiveness and everything would go smoothly until the next Whitsun.

He was also famous for having once shot, plucked, roasted, and eaten a whole crow. All purely out of scientific interest.

He loved telling our old Nyanya about this, probably because the story really did make her feel very queasy.

"There's nowt quite like it, my dear Nyanya. No, there's no flesh so full o' goodness like that of a crow. Brimful of satiety, and how! The ribs be a little sour, mind, the loins a little like human flesh. But the thighs—so rich, so dripping wi juice they are … After a meal of crow, it be a whole month till you next feel hunger. Aye, it's three weeks nah since I last put food in me mouth."

Nyanya gasped. "So you really…you really ate a crow?" she would ask.

"That I did, Nyanya—and washed it dahn wi good strong water."

The heroine of this tale, Kornelia the chambermaid, was another of these important, long-term servants. She was from a family of Polish gentry and some of her elegant mannerisms seemed affected. She was, therefore, known as "Pannochka"—Polish for "mademoiselle."

She had a plump, very pale face and bulging eyes. The eyes of a fish—yellow with black rims. Her fine eyebrows were like an arrow, cutting across her forehead and giving her a look of severity.

Kornelia's hair was extraordinary. She had long plaits that hung down below her knees but which she piled up in a tight crown. All rather ugly and strange, especially since her hair was a pale, lackluster brown.

Kornelia was slow and taciturn, secretly proud. She spoke little, but she was always humming to herself through closed lips.

"Kornelia sings through her nose," Lena and I used to say.

In the mornings she came to the nursery to comb our hair. Why she had assumed this particular responsibility was unclear. But she wielded the comb like a weapon.

"Ouch!" her victim would squeal. "Stop! Kornelia! That hurts!"

Calm and deliberate as ever, Kornelia just carried on, humming away, her nostrils flared and her lips pursed.

I remember Nyanya once saying to her, "What a slowpoke you are! For all I know, you could be asleep. You working or not?"

Kornelia looked at Nyanya with her usual severe expression and said in Polish, "Still waters break banks."

She then turned on her heels and left the room.

Nyanya probably couldn't make head or tail of these words, but she took offense all the same.

"Thinks she can scare me, does she? Coming out with gobbledygook like that—the woman's just plain work-shy!"

On Sundays, after an early lunch, Kornelia would put on her best woolen dress—always decorated with all kinds of frills and bows—and a little green necktie. She would slowly and carefully comb her hair, pin it up, throw a faded lace kerchief over her shoulders, tie a black velvet ribbon with a little silver icon around her neck, take her prayer book and rosary, and go to a bench near the icehouse. She would then solemnly sit down, straighten her skirt, and begin to pray.

Lena and I were intrigued by Kornelia's way of praying. We always followed her to the icehouse and observed her for a long time, unabashed as only children and dogs can be.

She would whisper away to herself, telling the long oval beads of her rosary with her short, podgy fingers and looking piously up at the heavens. We could see the whites of her bulging eyes.

The hens bustled about and clucked. The cock pecked away crossly, right next to Pannochka's fine Sunday shoes. Rattling her keys and clattering her jugs, the housekeeper went in and out of the icehouse.

Aloof as ever, her pale, plump face plastered with face cream, Kornelia seemed not to notice any of this. Her beads clicked quietly, her lips moved silently, and her eyes seemed to be contemplating something unearthly.

She ate her meals apart from the other servants, fetching a plateful of food from the kitchen and taking it to the maids' room. Arching her neck like a trace horse,[1] she always put her spoon into the right-hand corner of her mouth.

One summer, we arrived from Moscow to find all our servants present as usual, except that Kornelia was now living not in the maids' room but in the little white annex beside the laundry, right by the pond. We were told that she had married and was living with her husband, Pan Perkawski, who did not yet have a position on the estate.

Kornelia still came to do battle with our hair in the mornings and she still prayed on Sundays, now sitting outside her new home, where there was a sprawling old willow. One of its two trunks leaned over the pond; the other grew almost horizontally along its banks. It was on this second trunk that Kornelia now sat, her prayer book in her hands, her velvet ribbon around her neck, and her skirt spread out decorously beneath her.

Her husband was nothing to write home about. Dull, pockmarked and—like Bartek—rather short. Most of the day he just hung about smoking. He'd acquired a chicken that he used to bathe in the pond. The chicken would struggle to get free, letting out heartrending squawks and spattering him with water—but he was unflinching. Grunting and grimacing, with the air of a man who has sworn to fulfill his duty no matter what, he would plunge the chicken into the water.

In other respects Pan Perkawski had little to distinguish him.

It was a rowdy and merry summer.

There was a regiment of hussars stationed in the nearest town. The officers were frequent visitors to our house, which was always full of young ladies—my elder sisters, our girl cousins, and a great many friends who had come to stay. There were picnics, expeditions on horseback, games, and dances.

Lena and I did not take part in all this and we were always being sent away just as things were getting interesting. Nevertheless, we entirely agreed with the housekeeper that the squadron commander was a splendid fellow. He was short and bowlegged, and he had a mustache, a topknot, and whiskers just like Alexander II. He would arrive in a carriage drawn by three frisky gray horses, caparisoned with long colorful ribbons. On each side of the painted shaft bow was an inscription. On the front: "Rejoice, ladies—here comes your suitor!" On the back: "Weep—he is already married."

The squadron commander was, in reality, a long way from being married. He was in a state of permanent infatuation, but with no one in particular. He offered his hand and his heart to each young lady in turn, took their refusals in his stride, entirely without resentment, and sped on to his next choice.

And he was not the only one to be in love. Love was the prevailing mood. Young officers sighed, brought bouquets and sheets of music, sang songs, recited poems, and, narrowing their eyes, reproached the young ladies for their "be-eastly cruelty." For some reason, they always pronounced the word *beastly* with a particularly long *e*. As for the young ladies, they grew more mysterious by the day. They laughed for no reason, spoke only in hints, went for walks in the moonlight, and refused to eat anything for supper.

It was a shame that we kept being packed off to the nursery at the most interesting moment. Some of those moments have stayed with me to this day.

I remember a tall, pockmarked adjutant translating some English poem for one of my cousins:

> Clouds bow down to kiss mountains...
> Why should I not bow to kiss you?[2]

"What do you make of the poem's last line?" he then asked, bowing every bit as impressively as the clouds.

The cousin turned around, caught sight of me, and said, "Nadya, go to the nursery!"

Even though I too might have been interested in her opinion.

Other enigmatic dialogues were no less intriguing.

She (pulling the petals off a daisy): "Loves me, loves me not. Loves me, loves me not, loves me. Loves me not! Loves me not!"

He: "Don't trust flowers! Flowers lie."

She (glumly): "I fear that non-flowers lie still more artfully."

At this point she noticed me. Her look of poetic melancholy changed to one of more commonplace irritation.

"Nadezhda Alexandrovna, it's high time you were in your nursery. Please go on your way."

But this didn't matter. What I'd already heard was enough. And in the evening, when little Lena bragged that she could stand on one leg for three days on end, I deftly cut her down to size: "That's a lie. You just lie and lie, like a non-flower."

That summer's chief entertainment was riding. There were a lot of horses, and the young ladies were constantly running out to the stables, bearing gifts of sugar for their favorites.

It was around this time that everyone became aware of the exceptional good looks of Fedko the groom.

"He has the head of Saint Sebastian!" enthused one of my sister's student friends. "What a complexion! I really must find out what he washes with, to have skin like that."

I can still remember this Fedko. He couldn't have been more than eighteen. Creamy pink cheeks, bright, lively eyes, dark hair cut in a fringe, and eyebrows so defined they could have been drawn with a brush. All in all, handsome as handsome can be. And he seemed well aware of his charms: he arched his eyebrows, gave little shrugs, and smiled contemptuously. He could have been a society beauty.

And so the young ladies began plaguing Fedko with questions, wanting to elicit from him the secret of his good looks.

"Tell me, Fedko," said my sister's friend, "what do you wash with, to have such a fine complexion?"

He did not seem in the least taken aback. "With ear-r-rth, Pan-nochka. Ear-r-r-th."

"What do you mean?" squeaked the young ladies. "Earth isn't liquid!"

"So what?" replied Fedko, preening himself. "I rub some ear-r-rth on me face, wipe it away—an' I'm set."

Probably he would have liked to top this with something still more startling. But since nothing came to mind, he just said, "Aye, that's how I am."

The young ladies realized they'd forgotten to bring any sugar. So I was sent to Kornelia.

Kornelia must have been halfway through her elaborate coiffure. She finished it in a hurry and, just as she got to the stables, her hair cascaded down to her knees.

"Jesus Mary!" she exclaimed affectedly.

"Kornelia!" my sister's friend exclaimed in astonishment. "You're a *rusalka*—a real Russian mermaid! Isn't her hair remarkable, Fedko?"

"Her 'air? There be enough on 'er for four mares' tails."

Sensing that these words had not gone down particularly well, he added, with a languid sigh, "Beauty—our world be not without beauty!"

Probably, though, it was his own beauty that he had in mind.

At this point I turned to look at Kornelia. Her jaw had dropped, her cheeks had gone pale, and her bulging, fishlike eyes were fixed on Fedko. It was as if her whole being had frozen in some intense, as-tonished question. Then she gasped and dropped the plate of sugar. Without picking it up, she turned around and walked slowly out of the stable.

"Kornelia's upset," whispered the young ladies.

"Silly girl! What's there to get upset about? On the contrary."

There are moments when the line of our fate suddenly fractures. And moments of this kind are not always noticeable. Sometimes they bear no sign or seal and are lost among our ordinary routines. We watch without interest as they slip by and only later, when we look back after some train of events has reached its conclusion, does their fateful impact become clear.

Kornelia still came every morning to yank at our hair. She was still as quiet and slow as ever. She would still sit every Sunday on the bough of her old willow. Only, instead of reading her prayer book and telling her rosary, she'd be combing her hair with a large comb. And instead of singing "through her nose," she'd be singing aloud. One and the same Polish song: "Golden plaits, golden braids..."

She sang quietly and with poor articulation. Apart from these golden plaits and braids, there was barely a word we could make out.

"She's singing about the Lorelei!" my eldest sister said in surprise. "The fool really does seem to fancy she's some kind of *rusalka*!"

One evening, Lena and I went out with Nyanya to water the flowers. First we went down to the pond to fill our watering cans. We heard a lot of splashing, which turned out to be Kornelia and Marya the washerwoman bathing. Kornelia's hair was like a long cloak, floating behind her. When she raised her head, however, it seemed more like the skin of a walrus, fitting perfectly over her strong, gleaming shoulders.

Loud shouts rang out from somewhere off to one side: "Hey there! *Rusa-a-alka*!"

Fedko and another man were bathing the horses.

Marya screamed and plunged down deeper. All we could see of her was the top of her head.

But Kornelia quickly turned her whole body away from us, toward the shouting. She stretched out her arms and began to shake with hysterical, staccato laughter. Then she began to leap up and down, her whole upper half rising out of the water. Her nostrils flared and her eyes opened wider than ever—round, yellow, and full of wild, animal joy. With the fingers of her outstretched hands she seemed to be beckoning.

"The horses! Kornelia's luring the horses!" cried Lena.

This startled Kornelia. She shot up higher still, then sank out of sight, deep into the pond.

Then came more shouting, "Hey, *Rusa-a-alka*!"

Nyanya grabbed us crossly by the hand and led us away.

Autumn was approaching.

Like a noisy flock of birds, the love-sick officers took off and left. Their regiment was being posted elsewhere.

The young ladies quieted down and grew less interested in riding. They ate more, dressed worse, and ceased to speak in subtle hints.

Those who were studying talked more often about the exams they had to retake. Or rather, other people began to mention these exams more often. It was not a subject the girls were keen to bring up themselves.

Soon we would all be leaving. This was sad and unsettling.

One evening, after supper, Nyanya decided to go down to the laundry to ask about a missing pillowcase.

I trotted along at her heels.

The laundry was in the annex, next to where Kornelia now lived with her husband. Just by the pond.

Water, damp, slime. The square orange window looked out onto the path, close to the water. Through the murky glass I could see a table. On it were a small lamp and a plate of food. And a quiet, dark figure was sitting there, barely moving. Who was it? Kornelia's husband—her *Pan*?

Marya met us on the threshold and at once started whispering to Nyanya.

"Lord have mercy!" Nyanya sighed. "Anyone else would have chased her away with a stick."

More whispering. And then, once again, I made out a few words of Nyanya's: "So he just sits there, does he?"

She must have been asking about the still, silent figure at the table.

"Bathing at night! The housekeeper said she'd speak to that priest of theirs."

"Her sort shouldn't be allowed Communion. And there's no getting away from it—she smells of perch. We should speak to the mistress, really—but do our masters ever believe us?"

Whisper, whisper, whisper.

"Are you all right here, Marya? You don't feel frightened? Sleeping here, I mean?"

Yet more whispering.

"Does she still wear her cross?"

As we left, Nyanya took my hand and didn't let go of it until we were back inside the house.

We heard a low moan from the pond. Was someone singing? Or crying?

Nyanya stopped for a moment and listened. "Howl all you like!" she said fiercely. "But wait till he grabs you by the legs and drags you down under—that'll put an end to your howls!"

When she came to the nursery the following morning, Kornelia's eyes were red from crying.

Nyanya didn't allow her into the room.

"Get out!" she said sternly. "This nursery's no place for your sort. Go plait the beard of the pond sprite. Tie him a tithe of harvest wheat."[3]

Kornelia did not seem in the least surprised. She turned around and left without a word.

"Fish tail!" hissed Nyanya. "Slimy and slippery."

"Nyanya," asked Lena, "is Kornelia crying?"

"Crying! Her sort are always crying. But don't you go pitying *her*—every tear will cost you dear. Why oh why has the mistress not noticed? But do our masters ever believe us? More foolish than fools, they are. God help us."

And that was the last we saw of Kornelia in the nursery.

I can recall that day clearly. I'd had a headache all morning and the bright sun hurt my eyes. And little Lena was whimpering, stumbling, and knocking against my shoulder. Her eyes looked murky, bleary, and we were both feeling sick. In the blur around us we could hear a tambourine and the squeals of a violin—a village wedding.

The bridegroom turned out to be Fedko. He was red-faced, sweating, and a little drunk. He was dressed in white—in a new Ukrainian smock. Around his neck was the little green tie that Kornelia used to wear on Sundays, when she sat outside and prayed.

The bride was young but startlingly ugly. Her long, pockmarked nose poked out from beneath the white linen cloth that, in those parts, took the place of a Russian bridal headdress.

Along with Fedko, she threw herself several times at Mama's feet, offering her the wedding *karavay*—a round loaf of pimply, sour-smelling rye bread.[4]

It was strange to see a woman with pockmarks like hers beside the handsome Fedko.

People began to dance in the huge hall, from which our two giant tables of Karelian birch had been temporarily removed. Young boys and girls whirled around, stamping away grimly in their heavy boots. Bartek the footman, sticking out his lower lip with a look of contempt, wandered about with a tray of hard candies and small glasses of vodka. The violin continued its plaintive squeals.

Lena and I huddled in a corner of the sofa. Nobody paid any attention to us. Lena was quietly crying.

"Why are you crying, Lena?"

"I'm sca-a-ared."

All around us were rough, scary people we didn't know. Stamping and leaping.

"Look, there's another wedding going on over there!"

"Where?"

"There."

"But that's a mirror!"

"No, it's a door. Another wedding!"

And I too begin to think that it's not a mirror but a door, and that beyond it are other guests, celebrating another wedding.

"Look! Kornelia! She's dancing!"

Lena closes her eyes and lays her head on my shoulder.

I half get to my feet. I'm looking for Kornelia. The people in this other wedding are all rather green—cloudy and murky.

"Lena! Where *is* Kornelia?"

"There!" she gestures, not opening her eyes. "Kornelia's weeping."

"What did you say? Weeping? Or leaping?"

"Don't know," Lena mutters. "I don't know what I'm saying."

I look again. My head whirls. And green, evil people are whirling around, stamping stubbornly, as if trampling someone into the ground. And isn't that Kornelia, all dark and blurry? With huge, staring, fishy eyes? And then she leaps up, like that time in the pond, naked to the waist. She stretches out her arms and beckons, beckons. Below her breasts she is all fish scales. Her mouth is wide open and she half sings, half cries, "O-o-ee-o-o!"

In a frenzy, trembling all over, I shout back, "O-o-ee-o-o!"

Then came a whole string of long days and nights. Heavy and murky. Strangers came and went. There was an old man, a water spirit, who tapped on my chest with a little hammer and pronounced, "Scarlatina, scarlatina. Yes, they've both got scarlatina."

Spiteful old women kept whispering about Kornelia, "I don't believe it! How could she? Some evil spirit must have dragged her down."

I had no idea who these old women were.

Apparently, the pond had been drained.

"They searched and they searched, but they found nothing."

"Not till they looked in the river, behind the mill."

That is all I know about Kornelia's life. And only many years later did I realize what it was they had found in the river. Nobody ever said anything more in our presence. And when I got over my scarlet fever and began to ask questions, all I ever heard was "She died." And, on another occasion, "She's gone."

Once we had recovered, we were taken back to Moscow.

What are we to make of this story? Did Kornelia love this Fedko? It's not impossible ... Fedko in his white caftan, with her little green tie ... Kornelia dying on the very day of the wedding ...

Or did love have nothing to do with it? Did Kornelia simply go mad and slip away, like a *rusalka*, into the water?

But if I'm ill, or lying half asleep in the small hours, and if among the clouded memories of childhood I glimpse her strange, distant image, then I believe that the real truth is the truth we two little sick children saw in the mirror.

Translated by Robert and Elizabeth Chandler

SHAPESHIFTERS

SOMETIMES, you hear a dog howling plaintively all night. A long, modulating howl.

"Whose is it?" you wonder, as you go out to have a look.

Your own dogs are all where they should be. Quieter than ever on a night like this. Clearly frightened.

You make your way toward these howls, listening intently and moving cautiously, so as not to scare the creature away. And then, you see it. Somewhere out of the way—in the tall grass, in a backyard or kitchen garden—a dog is howling at the moon.

At first glance, the dog looks real, but no one with any experience will be fooled. This type of dog is always white and rather large. Down its back runs a wide stripe, like a long plait, reddish-brown or almost black. Look closely, and you'll see that this dog casts no shadow. And then you know: you are in the presence of a turn-skin, a shapeshifter.

You also often come across were-cats. Unlike their canine counterparts, these like to nose around near human beings. They are always large and black, with a distinctive mark: most often a white paw, or else a stripe down their back. They have long necks and are skinny and sinewy. And of course—no shadow.

The shapeshifters that hang around people's yards and gardens tend to be female. Usually they come out of spite, or because they're jealous and seeking revenge, but some are moved simply by anguish. Those in the very deepest anguish will take the shape of dogs, so they can howl at the moon. They need to release this anguish—to howl it away.

Cat shapeshifters, on the other hand, are always spying, trying to find something out. They like to cause mischief. And so they look for things they can gossip about later, back in their human shape.

Cats like this are hard to hide from—and you probably wouldn't even think to try.

Some old fellow, perhaps, decides to bury his money box in the back garden. He chooses a dark night, so he won't be seen. Although a cat does nip past his feet . . .

The following morning, there's a woman standing by his gate.

"So," she says, "you like turning over the earth, do you?" And she stares at him without blinking.

She knows something. No doubt about it.

But how can she?

He racks his brains. And then he remembers that cat—where had it come from? There's no cat like that in his own home. The neighbors have a small ginger cat, but last night's cat was big and black. And why was it nosing about in his garden just then?

He keeps an eye on this woman. Says a word or two to one person, then to another—and then the rumor mill really gets going. And the woman is caught.

Once I heard of another such woman. In Belarus. One day, as everyone was going off to work in the fields, she didn't come out of her hut. Her neighbor called around and found her lying on the stove, groaning in pain. "Yesterday evening," she said, "I was on my way to bring in the sheep when I tripped over the harrow. Twisted my ankle. Lucky I didn't break it."

The neighbor told people what she'd said. "A likely story," someone replied. "We know about her harrow, all right. Last night a cat darted right under Maxim's feet, so he chucked a log at it. Broke its paw. So much for her harrow."

The woman could well have been lynched. But then the local landowner suddenly died—which gave everyone in the village something else to think about.

The most sinister shapeshifters of all are the wolves. Werewolves are invariably harbingers of misfortune.

Nearly always she-wolves—only rarely male—they lure hunters

into danger: into bogs in the autumn, onto patches of thin ice in winter. Or they trick a hunter into entering an estate where he is far from welcome. He need only show his face there for some tragic course of events to be set in motion, leading perhaps to his death or the death of one of his family.

Western cultures too have their werewolf legends. In some of these legends the she-wolves have no wish to do evil; they simply want to be free. A wife, perhaps, trapped in a forbidding castle, and always under the watchful eye of a cruel and unloved husband. Something inside her longs to break loose. She longs to roam field and forest, free and unbridled. And she doesn't want to slip into the skin of a timid rabbit or a cautious fox. She doesn't even choose the guise of a strong yet good-natured bear. Desperate to escape the yoke, she dreams fangs and claws. A dark and mighty strength, swift legs, a sinister howl. The imprisoned soul yearns for freedom; she who has been chained to the spot longs to run wild. The frightened heart seeks to frighten; the ruined, to avenge and ruin.

Once, I was staying with some friends. They'd bought their estate from a merchant who had only owned it for a short time. He'd built a new house—then almost immediately decided to sell the place. He'd hoped to rent it out as a dacha over the summer, but it was somewhere rather out of the way and not especially picturesque. And besides, the nearest town was quite small and everyone there had their own garden. People stayed in their homes all summer long and didn't need dachas. So the merchant had decided to sell.

Everything about this estate was somehow off-kilter. In front of the little two-story, green-roofed wooden house was a round meadow with two huge but strangely positioned fir trees. Beyond this meadow lay a magnificent park. But this too had something strange about it. Rather than being at a right angle to the main house, as you'd expect, the paths and avenues ran parallel to it.

Not wishing to offend, I remarked that it was all most unique. My host then explained that the main house had once stood on a slightly different site, with the two firs flanking the front door. But the house had long ago fallen into disrepair. The best the merchant could do was to reuse a few of the stones for the foundations of a new building close by. He'd felt he must start afresh, since the old house had been considered ill-starred; long ago, supposedly during the days of Catherine the Great, the master of the house had shot his wife dead. After that, he had either been executed or sent into exile. For decades, the estate had been abandoned; no one had lived there at all. In winter, wolves had roamed freely about the park. Though the merchant had, of course, tidied everything up when he was hoping to rent out the property.

Such places always bear an imprint of the tragedies they have seen unfold. You feel uneasy there. However peaceful their night may seem, however bright their sun may shine, you can't quite believe in it. Something has snapped; something is out of true. The earth's pulse and the vibrations of everything around it have been disrupted, never to return to their former state.

Once, I spent a night in that house. A moonlit night.

Even with the curtains drawn, I could sense the bright moon. I couldn't sleep.

I went over to the window. A large, humpbacked dog—or maybe wolf—was trotting quietly across the meadow. It was limping on one forepaw, which was entirely white, and its rough fur glittered in the moonlight like needles. This strange creature ran behind the fir trees, to the site of the old house—and vanished.

In the morning, everyone had a good laugh when I told them about my "wolf with a white paw." "Sure it didn't have a collar?" they asked. "Or a muzzle?"

Yet there was not a single dog on the estate that matched my description.

For some time afterward I felt troubled, unable to shake off the impression left by that off-kilter estate, by that anguished and inordinate moon, and—above all—by that strange humpbacked half wolf.

I never went back there, but I did come across the owners again, in town the following winter. They told me a story they had not known at the time of my visit.

Apparently, the estate used to belong to a retired hussar. After inheriting it, he took a wife from somewhere in Lithuania. She was, as always in stories of this kind, a perfect beauty. The hussar was both severe and jealous, and he kept his wife locked away, never allowing anyone else to see her. He never took her with him when he went out hunting or to visit a neighbor. He even appointed a former soldier of his as a special guard—to keep a close eye on her. For her part, she was quiet and submissive, obeying her husband in everything. And yet, for some reason, this hussar seemed unable to trust her.

One day he went over to his neighbors to go shooting with them. Late in the evening, as he rode back, he sensed that something was agitating his horse. He looked around—and saw a fully grown she-wolf running along the edge of the forest, a little ahead of him. He spurred on his horse. The wolf ran faster—but still in the same direction, heading straight for his estate. The hussar reached for his gun and fired. The wolf then began to limp on one forepaw but kept on running. She reached the fence, crouched down to slip through a gap—she clearly knew her way around—then disappeared into the park. The hussar galloped back to his house. Everything there was as quiet as ever—not a sound from the dogs. He left his horse with the groom, went upstairs, woke his wife, and told her about the wolf. She refused to believe a word he said.

"Never heard anything like it!" she exclaimed. "You must have been dreaming."

She'd pulled the bedclothes right up to her chin, and she looked as pale as can be.

When the hussar woke in the morning, his wife didn't want to get up. She didn't feel well.

This alarmed him. He pulled back the blankets and saw a bandage around one of her hands.

"I went out to pick cherries," she said. "I was climbing up the ladder and a rung snapped. I cut my hand."

He believed her, of course, and felt sorry for her.

But then he began to have doubts. "It's autumn," he thought. "How can she have been picking cherries?"

He went into the garden and found the ladder. All the rungs were intact.

He thought and thought—but nothing made any sense to him.

After a while, his neighbors invited him to go shooting again. He rode off, giving strict orders both to his wife—not to venture outside; and to the soldier—to keep a close watch on the house.

Late that night, he was riding back home again, looking around alertly. He caught sight of the she-wolf. This time she was running straight ahead of him. She was still limping; one forepaw was wrapped in a white bandage.

He understood yet dared not understand. He spurred on his horse to a gallop and chased after her, scarcely able to breathe. But the wolf was too far ahead; he couldn't catch up with her. His house was already in sight. His horse was wheezing and panting, at the end of its strength. As they neared the park, the wolf crouched down, ready to disappear once again through her gap in the fence. That was it—he could no longer hide from the truth. Hardly knowing what he was doing, he seized his gun, made the sign of the cross over the barrel, took aim, and fired. With a strange groan, the wolf sank to the ground.

The hussar leaped from his horse, ran over to the wolf, and bent down. It was too dark to see anything. He squatted still lower. In front of him lay his wife: quiet as ever, in anguish, her dress all torn. She looked at him with bitter reproach—and then her eyes rolled back. She was dead.

He was tried in court, but no one believed him. He was found guilty of murder.

That was a tale from long ago, from the days of Catherine the Great. But I can tell you another tale that is only too modern. It is set in today's Petersburg, and it is entertaining.

True, I can't say for sure just when it happened. I can never remember dates; I find it hard to label years by numbers. What matters to me is events; it is what took place during a particular year that determines its shape.

The time I want to tell you about can be called an era of "occult-omania." I say this with regard both to our own small literary milieu and to all our followers, well-wishers, and patrons. Everyone then was conjuring and casting spells, studying medieval witch trials, and writing stories and poems about wizards, vampires, and shapeshifters. Briusov published his *Fiery Angel*. Sologub played the sorcerer in poetry, in prose, and in his everyday life. Kondratiev wrote about *rusalkas* and the unclean dead.[1] A mass readership learned for the first time about Sologubian petty demons, Roman *larvae*,[2] and many other such wonders.

Friends of the arts, those whom Alexander Blok christened "pharmacists,"[3] soon caught on to this new fashion. Needless to say, they didn't know how to pronounce the name of Sologub's *nedotykomka* and they confused the *larvae* of ancient Rome with the ancient cave monastery of Kiev Lavra[4]—but they did their very best to appear interested.

These pharmacists really were very sweet. They visited exhibitions, filled the most avant-garde theaters, and attended every literary gathering, lecture, and public discussion. And however shaky their grasp of matters artistic, they always knew what and whom they should love, and what and whom they should loathe. They sacrificed both time and money for the sake of feeling involved with a literary world they must have found tedious and incomprehensible.

Among them were photographers, young lawyers, and the dentists who took care of the artists' teeth. And there were relatives—the brother of a writer's wife, or the husband of an actor's sister.

With all their fiancées, nieces, wives, daughters, and aunts, these pharmacists made up quite a crowd. And this helped to create the right atmosphere, to saturate the air with the appropriate ecstatic emanations.

They did not find it easy to understand the appeal of sorcery. They were hard put to distinguish between necrophilia and philately—but they wanted to keep up with the times.

Budding poets liked to write about stern wizards. They flocked to the Harz Mountains to see the Brocken specter.[5]

Shapeshifters were also held in great esteem.

One poetess wrote:

> Starry sky, still and quiet.
> Cloudy dreams swirl and riot.
> I, a she-wolf on the prowl,
> Bound by forest law to howl;
> You, my consort, most lupine
> You, dear white-fanged wolf of mine.
> In the dying rays of sun
> Our hunt has only just begun.
> Light of foot, you make no sound,
> Dark shadow creeping o'er the ground—
> Your pointed ears a source of fear
> To feeble-hearted elk and deer.

Her husband, who had the most unfortunate pointed ears, took offense. Bringing public attention to his inadequacies was, in his view, out of order. These lines occasioned a serious family rift.

Many of us truly did long to fly away to a witches' sabbath. But fantasy alone could not transport us there. Somehow we had to procure the magic ointment that witches smear on their bodies.

Piotr Potiomkin once discovered a detailed recipe in a book of witchcraft.[6] Sadly, however, he could find no chemist willing to follow it, since every ingredient required was a deadly poison.

And so, we had to make do with fantasy.

While we were still all in thrall to demonism, someone most unusual appeared in our little circle—or rather, on its periphery.

This petite woman, whom we knew as Baroness Liza, had green eyes and a sharp nose. She was extremely thin, like a dried flower pressed between the pages of a book, but her hair was splendid and luxuriant, like a golden chrysanthemum. Though born and raised in England, she had Russian nationality. Two years earlier, she had gone to Switzerland in order to die of consumption. There she had met a captivating Russian lady, who beat her cruelly, brought her back to Saint Petersburg, then threw her out onto the street.

We loved these mad stories of hers, all the more so since she was an excellent pianist and composer and used to set our poems to music (though without understanding a word of them, since she knew no Russian at all).

The baroness was always falling in love—but only with women, which was also very much in fashion.

She remained in Petersburg for a year at most. I remember her frequent laments about Russia's lack of a proper revolutionary hymn. Come the Revolution, what would the poor Russians sing? She kept trying to compose such a hymn herself—but without success. It always ended up sounding like either "La Marseillaise" or "La Carmagnole."[7]

The manner of the baroness's departure from Petersburg was as mysterious as that of her first appearance there. It was rumored that she had moved to Germany. Apparently, she'd adopted the pseudonym "Eugene Onegin," begun wearing a man's suit, and taken a wife.

A lady in our circle managed to discover her new address. She was passing through this small town anyway, so she resolved to pay her a call. The baroness was not at home, but her landlady spoke of her with the greatest respect.

"*Herr Onegin*," she said, "*ist ein braver Mann.*"[8]

But I don't need to say any more about this baroness—though a shapeshifter, of course, she most certainly was. What matters is the role she plays in the story I'm about to tell you.

I had invited a few people to my apartment—among them this same baroness and a sweet young lady called Ilya, also from the periphery of the literary world. She wrote a little, did a little translating, and was intelligent and endowed with good taste.

I've no idea why, but Ilya and the baroness took a strong dislike to each other.

Ilya was watching sullenly as the baroness rhapsodized over a gift I'd been sent—a black plush kitten in a basket of white roses.

"I can't stand cats," Ilya snarled. "Even this toy kitten disgusts me."

The baroness carried on seeking attention. "Look!" she said, balancing the kitten on her shoulder. "Don't I look good with this black cat? Don't I look the very picture of a young sorceress?"

"You certainly do! You look like Carabosse, from *The Sleeping Beauty*. In a coach-and-six—drawn by six rats."

This upset the baroness. Her eyes suddenly looked like two needles. Carabosse, after all, was a hunchback, with a long nose.

"Really?" she replied. "How very sweet you are! I am indeed Carabosse. And to prove to you the power of a wicked godmother, I'm going to turn you into a cat. Maybe that'll prove just what you need. Seeing the world through a cat's eyes may teach you to love them."

Seeing how angry they both were, I quickly changed the subject.

The next day, Ilya called around, deeply troubled. "I think I've gone mad," she said. "Please don't say anything to anyone, but something very strange has happened to me."

"What do you mean?"

Blushing, and with an awkward smile, she whispered, "I'm a cat."

"*What?*"

"A cat," she repeated, in embarrassment.

The story she then told me was surprisingly coherent.

"You know me," she began. "I've never been one for all this witchcraft and sorcery of yours. I know it's not fashionable to say so, but I've never believed in all that mumbo jumbo. I'm someone who prefers to be rational—a positivist, you might say.

"And I certainly wasn't frightened by that vicious Carabaroness of yours. I forgot everything she said then and there.

"But then something woke me in the middle of the night. A breath of air. I looked across at the window and saw that the little pane at the top was open. I began to get out of bed. I didn't fall—but somehow I found myself on all fours. Without standing up again, I went over to the window. A quick leap—and there I was on the windowsill. I sat for a moment, wondering what on earth was going on with me. I put my hand to my forehead, but it wasn't a hand. It was a paw. I looked at the rest of myself—there was a streetlamp close by—and realized I was all soft and gray and silky. 'Heavens!' I thought. 'I'm a cat! Whatever am I to do?'

"I stretch my paws up to the open pane, then jump down onto the ledge outside.

"You know very well, my dear, what a nervous soul I am, and how scared I am of heights. So imagine my surprise when I look down from the third floor and find the sensation quite pleasant. This makes me want to test myself. I'm scared, of course, yet curious. I walk along the ledge. It's all right—I don't even feel in the least dizzy. And I have a sense of my own body like I've never known before. Supple and bendy, everything doing as I ask. Next I remember the Martsevs—their apartment's on the other side of the staircase. I look in through a window, but it's dark. I can't make out a thing. Then someone in white moves slowly toward me. This alarms me and I run away. Imagine it! Me, running along a ledge! On the third floor!

"I get to the end of the ledge. Beyond it lies the roof of the priest's house. I jump across. Black, crisp shadows and a bright moon—a glorious night. I go right to the edge of the roof and look down. I'm not afraid! I even spin around a few times on purpose—and still don't feel in the least dizzy. But then I sense I'm being watched. I turn around to see an enormous tomcat slip out from behind the chimney. His hackles are up. His eyes are round and frightening. He looks like a tiger—I've never seen such a huge cat. Now, of course, I can see that it was more a matter of how small I'd become myself. Back then, though, I was terrified. Leaping from roof to roof, from ledge to ledge, I race back. But my little pane has blown shut. Imagine my despair! What can I do? I go down into the yard. The door to the back stairs turns out to be open. Up I go.

"'It's already getting light,' I say to myself. 'The milkmaid will be here soon, and I can sneak in behind her.' Cats, though, aren't allowed in our apartment. Praskovya, the cook, will throw me out the moment she sees me. But what else can I do? I hide in the corner and wait. Then I hear the clatter of cans—the milkmaid climbing the stairs. Praskovya opens the door. 'No,' I think. 'I'll never be able to get past her.' And then . . . 'Wait here a second,' I hear Praskovya say. 'I've got some crusts for your cow.'

"'Thank God for that!' I say to myself. The moment Praskovya turns her back, I dart through into the corridor—and behind a cupboard. Little by little, I make my way back to my room. Luckily, the door is ajar. I jump up onto the bed and slip under the blanket. 'Now I'll go to sleep,' I think, 'and when I wake up everything will be all right again. After all, I can't stay a cat forever.' And then I remember that vile baroness. Was this some trick of hers? I have a little cry, then fall asleep.

"In the morning, Nastya wakes me up. As usual, she brings in my tea.

"'Time to get up,' she says. 'It's gone nine o'clock.' Afraid it may still be a paw, I slowly bring one hand out from under the blanket. But that silly dream—thank God—is now over and done with. It's even starting to seem funny.

"But Nastya goes up to the window. 'What are these marks?' she asks. 'They look like paw prints. Leading straight from your bed.'

"Nastya looks first at me, then at the paw prints, and then at me again. She clearly suspects something. I'm horrified. My mind blanks out. I almost faint.

"Without a word, Nastya leaves the room. I go back to sleep. And then, once again, I'm woken by a woman's voice: 'Time to get up, young lady!'

"I open my eyes. It's Nastya again, bringing me my tea. Nothing makes any sense. I feel shattered, my head's like a lead weight. I ask Nastya the time.

"'Gone nine,' she replies.

"After deciding that I must have dreamed her previous appearance, I go back to sleep. Less than half an hour later, I wake up again. There on the bedside table is a tray with an untouched cup of tea. Which of Nastya's two appearances—I wonder—was a dream? And which was real?

"I start to get dressed. I see a bruise on my elbow and remember jumping onto a ledge, hurting my paw. Then I go along to say good morning to my mother. I find her with Praskovya, telling her what to prepare for supper.

"'Praskovya,' I ask, 'does our milkmaid have her own cow?'

"'Of course she does. I often give her old crusts for her cow. Today I gave her a whole bagful—she was overjoyed!'

"At this, of course, my head starts to spin.

"But that's not the end of it. Listen to what comes next. Our neighbor, Madame Martseva, joins us for breakfast. When she sees me, she laughs and says, 'Last night I saw a vision. I felt someone looking at me from outside. I went toward the window and realized it was a cat. And then I saw that this cat had your face. Yes, it was the spitting image of you. Strange, isn't it? After all, you don't really look in the least like a cat.'

"This was awful. It was all I could do not to rush out of the room. As soon as we were through with breakfast, I came straight here. So please, tell me what I should do. I can't spend another night at home—I'm terrified. I haven't really turned into some kind of were-creature, have I?"

A wild, crazy story. I felt sorry for poor Ilya, but I also found it rather funny. And I had to think of something to say.

"You've experienced a psychotic episode," I pronounced.

"Well, if that's what it's called," Ilya replied calmly, "please help me out of it. But what about all the coincidences? You must admit they are rather striking!"

After much thought, we came to a decision. Ilya would leave Petersburg straightaway to spend a month in Moscow. But before she left, she would send that accursed baroness a gift: a pretty little angora cat, in a basket of flowers, with the very sweetest of accompanying notes:

To the most enchanting sorceress,
Enchantedly yours, etc, etc.

And so Ilya did.

It was soon after these events that the baroness disappeared from our lives. As for Ilya, I ran into her again about a year and a half later.

"Do you remember—" I began, with a smile.

"For the love of God," she interrupted, "please don't go bringing up any of *that*! Surely you understand that such distressing episodes are best forgotten?"

Translated by Robert and Elizabeth Chandler
and Sian Valvis

THE DOG

(A story told to me by a woman I did not know.)

Do you remember that tragic death? The death of that artful Edvers? The whole thing happened in front of my eyes. I was even indirectly involved.

His death was extraordinary enough in itself, but the strange tangle of events around it was still more astonishing. At the time I never spoke about those events to anyone. Nobody knew anything except the man who is now my husband. There was no way I could have spoken about them. People would have thought I was mad and might well have suspected me of something criminal. I'd have been dragged still deeper into that horror—which was almost too much for me as it was. A shock like that is hard to get over.

It's all in the past now. I found some kind of peace long ago. But, you know, the further my past recedes from me, the more distinctly I can make out the clear, direct, utterly improbable line that is the axis of this story. So if I am to tell this story at all, I have to tell you all of it, the way I see it now.

If you want to, you can easily check that I haven't made any of this up. You already know how Edvers died. Zina Volotova (née Katkova) is alive and well. And if you still don't believe me, my husband can confirm every detail.

In general, I believe that many more miracles take place in the world than we think. You only need to know how to see—how to follow a thread, how to follow the links in a chain of events, not rejecting something merely because it seems improbable, neither jumbling the facts nor forcing your own explanations on them.

Some people like to make every trivial event into a miracle. Where everything is really quite straightforward and ordinary, they introduce all kinds of personal forebodings and entirely arbitrary interpretations of dreams, tailored to fit their stories. And then there are other, more sober people who treat everything beyond their understanding with supreme skepticism, dissecting and analyzing away whatever they find inexplicable.

I belong to neither of these groups. I don't intend to explain anything at all. I shall simply tell you everything truthfully, just as it happened, beginning at what I see as the story's beginning.

And I myself think the story begins during a distant and wonderful summer, when I was only fifteen.

It's only nowadays that I've become so quiet and melancholic—back then, in my early youth, I was full of energy, a real madcap. Some girls are like that. Daredevils, afraid of nothing. And you can't even say that I was spoiled, because there was no one to spoil me. By then I was already an orphan, and the aunt who had charge of me, may she rest in peace, was simply a ninny. Spoiling me and disciplining me were equally beyond her. She was a blancmange. I now believe that she simply wasn't in the least interested in me—nor did I care in the least about her.

The summer I'm talking about, my aunt and I were staying with the Katkovs, who lived on a neighboring estate, in the province of Smolensk.

It was a large and very sweet family. My friend Zina Katkova liked me a lot. She simply adored me. In fact the whole family were very fond of me. I was a pretty girl, good-natured and lively—yes, I really was very lively indeed. It seemed there was enough joy in me, enough zest for life, to last me till the end of my days. As things turned out, however, that proved far from the truth.

I had a lot of self-confidence then. I felt I was clever and beautiful. I flirted with everyone, even with the old cook. Life was so full it filled me almost to bursting. The Katkovs, as I've said, were a large family and—with all the guests who'd come for the summer—there were usually about twenty people around the table.

After supper, we used to walk up a little hill—a beautiful, romantic spot. From it you could see the river and an old abandoned mill. It was a mysterious, shadowy place, especially in the light of the moon, when everything round about was bathed in silver, and only the bushes by the mill and the water under the mill wheel were black as ink, silent and sinister.

We didn't go down to the mill even in daytime—we weren't allowed to because the wooden dam was very old and, even if you didn't fall right through it, you could easily sprain your ankle. The village children, on the other hand, went there all the time, foraging for raspberries. The canes had become dense bushes, and the raspberries themselves were now very small, like wild ones.

And so we would often sit in the evenings on the little hill, gazing at this old mill and singing all together, "Sing, swallow, sing!"

It was, of course, only us young who went there. There were about six of us. There was my friend Zina and her two brothers—Kolya, who was two years the older, and Volodya, who is now my husband. At the time he was twenty-three years old, already grown up, a student. And then there was his college friend, Vanya Lebedev—a very interesting young man, intelligent and full of mockery, always able to come up with some witticism. I, of course, thought he was madly in love with me, just trying his best to hide it. Later the poor fellow was killed in the war. And then there was one more boy—red-haired Tolya, the estate manager's son. He was only about sixteen and still at school. He was a nice boy, and even quite good-looking—tall, strong, but terribly shy. When I remember him now, he always seems to be hiding behind somebody. If you happened to catch his glance, he would smile shyly and quickly disappear again. Now, this red-haired Tolya really was head over heels in love with me. About this there could be no doubt at all. He was wildly, hopelessly in love with me, so hopelessly that no one had the least wish to tease him about it—or to try and laugh him out of it. No one made fun of him at all, though anyone else in his position would have been treated mercilessly—especially with someone like Vanya around. Vanya even used to make out that Fedotych the old cook was smitten with my charms. "Really,

Lyalya, it's time you satisfied poor Fedotych's passion. Today's fish soup is pure salt.[1] We can't go on like this. You're a vain girl. *You* may enjoy his suffering—but what about *us*? Why should *we* be punished?"

Tolya and I often used to go out for walks together. Sometimes I liked to get up before dawn to fish or pick mushrooms. I did this mainly because I liked to surprise everyone. People would walk into the dining room in the morning for a cup of tea and say, "What's this basket doing here? Where have all these mushrooms come from?"

"Lyalya picked them."

Or fish would unexpectedly be served for breakfast.

"Where's this come from? Who brought it?"

"Lyalya went fishing this morning."

I loved all the oohs and aahs.

So, this redheaded Tolya and I were friends. He never spoke to me of his love, but it was as if there were a secret agreement between us, as if everything was so clear and definite that there was no need to talk about it. Tolya was supposed to be a friend of Kolya Katkov, although I don't really think there was any particular friendship between them. I think Tolya just wanted to be a part of our group— so he could stand behind someone and look at me.

And then one evening we all, including Tolya, went off up the hill. And Vanya Lebedev suddenly took it into his head that each of us should retell some old tale or legend, whatever they could remember. The scarier, the better—needless to say.

We drew lots to decide who should begin. The lot fell to Tolya.

"He'll just get all embarrassed," I said to myself, "and he won't be able to think of any stories at all."

But, to our general astonishment, Tolya began straightaway: "There's something I've been meaning to tell you all for a long time, but somehow I've never gotten around to it. A story about the mill. The story's quite true—only it's so strange you'd swear it was just a legend. I heard it from my own father. He used to live ten versts away, in Konyukhovka. It was when he was a young man. The mill had already been out of use for many years. And then a German with a huge dog suddenly came along and rented the place. He was a very strange old man indeed. He never spoke to anyone at all; he was always silent. And the dog was no less strange; it would sit opposite the old man for days on end, never taking its eyes off him. It seemed that the man was terribly afraid of the dog, but unable to do anything, unable to drive it away. And the dog just kept on watching him, following his every movement. Every now and then the dog would bare its teeth and growl. But the peasants who went there for flour said the dog never harmed them. All it ever did was look at the old man. Everyone found this very odd. People even asked the old man why he kept such a devilish creature. But there was no chance of getting any reply out of him. He simply never uttered a word . . . and then it happened. All of a sudden this dog leaped on the old man and bit through his throat. Then the peasants saw the dog rushing away, as if someone were chasing it. No one ever saw the dog again. And the mill's never been used since."

We liked Tolya's old legend. Vanya Lebedev, however, said, "That's splendid, Tolya. Only you could have told it better—it should be more scary. You should have added that the mill's been under a spell ever since. Whoever spends one whole night there will be able, if ever he wishes, to turn himself into a dog."

"But that's not true," Tolya replied shyly.

"What makes you say that? Maybe it *is* true. Something tells me that's the way it is. It's just that no one's tested this out yet."

We all laughed. "But why? What's so special about turning into a dog? If one could turn oneself into a millionaire, that would be another matter. Or some hero or other, or a famous general—or a great beauty. But who wants to turn into a dog? Where would that get you?"

There were no more stories that evening. We talked about this and that, then went our separate ways.

The following morning Tolya and I went out into the forest. We picked some berries, but there were too few to take back to the dining room so we decided I might as well eat them myself. We sat down beneath a fir tree, me eating berries and Tolya just looking at me. Somehow this began to seem very funny.

"Tolya," I said, "you're staring at me the way that dog of yours stared at the miller."

"Really I wish I could turn into a dog," he answered glumly, "because you're never going to marry me, are you?"

"No, Tolya, you know I'm not."

"So," he went on, "if I remain a man, I won't be able to stay by your side all the time. But if I turn into a dog, no one will stop me."

I had a sudden thought. "Tolya, darling! You know what? Go to the mill and spend the night there. Please do! Turn into a dog, so you can stay beside me. You're not going to say you're scared, are you?"

He turned very pale—I was surprised, because all this was just stuff and nonsense. Neither of us, it went without saying, believed in that dog. But Tolya, for some reason or other, turned pale and replied very gravely, "Yes, I'll go. I'll go and spend the night at the mill."

The day went by in its usual way and, after this early-morning walk, I didn't see Tolya. I didn't even think of him.

I remember some guests coming around—newlyweds from a neighboring estate, I think. Crowds of people, and much noise and laughter. And it was only in the evening, when everyone except family had left and we youngsters set out for our usual walk, that I began to think about Tolya again. It must have been when I saw the mill—and when someone said, "Doesn't the mill look dark and spooky this evening?"

"That's because we know the kind of things that go on there," replied Vanya Lebedev.

Then I started looking for Tolya. Turning around, I saw him sitting a little apart from the rest of us. He was completely silent, as if deep in thought.

Then I remembered his words, and somehow this made me anxious. At the same time, I felt annoyed with myself for feeling anxious, and this made me want to make fun of Tolya.

"Listen, ladies and gentlemen!" I called out merrily. "Tolya's decided to conduct an experiment. Transformation into a dog. He's going to spend the night at the mill."

No one took much notice of this. They probably thought I was joking. Only Vanya Lebedev replied, saying, "Yes, why not? Only please, dear Anatoly, be sure to turn into a proper hunting dog. Not a mere mongrel—that would be common."

Tolya didn't respond at all. When we were on our way home, I purposely lagged behind a little and Tolya joined me.

"So, Lyalechka," he said, "I'll go. I'll go tonight."

Looking very mysterious, I whispered, "Go then. You have to. But if, after this, you have the nerve *not* to turn into a dog, I never want to set eyes on you again!"

"I promise to turn into a dog," he said.

"And I shall be waiting for you all night," I replied. "As soon as you've turned into a dog, run straight back and scratch on my shutter with your claws. I'll open the window—and then you can jump into the room. Understand?"

"Yes."

"Off you go then!"

And so I went to bed and began to wait. And just imagine—that night I didn't get a minute's sleep. Somehow I was terribly anxious.

There was no moon that night, but the stars were shining. I kept getting up, half opening the window, and looking out. I felt very scared of something. Too scared even to open the shutters—I just peered out through a chink.

"Tolya's a fool," I said to myself. "What's got into him? Spending a whole night on his own in a dead mill!"

I fell asleep just before dawn ... and then, through my dreams, I hear scratching. Somebody scratching on the shutter.

I jump out of bed to listen better. Yes, I can hear claws against the shutter. I'm so scared I can hardly breathe. It's still dark, still nighttime.

But I steel myself, run to the window, throw open the shutters—and what do I see? Daylight! Sunshine! And Tolya's standing there laughing—only he looks very pale. Overcome with joy, I grab him by the shoulders and fling my arms around his neck.

"You scoundrel! How dare you not turn into a dog?"

He just kissed my hands, happy that I had embraced him.

"Lyalechka," he said, "can't you see? Or maybe you simply don't know how to look properly. I *am* a dog, Lyalechka. I am your faithful hound forever. How can you not see? I shall never leave you. But some evil force has put a spell on you that stops you from understanding."

I grabbed a comb from the table, kissed it, and threw it out the window.

"Fetch!"

He rushed off, found the comb in the grass, and brought it to me between his teeth. He was laughing, but there was something in his eyes that almost made me burst into tears.

"Well," I said, "now I believe you."

All this happened as summer was drawing to a close.

Three or four days after that night, my aunt and I went back to our village. We needed to get ready to return to Petersburg.

I was a little surprised by Volodya Katkov. He'd got hold of a camera from somewhere and went on and on taking photographs of me.

Tolya kept at a distance. I barely saw him. And he left before me. For Smolensk, where he was studying.

Two years passed.

I only saw Tolya once. He'd come to Petersburg for a few days to attend to some practical matter, and he was staying with the Katkovs. He had changed very little. Still the same round, childish face, with gray eyes.

"Greetings, my faithful hound! Let me take your paw!"

He didn't know what to say. Terribly embarrassed, he just laughed.

Throughout his visit Zina Katkova kept sending me little notes: "You really must come around this evening. Your hound keeps whining." Or: "Come around as soon as you can. Your hound is wasting away. Cruelty to animals is a sin."

Everyone kept quietly making fun of him, but he behaved very calmly indeed. He didn't seek me out, and he went on hiding behind other people's backs.

There was just one occasion when Tolya seemed to go a bit wild. Zina was telling me that, since I had such a wonderful voice, I really must go and study at the conservatory—and Tolya suddenly came out with, "Yes, I knew it! The stage! How utterly, utterly wonderful!"

Immediately after this, needless to say, he seemed overcome by embarrassment once again.

He was only in Petersburg for a few days. Soon after he left, I received a huge bouquet of roses from Eilers.[2] We all racked our brains, wondering who on earth could have sent it, and it was only the following day, as I was changing the water in the vase, that I noticed a little cornelian dog, tied to the bouquet by a thin gold thread.

I didn't tell anyone the flowers were from Tolya. I somehow started to feel awfully sorry for him. I even started to feel sorry for the cornelian dog. It had small, shiny eyes, as if it were crying.

And how could someone as poor as Tolya have found the money for such an expensive bouquet? It was probably money his family had given him to go to the theater, or to buy things he really needed.

For all their expensive splendor, these flowers had an air of poignant sorrow utterly out of keeping with Tolya's round, childishly naïve face. I even felt glad when the flowers withered and my aunt threw them out. Somehow I hadn't dared do that myself. As for the little dog, I tucked it away in a drawer so I could forget about it. And I forgot about it.

Then came a very chaotic period in my life. It started with the conservatory, which disappointed me deeply. My professor praised my voice, but he said I needed to work on it. This, however, wasn't my way of doing things at all. I was used to doing very little and being showered with praise for it. I would squeak out some little song and everyone would say, "Ooh! Aah! Such talent!" As for any kind of systematic study, that was entirely beyond me. It also became clear that the generally held belief in my exceptional talent was somewhat mistaken. In the conservatory I did not stand out in any way from the other girls. Or if I did, it was only because I didn't even once bother to prepare properly for a lesson. This disappointment did, of course, have its effect on me. I became anxious and irritable. I found solace in flirtations, in pointless chatter, and in endlessly rushing about. I was in a bad way.

I heard only once from Tolya. He sent me a letter from Moscow, where he'd gone to continue his studies.

"Lyalechka," he wrote, "remember that you have a dog. If ever you're in trouble, just summon it."

He did not include his address, and I did not reply.

The war began.

The boys from my old circle all turned out to be patriots, and they all went off to the front. I heard that Tolya went too, but somehow I hardly thought about him. Zina joined the Sisters of Mercy, but I was still caught up in my mad whirl.

Things at the conservatory were going from bad to worse. And I'd fallen in with a wild, bohemian crowd. Aspiring poets, unrecognized artists, long evenings devoted to discussing matters erotic, nights at the Stray Dog.[3]

The Stray Dog was an astonishing institution. It drew in people from worlds that were entirely alien to it. It drew these people in and swallowed them up.

I shall never forget one regular visitor. The daughter of a well-known journalist, she was a married woman and the mother of two children.

Someone once happened to take her to this cellar, and one could say that she simply never left. Young and beautiful, her huge black eyes wide open as if from horror, she would come every evening and remain until morning, breathing the alcoholic fumes and listening to young poets howling out verses of which she probably understood not a word. She never spoke; she looked frightened. People said that her husband had left her and taken the children with him.

Once I saw her with a very sickly-looking young man. His dress and general air were sophisticated and "Wildean."

Seeming cool and aloof, he was sitting beside her at a table, writing or sketching something on a scrap of paper just under her nose. These words or signs evidently agitated her. She kept blushing and looking around: Had anyone seen anything? She would grab the pencil from the young man and quickly cross everything out. She would watch tensely while he lazily scribbled something new. Then she would blush once more and snatch back the pencil.

Something about this degenerate was so horrible, so deeply disturbing that I said to myself, "Can there, anywhere in the world, be a woman so idiotic as to allow that creature anywhere near her? A woman who would trust that man in any way, let alone be attracted to such a repulsive little reptile?"

In less than a fortnight I proved to be just such a woman myself.

I would prefer not to dwell on this disgusting chapter of my life.

Harry Edvers was a "poet and composer." He composed little songs, which he half read and half sang, always to the same tune.

His real first name and patronymic were Grigory Nikolaevich. I never found out his surname. I remember I once had a visit from the police (this was later, under the Bolshevik regime) to ask if a certain Grigory Ushkin was hiding in my apartment. But I don't know for sure if it was him they were inquiring about.

This Harry entered my life as easily and straightforwardly as if he were just letting himself into a hotel room, opening it with his key.

Needless to say, it was in the Stray Dog that our acquaintance began.

I was onstage for part of that evening and sang Kuzmin's little song, "Child, Don't Look for a Rose in Spring."[4] At the time it was still very much in vogue. At the end of the first phrase someone in the audience piped up, "Rose lives in Odessa."

It had been someone at the same table as Harry. As I was on my way back to my seat, Harry got to his feet and followed me. "Please don't take offense," he said. "Yurochka was just playing the fool. But you really shouldn't be singing Kuzmin. You should be singing my 'Duchesse.'"

And so it began.

Within two weeks I'd had my hair cropped and dyed auburn, and I was wearing a black velvet gentleman's suit. A cigarette between my fingers, I was singing the drivel composed by Harry:

> A pale boy, fashioned from papier-mâché
> And now the darling of the blue princess,
> He had a certain *je ne sais quel cachet*
> Betokening voluptuous excess.

I would raise my eyebrows, shake the ash from my cigarette, and go on:

> The princess had the bluest, sweetest soul,
> A dainty, pear-like soul—a true *duchesse*—
> A soul to savor, then to save and seal,
> A soul for lovers of *vraie délicatesse*.

And so on, and so on.

Harry listened, gave his approval, and voiced corrections.

"You must have a rose in your buttonhole—some quite extraordinary, unnatural rose. A green rose. Huge and hideous."[5]

Harry had his retinue of followers, an entire court of his own. All of them green, unnatural, and hideous. A green-faced slip of a girl, a cocaine addict. Some Yurochka or other, "whom everybody knew." A consumptive schoolboy. A hunchback who played quite wonderfully on the piano. They all shared strange secrets that bound them together. They were all agitated about something or other, suffering some kind of torment and, as I now realize, often just making mountains out of molehills.

The schoolboy liked to wrap himself up in a Spanish shawl and wear ladies' shoes with high heels. The green-faced girl used to dress as a military cadet.

It's not worth describing all this in detail. These people don't matter; they're neither here nor there. I mention them merely to give you some idea of the circles into which I'd descended.

At the time I was living in furnished accommodation on Liteiny Prospekt. Harry moved in with me.

He latched on to me in a big way. I still don't know whether he truly fancied me or whether he just thought I had money. Our relationship was very strange. Green and hideous. I don't propose to tell you about it now.

The strangest thing of all is that when I was with him, I felt repelled by him. I felt a sharp sense of disgust, as if I were kissing a corpse. But I was unable to live without him.

And then Volodya Katkov arrived on leave. Full of joy and excitement, he rushed into my apartment, saw my red hair, and exclaimed, "Why on earth? What a one you are! Still, you really are awfully sweet!"

He turned me around, to look at me from all sides. It was clear that he really liked me. "Lyalechka, I'm only here for a week, and I'm going to spend every day of it with you. I've got a lot to say to you— and it can't wait any longer."

But then Harry came in. He didn't even knock. And I could see that he took an immediate dislike to Volodya. He must have felt jealous. And so he sprawled out in an armchair and began nonchalantly doing something he'd never done before: addressing me with extreme familiarity, not as *vy* but as *ty*.

Volodya must have felt very confused indeed. For a long time he just kept looking from me to Harry and back again, without a word. Then he got resolutely to his feet, straightened his field jacket, and said goodbye.

It greatly upset me to see him leaving like this, but I too had been confused by Harry's rudeness. I could think of nothing to say and I didn't know how to stop Volodya from leaving. I felt there had been a terrible misunderstanding, but there seemed to be no way to put it right.

Volodya didn't call again. Nor did I expect him to. I felt that he had gone away, that his heart had gone away, forever.

Then came a period of isolation.

In spite of all he'd done to avoid this, Harry was about to be sent to the front. He went to Moscow to make representations.

I was on my own for more than a month.

It was an anxious time for me, and I had no money. I wrote to my aunt in Smolensk Province, but I heard nothing back.

Eventually, Harry returned. Entirely transformed. Tanned and healthy-looking, wearing a fine sheepskin coat trimmed with astrakhan, and with a tall Caucasian hat, also astrakhan.

"Have you come from the front?"

"In a way," he answered. "Russia needs brains, not only cannon fodder. I'm supplying the army with motorized vehicles."

Harry's brain may have been working magnificently, and it may have been needed by Russia, but he was still short of money.

"I need funds. Can you really not get hold of any for me? Are you really that lacking in patriotism?"

I told him I had no money and mentioned writing to my aunt. He seemed interested and asked for her address. After hurrying about the city for a few days, he set off again. By then I'd learned that the secret of his new "soldierly" look lay in two small pots of pink and ochre powder. To give him his due, this really did make him look very handsome.

By this time the mood of our little world of aesthetes had grown distinctly counterrevolutionary. Before leaving, Harry had composed a new ditty for me:

> My heart hangs on a little white ribbon.
> White, white, white—remember the color white!

I now wore a white dress when I performed; we were all pretending to be countesses or marquises. The song was received well. So was I.

Soon after Harry left, Zina Katkova came back unexpectedly from the front. She at once began telling me a story I found deeply troubling.

"Our field hospital was on the edge of a forest. We had a great deal to do—and we had orders to leave the next morning. We were being rushed off our feet. At one point I went out for a smoke—and suddenly there was a young soldier calling my name. Who do you think it was? It was Tolya. Tolya the Dog. 'Forgive me, darling,' I said, 'I'm in a desperate rush.' 'But I just want to know how things are with Lyalechka,' he answered. 'She isn't in trouble, is she? For the love of God, tell me everything you know.' But just then I heard someone shouting for me. 'Wait, Tolya. I'll be back in a moment.' 'All right,' he answered, 'I'll wait for you by this tree. We certainly won't be going anywhere before tomorrow.' And so I rushed back in to my wounded. It was a terrible night. The Germans had gotten the range of our position—and we had to have everything packed up by dawn. We didn't lie down for even a minute. I got a little behind with everything and I had to run to get to roll call in time. A miserable morning, endless gray drizzle. I'm running along—and suddenly—oh Lord! What do I see? Tolya, gray and ashen, standing beside a tree. He's been waiting for me all night long. He looks pitiful. His eyes sunken, as if staring out from under the earth. And smiling! And probably with not long to live. Imagine—he'd been standing there all night long in the rain. Just to hear news of you. And I still couldn't stop for one moment. There was no time for anything. He thrust a slip of paper at me with his address. I shouted over my shoulder, 'Don't worry about Lyalya. I think she's getting married soon.' And then I worried I'd said the wrong thing. I might have upset him. Who knows?"

All this greatly disturbed me. I was in a bad way and I needed the friendship of a good man. And where would I find a better man than Tolya? I felt moved. I asked for his address and tucked the slip of paper away.

During this visit I really turned against Zina. First, she'd grown ugly and coarse. Second (though really, I suppose, this should come first), she treated me very coldly. More than that, she went out of her way to show her complete lack of interest in me and everything about my life. It was the first time, for example, that she'd seen me with short red hair, but for some reason she behaved as if this wasn't in the least surprising or interesting. I naturally found this hard to believe. How could she not want to know why I'd suddenly cut my hair so very short? This apparent lack of interest was clearly Zina's way of showing her contempt for me and my dissipated life—as if, from her exalted heights, she barely noticed my foolish antics.

She did not even ask whether I was still having singing lessons, or what I was up to more generally. To get my own back, I was extremely rude. "I just hope the war comes to an end soon. Otherwise you'll lose every last semblance of humanity. You've become a real old harridan."

I then gave a mannered smile and added, "I for my part still acknowledge art alone. The world has no need for your and your comrades' heroic deeds. They will all be forgotten. Art, however, is eternal."

Zina looked at me with a certain bewilderment and left soon afterward. Probably, she wanted simply to shake my dust off her feet.

That evening I wept. I was burying my past. I understood for the first time that there was no going back. The paths I had taken had now all been entirely destroyed—blown up like railway track behind the last train of a retreating army.

"And what about Volodya?" I thought bitterly. "Is that how a true friend behaves? He didn't ask any questions. He didn't take the trouble to find out what was really going on. He just took one look at Harry, turned around, and left. If they all think I've gone mad, that I've lost my way in life, then why don't they come and help instead of walking away? Why don't they support me and try to make me see reason? How can they be so cool and indifferent? How, at such a black and terrible time, can they abandon someone they once held dear?

"Very virtuous they all are!" I went on. "And they certainly rub your nose in their virtue. But is it really so very praiseworthy? How many temptations are there going to be for a woman with a mug like Zina's? And Volodya has always been cold and narrow-minded. His petty little soul's as straight and narrow as they come. When did *he* last feel the intoxication of music or poetry? How much more I love my dear Harry, my dear and dissolute Harry, with his tender little song:

> My heart hangs on a little white ribbon.
> White, white, white—remember the color white!

They would say this is rubbish. *They* would rather have Nekrasov—and his plodding, four-square poems in praise of civic virtue."[6]

My green and hideous monsters now seemed nearer and dearer to me than ever.

They understood everything. *They* were my family.

But this new family of mine was disappearing too. The cocaine addict was fading away in a hospital. Yurochka had been packed off to the front. The consumptive schoolboy had volunteered for the cavalry because "he had fallen in love with a golden horse" and could no longer bear being with people. "I don't understand people any more or feel anything for them," he kept saying.

From Harry's large retinue there remained only the hunchback. He used to play "Waves of the Danube"[7] on a beaten-up piano in a tiny cinema grandiloquently called the Paris Giant—and he was slowly starving to death.

This was a grim time for me. I was kept going only by my anger with those who had wronged me and by my overwrought and carefully nurtured tenderness toward my one and only Harry.

At last, Harry returned.

He found me in an anxious state. I greeted him so joyfully that he was positively embarrassed. He'd never seen me like that before.

Then he kept disappearing for days on end. It seemed he really was buying and selling something. It was all very strange.

After hurrying about for a couple of weeks, he decided that we must move to Moscow: "Petersburg is a dead city. Moscow's seething with life. There are cafés springing up everywhere. You can sing there. You can read poems. One way or another you can earn a few rubles."

Moscow also apparently offered more scope for his own new commercial activities.

We packed up and moved.

Life in Moscow really did turn out to be more animated, more exciting, and more fun. There were a lot of people I knew from Petersburg. It was a familiar world and I fit in easily.

Harry kept on disappearing. He seemed preoccupied and I saw very little of him.

And he forbade me, incidentally, to sing his "Little White Ribbon." Forbade me. He didn't *ask* me not to sing it—he *forbade* me. And he seemed angry: "How can you not understand that that song has now become superfluous, superficial, and utterly inappropriate?"

And he also happened to ask several times whether I knew the address of Volodya Katkov. I put this down to jealousy on his part.

"He's somewhere in the south, isn't he, with the Whites?"

"Of course."

"And he's not planning to come to Moscow?"

"I don't know."

"And none of his family are here?"

"No."

He was strangely inquisitive.

Just what Harry was up to I couldn't work out. It seemed he was once again involved in some kind of business activity. The good thing was that every now and then he would bring back some ham, flour, or butter. Those were hungry days.

Once, as I was going down Tverskaya Street, I caught sight of a shabby-looking figure. After looking straight at me, this man hurried across to the other side of the road. Feeling I'd seen him before, I looked again. It was Kolya Katkov! Volodya's younger brother, the friend of my dog Tolya. Why hadn't Kolya called out to me? He had clearly recognized me. Why had he been in such a hurry to slip away?

I told Harry about this encounter. For some reason this made him agitated. "How can you not understand?" he said. "He's a White officer. He doesn't want to be noticed."

"But what's he doing here in Moscow? Why isn't he with the White Army?"

"He must have been sent here on some mission. How stupid of you not to have stopped him!"

"But you just said he doesn't want to be noticed!"

"Makes no difference. You could have asked him back. We could have sheltered him here."

I was touched by Harry's generosity. "Harry, wouldn't you have felt scared to be sheltering a White officer?"

He blushed a little. "Not in the least," he muttered. "If you see him again, you really must bring him back with you. Yes, you really must!"

So Harry was capable of heroic deeds! More than that, he was even eager for a chance to prove his heroism.

It was a hot, sultry summer. A peasant woman who traded apples under the counter suggested I go and live in her dacha just outside the city. I moved in with her.

Now and again Harry made an appearance. Once he brought some of his new friends along too.

They were the same young Wildean poseurs as before. Green faces, the eyes of cocaine addicts. Harry too had recently taken to snorting a fair amount.

Most of his conversations with these new friends of his were about business.

Soon afterward someone I knew showed up. He was from Smolensk Province, from near our family home, and he brought me a strange little letter from my aunt.

"I've been carrying this letter around for the last two months," he said. "I tried to find you in Petersburg, but it seemed impossible. I gave up all hope. It seemed I was never going to find you. Then I happened to meet an actress who told me your address."

"Evidently my letters aren't reaching you," my aunt wrote. "But at least the money is in your hands now, and it comforts me to know this. I like your husband very much. He seems enterprising—a man with a future."

I didn't understand. What husband? What money? And just what was it my aunt found so comforting?

Harry appeared.

"Harry," I said, "I've just received a letter from my aunt. She says she's glad the money is in my hands now."

I stopped, struck by the look on his face. He was blushing so furiously that it had brought tears to his eyes. Finally, I understood: Harry had called on my aunt and introduced himself as my husband—and the silly old woman had given him my money.

"How much did she give you?" I asked calmly.

"Around thirty thousand. Nothing much. I didn't want us to

squander it all on trifles, and so I put the money into this transport business."

"Mr. Edvers," I said, "in the whole of this story there is only one thing I find truly surprising: the fact that you can still blush."

He shrugged. "What I find surprising," he said, "is that you haven't once wondered what we've been living on all this time and how we found the money to move here from Petersburg."

"So I've been paying my way, have I? Well, I'm glad to know that."

He left. A few days later, however, he made another appearance—as if this conversation had never happened. Two of his friends came as well, the same two friends as before. They'd brought some vodka and something to eat with it. One of them began flirting with me. They addressed each other—jokingly, I thought—as "comrade." Edvers too was a "comrade." They asked me to sing. My admirer—whom I'd prefer not to name—rather appealed to me. There was something world-weary and depraved about him, something that reminded me of people from our "hideous green" Petersburg world. Without giving it any particular thought, I sang our "Little White Ribbon."

"It's a sweet tune, but the words are idiotic!" said Harry. "Wherever did you get hold of such antediluvian nonsense?" And he hurriedly changed the subject, evidently afraid I would tell everyone the name of the song's composer.

Three days later I was supposed to be singing in a café. Our manager looked very embarrassed when he saw me and muttered something about it no longer being possible for me to sing that night. I was surprised, but I didn't insist. I sat down in a corner. Somehow nobody seemed to notice me. The only person who did was Lucy Lyukor. In a poisonous tone of voice, the little poetess said, "Ah, Lyalya! Word goes you haven't been wasting time. I hear you've dyed your little white ribbon red!"

Sensing my bewilderment, she went on: "Only the other day you were singing for a group of Chekists.[8] I don't imagine you treated them to your Little White Ribbon!"

"What Chekists?"

She gave me a sharp look, then named the comrade who'd flirted with me.

I didn't reply. I just got up and left.

I was terribly frightened. Harry had truly landed me in the dirt!

The incident with my aunt hadn't shocked me so very deeply. Nobody in our bohemian world was particularly scrupulous about money. Though it was unpleasant, of course, that he'd kept the whole business a secret from me. But what Lucy had just told me was another matter altogether. How could I stay with Harry now? He was crazed by cocaine and in cahoots with the Cheka. No, I couldn't let comrade Harry call the tune any longer—not after he'd tried to use me to lure a White officer into a trap. It was not just out of the goodness of his heart, I now realized, that he'd wanted me to invite Kolya Katkov to stay.

I was in despair. Where could I go? There was not a single close friend or relative I could turn to, no one I could count on to show me even just a little everyday kindness. My aunt? But I would have to obtain a travel permit, and besides, I didn't have a kopek to my name.

I went back home.

There was no sign of Harry. It was several days since I'd last seen him.

I did all I could. I made the rounds of different institutions. I wrote petitions and applications. I tried to get myself registered with the newly reconstituted Artists Union. That would make it easier for me to get a travel permit.

And then one day I was walking down the street and all of a sudden . . . you could have knocked me down with a feather. Kolya. Kolya Katkov. There—right in front of my eyes.

"Kolya!" I shouted.

He appeared not to see me and quickly turned down a side street. After a moment's thought, I followed. He was waiting for me.

I now realized why I'd been slow to recognize him the previous time. He had grown a beard.

"Kolya," I said, "what are you doing here? How come you're in Moscow?"

"I'm leaving today," he replied. "But you shouldn't have let it be seen that you know me. Isn't that obvious?"

"You're leaving today?" I exclaimed—and felt more despairing than ever. "Kolya," I said, "for the love of God, save me! I'm lost."

He evidently began to feel sorry for me.

"There's nothing I can do now, Lyalechka. I'm a hunted beast. And anyway, I'm leaving today. There really is nothing I can do. I'll ask someone to call around."

I remembered Harry and the people he was now bringing back with him.

"No," I said, "you mustn't send anyone around."

And then I had another thought, a thought that warmed my heart.

"Kolya," I asked, "is there any chance you'll be seeing Tolya?"

"It's certainly possible."

"Tell him, for the love of God, that Lyalya is calling on her dog for help. Remember my words and repeat them exactly. Promise me. And tell him to leave a note for me in the café on Tverskaya Street."

"If all goes well," Kolya replied, "I'll be seeing him in about five days."

Kolya was in a great hurry. We parted. I was crying as I walked down the street.

Back home I thought everything through and decided not to say anything to Harry. Instead I would try and trick him into handing over some of the money—money that did, after all, belong to me.

My efforts to get hold of a permit met with success, and soon nearly everything was ready.

The day came.

I'm on my own in the dacha, leafing through some papers in my desk, when I sense that someone is looking at me. I turn around— a dog! Rust-colored, large but lean, with matted fur—a German shepherd. Standing in the doorway and looking straight at me. "What's going on?" I think. "Where on earth's this dog come from?"

"Kapitolina Fedotovna!" I call out to my landlady. "There's a dog in here!"

My landlady comes in, very surprised. "But the doors are all shut," she says. "How can it have gotten in?"

I wanted to stroke the dog—there was something so very expressive about the way it was looking at me—but it wouldn't let me. It wagged its tail and backed into a corner. And just kept on looking at me.

"Maybe we should give it something to eat," I say to Kapitolina. In reply, she mutters something about there not being enough food any longer even for people, but she brings some bread anyway. She throws a piece to the dog. The dog doesn't touch it.

"Better throw the dog out!" I say. "It's acting strange. It might be sick."

Kapitolina flung the door open. The dog went out.

Afterward we recalled that it never once let us touch it. Nor did it bark, nor did it ever eat anything. We saw it—and that was all.

Later that day Harry appeared. He looked awful—completely exhausted. His eyes were bulging and bloodshot, his face taut and sallow. He walked in, with barely a word.

My heart was thumping. I had to speak to him—for the last time.

He slammed the door shut. He seemed terribly edgy. Something had gone badly wrong—or else he'd overdone the cocaine.

"Harry," I began, steeling myself, "we need to talk."

"Hang on a moment," he said confusedly. "What's the date today?"

"The twenty-seventh."

"The twenty-seventh!" he muttered. "The twenty-seventh!"

Why this so mattered to him I don't know, but his despairing tone made the date stick in my mind. And later, this turned out to be important.

"Where's that dog from?" he shouted all of a sudden.

I turned around—there in the corner of the room was the dog. Taut, pointing, it was looking at Harry intently, as if it were nothing but eyes—as if its eyes were now its entire being.

"Get that dog out of here!" Harry shouted.

There was something excessive about his fear. He rushed to the door and flung it open. Slowly the dog began to move toward the door, not taking its eyes off Harry. It was slightly baring its teeth, its hackles raised.

Harry slammed the door after it.

"Harry," I began again, "I can see you're upset, but I just can't put this off any longer."

He looked up at me, and then his whole face twisted in horror. He was now looking not at me but past me—somewhere behind me. I turned around: there outside the window, with both front paws on the low sill, was the reddish-brown dog. Perhaps startled by my movement, it dropped back down at once. But I managed to glimpse its raised hackles, the muzzle it had thrust alertly forward, its bared teeth and terrible eyes—still fixed on Harry.

"Go!" Harry yelled. "Go away! Make it go away!"

Trembling all over, he rushed out into the hallway and bolted the door.

"This is terrible, terrible!" he kept repeating.

I sensed that I too was trembling all over, and that my hands had gone cold. And I understood that we were in the middle of something truly awful, that I ought to do something to calm Harry, to calm myself, and that I'd chosen a very bad moment indeed—but for some reason I was unable to stop and I hurriedly, stubbornly, went on, "I've come to a decision, Harry."

His hands trembling, he struck a match and lit a cigarette.

"Oh have you?" he said with a nasty smirk. "How very interesting."

"I'm leaving. I'm going to my aunt's."

"Why?"

"It's better not to ask."

A spasm passed across his face.

"And if I don't let you?"

"What right do you have to stop me?"

I was speaking calmly, but my heart was racing and I could hardly breathe.

"I have no right at all," he answered, and his entire face trembled. "But I need you now—and I won't let you go."

With these words he pulled open the drawer of my desk and at once saw my new passport and papers.

"Ah! So it's like that, is it?"

He snatched the whole sheaf and began tearing the papers first lengthways and then crossways.

"For your dealings with the Whites I could easily—"

But I was no longer listening. I leaped on him like a madwoman. I was shrieking; I was clawing at him. I hit him on his hands and arms. I tried to tear the papers out of his hands.

"Chekist! Thief! I'll kill you! I'll kill you!"

He grabbed me by the throat. Really he was not so much strangling me as just shaking me; his bared teeth and staring eyes were wilder and more frightening than anything he actually did. And the loathing and hatred I felt for those wild eyes and that gaping mouth made me start to lose consciousness.

"Help!" I gasped. "Help me, somebody!"

What happened next was truly weird. There was the sound of smashing glass, and something huge, heavy, and shaggy jumped into the room and crashed down on Harry, bringing him to the floor.

All I can recall is the sight of Harry's legs twitching. They were poking out from under the red, tousled mass that covered the rest of his body, which now lay almost completely still.

By the time I came to, it was all over. Harry's body had been taken off to the morgue; his throat had been clean ripped out.

The dog had disappeared without a trace.

Apparently, some boys had seen a huge hound, leaping across fences as it streaked past them.

All this happened on the twenty-seventh. That is important. Much later, when I was a free woman, in Odessa, I found out that Kolya Katkov had passed on to Tolya my appeal for help, and that Tolya had dropped everything and rushed to my rescue. That meant trying to slip through the Bolshevik front line. He was tracked down, caught, and shot—all on the twenty-seventh. The twenty-seventh, that very day.

That's the whole story; that's what I wanted to tell you. I've made nothing up; I've added nothing; and there's nothing I can explain—or even want to explain. But when I turn back and consider the past, I can see everything clearly. I can see each separate event and the axis or thread upon which a certain force had strung them.

It had strung the events on the thread like beads and tied up the loose ends.

Translated by Robert and Elizabeth Chandler

THE KIND THAT WALK

FIRST to raise the alarm would be the two young pointers always playing by the gates.

They would come out with a peculiar warning bay—a dog's way of saying "Bewa-a-are! Bewa-a-a-re!"

At this, the entire pack of village dogs slumbering by our front door would leap to their feet—big dogs, little dogs, pedigrees, half-breeds, and stray mutts with no breeding whatsoever.

From the kennel would emerge a great shaggy dog named Watcher, who looked like an old man wearing a sheepskin coat inside out. He would fly into a rage, barking himself hoarse as he got up on his hind legs and tugged at his chain.

This canine concert marked an event that was quite straightforward and by no means unusual: Moshka the carpenter coming in through the gates.

Why the dogs grew so agitated at the sight of him, I can't understand even now.

Moshka was old, very thin, long and bent. On his head was a yarmulke and he had sidelocks, a long black *rekel* coat, and galoshes. For our part of the world, in short, he looked entirely ordinary.

What was remarkable about him was not his appearance but other things—which the dogs could hardly have known.

First, he had a reputation for unswerving honesty. He did every job well, on time, and at a fair price, and without asking for a deposit.

Second, and this too the dogs could not have known, he was a man of few words. I don't know whether he ever talked at all. Maybe he only winked and shook his sidelocks.

But what was truly remarkable about him was a legend that shed some light on his strange ways. Apparently, one Yom Kippur some thirty years ago, while he and his fellow believers were praying and repenting of their sins in the synagogue, there occurred an incident that Jewish belief held to be entirely within the bounds of possibility: poor Moshka was dragged off by a devil.

There were, of course, people who had seen with their own eyes how Moshka flew up into the air and was carried off by some foul being who looked like nothing so much as a ram. They'd wanted to help Moshka by making the sign of the cross over the devil, but then they'd thought better of it: the cross might get Moshka even deeper into trouble.

One old woman saw not a ram but "summat like a ball wi flames coming out its nose."

How a ball can have a nose, this old woman made no attempt to explain; she just spat over her shoulder.

Whatever the truth, Moshka disappeared for the best part of thirty years. Then he reappeared—from goodness knows where—settled down beyond the cemetery in an abandoned bathhouse, and began going from one landowner to another, doing odd jobs of carpentry. His work was good. How he'd learned his trade during his years with the devil no one knew.

As always, there were people who knew better—who said with a little smirk that Moshka had simply been dodging his military service and must have spent all those years in America.

Few people liked this reasonable explanation; many even found it offensive. "What stories people come up with! When, with our very own eyes, we saw him being dragged away by the devil! Besides, if Moshka really had been in America, don't you think he'd be telling us about it? People are real loudmouths when they come back from America. If you don't brag when you come back from America, when *are* you going to brag? But Moshka just holds his tongue. Why? Why do you think? Because he's bound by a vow of silence! Maybe he has to atone for some sin. And why's he so honest? Don't tell me *that's* from being in America! Ha ha! And as for him not wanting to be paid in advance, well, that's because he's afraid the devil might drag him off again and the money would simply be lost."

I remember those "Moshka" days well.

An outbuilding; a small, empty, whitewashed room; planks, boards, and sawdust.

A long black figure, bending over a wide board and running a little box along it. Cascading from beneath the box—delicate, silky curls of fragrant shavings.

My sister and I would stand in the doorway, watching with bated breath. I think we sometimes stood there for hours on end.

Moshka said nothing; he paid no attention to us at all. He planed, sawed, and chiseled. His eyes were half closed and his movements very slow, as if unconscious. All this lulled us into a kind of trance. Our eyes, too, would half close and we would breathe deeply and evenly, as if asleep. Something strange, pleasant, and irresistible would come over us, enchanting us, bewitching us, taking away our strength and will.

At a call from our elders we would, with difficulty, come back to ourselves and return to the house. At table, our mother would remark on how pale we looked.

But the moment we were left to our own devices, off we ran to watch Moshka again. Something about this quiet, dark man held an inexplicable attraction for us.

Many years later, a landowner from Simbirsk told me how a Kalmyk once cured his six-year-old son of childhood epilepsy. The Kalmyk asked for a pound of pure silver, took a little hammer, and began beating out a hollow cone. For nine days he shaped the silver, humming softly as he tapped away and slowly rotated the shining chunk of metal. The sick boy was told to stand beside him and watch. The boy grew calm and sleepy. After nine days, the cone was finished and the boy was cured.

There must have been something in old Moshka's movements that had a similar hypnotic effect on us.

Moshka, however, was no ordinary carpenter. The legends around him couldn't but inflame people's imaginations.

Just think—a man who has been carried off by the devil! How often, in our humdrum world, do we come face-to-face with such a person?

Once the story of his disappearance had been thoroughly picked over, it began to seem inadequate. It was not so easy to leave it at that. And so people's minds set to work.

The housekeeper would bustle in. The laundress would start whispering.

"Why d'you keep running off to see Moshka?" Nyanya would grumble. "You shouldn't watch him like that. His kind bring wrong—don't look at 'em long."

"What kind? What kind is Moshka's kind?"

"The kind that walk."

This sounded macabre and mysterious.

"Where does he walk, Nyanya?"

"Here. He ought to stay *there*, but he comes and walks *here*. No good'll come of it."

"But where's *there*?"

"Where he was put in the ground!"

The way Nyanya said this, we didn't dare ask more. After being put in the ground, it seemed that Moshka had somehow got back out again.

In the evening we heard the housekeeper whispering something about the cemetery. It was scary. We understood that Moshka had been buried in the cemetery—and now here he was, coming *here* from *there*.

There was another Jew working on our estate at the time. A talkative, sociable fellow. He was making bricks for the barn and he kept promising to build me and Lena a little house. Knowing he had a loose tongue, we decided to ask him about Moshka.

Thanks to our house-building plans we were on the friendliest of terms. Yes, he was sure to tell us everything.

And so off we went.

"Itska, tell us about Moshka. Is it true he was once put in the ground?"

Our question didn't surprise Itska, although I suspect now that he simply didn't understand. But his response was so eloquent that it has stayed with me throughout my long life: "Moshka? Oy, again with Moshka! Ant vhy always Moshka? Vhy not not-Moshka? Let me tell you vunce ant for all—Moshka is jus' plain Moshka."

And that was that.

Early that evening, a general meeting was held in the nursery. Among those present were the housekeeper, the laundress, the kitchen woman, and some witch in a brown head scarf whose connection to the household seemed somewhat tenuous; she may have been the coachman's mother-in-law.

The news everyone had come to discuss was astonishing. Moshka's carpentry work, it turned out, was merely a cover. The sly fellow was using it to divert attention from his real business: he was running a bathhouse for the dead.

Everything had been confirmed by statements from witnesses. Someone had a friend who'd left town late on a Sunday evening. He'd had a bit too much to drink, so he went the wrong way and ended up at Moshka's bathhouse. And then—heavens above! Knocking and crashing, like metal pails tumbling about on the floor. And what sounded like angry voices, except that the voices weren't human. The man ran off in terror. But he went back the next morning and looked through the window: shelves had been overturned, boards were lying about on the floor, and pails had been thrown all over the place. No doubt about it, something had been going on. He spoke to a friend— a clerk and a man of the world. This man of the world just grinned at him.

"Where've you been all these years?" he asked. "It's common knowledge. Any fool could have told you that Moshka runs a bathhouse for the dead. Why else would the bathhouse have been built right next to the cemetery?"

"But . . . that bathhouse hasn't been used for years."

"Of course it hasn't," said the man of the world. "There's not many people go to a place like that. Only the kind that walk. Was all this on a Sunday?"

"Yes."

"What Christian soul would go to the bathhouse on a Sunday? And don't pretend you're a child—you know what I mean."

All this was said in whispers, punctuated with little gasps.

Then we heard about the aunt of some woman who made Communion bread. One night her husband's brother had gone to this bathhouse—he'd wanted to see for himself. He'd looked through the window and seen two naked dead men steaming themselves with cold water. The brother-in-law took such a fright that he was struck dumb for the rest of his life.

And now this same mute brother-in-law was telling everyone to knock out the bathhouse windows, take the door off its hinges, and keep a good watch on the place. It was time to smoke Moshka out. Why should anyone around here give him work if he was *the kind that walks*?

Soon after this, Moshka disappeared. Some said he must have gone to Kiev to find work; others had seen with their very own eyes how he'd been dragged off again by the devil.

Then it emerged that while Moshka was working for us in his usual way, planing his boards, someone had indeed gone to the trouble of smashing in the bathhouse windows and making off with the bathhouse door. And Moshka could hardly go on living there with no windows or doors. He needed to be able to hide from people.

I may only have been little, but I could see that anyone would find it hard to get by without windows or doors. Although such things might not have mattered to Moshka. After all, he wasn't going to catch cold if he was *the kind that walks*.

But the story of him going to Kiev was, of course, no more than idle gossip. Because what did our herdsman find, on a birdhouse near an outbuilding, but an old galosh? Who could it have belonged to, if not Moshka? And how did it get there? It had fallen from the sky, of course, as Moshka was being carried off by the devil.

All in all, people felt sorry for Moshka.

"He was a good sort. Quiet, hardworking, honest. The trouble is, he wasn't a human being. If he had been, none of this would have happened. It's just as well he went away of his own accord. Otherwise . . . well, people were already muttering about aspen stakes."

The galosh was solemnly burned. Because everyone knew that, unless it was destroyed, Moshka was sure to come back for it. If not now—then in thirty years.[1]

"Better he doesn't walk any more," said the kitchen woman. "Enough's enough."

Translated by Anne Marie Jackson

WONDER WORKER

Childhood memories can be astonishingly vivid.

Later, when we are grown up, we see much that is both wonderful and full of meaning, but it merely flits across our heart and fades away. Our memory fails to get a grip on it.

Yet a trifling scene from our earliest years can stay with us till our dying day.

I still have a vivid memory of our coachman Slavitsky biting into a black radish. It couldn't be clearer. Picture-perfect. It has lost none of its life or color.

A fine summer day. A marvelous smell of hot straw and beech bark. My sister and I are playing a game by the back porch, underneath the awning for the firewood.

It's a splendid game. Using only your heel, you make a hole in the ground. It has to be perfectly round. To make the earth softer, you can spit in the hole.

The work goes with a swing. We keep up a constant refrain.

"Look! I can and you can't!"

"No, *I* can and *you* can't."

There's nothing like a little friendly competition to move things along. Our stockings are torn, our legs are muddied up to the knee, and one of my sister's heels has snapped off.

Suddenly our mother's maid bursts out of the house, her starched skirts crackling like thunderclaps.

"Dasha! Dasha! Where are you going?"

"To the coachman. Your mama said to get the horses ready."

At once, without another word, my sister and I grab each other by the hand and run after her.

The coachman lived next to the stables, which were strictly out of bounds to us. Once we'd been caught by the stable door, gazing reverently at the horses' long hind quarters. Hanging down between them, their tails looked like a young girl's plaits.

"Horses can kick."

"Not when we're this far away!" we'd squealed.

To which our military cadet brother had replied, sounding knowledgeable, "A horse's hoof can reach ten whole yards."

And so we were forbidden to enter the stables.

Dasha ran into the coachman's hut. We stood in the doorway and watched.

Beside a table in a dingy, poky little room loomed a giant, some three times my height. He was wearing a drab coat and he stood sideways to the table, his face toward us, munching away and letting out little grunts. He was eating thin slices of black radish, taking them in his fingers from a bowl on the table.

The impression this left on us was ineradicable. Whether this is because he was eating while standing—and not even facing the table— or because he was eating something so vile with such gusto, or simply because he was using his fingers, I can't tell you. But in all my life I've never been able to forget it. And I was not in the least surprised when, thirty years later, my sister asked, "Do you remember Slavitsky the coachman eating a black radish?"

I also remember our head gardener. His name was Panas, the Ukrainian equivalent of Afanasy.

Small, grizzled, with only one eye, Panas was stern and taciturn. We were a little afraid of him.

Children were not allowed in the strawberry patch until the year's supply of jam had been made. That was an established rule.

But we were well organized. We would post a lookout on the nearby path. At the sight of Panas, she was supposed to sing, in a loud voice:

Many moons have waxed and waned
Since we went our separate ways.

Sometimes the lookout would play a mean trick. She would start singing, wait for the startled gluttons to come rushing out, then quickly take their place in the strawberry patch.

It wasn't really that we were afraid of Panas telling on us. It was more that we found something frightening about his very being.

He was the village wise man. And as such, he could perform all kinds of wonders. He could foretell the weather. More than that—he could also command it. He could scatter storm clouds.

I remember an occasion when we children had been promised we could go to the all-night vigil. And then someone looked up and saw that the sky had gone dark. A storm was brewing. It was decided, of course, that "the children had better stay at home." And that was that.

But Dasha the maid clearly had reasons of her own for wanting us out of the house. She thought for a moment, then said firmly, "I'll go and have a word with Panas."

My sister and I tagged along behind her. We found one-eyed Panas in the apple orchard. He was pruning and tying back branches, muttering into his beard, "Now then. Why so contrary, eh? You can't just take and take, you know. No, it's really not right. We all want a place in the sun, don't we?"

Dasha waited respectfully. When Panas was done with scolding the apple tree, she said, "Uncle! Can you send that black cloud away? The family need to go to church."

Panas gave Dasha a sharp look out of his one eye, as if to check whether or not she was telling the truth. Then he frowned, squinted, and looked up. He whispered something, then blew a little. He lifted an arm. He pulled down the sleeve of his caftan and flapped it about. He flapped the end of this sleeve a little more. He blew and he whispered. His thin beard shook. Then he rolled the sleeve back up again.

"There you are," he said. "You can go to church now. There'll be no rain."

We looked up. In the middle of the dark cloud was a small, round window of blue. It was growing bigger. The storm was moving away.

The grown-ups, for their part, were not afraid of Panas. He had secret knowledge, but he did not use it for ill. A wonder worker, it seems, is not meant to do ill.

Only when his assistant gardener, young Trifon, went and married a pockmarked girl with no dowry did people start saying that Panas must have worked a spell on him. But no one set much store by this rumor and it was, of course, groundless. It's simply that it's human nature to try and explain the inexplicable. Assistant head gardener, a young man with exalted prospects—and then, a pockmarked bride? The only answer could lie in the world of wonders.

What I remember next is how Panas left us.

It was all very strange.

He turned up unexpectedly, asking to be paid for his last days of work, since he had to hurry back home to die.

"But Panas, you're not unwell, are you?" someone asked in astonishment.

"I'm well enough for the time being. But the trees have got it in for me, you see. My time must be up. Just the other day a branch grabbed hold of me in the gooseberry patch an' wouldn't let go. Then I put a graft on an apple tree—but it wouldn't listen to me, would it? No, I'll not be staying here."

That day he was all spruced up, almost shining, and he wore a bright green ribbon in the collar of his linen shirt. His dignified appearance emphasized the gravity of his decision.

And so he left. But not completely. That is, the servants understood that he had not left completely—and so did we children.

Some chicks had hatched in the henhouse. They were all yellow except for one black one. The black one liked to keep to himself; the others all stayed together.

The other chicks got bigger and grew feathers, but the black one remained almost bald, with just the odd feather here and there. Almost a hunchback, and one-eyed into the bargain—even though no one had ever laid a finger on him. How come? What had happened to his other eye?

The wiseheads among us began to have their suspicions.

"That chick there—eh? Don't ye think?"

"Oh my God . . . Are you tellin me it's Panas?"

"What'll happen now?"

"Summat'll happen. That's for sure!"

This chick turned out to be quite a wild one. A vicious little thing.

We used to run along to look at him. He'd be standing on the very top of the dung heap. Alone, small, hunched, and bald. Head cocked, blinking his one eye. Hopping up and down furiously, not letting the other chicks anywhere near him.

The other chicks went on growing. They began to crow in their young cockerel voices, but this vicious one didn't grow at all. He stayed small and stunted. But the housekeeper said he demanded more feed than a dozen fully grown cockerels.

"What's the use of keeping a chick like that?" someone asked.

"Just you try slaughtering it!" came the answer. "That chick'll show you a thing or two!"

The chick was given the name Koldun—"Sorcerer." No one dared come right out and call him Panas.

His story ends strangely.

According to a number of witnesses, Koldun suddenly threw back his head and—in broad daylight—began to crow. After a loud "Cock-a-doodle-doo," he ran off into the forest. The forest began right there, beside the henhouse.

Since when have cockerels run off into the forest? And very fast, too! As if in answer to a summons.

He let out a loud crow—and off he ran. And never came back.

"Was that really Panas?" we asked. "What on earth made him come back as a chicken?"

"How are we to know?" replied the village wiseheads. "If he came back, then he was meant to come back. Must we really understand *everything*?"

Translated by Anne Marie Jackson

WATER SPIRIT

THE TOWN was just thirty versts from the railway station, and it was forest, bogs, and more forest all the way. Rickety wooden bridges dancing across wild streams. Backwoods. The back of beyond. Dreary, dreadful, godforsaken.

By the time Klaudia Petrova reached the town, it was already evening. She told the coachman to take her straight to the mill, which her husband had arranged to rent.

Klaudinka felt apprehensive. She didn't altogether trust her husband—he wasn't the most sensible or practical of men. But they hadn't been able to go to the mill together. He'd been due to take up his new post—and she'd been busy selling the last of the furniture and winding up other domestic affairs. So she'd left it to him to find somewhere to live. And as it was nearly summer, people told him to try the little house next to the mill. Some town official had lived there for a couple of years and had fixed the place up, painting the floors and hanging wallpaper. It would do nicely, at least for the summer—and come autumn they could find somewhere in town.

It seemed a beautiful place—a little wild, overgrown by bushes. The track didn't go all the way to the house. From the mill you had to follow a path by the river.

Klaudinka clambered out of the old carriage. She felt shattered. The coachman walked behind, carrying her belongings.

It felt damp. It smelled damp. A real backwater.

"When did he last do anything right?" she said to herself.

An old woman emerged from the house. She was terribly thin and had a nose like a beak. Her white kerchief was pulled down over her

forehead. Without a word of greeting, she handed Klaudinka a letter.
It was from her husband:

> I've been called away on business. An audit. I'll be back in two
> days. Get yourself settled in. I've hired a housekeeper. Every-
> thing's as it should be—you'll be pleased. Kisses to your dear
> little eyes and your darling baby blue hands.
>
> Volodya

"Darling baby blue hands?" she muttered. "The usual muddle!"

"So the master's asked you to work for us?" she said to the beak-
nosed woman. Her face was narrow as a sword, and the circles under
her eyes were as black as if they'd been smeared with coal.

"Yes, madam. Cooking. Milking. Or whatever."

"Oh, do we have a cow?" Klaudinka asked in surprise.

"How'd I know?" the woman replied huffily. "Only got here yesterday."

Klaudinka went inside. The rooms were small and damp. Branches
from the chokecherry tree were pressing against the windows, block-
ing the light. She began to shiver, as if she'd caught a cold.

She looked around. On a hot day it might all be pleasant enough,
but right now it was difficult to tell. There was hardly any furniture.
In all three rooms—just a bed, a small sofa, and three chairs.

"Aren't there any lamps?" she asked.

"No," the woman answered, from the kitchen.

"So how am I supposed to manage?"

"What d'you need light for? It's the white nights now. But as you
wish. Give me money—and I can go into town and get you a candle."[1]

"Good. And can you heat the samovar?"

"Give me the money and I can get charcoal too."

Klaudinka gave the woman some money and told her to buy some
food as well. The woman left the house—and disappeared.

Everything was cold, damp, dark, and dreary. Klaudinka wrapped
herself in a blanket and dozed off. Then the door slammed.

"Well? Have you brought a candle?"

No answer. And the woman entered, then stopped.

Klaudinka looked around.

A woman was standing in the doorway—but not the one from before. A stranger. Tall and broad-shouldered, hefty as any man. And with a dark kerchief on her head.

"What do you want?" asked Klaudinka.

"I'm here as a maid—on your husband's orders," the woman replied in a deep voice.

"So my husband's taken you on, has he? Have you been in service before? You know what to do?"

"Of course!" the giantess answered good-naturedly. "It's all simple enough."

"There's a lot to sort out," said Klaudinka. "But it's dark—I can't see a thing. I've sent someone into town to get a candle. What's your name?"

"Klasha."[2]

"All right, Klasha. First, attend to this bundle here. And make up my bed."

Klasha briskly unpacked the bundle, sorted everything out, then went outside. Klaudinka saw her standing beside the river, facing the water, and waving her arms as if beckoning to someone.

In time, Beak-Nose came back with the shopping. She lit the candle and made her mistress some tea.

There was something unsettling about this woman. Always twitching, and a strange gleam in her eye. Her kerchief kept shifting about; when it slipped back, you could see little bristles, as if she'd had her head shaved after a bout of typhus.

"What strange servants!" Klaudinka said to herself. "What on earth was Volodya thinking!"

That night she slept badly. She just couldn't get warm, and a mosquito kept whining close to her ear.

"A few more weeks," she said to herself, "and the place will be swarming with them."

In the morning, she woke with a headache. On the table, next to some things from her valise, she saw a passport. She picked it up and looked inside. "Klaudia Petrova," she read. "Widow."

For a moment everything went dark.

"Why my name? And why widow? Seems I really have fallen ill!" She looked again. No doubt about it. "Klaudia Petrova—Widow." She read on. "Age: 30. Peasant. Resident of Vologda Province."

"Oh, it must be Klasha—but how silly that we have the same name and surname."

All this was scary and horrible. As if she'd met her double.

She went into the kitchen—and found Beak-Nose, on her own.

"Give me some tea," said Klaudinka.

Beak-Nose jumped, dropping her knife. She'd merely been peeling potatoes, but it was as if she'd been caught in some unimaginable crime.

"Tell me," said Klaudinka, "is Klasha's last name Petrova?"

"Petrova. Yes, Petrova," Beak-Nose muttered warily.

"And what's your name?"

Beak-Nose turned away.

"Marya," she said crossly. "As if it matters."

She had strange ways, this Marya. She never looked you in the eye, and she turned away when answering a question.

"Where *is* Klasha?"

"In the river. Where else? That's where he's from."

"Where *who's* from?"

"Who do you think? Klasha!"

Marya, evidently, was soft in the head.

Klaudinka went back to her room. Outside the window was a thick mist, white as steam. The room was damp. In the corners the wallpaper was peeling away.

Marya brought in the tea and milk, and some pretzels. She set everything down on the table, glanced behind the door and out of the window, then went right up to Klaudinka.

"Promise you won't tell on me," she whispered, "but Klasha's not really Klasha. She's Ivan."

Klaudinka's eyes widened.

"Don't let on," Marya continued, "but she worked here for two years as a coachman."

"I don't understand!" said Klaudinka in bewilderment. "How come she's a maid now?"

"Well, you don't have any horses—so what else could she do? She can't go anywhere else, can she? And the mill's not working."

Marya leaned right forward. Her face was so close that Klaudinka could smell the salted cucumbers on her breath.

"A spirit," she whispered, "an unclean spirit. From the river, she is. Yes, this Ivan of yours is from the backwater behind the mill."

She drew herself up and began to walk toward the door, but then she stopped and turned around.

"Not an icon in the house," she said in a loud voice. "No wonder you end up with beings like him. And there'll be worse to come, I tell you."

"She's out of her mind!" thought Klaudinka, "Oh God, I hope Volodya comes soon." Her head ached. Spots danced before her eyes.

"I'll have a rest, then go into town. I need to talk to someone—even if it's only the pharmacist. I don't know anyone here at all!"

She had a little cry. Then she lay down, tucked herself up, and fell asleep. When she woke, she realized she'd slept through nearly the whole day. What had woken her was the sound of someone else in the room. Huge and imposing, Klasha was standing by the table with a plate in her hand, evidently putting things out for supper.

"Klasha," said Klaudinka, "is it true you used to work as a coachman?"

Klasha came over to the bed. Up close, her face looked puffy, with bright eyes and white lashes, like a little calf.

"A coachman?" she repeated calmly. "Well, we all have to work, don't we?"

"So it's true?"

Klasha did not answer.

"Tell me, Klasha, do you know this Marya well?"

"Marya Sova?[3] Of course I know her. Who doesn't?"

"What do you mean?"

"Spent eighteen months inside. Food for prison bedbugs, she was."

Klaudinka sat straight up in bed. "Why? Did she steal something?"

"*Steal something?* No. She killed her husband."

"Why…why on earth did they let her out?"

"This is why," said Klasha, tapping her forehead. "Her kind aren't so easy to keep in prison."

"You mean she's dangerous?" said Klaudinka, taking fright.

Klasha shrugged and went out of the room.

"Good God! What is all this? I'd better get dressed right away and go into town. I can't stay here with these crazy women."

Klaudinka got up and checked the door. Seeing that it could be bolted, she calmed down a little.

"One way or another I'll get through the night—and Volodya will be here tomorrow. Anyway, where would I go in town? There probably aren't any hotels at all."

Marya came in and asked what to make for dinner.

"Oh, anything really," answered Klaudinka, eyeing Marya cautiously. "Perhaps some fish?"

Marya looked around fearfully and shook a finger at Klaudinka.

"Shhh! Ivan will be angry! When he's around, you must treat fish with respect!" She bent down. Once again bringing her face very close to Klaudinka's, she went on in an emphatic whisper, "Can't you see? Ivan's from the river!"

Klaudinka cowered against the wall, staring in horror at the madwoman in front of her. "On second thought, Marya, I'm not hungry. I'll just have some tea."

Marya winked at Klaudinka, glanced pointedly at the door, and went out.

Klaudinka shut the door and bolted it for the night. She opened the window a crack. It was a light night, very quiet. She could hear the whine of mosquitoes. Across the river, someone was singing in a heartrending voice:

> Little torch, burn away,
> I'll burn along with you today…

Klaudinka threw a shawl over her shoulders and sat by the window.

A pale, starless night was quietly unfolding. A thin strip of pink stretched across the sky. And she could hear the lazy plash of the river.

Out of the bushes appeared a skinny, dark figure with something white on its head. It was Marya. She came up to the window.

"Madam," she whispered, and laughed. "Come and have a peek over here. Under the willow. It's our Klasha. You'll have a right laugh, you will. Just climb out your window. But quiet—mind you don't scare her. You'll have a right laugh, I'm telling you."

Perhaps because Marya was laughing herself, Klaudinka didn't feel in the least scared. She sat on the windowsill, then jumped lightly down to the ground.

"Here, over here! Have a look," Marya whispered, now laughing still more.

Not understanding a thing, Klaudinka took a few steps, over toward the bank. There, under the willow, was a pale shape. Klasha?

She went closer.

No, it wasn't Klasha. Sitting beneath the willow with his feet in the water, wringing out his long gray beard, was a naked old man. The water from his beard was streaming straight into the river.

"Who's that?" Klaudinka called out.

The old man turned around, then slipped beneath the branches of the willow and disappeared. There was just the glimmer of his bright eyes and white lashes. Or had she imagined it?

She waited a moment, then went back in through the window. Marya had disappeared.

"How absurd!" she said to herself. "Why say it's Klasha when it's some old man?"

She closed the window, checked the bolt, and went around the room, making the sign of the cross in all four corners. Then she lay down and pulled the covers up to her chin.

In the morning, she was woken by a cheery voice: "Klaudinka! Open up! It's me, Volodya!"

*

Klasha had vanished into thin air—or maybe into the water?

And it turned out that Volodya hadn't even spoken to any possible maid, let alone hired one. The only woman he'd hired was Beak-Nose. He'd been in a hurry and hadn't made any inquiries about her. He hadn't known that she was unwell.

"But what about her passport?" said Klaudinka. "I saw her passport! I could hardly believe it. We have exactly the same name! Klaudia Petrova!"

"You must have been looking at your own passport," reasoned Volodya.

"Certainly not! It said she's thirty years old and a peasant and a widow. And I'm only twenty. And you're alive!"

"Now don't go upsetting yourself, that's the main thing," Volodya replied, his hands shaking as he stroked his wife's head. "I asked Marya. She says there was no one else here at all. Only her."

Klaudinka threw up her hands in despair.

"But why? What makes her say that? When she told me herself that Klasha was really Ivan!"

Volodya gave his wife a frightened look and began to gabble. "You must have just imagined it, darling. We all imagine things when we have a fever. Now lie down in bed and keep still. I'll go into town and fetch the doctor. To check your temperature, I mean—I believe every word that you say. No need to be afraid now—I'll take Marya with me. Best if she stays in town. And try not to upset yourself. That's the main thing."

He smiled weakly, his lips trembling. He grabbed his wallet from the table and tried to put it into his pocket—but it dropped to the floor. He picked it up a second time—and once again it slipped past his pocket and dropped to the floor. With a look of despair, he ran out of the room.

Translated by Robert and Elizabeth Chandler and Sian Valvis

WOLF NIGHT

In the morning, the gardener came to light the stove in the bedroom. During the night, he said, wolves had made off with two dogs that belonged to someone leasing a house in Shepetovka. It had been a terrible year and wolves were no longer scared of anything. People said this meant war.

"But they don't bother people, do they? They don't bite *people*?" asked Ilka. She blushed. The old gardener would realize she was afraid. "Gentry should know better!" he was probably saying to himself.

But he appeared not to think any the worse of her.

"What do you mean?" he replied. "They bite people all right! Only the year before last, there was a beggar woman in Lychovka. Gnawed to death, she was. Wolves have gotten brazen nowadays—worse than people."

What he said was frightening, but Ilka liked talking to this old man. He was so calm and methodical. First he lit the kindling. Then he set the taper at an angle, to make a taller flame. The resinous wood smelled good as it burned. Very good. And there was little in her life that was good.

Everything was too bright, too strong, too blaring. Yesterday, at dinner, she had said, "I can't drink water. It's too wet."

And everyone had laughed.

Stanya had laughed too. He shouldn't have. He was her husband and he should have stood up for his sick wife. She was very sick and very unhappy.

And this would go on for another three months.

If she'd known that everything would turn out so horribly, nothing would have induced her to marry. She would have studied. Not that that would have been easy. She'd had enough of studying.

But how could she have imagined the horror of village life? Always someone being slaughtered. If it wasn't a hen, it was a goose. If it wasn't calves, it was chickens. Fattened up. Squeezed and groped. Then killed and eaten. And if not killed and eaten, then sold, so that someone else could kill and eat them.

All so vile and frightening. Life was cruel.

And so very joyless.

At first Ilka had liked the cat. It was soft and warm. And then she'd seen it in the kitchen garden. It walked along very silently, as if across a cinema screen, ate some kind of grass, and vomited. After that, the cat disgusted her.

And her country Stanya was not the Stanya she'd known in the city. There he had been smart and fashionable.

"Your fiancé's so chic!" other young ladies had said to her.

Here he was boring and lethargic. He didn't answer her questions. All he ever did was smoke—and slap down his cards while playing patience.

Talking to him was impossible. She'd realized this long ago. Yet she went on trying, simply because there was no one else to talk to. Just two old aunts and some distant relative, a hanger-on who was stone deaf. They could hardly be called human beings.

The evenings were long, boring, and frightening. They all sat together in the dining room. And if you went through the study and into the living room, right up to the garden windows, there was no longer any light from the door. You were all on your own, with nothing between you and the black night.

If you put your forehead to the glass, you could make out a few trees—faint, uncertain shadows. She knew that behind them was a fence, a track, and some woodland. On the track people had seen the paw prints of wolves. At night the wolves came right up to the fence, looked through the slits, and howled at the house and its lit windows.

*

"Stanya!" Ilka says to her husband. "I'm frightened. Wolves have eaten a beggar woman."

Stanya shrugs. "What's there to be frightened of?" he says crossly. "You're sitting safely at home."

He doesn't understand! She isn't frightened for herself—she's just frightened. Frightened because such things happen, because this is what it's like in the world.

"The weather's gotten better at last," he says with a yawn. "We could have a Christmas Eve picnic. We could invite a dozen people from town and have lunch together over in your Kalitovka. I'd go over the day before and have the stoves lit in the dining room and the living room. I could get the chef from the club. Then you could come in the morning. And we could go back with everyone else. Or perhaps stay the night. What do you think?"

Kalitovka was a small estate belonging to Ilka's grandmother. A large house right in the middle of the forest. Nobody lived there.

"It won't be very nice there at night," she says. "And the furniture's under wraps, and the windows are all naked."

"So what? It's easy enough to remove the dust sheets."

Stanya was stubborn. Always had to have his own way.

"Stanya! I don't want to go. And I don't want guests!" she says. "I'm not well." And she begins to cry.

And there's no knowing whether or not he'll give way.

In the night it is quiet and black. Not dark, but black, pitch-black. Through the half-open shutters she can see the white of the window frames.

Cocks are crowing out in the yard. Like the whistle of a distant locomotive.

She's already dozing. The bell keeps ringing and ringing. The very last guests are drawing up outside.

God, how tired she feels! And this empty house is so cold!

A long, long table in the huge dining room. Where's it from? There are plates and glasses on it, but nothing else.

Stanya greets the guests, apologizes for something or other, and makes small talk. There are a great many guests and she doesn't know any of them. And no one says even a word to her. It's as if they don't see her. Perhaps because they're all so smart, while she's in her old school pinafore.

Then everyone sits down at the table. She sits down too.

Behind her are three huge windows. Huge, black, and naked.

The guests are wildly cheerful. All speaking at once and laughing. Shouting, clattering plates, making a hubbub.

And then—a sudden silence. Everyone freezes. Wide-open staring eyes. Horror on every face. Everyone is looking outside, through the naked black windows.

There must, Ilka realizes, be something dreadful out there. Very slowly, hunching her shoulders, she turns around.

What is it?

The window is alive with points of green light. Points of living green light. Twinkling. Shifting about a little, and always in pairs.

"Wolves!" someone whispers. "Be quiet! Don't move! We're surrounded by wolves."

It's happened! Just what she was afraid of. She'd seen it coming.

"A-a-a-ah! I'm sca-a-a-ared!"

"What's the matter?" says an unfamiliar voice. "Wait, I'll light a..."

A blinding light.

"Well? What is it?"

No, it's a familiar voice.

"Stanya, my dear, please let's not go to Kalitovka! I'm frightened!"

"Idiot!" Stanya grumbles. "Screaming your head off at night! Instead of saying anything sensible, you wake the whole house!"

The whole house, of course, meant Stanya.

Still, let him grumble. Really, she quite liked it. It calmed her down.

All went dark again. For a long, long time. Out in the yard, the cock crowed. No, it was the bell. Who could it be?

"Must be a telegram," Stanya says. "Go and open the door. The servants haven't heard, and I've got a cold."

She doesn't want to get up.

"Go on," Stanya says. "You're my wife and you must do as I say."

She gets up. Without lighting a candle, she fumbles her way out of the room. She reaches the stairs. Very carefully, gripping the banister, she goes down into the hall.

Another sharp ring.

Beside the front door is a little window. Through it she can see the porch. She looks out.

The moon! A miracle—it hadn't been there before. And now there it was—round, clear, and malevolent. Glittering on the snow.

And she can see dogs. But there's something strange about them. All in a half-circle, sitting back on their tails. Heads pulled down into their shoulders, as if they've caught colds too. All staring at the porch, tongues lolling out.

There on the porch is another, bigger dog. It's restless, stamping up and down. Then it leaps up and seizes the bell rope between its teeth. As it leaps, Ilka sees that its tail is straight and thick.

A wolf.

Yes, these were wolves.

"They've gotten brazen," the old gardener had said. "Worse than people."

Ilka huddles in the corner, afraid to move. She no longer looks out of the window.

Ever so slowly, the front door starts to open.

"It's the moon!" Ilka thinks. "The moon's opening the door to them! It's in league with them! Oh my God!"

"This is getting to be quite impossible," the moon says indignantly. "You've turned into a regular hysteric. You need a bucket of cold water thrown over you every morning. There's no other way we'll get any sense out of you."

There's something familiar about this voice. Something that isn't so frightening. Of course, it's Stanya!

"Stanya! Quick! Light a candle!"

"Please! Do me a favor! Go and stay with your oh so clever mother. A fine way she must have brought you up, to make you into such a hysteric. Crying all day, yelling all night! Enough to wear out anyone's nerves!"

Stanya is boring. Evil-tempered. He curses and rants, but still— better him than the moon or the wolves. Yes, no doubt about that.

"Stanya," she says gently. "Stanya, be patient. Wait till it's light. Then you can rant at me all you like. Say something nice to me now. What do you think? What shall we call our little one?"

Translated by Robert and Elizabeth Chandler

PART FIVE
from *Earthly Rainbow* (1952)

BABA YAGA

IN THE words of the magic tales: "Baba Yaga Bone-Leg rides in a mortar, pushes herself on with a pestle, and sweeps away her tracks with a broom."

And in the words of teachers of literature: "Baba Yaga is the goddess of whirlwinds and snowstorms."

In children's books, Baba Yaga was depicted as a wild, gaunt old woman, with evil green eyes, tousled gray hair, and a fang sticking out of her mouth. She was thin and bony. She was very, very frightening—and she ate children.

The word "goddess" conjured up images of beauty—of Venus or Diana. We'd seen statues of them, images of perfection. We'd heard people say, "She looks like a goddess." And then it turned out that our own goddess, our own Russian goddess, was this terrible witch—a hideous and vicious old woman. It seemed ridiculous and absurd.

But if we're to be honest about it, can any of our ancient gods be called beautiful? Lel', perhaps, the god of spring? But he wasn't so very popular and has not survived in folk memory.

The figures who have survived are the house spirit, the forest spirit, and Baba Yaga. Nowadays the names of all three are used for insults.

The house spirit—a stern little monster—may have been a guardian of the hearth, responsible for keeping a home in good order, but he behaved like some old-style landowner. He brawled. He made a racket. He tormented the horses and got up to all kinds of mischief in the stables. He pinched the maids till they were black and blue all over. He had a sense of justice, but he was willful and autocratic:

"Maybe I'll take a liking to you, or maybe I won't. And if I don't, you'll soon wish you were dead."

As for the forest spirit, it takes courage even to mention him. He made wild hooting noises, confused people and led them into impassable thickets. He did not have a single good deed to his name. He had an evil temper. His only aim, his only role was to frighten, to lead astray—to bring someone to a bad end and then plait a tangle of grasses and weeds over the scene of the crime.

Only the *rusalka* was beautiful. But if she let you see her—if you were unable to take your eyes off her—it was because she wanted to lure you to your doom. She used her sweetness and delicate beauty as a lure, to make you feel sorry for her. You'd see her sitting there on a branch—a little woman, though she wasn't really a woman at all, since her lower half was the tail of a fish. There she would sit, just above the water, hiding this tail of hers in the weeds. A little woman, shy and delicate—and always weeping bitterly. Had she merely sat there and beckoned, few people would have come any closer. But how could they help going closer when they saw her weeping? They felt sorry for her. Her lure was pity. A very dangerous goddess indeed.

But Baba Yaga is still more terrifying—and more interesting. And more Russian. Other nations did not have goddesses like Baba Yaga.

Baba Yaga lived on the edge of the forest, in a windowless, doorless hut standing on chicken legs. Though, in fact, the hut always did have a door—facing the forest. So a sneaky young hero, having somehow learned the words of the spell, had only to say, "Little hut, little hut, turn your face toward me and your back on the forest!" And the hut would turn around.

Baba Yaga lived alone. Except for a cat. Total solitude was too much even for Yaga. The cat gave off a sense of warmth and coziness. He purred and had soft fur. That was why Yaga liked to have a cat around. As for people, she hated them and never sought them out. People came to her of their own accord to learn various wise secrets, and they always managed to cheat her. She knew only too well that every human approach brought with it deception and hurt.

"I can smell the smell of a Russian," she would sometimes say to herself. And this smell always brought trouble.

Some brave young hero would tell her a pack of lies, make false promises, elicit from her whatever he needed to know, cheat her, and then slip away. She could expect neither gratitude nor honest payment.

And every time she heard the words of the spell, every time the hut turned on its chicken legs, Yaga knew what was coming. And every time, she still stupidly believed in the honesty of the human soul: "It's just not possible. They can't all be like that."

One day a poor little orphan girl turns up. Her stepmother has thrown her out of the house, sending her off to certain death. But Yaga has seen this before—she knows only too well that no human whelp, however little, however poor and pitiful, is without its share of guile. And as well as guile, this little pup of a girl will have with her a little comb, a little towel, and a piece of fatback. She will give this fatback to the cat—and the cat will betray his owner. That warm, soft, purring puss, that flatterer and caresser—he too will betray her. And the squeaking gates will betray her—the girl will just smear them with oil. Nothing but treachery and betrayal. All so sad and bo-o-oring.

There Yaga sits, cross as cross can be, sharpening her one fang.

"I should eat up every one of these boys and girls. But they're cunning, they always manage to slip away. They appear out of nowhere. They pay homage to my great wisdom. They lie and cheat—and then they take to their heels, time and again."

The treacherous cat and the dishonorable gates release the sly little runt of a girl. Yaga rushes off in pursuit. The girl throws down her comb—and a dense forest appears. Yaga gnaws her way through the trees. The girl throws down her towel—and a broad, flowing river appears. Yaga begins to drink up the river—but the girl is soon far away, out of reach. And the vile little creature has made off with all of Yaga's secrets.

So there she is once again. Staring out from her chicken-leg hut, nose almost touching the trees. She feels b-o-r-e-d. Would winter never come?

Spring brings anxiety. Nature starts to live it up. People and animals make love. They give birth to cunning little children—which means trouble. Then comes summer. In the heat, the forest seethes with life. The trees do their work; the wind scatters their seeds. The forest feels pleased with itself. Stupid old fool of a forest. It loves life, the immortality of the earth.

Then—autumn. A first dusting of snow. Yaga cheers up.

And then, at last, winter.

The winds begin to blow. The eight grandsons of the god Stribog.[1] Fierce and vicious—beings after her own heart. Soon paths will be hidden by blizzards. Whirlwinds will whirl their crystal dust, snowstorms will sing their songs. At last!

Yaga gets into her mortar and pushes off with her pestle. The mortar knocks against hillocks; it bumps, leaps, and jumps; it soars through a whirl of snow. She has strands of ice in her hair; her bony knees poke out. She is terrible and powerful. Free as free can be. She flies over the earth like the song of the storm.

Who has ever seen her? As knights dying on a battlefield glimpse the Valkyries, so people freezing to death see Yaga through their closed eyes.

Yaga leaps out of her mortar. She sings and dances. She seizes a soft young birch. She twists, twirls, bends, and snaps it. A loud moan—and powdered snow flies up into the air like silver smoke. Then Yaga throws herself at a scarecrow. He's stuffed with straw and someone's wrapped him around some rosebushes for the winter. She throws her arms around him and dances with him. Wild and drunken, she shakes him about, then hurls him to the ground.

"Let me go!" begs the scarecrow. "Don't torment me. I don't want you! I've got a rose for a heart."

Baba Yaga howls and weeps. On she whirls, crazed and vicious. Roaming the fields and valleys again, looking for someone new to torment.

A traveler. He's just gotten out of his sleigh, he's trying to find the road. Aha! She spins him around, knocks him into a snowdrift, and flings snow into his eyes.

Where was he going? To some Masha or other. Some sweet, jolly, warm little Mashenka. What does he want with her now? He's all white now, whiter than white. His eyelashes and eyebrows are white. Icy white curls poke out from under his cap. Wonderful—free and wonderful is the song of the blizzard. It enchants him. Mashenka? What does he care about Mashenka now? No more than he cares about a colorful piece of cloth on a fence. Can he even remember her? Eyes of green crystal are looking into his soul. They fill him with terror and joy, and his soul sings and laughs. Never, never has it known such delight.

Baba Yaga! Terrible old hag! Accursed man-eater! How wonderful you are with your song and your crystal eyes! You are a GODDESS. So take me into your death—which is better than life!

The blizzard falls silent. It's warm and dark in the little hut on chicken legs. The broom stands in the corner, exchanging winks with the pestle. The faithless cat purrs sleepily, stretching his back, pretending...

Baba Yaga is lying on the stove. Water drips onto the floor from her icy hair. A bony leg sticks out from under some rags.

Boring. Boring. B—o—r—i—n—g.

Translated by Robert and Elizabeth Chandler

VOLYA

O to live free, freer than free;
O to live free as the wind.
                              —Novgorod folk song

"SEE, summer's here!"

"Spring's come. It's May. Spring."

How can you tell? Spring? Summer? A few days of stifling heat—
and then: rain, a little May snow, and it's back to lighting the stove.
And then: it's stifling hot again.

It wasn't like that for us. Our northern spring was a real event.

The sky changed—and so did the air, the earth, the trees.

Secret powers—all the secret saps and juices accumulated during
the winter—would suddenly burst free.

Animals roar; wild beasts snarl. The air fills with the sound of
wings. High up, just beneath the clouds, like a heart soaring over the
earth—a triangle of cranes. The river—all crashing ice floes. Streams
babble and gurgle along ravines. The whole earth trembles with light,
with ringing, with rustles, whispers, and loud cries.

And the nights did not bring calm, did not cover our eyes in
peaceful darkness. Day would fade; it would turn a pale pink but
never depart.

People would wander about, pale, languid, listening intently—like
poets in search of a rhyme for an image already clear in their minds.

It grew difficult to live an ordinary life.

What could one do? Fall in love? Write poems about love and death?

Not enough, not nearly enough. Our northern spring is too powerful. With all its light, with all its whispers, rustles, and ringing it lures us away—toward the open horizon, toward free *volya*.

Volya is not at all the same as freedom.

Freedom—*liberté*—is the rightful state of a citizen who has not infringed the laws governing his or her country.

"Freedom" can be translated into all languages and is understood by all peoples.

Volya is untranslatable.

When you hear the words "a free man," what do you see? You see this: A gentleman walking along the street, cap tilted slightly back, cigarette between his teeth, hands in his pockets. Passing a watchmaker's, he glances at the clock, nods—yes, he still has time—and goes off into the park, along the embankment. He strolls about for a while, spits out his cigarette, whistles a few notes, and enters a little café.

What do you see when you hear the word *volya*?

An unbroken horizon. Someone striding along, sure-footed but not thinking about tracks or paths, not going anywhere in particular. Bareheaded. The wind ruffles his hair and blows it over his eyes—since for his kind, every wind is a tailwind. A bird flies by, spreading its wings wide, and this man waves both arms high in the air, calls out to the bird in a wild voice, then bursts into laughter.

Freedom is a matter of law.

Volya takes no account of anything.

Freedom is an individual's civil status.

Volya is a feeling.

We Russians, the children of Old Russia, were born with this feeling of *volya*.

Peasant children, children of the rich bourgeoisie, children of the intelligentsia—regardless of background and upbringing, all sensed and understood the call of *volya*.

Thousands of vagrants, such as you'd never see in any other country, answered this call. And if there were fewer vagrants in other countries, this was not because their better living conditions and stricter laws meant that there was neither need nor opportunity to leave the home nest. We too treated vagrants strictly. We arrested them, sentenced them, and tried to force them to settle. Anyway, it's not as if every Russian who left their home had a hard life there. No, there must be some other explanation.

Was it simply a love of journeying?

But if you buy one of these vagrants a ticket, send them with money, in luxury, to some wonderful destination, to the Caucasus or the Crimea, they will jump out somewhere near Kursk, drink away the money, and head off to Arkhangelsk on foot. Why?

"Wood tar's cheap up there."

"And why do you need wood tar?"

"Well, you never know."

The point isn't the tar, it's the need for movement. To follow your nose, to go where your eyes look.

There we have it—the eternal aim of the Russian soul.

To go where your eyes look.

Like in the old fairy tales—to go thither, I know not whither.

Old and young walk and walk. They walk the length and breadth of Russia—this way and that way, along her roads, along her paths, across her virgin soil.

Catch one of these wanderers, take them back to their birthplace—and they're off again at once. In the north we used to call them Spiridon Turnabouts.[1]

A Spiridon Turnabout strides along the road, wearing heaven knows what kind of hat—a Jewish kippah, a monk's skullcap, a crush hat, a Panama hat without a brim or even a Panama without a top. You name it—even a woman's kerchief. Shoes falling apart and no footcloths,[2] a knapsack or cloth bundle on his back. A tin kettle hanging at his side.

He strides along as if that were his be-all and end-all in life, but he has no idea where he's heading, or why.

Among these Spiridon Turnabouts are representatives of every class—from runaway monks to the sons of village priests or rich merchants.

In Novgorod Province—as I remember—there lived an old district police superintendent. As in a fairy tale, he had three sons. Except that it was not only the two eldest who were normal and sensible. All three were regular, sensible boys, and all three went to military school. The eldest, who was in good health and good spirits, graduated from the school and received his commission. Then he went back home for a few days. He seemed lost in thought. But not for long. One morning they found his boots and uniform in his room, but no sign of the boy himself. Where he'd gone and what he was now wearing, no one knew.

A few months later, he returned. Though that's hardly the word— he made a brief appearance, and in such a state that it would have been better if he hadn't shown up at all. He was drunk, dressed in rags—yet full of joy, even ecstatic.

His father was in despair. He did all he could. He revoked his paternal blessing. He cursed and wept. He offered his son money. He took to drink himself. Nothing helped.

The only response to his arguments and entreaties was a load of balderdash about the importance of understanding the fern flower,[3] and about the birds in heaven—how they pray to God every dawn.

And with that the boy went on his way.

And two years later, the second son left home in exactly the same fashion.

When the third son turned sixteen, the father decided not to wait for him to get lost in thought. He summoned three policemen and ordered the boy to be flogged. Strangely enough, this had a positive effect. The boy graduated successfully and even got started on his military career. Maybe he'd have been all right anyway; maybe he wouldn't have gotten lost in thought and his father's heroic measures were neither here nor there. But we didn't keep in touch, and I've no idea what became of him.

Until recently there were always pilgrims in Russia. They went from monastery to monastery and were not always led by religious feeling. What mattered was simply to be on the move. They felt the same pull as migratory birds. A mysteriously strong pull. We Russians are not so cut off from nature as Europeans. We have only a thin overlay of culture; nature can quickly and easily pierce through it. In spring, when the earth awakes and her voices grow louder, summoning us to *volya*, we have no choice but to follow her resonant call. We are like mice in thrall to a medieval sorcerer playing a pipe.

I remember how my first cousin, a fifteen-year-old cadet, a quiet, obedient boy and a good student, twice ran away from his military school and made his way deep into the northern forest. When he was tracked down and returned to his home, he was quite unable to explain himself. Both these occasions were in early spring.

"What were you thinking of?" we asked.

He smiled shyly. "I don't know. Something was pulling me."

Later, as an adult, he would look back on this chapter of his life with a kind of tender astonishment. He was unable to understand or explain what it was that had so pulled him.

He had been able to imagine his mother's anguish and had felt desperately sorry for her. And he'd known very well what a hullaba-loo there'd be at his military school. But all that had been a mere blur. His ordinary life had seemed like a dream. And his wonderful forest life had felt real. He even found it hard to understand how he could have lived such a tedious, difficult, and unnatural life for so long—for fifteen whole years.

But he hadn't done very much thinking. For the main part, it had been a time of feeling. He had felt *volya*: "Dense forest. You wander along without a path. Only pine trees and sky—no one else in the world. And suddenly, with all your might, you let yourself go. At the top of your voice, you let out a cry of such wild, primal joy that for hours afterward all you can do is laugh and shake."

Later, he said more: "Once I was lucky enough to see a bear enjoying music. He was lying on his back beside a giant tree felled by a storm. It was a very old tree. The trunk had split apart and the wood was all splintered. And there was the bear, stretching out a front paw and plucking the wood. The slivers hummed and buzzed, creaked and cracked. And all the time, the bear was letting out quiet growls of pleasure. He certainly liked this music . . . then he seized some more slivers and played with them too. I'll never forget the sight. A white night, a northern white night. In the Far North, by the way, a white night isn't as pale as, say, in Petersburg. In the Far North it's pinker, because there's always a glow in the sky. Dawn starts to brighten before the evening light fades. There's a rosy haze in the forest and, in this haze, a remarkable picture: a bear making music and a boy watching him from the bushes and almost crying—maybe he really does cry—out of love and delight. Who could ever forget this?"

This boy, incidentally, had been hard to track down. Information about him had been sent to police all over northern Russia, but it was only by chance that he was caught—in the north of Olonets Province. On his way through a village, he stopped at an inn. He'd spent the night in the woods. It was a cold day and was raining. He was chilled to the bone and he wanted a hot meal. He asked for some cabbage soup.

"What kind?"

"With meat," he replied.

The innkeeper was shocked. "What do you mean? It's Friday. What kind of person eats meat on a Friday?" And he sent for the constable.

The constable came and asked for his passport. The boy, needless to say, didn't have a passport. He was arrested and questioned. He burst into tears and confessed all. And so ended his days of *volya*.

Nowadays, you often hear talk like this: "Oh to be in Russia. Even for just one day. I'd go to the forest—*that* can't have changed. I'd go for a good wander. I'd get a lungful of sweet *volya*."

I too have my memories. There, it's always spring. A white night. The small hours, perhaps two o'clock. It's light, there's pink in the sky.

I'm standing on a terrace. Below me, beyond the flower garden— a river. The muffled sound of a bell, and the cries of a young boy goading his oxen along the towpath. A barge is being towed toward the distant Volga.

My heart misses a beat, and my tired, sleepless eyes half close in the pink light.

Across the river, someone overwhelmed by joy belts out a wild, senseless, ecstatic song:

> The boy lived free, freer than free;
> The boy lived free as the wind.
> If a bird flew by, high in the sky,
> He shot—not once did he miss.
> If a maiden came by,
> Brightening his way,
> He swiftly gave her a kiss.

And then the refrain—heartrending, piercingly joyful, like a sudden yelp, coming from somewhere too deep in the soul:

> O to live free, free as the wind!
> Sing *Volya*, *Volya*, *Volya*!

And somehow, not knowing what I'm doing, I raise my hand and wave at the dawn and this wild song. And I laugh, and cry out, "*Vo-o-o-ly-a-a-a!*"

Translated by Robert and Elizabeth Chandler
and Maria Evans

AFTERWORD

Spirits of Home, Forest, Field, and Water

FOR PEASANTS in Russia, Ukraine, and Belarus, every building and place had its resident spirit. Some were thought to be benevolent, others malevolent. Their origin is ancient, though some of their characteristics changed over time.

The most important of these spirits, the house spirit or *domovoy*, was generally seen as helpful and protective, though sometimes bad-tempered and quick to take offense. The Russian writer and scholar Andrey Sinyavsky describes him as follows:

> The *domovoy* is the secret inhabitant and secret master of the house. Every peasant hut has its own *domovoy*. He is often referred to as "master," and even more often as "grandfather," a very deferential form of address. This has to do with the fact that the *domovoy*, evidently, in deepest antiquity, goes back to the clan's worshiped forefather, to the family's founder. In other words, the *domovoy* continues the religion connected with the worship of ancestors who became protectors of the clan, preservers of the family hearth and home. That is why the *domovoy* is usually busy by the hearth. In the peasant hut, he lives over the stove, behind the stove, or under the stove.[1]

Willful and fiercely conservative, the *domovoy* was an upholder of tradition. If angered, he could cause serious disruption, harming livestock, banging pots, tangling needlework, making furniture creak, spreading manure on the door, or even choking people in their sleep.[2]

In some regions, the *domovoy* was responsible for everything relating to a peasant home, including the livestock; in others there was a subordinate yard spirit, or *dvorovoy*, who took care of everything outside the hut itself. The barn, the threshing floor, and other smaller buildings also had their particular spirits.

Another important figure was the bathhouse spirit, the *bannik*— or bathhouse devil (*banny chort*), as Teffi calls him. Unlike the *domovoy*, the *bannik* was malevolent. In part, this probably reflects objective dangers relating to the building itself. The village bathhouse was usually a dilapidated log shack with a rudimentary stove; these buildings were known to catch fire and people sometimes suffocated in the steam or from lack of oxygen.[3]

The bathhouse, however, was also dangerous in other ways. According to Sinyavsky,

> it served as a haven for all sorts of evil spirits. This may be because of the bathhouse's connection with dampness, with soot, with darkness (evil spirits love dark, boggy water), as well as because, while steaming in the bathhouse, people sloughed off their illnesses and sins, which trickled down under the floorboards. [...] Russian families usually washed in three shifts, and never late in the evening. They were afraid of the fourth shift because that was when devils, forest spirits and the *bannik* himself washed. [...] But because the bathhouse was home to evil spirits, young girls went there to learn their fortunes.[4]

William Ryan, author of *The Bathhouse at Midnight*, writes, "The communal village bathhouse and midnight represent the conditions *par excellence* for popular magic and divination in Russia—hence the title of this book."[5]

Given all this, it may seem surprising that the bathhouse was also where peasant women most often gave birth. The reasons for this may have been mainly practical; it was easy to wash and clean up afterward and the bathhouse was relatively secluded. It can also, however, be seen as an indication that there was a certain ambivalence about all of these spirits. Few, if any, were entirely good or entirely evil.

Fields, meadows, forests, and stretches of water also had their resident spirits. The field spirit (*polevoy*) and meadow spirit (*lugovik*) were relatively benevolent. The forest spirit or *leshy*—a more important figure—was seen as a dangerous trickster; there are many accounts of him taking pleasure in misleading people and confusing them. Like all these spirits, he can best be understood as the master of a particular realm. According to the ethnographer Dmitry Zelenin, "All forest animals are obedient to the *leshy*, and sometimes he loses them at cards to his neighbors. This happens especially often with hares and squirrels, which is how people explain the mass migrations of these creatures."[6] Teffi does not write about the *leshy*, but she devotes an entire story to his less common female equivalent, the *leshachikha*. The *leshachikha* often appears as the wife of the *leshy*, but sometimes she is independent; in Teffi's story, she is presented as powerful and frightening.

The water spirit, or *vodyanoy*, was more dangerous still. Sinyavsky quotes a folk saying: "The *domovoy* teases you, the *leshy* misleads you, but the *vodyanoy* drowns you." He continues: "Of the three, the *vodyanoy* is the most wicked and dangerous. He is closest of all to the unclean force. Sickening to behold, he is usually depicted as a naked old man with a green beard tangled with slime, a swollen belly and a face bloated from drink."[7] Like the *leshy* and the *domovoy*, the *vodyanoy* is the ruler of his realm, the master of the fish in his river or lake. He is also associated with water mills; millers were often thought to be sorcerers, and the *vodyanoy* and the *vodyanitsa*—who liked to hide in deep water close to a mill—were sometimes his helpers.

The *rusalka* stands apart from the other spirits. Though associated with water, and to a lesser degree with trees, she is not the ruler of any particular place. She was associated, above all, with the unclean dead—suicides, unbaptized children, and all who did not receive a proper Christian burial. Being unclean, a *rusalka* was thought capable of damaging crops and causing illness and death. According to

Zelenin, *rusalki* remained on earth, in the place where they died, for as long as they could have been expected to live in normal circumstances.[8] According to Sinyavsky,

> Sometimes they come ashore and climb up into the trees. This is an important sign: trees, according to the religious beliefs of the ancient Slavs, were the dwelling places of the dead. *Rusalki* are afraid to go far from the water: if they dry off, they will perish. Just in case, they have a comb with which they comb their hair, and water streams down. Sometimes they rob women of their spinning and unravel it while swinging from the trees. All this attests to the very ancient origin of *rusalki*. [...] *Rusalki* combine several fundamental and related symbols: *water—woman—death—hair—spinning—fate*.[9]

Much of *Witch* is based on Teffi's recollections of her childhood summers in Volhynia.[10] A few close textual parallels show us that Teffi also drew on one of the most authoritative sources then available, a book by Sergey Maximov about Russian house and nature spirits, first published in 1903.[11] Teffi writes vividly, wittily, and with deep psychological understanding; her stories are also ethnographically sound.

—R. C.

A NOTE ON RUSSIAN NAMES

A RUSSIAN has three names: a Christian name, a patronymic (derived from the Christian name of the father), and a family name. Thus, Agafya Petrovna is the daughter of a man whose first name is Piotr, and Grigory Nikolaevich is the son of a man called Nikolay. The first name and patronymic, used together, are the normal polite way of addressing or referring to a person; the family name is used less often. Close friends or relatives usually address each other by one of the many diminutive, or affectionate, forms of their first names. Lena, for example, is a diminutive of Yelena, Grisha of Grigory, and Varya of Varvara. Volodya and Volodka are both diminutives of Vladimir, Klasha and Klaudinka are both diminutives of Klaudia, and Masha and Manya are both diminutives of Marya. Less obviously, Tolya is a diminutive of Anatoly, Kolya of Nikolay, Tyoma of Artyom, and Venyushka of Avenir. Ganya and Ganka are both diminutives of Agafya. There are many double diminutives; Varenka is a double diminutive of Varvara, Vanechka of Ivan, and Manechka and Marusenka are both double diminutives of Marya.

Married or older peasants are often addressed and referred to by their patronymic alone, or by a slightly abbreviated form of it. Thus, the cook mentioned in the first pages of "The Dog" is referred to simply as Fedotych.

Many traditional Russian and Ukrainian names are derived from Greek. Yavdokha, for example, comes from the Greek Eudokia (*eudokeo* meaning "to be well pleased"). Ustiusha is a diminutive of Ustinya, a Russian equivalent of the Latin Justina (*justin* meaning "fair").

Most of the stories from *Witch* are set in the province of Volhynia, then part of the Russian Empire and now a part of Ukraine. At the time, Polish, Yiddish, and Ukrainian were all widely spoken there and several of Teffi's characters bear Polish names. Teffi, naturally, transliterates those into the Cyrillic alphabet, but we have reverted to the original Polish spellings. Jadzia (pronounced Yadya) is a diminutive of Jadwiga, which is derived from the Old German Hedwig (a compound word meaning "battle fight"). Kornelia is a variant of Caroline, and Eleonora of Helen.

Lastly, a Russian *nyanya* differs in many ways from an English nanny. We have therefore chosen to transliterate the word rather than translate it. A *nyanya* was typically employed first as a wet nurse and then as a more general household servant, often becoming an integral part of the family. It was common for a *nyanya* to be more deeply and intimately involved in a child's life than his or her mother. Pushkin's *nyanya* was deeply important to him, and *nyanyas* play a prominent role in many classic works of Russian literature.

—R.C.

THIS TRANSLATION

TEFFI is difficult to translate. I have said a little in the foreword about her Pushkinian grace and deft use of repetition. She also makes the most of two freedoms—the freedom to omit words and an extreme freedom of word order—that are available only in a highly inflected language like Russian or Latin. And the precision of her psychological understanding, visual descriptions, and references to details of nineteenth-century Russian life leaves a translator with no room to maneuver.

Her use of dialect and substandard speech presents a particular difficulty. Many of the stories are set in Volhynia, in what is now western Ukraine, and the peasants and less educated characters speak a language heavily influenced by both Ukrainian and Polish. There is no logically satisfactory way of translating such speech. On the one hand, much of the texture of these stories is lost if all the characters—educated and uneducated alike—are made to speak the same standard English; on the other hand, translating their speech into a particular English or American dialect risks disorientating a reader, making him or her feel they have suddenly been transported to, say, Somerset, Yorkshire, or Appalachia. In the end, the latter risk seemed worth taking—if only because I had the good fortune to know two translators, Pavel Gudoshnikov and Sian Valvis, both of whom have an unusual gift for reproducing Yorkshire dialect. With their input, our versions of several of these stories—especially of some from *The Lifeless Beast*, where Teffi deviates most boldly from standard Russian—have gained greatly in poetry, humor, and vividness. I should also explain that I asked Valvis to introduce a hint of Scots into the dialogue of "Solovki," which is set in the Far North of European Russia.

All these translations are the fruit of collective vision and revision. All those credited as translators of individual stories have also read the entire book and made helpful suggestions with regard to many of the other translations. And I have used most of the stories as texts for translation workshops at Pushkin House, in London. Participants have often come up with good, lively turns of phrase that my wife, Elizabeth, and I have eagerly incorporated in our final versions. Native speakers of Russian have also drawn my attention to many passages in the original that I had initially misunderstood. Teffi's apparent simplicity often veils unexpected subtleties; I almost always underestimate her work on first reading.

If we read Teffi in Russian, we feel that we are listening to a living, speaking voice—not just reading words intelligently arranged on a page. The greatest difficulty for a translator lies in reproducing this immediacy, this illusion of spontaneity. The simplest words, paradoxically, are often the hardest to translate. Two short sentences about Baba Yaga, for example, proved surprisingly difficult. Though not especially original, the Russian is pithy: "*Sku–u–u–uchno* (B-o-r-i-n-g). *Skoree* (sooner) *by* (if only) *zima* (winter)." We published an earlier version of our translation of this article in the anthology *Russian Magic Tales from Pushkin to Platonov*.[1] There we translated these two sentences as "She feels b-o-r-e-d. If only winter would come soon!" This is accurate, but I can't hear the intonations of Baba Yaga's voice. It was only recently that we changed it to "Would winter never come?" This has the ring of speech—and the right plaintive tone.

One of the joys of running a translation workshop is that almost every participant makes at least a few valuable contributions. Even someone relatively unschooled or inexperienced will sometimes suggest a brilliant solution I would never have thought of myself. In a description of a group of people walking across a grass-covered bog, Teffi writes that "beneath the velvety green carpet they could sense sticky, viscous, quagmiry death." In the original, the last four words (*lipkaya, tyaguchaya, tryasinaya smert'*) are expressive, even onomatopoeic. We struggled over them for some time. The word "viscous" was clearly unsatisfactory. It is a dull, rather scientific word, and too similar in meaning to "sticky." It was a secondary-school student, Sophie Benbelaid, then only seventeen and less than half the age of anyone else present, who came up with "treacly." We all immediately recognized that this was perfect—above all, perhaps, for being so unexpected an adjective to use of death. And we quickly agreed on a final version: "Hidden under the velvety green carpet lay sticky, treacly, quagmiry death."

There are many features of Teffi's style that I first consciously noted only while working on this book, as I tried to understand what made a particular sentence seem dull and pedestrian in our draft even though it was lively and graceful in the original. Teffi's pacing, her handling of transitions, is fluent and delicate; our first drafts, in contrast, often sounded either ponderous or jerky and disconnected. And Teffi's syntax is unusually flexible. The first sentence of "Water Spirit" is performative; the syntax enacts the narrator's growing anxiety as she travels alone through remote countryside. The first third of the sentence reads as if lifted from a dull guidebook. The syntax then becomes less controlled, and the tone more desperate. By the end of the sentence, the syntax has fallen apart; the last three words—*gloosh'*, *dal'*, *oozhas*—sound like wild exclamations rather than descriptive statements.

In English, Teffi's single long sentence seemed to work best as a series of short sentences. Our final version runs as follows: "The town was just thirty versts from the railway station, and it was forest, bogs, and more forest all the way. Rickety wooden bridges dancing across wild streams. Backwoods. The back of beyond. Dreary, dreadful, godforsaken."

It is those last three words—*gloosh'*, *dal'*, *oozhas*—that were hardest to translate. The repeated long vowels—*oo*, *aa*, *oo*—are crucial; they do much to convey the narrator's sense of fear and horror. And two of these words have no English equivalent. The noun *gloosh'* is cognate with *glookhoy*, a common adjective meaning "deaf," "muffled," or "muted." Nicolas Pasternak Slater writes, "*Gloosh'* is untranslatable. It carries the feeling of a dull sound that is almost silence, at the same time as the remoteness of the back of beyond."[2] *Dal'* means something like "distance," but it is more colloquial and expressive. *Oozhas*, at least, is relatively translatable—except that "horror," while conveying the dictionary meaning, lacks the long *oo* that is so important in the original.

Our version evolved only gradually. Since a literal translation is not even possible, we tried to compensate for the inevitable losses by means of alliteration, assonance, and repetition. "Backwoods" evoked "back of beyond." "Dreary" and "dreadful" seemed a natural pairing; for some time our last sentence read simply, "Dreary and dreadful." Eventually, however, I realized that this sounded too neat, that it lacked the necessary emotional intensity. The addition of "godforsaken" allowed the sentence to echo on in the mind. I was pleased when my friend and colleague Maria Bloshteyn wrote, in response to this last change, "It now sounds almost like a hex or a spell. Teffi would have loved that."

It has been said that the first letter of the Hebrew Bible is untranslatable. Nevertheless, the Bible as a whole evidently *can* be translated. Something similar is probably true of any great work of literature, however universally it has been recognized; there will always be at least an occasional sentence where the author has made such creative use of the most specific resources of a particular language that any attempt to reproduce this sentence in another language is bound to fail. Since Teffi's linguistic creativity—the poetry of her prose—has yet to be properly acknowledged, I shall end by quoting a virtuoso passage from "Shapeshifter": *I dolgaya, dolgaya, tianulas' doroga. Sierdtse bolielo ot bieloy toski bespriediel'nykh snegov.* Literally, this means, "And long, long, stretched the road. Heart ached from white anguish of boundless snows."

Like the sentence quoted earlier, this sentence is performative. The repetitions of the word *dolgaya* and of the syllable *iel* enact the sheer vastness of these white spaces. The final occurrence of *iel* is especially effective, since *bespriedyel'nykh* ("boundless") would stand out anyway because of its length. As for "white anguish," this is as unusual in Russian as in English; it gains added resonance, however, from its similarity to "white fever" (*bielaya goriachka*)—a standard term for delirium tremens.

Our final version of this sentence is acceptable, but no more than that: "The white anguish of the boundless snows, the monotonous jingle of our bell, the motionless, evil figure beside me—all this made my heart ache." This conveys the meaning of the original and some of its feeling, but it is not—like the Russian—something that anyone is likely to remember by heart. Nevertheless, as often happens, English then offers us at least partial compensation for these losses. Our next two sentences read, "The driver swayed silently in his seat, as if dead. Ahead loomed the dead of night." The curt final sentence works extremely well in English. In the original, "dead" serves merely as an ordinary adjective, agreeing with "night." English allows us to use the more idiomatic "dead of night." The bleak context reinvigorates the idiom, and the repeated "dead" takes on still more weight from the rhyme with "ahead."

One of the many reasons I so often choose stories by Teffi for translation workshops is that she has an unusually wide appeal. Regardless of age or literary taste, most readers warm to her. Erica Wagner concluded a London *Times* review of *Memories* with the sentence, "Teffi is a courageous companion for anyone's life." Nicholas Lezard began a *Guardian* review of *Subtly Worded*, our first collection of Teffi's stories and articles, by saying, "Pushkin Press has done it again: made me fall in love with a writer I'd never heard of." Other reviewers and readers have responded in a similar vein. There is no doubt that Teffi evokes in her readers an unusually strong sense of personal connection.

It is now well over fifteen years since Elizabeth and I translated two of Teffi's stories for our first Penguin Classics anthology, *Russian Short Stories from Pushkin to Buida*—and we can certainly say that she has been an engaging and rewarding companion. We admire her wit, grace, and courage more and more as the years go by. And she has a gift for bringing people together; my workshops and e-mail collaborations have been a constant joy—both at the time and in retrospect.

—R. C.

ACKNOWLEDGMENTS

My SPECIAL thanks to Mme Szydlowski for her remarkable generosity; to Christine Worobec for her help with many questions relating to both Orthodox and folk-religious beliefs, rituals, and traditions; and to Boris Dralyuk, Veronica Muskheli, and Alexander Nakhimovsky who have provided convincing answers to a great many complex questions.

Collaboration with others always reveals unexpected aspects of the original, as well as helping to free one from stylistic habits one may slip into too readily. It has been a joy to work with the following, all of whom have translated or co-translated at least one complete story: Maria Bloshteyn, Maria Evans, Pavel Gudoshnikov, Anne Marie Jackson, Sabrina Jaszi, Sara Jolly, Nicolas Pasternak Slater, Kathryn Thompson, and Sian Valvis. The contributions made by Jolly and Slater have proved especially valuable.

All the following have also made helpful suggestions: Anoushka Alexander-Rose, Leonie Barron, Sophie Benbelaid, Christine Bird, David Black, Maria Bozunova, Irena Brezowski, George Butchard, Ilona Chavasse, Richard Clarembaux, Elizabeth Cook, Douglas Doty, Anya Emmons, Tamara Glenny, Galina Griffiths, Gasan Gusejnov, Daryl Hardman, Stephen Holland, Jessy Kaner, Martha Kapos, Clare Kitson, Maria Kozlovskaya, Sophie Lockey, Elena Malysheva, Irina Mashinski, Melanie Mauthner, Naomi Mottram, Alice Nakhimovsky, Nargiz Najafli, Olga Nazarova, Yulia Kartalova O'Doherty, Natasha Perova, Anna Pilkington, William Powell, Lynda Proffitt, Susan Purcell, Donald Rayfield, Miriam Rossi, Francesca Sollohub, Jonathan Sutton, Natalia Tronenko, Elena Trubilova, Olga Utrivanova, Katia

Volodina, Marie-Claire Wilson. And there are many others who have responded helpfully to questions on e-mail forums or contributed to my Pushkin House workshops and summer schools.

For the main part, we have followed the texts of these stories as printed in the seven-volume collected edition published in Moscow by Lakom (1998–2005). For "Solovki," which is not included in the Lakom edition, we have followed the text as printed in *Vecherny den'* (Prague, 1924). Earlier versions of some of these translations have appeared as follows: "Kishmish" and "Solovki," in *Slav Sisters*, edited by Natasha Perova (Sawtry, UK: Dedalus Books, 2019); "Yavdokha," *Chtenia: The War to End All*, 8, no. 3, issue 27, edited by Boris Dral-yuk (Summer 2014); "A Quiet Backwater" and "The Kind That Walk," in Teffi, *Subtly Worded* (London: Pushkin Press, 2014); "The Dog" and "Baba Yaga," in *Russian Magic Tales from Pushkin to Platonov*, edited by Robert Chandler (New York: Penguin Classics, 2012).

RECOMMENDED READING

IN ENGLISH

Chandler, Robert. "Nezhivoi zver'" (a discussion of *The Lifeless Beast*) and "Ved'ma" (about *Witch*). *The Literary Encyclopedia*, available at litencyc.com.

———. *Russian Magic Tales from Pushkin to Platonov*. New York: Penguin Classics, 2012.

Haber, Edythe C. "The Roots of NEP Satire: The Case of Teffi and Zoshchenko." In *The NEP Era: Soviet Russia 1921–1928*, vol. I. Idyllwild, CA: Charles Schlacks, 2007.

———. *Teffi: A Life of Letters and of Laughter*. London: I. B. Tauris, 2019.

———. "Teffi." *The Literary Encyclopedia*, available at litencyc.com.

Hilton, Alison. *Russian Folk Art*. Bloomington and Indianapolis, IN: Indiana University Press, 1995.

Hubbs, Joanna. *Mother Russia: The Feminine Myth in Russian Culture*. Bloomington and Indianapolis, IN: Indiana University Press, 1993.

Ivanits, Linda. *Russian Folk Belief*. Armonk, NY: M. E. Sharpe, 1992.

Kelly, Catriona. *A History of Russian Women's Writing 1820–1992*. Oxford: Oxford University Press, 1999.

Kononenko, Natalie. *Slavic Folklore: A Handbook*. Westport, CT: Greenwood Press, 2007.

Pollock, Ethan. *Without the Banya We Would Perish: A History of the Russian Bathhouse*. Oxford: Oxford University Press, 2019.

Ryan, William. *The Bathhouse at Midnight: Magic in Russia*. London: Sutton, 1999.

Sinyavsky, Andrey. *Ivan the Fool: Russian Folk Belief.* Translated from the Russian by Joanne Turnbull and Nikolay Formozov. Moscow: Glas, 2007.

Teffi. *Memories.* Translated from the Russian by Robert and Elizabeth Chandler, Anne Marie Jackson, and Irene Steinberg. New York: New York Review Books, 2016.

———. *Subtly Worded.* Translated from the Russian by Anne Marie Jackson, Robert Chandler, Clare Kitson, and Natalia Wase. London: Pushkin Press, 2014.

———. *Tolstoy, Rasputin, Others, and Me: The Best of Teffi.* Translated from the Russian by Robert Chandler, Rose France, and Anne Marie Jackson. New York: New York Review Books, 2016.

IN RUSSIAN

Maximov, Sergey. *Nechistaia, nevedomaia i krestnaia sila.* Moscow: Kniga, 1989, first published 1903.

Teffi. *Izbrannye proizvedeniya*, 7 volumes. Moscow: Lakom, 1999.

Zelenin, D. K. *Vostochnoslavianskaya Etnografiya.* Moscow: Nauka, 1991.

NOTES

FOREWORD

1 Georgy Adamovich, review of *The Book of June*, *Illiustrirovannaya Rossiya* (April 25, 1931).

2 Teffi, *Izbrannye proizvedeniya* (Moscow: Lakom, 1999), 2:9. Edythe C. Haber quotes a similar passage in *Teffi: A Life of Letters and of Laughter* (London: I. B. Tauris, 2019), 152.

3 Teffi, "Katerina Petrovna," ibid., 4:45.

4 For more about *Witch*, including a discussion of "Seemings," which is set in a Siberian mining settlement and is omitted from *Other Worlds*, see Robert Chandler in *The Literary Encyclopedia*, available at www.litencyc.com/php/sworks.php?rec=true&UID=38906.

5 Teffi, *Izbrannye proizvedeniya*, 2:374.

6 Neither "Happiness" nor "Daisy" are included in *Other Worlds*. For more about *The Lifeless Beast*, see Robert Chandler in *The Literary Encyclopedia*, available at www.litencyc.com/php/sworks.php?rec=true&UID=38906.

7 Haber, *Teffi: A Life of Letters and of Laughter*, 18.

8 Ibid., 152.

9 Edythe C. Haber, "The Roots of NEP Satire: The Case of Teffi and Zoshchenko," in *The NEP Era: Soviet Russia 1921–1928* (Idyllwild, CA: Charles Schlacks, 2007), 1:92.

10 Ivanov's comments about Teffi are often misquoted. See, for example, Teffi, *Izbrannye proizvedeniya*, 2:5. Haber writes (personal email, June 25, 2020) that she found in her files a note of Ivanov's review in *Sovetskii patriot* of *Russkii sbornik* (1946) where he writes, "The first Teffi is a cultured, intelligent, good writer. The second is an unrepeatable phenomenon of Russian literature, a true miracle that people will still be wondering at in a hundred years' time, crying and laughing at once. ('*Pervaya Teffi kul'turnyi, umnyi, khoroshii pisatel'. Vtoraya—nepovtorimoye yavlenie*

russkoi literaturi, podlinnoye chudo, kotoroy cherez sto let budut udivlyat'sya, smeyas' pri etom do slez.')" It is not entirely clear which Teffi is the first, and which the second. It seems likely, though, that the first is the more serious Teffi and the second the more comic Teffi.

KISHMISH

1 *Nyanya* is often translated as "nanny," but the two words are not equivalent. See "A Note on Russian Names."

2 The Russian Orthodox refer to the first week of Lent as Clean Week. The faithful are expected to undergo spiritual cleansing through fasting, prayer, repentance, begging forgiveness of their neighbor, and taking the Eucharist. Throughout the six weeks of Lent, vegetable oils are substituted for butter and animal fats.

3 Teffi also uses this nickname in "Love" ("Lyubov," from the collection *Gorodok*), one of the finest of her semiaubiographical stories. Robert Chandler's translation of this is included in *Russian Short Stories from Pushkin to Buida* (New York: Penguin Classics, 2005).

SOUL IN BOND

1 Russians often used to drink tea by putting a cube of sugar into their mouth and sucking tea through the cube.

2 A tall domed loaf baked only at Easter. It is sweet and always glazed with white icing; often it is decorated with flowers.

CONFESSION

1 Kissel is made of pureed fruit or peas thickened with potato starch. Depending on the proportion of starch, it can be the consistency of a smoothie, a soup, or a blancmange.

2 Nyanya seems to be alluding to one of the many variants of a common folk belief that if you bridle a witch and ride her all through the night, she will turn into a horse and cease to make trouble. See Linda Ivanits, *Russian Folk Belief* (Armonk, NY: M. E. Sharpe, 1992), 194–95.

3 The eighth commandment in the Anglican and Orthodox traditions, seventh in the Catholic tradition.

4 Confession in a church or a monastery often took place behind a wooden screen. Penitent and confessor stood in full view of each other, while those waiting their turn stood on the other side of the screen. The confessor would stand beside an analogion—a wooden lectern

supporting a cross and a gospel. The penitent would stand too, often with bowed head. After reminding the penitent that they are confessing to the Lord, not to him, the confessor would ask a series of questions. The penitent would then kneel while the priest placed the end of his stole over the penitent's head and pronounced the absolution and blessing.

YAVDOKHA

1 Dr. A. D. Nurenberg was a well-known physician. In the autumn of 1914, shortly before this story was first published, he and Teffi were the subject of a major public scandal. Nurenberg was visiting Teffi when a man stormed in and fired five shots at him, hitting him in the neck, hand, and arm. He shot at Teffi, but missed. He then turned himself over to the police, saying he had warned Nurenberg not to go on visiting Teffi. Edythe Haber writes, "Nothing more is known about Teffi's relations with Dr. Nurenberg, but when he died in April 1917 (apparently of unrelated causes), she wrote an obituary describing his total dedication to his calling and his miraculous diagnoses"; *Teffi, Izbrannye proizvedeniya* (Moscow: Lakom, 1999), 72.

2 A standard measure of distance until the Revolution. Slightly longer than a kilometer.

A QUIET BACKWATER

1 Compare: "Dal' states that among the peasants [the Annunciation] was the most important religious festival. On this day and at Easter the souls in hell are not tormented. You may not spin or weave on this day, nor plait your hair, nor heat the stove, nor cook hot meals. Moles are blind because they dug on this day and cuckoos have no nest because they made nests on this day"; William Ryan, *The Bathhouse at Midnight: Magic in Russia* (London: Sutton, 1999), 132.

2 The day after Pentecost, "Whit Monday" in English. According to Russian belief, this was the day that the earth was created; it was wrong to dig in the earth since she was now pregnant with the harvest.

THE HEART

1 Teffi is referring to Johann Strauss's operetta *A Night in Venice*. Among the characters is a "fisher-girl."

2 Fedosya's physical appearance—her "sharp eyes" and "sharp nose"—would have been thought witchlike. And since fishing was a male occupation

and a fishing net was believed to have magical properties, the villagers would have had reason to be suspicious of Fedosya. They may have thought that she could use this net to place a hex on someone or even to capture a demon whom she could then use as her servant (my thanks to Christine Worobec and Veronica Muskheli for their help with this note).

3 In tsarist Russia, most Orthodox Christians confessed and took Communion only once a year, usually during Lent. Someone very devout might also confess and take Communion during one of the three other major fasts, but it was unusual for a layperson to take Communion more than twice in a year. Preparation for Communion was a serious matter. Before going to confession, a penitent was expected to abstain from certain foods for several days, to cut back on secular activities, and to pray in private or listen to special prayers in church. After confession, the penitent would fast until partaking of the Eucharist during Divine Liturgy the following day.

SOLOVKI

1 From the second half of the nineteenth century there was a huge increase in the number of pilgrims paying short visits to Solovki. The *Archangel Michael*, acquired in 1887, was one of three steamships operated by the monastery. The journey from Arkhangelsk took seventeen hours. The pilgrimage season started late in June and the most important feast day was August 8, the name day of Saints Zosima and Savvaty, the monastery's two founders.

2 A penance would include going to all services, a prescribed number of bodily prostrations, and the repetition of additional prayers.

3 An elite secondary school for boys.

4 To this day, pilgrims visiting a holy site often buy items of clothing for their burial. And it is customary for the deceased to wear a belt—into which a prayer has been woven—during an Orthodox burial, since he or she will need it when resurrected. Belts are symbolically important in Russian culture, suggesting order and dignity.

5 The Russian-speaking inhabitants of the country's northern coast of European Russia. They have developed a specific culture as a result of interaction and interbreeding with the region's indigenous peoples.

6 Probably these women had prayed to the monastery's patron saints and vowed to send their sons to Solovki (which did not accept women except as pilgrims on short visits) if their prayer was granted. The boys would

serve as laborers, also receiving some spiritual teaching. They were not trainee monks; in a year or two they would return to their homes.

7   To this day, some recluse monks on Solovki keep to a rule of complete silence, living alone and devoting their lives to prayer. It seems that some of Teffi's pilgrims did not understand this. It is also possible that the mutual incomprehension resulted from people speaking different dialects.

8   Their walk echoes the Procession of the Cross around the outside of a church on Easter Eve and certain other feast days.

9   Mustard was considered an aphrodisiac.

10 Demons in Russian iconography were usually depicted as shaggy, with webbed feet and twisting tails.

11 Being on the west wall, the Last Judgment was the last set of images a worshiper would see as he or she left the church; this makes the monks' surrender to temptation all the more ironic.

12 A lightly fermented drink made from rye bread.

13 The official is quoting from Psalm 37:45 (according to the Orthodox numbering), which is in the morning prayers for lay readers. In the King James Bible this is translated: "For my loins are filled with a loathsome disease: and there is no soundness in my flesh" (Psalm 38:7).

14 The period that these short-term visitors were allowed to stay. During these three days they were expected to avoid meat and dairy products; they were then ready to receive Communion.

15 In the mid-1880s the poet Konstantin Sluchevsky described Pomor women as "well dressed regardless of their social and economic status, wearing long colourful *sarafany*, and beautifully decorated headwear. [...] A distinctive feature of women's clothing in some parts of Pomor'e was an extensive use of pearls extracted from local rivers." Available at www.openbookpublishers.com/htmlreader/978-1-78374-544-9/ch8.xhtml.

16 See note 4. In their article "The Sea Is Our Field," Masha Shaw and Natalie Wahnsiedler write: "Sluchevsky was particularly impressed by the light and skilful movements of Pomor women in their long and richly decorated dresses as they steered their boats in rough and roaring waters"; in David G. Anderson, Dimtry V. Arzyutov, and Sergei S. Alimov, eds., *Life Histories of Etnos Theory in Russia and Beyond* (Cambridge: Open Book Publishers, 2019).

17 This marks the beginning of the most solemn part of the Liturgy. It is sung as the clergy—accompanied, it is believed, by angels—enter the sanctuary through the Holy Doors. It ends, "Let us now lay aside all earthly care."

18 The word means "whither." Teffi evidently chose it both for its sound and for its meaning. Unable to reproduce both, we have transliterated, reproducing the sound alone.

19 The celebration of Christ's resurrection through the mystery of the Eucharist was believed to provoke fear among demons, which in turn could prompt fits among those in a state of demonic possession.

20 Varvara's "Aida!" echoes the first woman's "Kuda!" And the word *da* means "yes."

21 Varvara would not normally have received Communion before completing her penance. Now, however, she is thought to be possessed and so not responsible for her state. In the words of John Chrysostom, "They that be possest in that they are tormented of the devil are blameless and will never be punished with torment for that: but they who approach unworthily the holy Mysteries shall be given over to everlasting torments"; quoted in *The Doctrine of the Russian Church*, R. W. Blackmore, trans. (Aberdeen: A. Brown and Co., 1845), 223n. And so Varvara is given the Eucharist: a small piece of bread dipped in wine.

22 Saint Tikhon of Zadonsk (1724–1783) was born, like Varvara and her husband, in the province of Novgorod. After serving for seven years as a bishop, he retired because of poor health to the monastery of Zadonsk, beyond the Don River. Eighty years after his death, he was canonized. Varvara imagines herself and Semyon making a pilgrimage to Zadonsk, stopping at other holy sites on the way.

THE BOOK OF JUNE

1 Alexey Konstantinovich Tolstoy (1817–1875) wrote lyric poems, acute satires, and verse plays on historical, religious, and legendary themes. He was not closely related to the famous novelist.

2 Viktor Vasnetsov (1848–1926) was one of the group of artists known as the Wanderers or Peredvizhniki. Many of his paintings are on themes from Russian folktales and the old oral verse epics known as *bylinas*.

WILD EVENING

1 The Russian *khrust* at one time referred to a particular silver coin. For Afanasy, though, it is probably just a slang word for "ruble."

2 Visitors to a holy well often made donations for prayers to be said both on behalf of the living—most often the sick—and on behalf of the dead.

3   An abbreviation of a formula found in old Russian *bylinas*: "If you wish
    for good, drink to the bottom. If you don't wish for good, don't drink
    to the bottom." ("*Esli khosh' dobra, tak pei do dna. A ne khosh dobra, tak
    ne pei do dna!*")

4   According to the ethnographer Dmitry Zelenin, Russian peasants saw
    some illnesses—especially fevers—as manifestations of the unclean
    dead. His description of a fever (*likhoradka*) is similar to Teffi's image of
    Cattle Plague: "with long, uncovered hair, without a belt, dressed in
    white like the dead"; in Dmitry Zelenin, *Izbrannye trudy* (Moscow: In-
    drik, 1994), 1:279.

SHAPESHIFTER

1   An organ of local government. Established in 1864, three years after the
    emancipation of the serfs, these democratically elected councils were
    central to the liberal movement during the last fifty years of tsarism.
    They were responsible for building schools, hospitals, roads, etc.

WITCH

1   There is nothing unusual about this. It was conventional for a social in-
    ferior to kiss a superior on the shoulder. In return, the superior would
    kiss the top of his or her head.

2   In each Russian province there was an Assembly of the Nobility, headed
    by an elected Marshal of the Nobility.

VURDALAK

1   The Russian equivalent of the biblical Abner. He first appears in the
    Book of Samuel as the commander of Saul's army.

THE HOUSE SPIRIT

1   For the story of the prophet Elisha raising the son of the Shunammite,
    see 2 Kings 4:18–37. Verse 34 reads, "And he went up, and lay upon the
    child, and put his mouth upon his mouth, and his eyes upon his eyes,
    and his hands upon his hands: and stretched himself upon the child;
    and the flesh of the child waxed warm."

2   Priscilla Roosevelt writes, "The nanny's replacement by the first govern-
    ess or tutor marked the cultural divide between a Russian infancy and a
    European childhood. [...] The nanny's fairy tales and fantastic visions
    were replaced by moral fables, in which children's virtue was tested and

evil punished"; in *Life on the Russian Country Estate* (New Haven, CT: Yale University Press, 1995), 181.

3 When upset, a house spirit often caused trouble in the stables. House spirits could not bear the smell of goats, so a goat's presence helped to protect the horses.

4 The poem Kolya reads aloud is a free translation of a poem by Byron that begins:

> When I dream that you love me, you'll surely forgive;
> Extend not your anger to sleep;
> For in visions alone your affection can live;
> I rise, and it leaves me to weep.

LESHACHIKHA

1 A female forest spirit. See the afterword.

2 "That charming little savage."

3 Polish for "mademoiselle" or "little lady."

4 "If you believe …"

5 "How I adore her and her wheat-blonde hair …"

6 See *Eugene Onegin*, act 6, scene 32, Stanley Mitchell, trans. (New York: Penguin, 2008):

> But now, as in a house forsaken,
> All it contains is dark and still,
> A home forever silent, chill,
> The windows shuttered, chalked and vacant,
> The mistress vanished from the place
> To God knows where, without a trace.

In other countries, too, windows are sometimes whitewashed if a house or shop is left vacant. As well as being a cheap antibacterial, the whitewash reduces heat from sunshine and deters the inquisitive.

ABOUT THE HOUSE

1 Compare Zelenin: "For Ukrainians and Belorussians, a witch's main activity is stealing milk from cows. If a witch milks a cow on the Feast of the Annunciation, on Easter, or on Saint George's day (April 23), only she can then continue to get milk from that cow. The milk flows from an aperture in one of the logs of the witch's home, if you turn on a tap there"; in D. K. Zelenin, *Vostochnoslavianskaya Etnografiya* (Moscow: Nauka, 1991), 421.

2 See the afterword. Teffi may have in mind the belief that some of these spirits are the unclean dead—former human beings who no longer have souls because they were denied a Christian burial.

BATHHOUSE DEVIL

1 The Grand Prince of Kiev Rus' from 1113 to 1125.

RUSALKA

1 A Russian troika is drawn by three horses abreast. The middle horse, attached to the shaft, is flanked by the two trace horses, in breast-collar harness and traces.

2 The poem "translated" by the adjutant is almost certainly Shelley's "Love's Philosophy." The second of its two stanzas reads:

> See the mountains kiss high heaven,
> And the waves clasp one another;
> No sister-flower would be forgiven
> If it disdained its brother;
> And the sunlight clasps the earth,
> And the moonbeams kiss the sea—
> What is all this sweet work worth
> If thou kiss not me?

3 A joking reference to the custom, common to many parts of Europe, of leaving a small patch of corn unreaped—to propitiate the fertility god or goddess and so ensure an abundant crop the following year. In Russia, the ears of unreaped corn were knitted together—and this was known as "the plaiting of the beard of Volos." William Ralston Shedden-Ralston writes, "The unreaped patch is looked upon as tabooed; and it is believed that if anyone meddles with it he will shrivel up and become twisted like the interwoven ears"; in *The Songs of the Russian People* (Miami, FL: HardPress, 2017), 251.

4 Also spelled *korovai*. Traditionally, seven women, including the bride, would help to make this large, rich, sweetened, and highly decorated loaf, which was presented to the bride and groom just before they married.

SHAPESHIFTERS

1 Valery Briusov (1873–1924) was a Symbolist poet, critic, and translator. *The Fiery Angel*, his novel on occult themes set in sixteenth-century Germany, was first published 1907–1909. The poet and novelist Fyodor

Sologub (1863–1927) came to fame with the publication in 1907 of *The Petty Demon*, a darkly comic novel about a provincial schoolteacher's descent into sadism and insanity. Alexander Kondratiev (1876–1967) was a Symbolist poet, novelist, and translator with a particular interest in Russian mythology. He subtitled his *On the Banks of the Yaryn* (1930) as "A Demonological Novel."

2   In Roman mythology, the unclean dead were known as *larvae*, or *lemures*.

3   A term introduced by the poet Alexander Blok to contrast the aristocratic patrons of art in the eighteenth and early nineteenth centuries with the urban bourgeoisie who were the main consumers of art in his own time.

4   The Kiev Pechersk Lavra is a large and important cave monastery. Founded in 1051 by Orthodox monks from Mount Athos, it is believed to contain the uncorrupted bodies of saints from the days of Kiev Rus, the Slav kingdom that embraced Christianity in 988.

5   A phenomenon most often seen in mountain fog: a person's huge shadow, sometimes surrounded by a rainbowlike halo, appears on clouds opposite the sun. Named after a peak in the Harz Mountains of northern Germany, this became a commonplace of Romantic poetry. Coleridge, for example, refers to it in "Constancy to an Ideal Object":

> And art thou nothing? Such thou art, as when
> The woodman winding westward up the glen
> At wintry dawn, where o'er the sheep-track's maze
> The viewless snow-mist weaves a glist'ning haze,
> Sees full before him, gliding without tread,
> An image with a glory round its head;
> The enamoured rustic worships its fair hues,
> Nor knows he makes the shadow, he pursues!

6   Piotr Potiomkin (1866–1926) wrote poetry, plays, and prose, and also worked as a translator. From 1908, he wrote regularly for the journal *Satirikon*. In October 1925, he and Teffi founded a theater in Paris. It staged several programs of miniatures but closed before the end of the year; see Edythe C. Haber, *Teffi: A Life of Letters and of Laughter* (London: I. B. Tauris, 2019), 122.

7   "La Carmagnole" is a French song, usually accompanied by a wild dance. During the French Revolution and later uprisings, it was almost as important as "La Marseillaise."

8   "Mr. Onegin is a most excellent fellow."

THE DOG

1 According to an old Russian saying, someone in love will use too much salt when cooking.

2 In the late nineteenth and early twentieth centuries, Hermann Friedrich Eilers supplied flowers to the court and owned a large florists opposite the Kazan Cathedral.

3 See the foreword.

4 Mikhail Kuzmin (1872–1936), a homosexual, was known as "the Russian Wilde." A gifted composer as well as a major poet, he sang his own songs at the Stray Dog, accompanying himself on the piano. Both in a newspaper obituary and in a later memoir, Teffi writes of him with respect, but she is critical (at least in the obituary) of his followers, whom she saw as affected and talentless.

5 Oscar Wilde used to wear a green carnation in his buttonhole. Wilde owed his fame in early twentieth-century Russia mainly to his trial and imprisonment, but many leading poets of the time—Konstantin Balmont, Valery Bryusov, Nikolay Gumiliov, Mikhail Kuzmin, and Fyodor Sologub—translated his work.

6 Nikolay Nekrasov (1821–77), the most popular poet of his time, was fiercely critical of serfdom and the autocracy. His most famous two lines are "You don't have to be a poet, / but you are obliged to be a citizen."

7 "Waves of the Danube" is a famous waltz composed in 1880 by Iosif Ivanovici, a Romanian. In the United States it has become known as "The Anniversary Song."

8 The Soviet security service, founded on December 5, 1917, was renamed many times; the most important of its names and acronyms, in chronological order, are the Cheka, the OGPU, the NKVD, and the KGB.

THE KIND THAT WALK

1 This seeming triviality points to an important understanding about the unclean dead: that what makes them continue to walk the earth is some kind of unfinished business. In her groundbreaking study of the beliefs of Transylvanian peasants, Gail Kligman writes, "Especially perilous are those deaths that pose dangers arising from unfulfilled lives. Briefly, it is believed that individuals who leave behind a mortal enemy, an unresolved love affair, or other unfinished matters will return in the forms of their bodies that they no longer inhabit"; in *The Wedding of the Dead* (Berkeley: University of California Press, 1988), 216.

WATER SPIRIT

1 Candles were expensive, and often very large. One large candle would have been enough to light the room.

2 See "A Note on Russian Names."

3 Her surname is the standard Russian word for "owl."

BABA YAGA

1 One of the ancient Slavic gods, probably a god of wind and storm.

VOLYA

1 Saint Spiridon (c. 270–348) is honored in both the Eastern and Western Christian traditions. According to the Julian calendar, his saint's day falls close to the winter solstice and so he is known as Spiridon Povorot or Spiridon Solntsevorot (Spiridon Turnabout or Spiridon Sunturn). In some regions, this term was used to describe people illegally returning home from exile. See Olga Atroshenko, *Russkii narodnyi kalendar'. Etnolingvisticheskii slovar'* (Moscow: Rossiiskaia akademiia nauk, 2015), 414–15.

2 Lengths of cloth wound around the foot and ankle—more common in Russia, until the middle of the twentieth century, than socks or stockings. By the 1950s, however, they had largely disappeared—except in labor camps and the army.

3 In Slavic and Baltic mythology, this is a magic flower that blooms on the eve of the summer solstice. In different versions of the myth, it bestows a variety of gifts on the person who finds it. These gifts include wealth, understanding of animal speech, and the ability to open any locked door, but they seldom, if ever, bring the finder any real benefit.

AFTERWORD

1 Andrey Sinyavsky, *Ivan the Fool* (Moscow: Glas, 2007), 108.

2 See Linda Ivanits, *Russian Folk Belief* (Armonk, NY: M. E. Sharpe, 1992), 53.

3 Ibid., 59.

4 Sinyavsky, *Ivan the Fool*, 115.

5 William Ryan, *The Bathhouse at Midnight: Magic in Russia* (London: Sutton, 1999), 50.

6 D. K. Zelenin, *Vostochnoslavianskaya Etnografiya* (Moscow: Nauka, 1991), 415.

7   Sinyavsky, *Ivan the Fool*, 108.
8   Dmitry Zelenin, *Izbrannye trudy* (Moscow: Indrik, 1994), 1:231.
9   Sinyavsky, *Ivan the Fool*, 123.
10 See the foreword.
11 Teffi, *Izbrannye proizvedeniya* (Moscow: Lakom, 1999), 2:378–79.

THIS TRANSLATION
1   New York: Penguin Classics, 2012.
2   Personal e-mail, June 2020.

OTHER NEW YORK REVIEW CLASSICS

For a complete list of titles, visit www.nyrb.com or write to:
Catalog Requests, NYRB, 435 Hudson Street, New York, NY 10014